VENGEANCE IN BLOOD

A *DETECTIVE LACY FULLER* NOVEL

VENGEANCE IN BLOOD

A *DETECTIVE LACY FULLER* NOVEL

LEE KELLY

Two Harbors Press
212 3rd Avenue North, Suite 290
Minneapolis, MN 55401
612.455.2293
www.TwoHarborsPress.com

This book is a work of fiction. All references to names, characters, places, incidents, or potential situations are a product of the author's imagination or are used fictitiously to create a sense of authenticity.

ISBN-13: 978-1-937293-60-4
LCCN: 2011941724

Distributed by Itasca Books

Cover Design and Typeset by James Arneson

Printed in the United States of America

For Momma and Daddy:

Not a day passes that I don't miss you both or feel grati-tude for having been blessed with the most wonderful parents in the world.

CHAPTER 1

Atlanta, GA July 23, 2004

The bastard! Shelly Farnsworth Stevens looked at the photograph from her wedding day. She'd been so happy standing next to that son-of-a-bitch, even though he'd insisted on wearing that ridiculous looking tuxedo that belonged to his father. The wide lapels made her think of the cheesy television programs she'd watched as a child. She should have realized then that he would only bring grief into her life. She hurled the picture across the room and cringed as she heard the loud crash. Just her luck; she shattered not only the picture frame, but also the antique mirror it hit. She wondered if she would have the luxury of even having seven years of life, with or without bad luck.

Why had he cheated on her? Sure, they didn't have a perfect marriage, but nobody did outside of romance novels and movies. She was attractive, wealthy, and his wife, for God's sake. She worked hard at staying attractive through constant dieting and exercise programs. Of course, the numerous cosmetic procedures she'd undergone over the years had also helped. She closed her eyes and took a deep breath, wondering why he had been unfaithful. She would ask him when he came home and hope for an honest reply.

Todd had an annoying way of never truthfully answering a question, and she hated his lies. Rising, she went to the closet, took a shoe box down from the top shelf, and removed the lid. Merely holding the pistol gave her a sense of peace and power. Perhaps this would help her get the answers she needed from the bastard. She heard the front door open and her husband's voice call out to her.

Todd Stevens loosened his tie and made a beeline to the refrigerator. He took out a beer, opened it, and took a long swig. As he set the bottle on the counter, he heard a distinctive click behind him. Turning slowly, he was met with the muzzle of the blue steel gun held expertly in front of his wife's steel blue eyes.

"Who was she?" Shelly's voice was an eerie whisper.

"Who was *who*?" Todd replied.

"Whoever you fucked, Todd. Did you know she made you sick? Huh? Did you know she had AIDS?"

Her husband stared at her blankly.

"Answer me, Todd. Who was she? Was she worth dying for?" Shelly's voice remained as calm as the unwavering manner in which she held the gun.

"Shelly, what in the hell are you talking about? I've never fooled around on you, not once. I never would!" Todd told a half-truth, for though he'd never had an affair, he would if the opportunity presented itself.

Shelly could see the lie on his face and her eyes filled with hatred and anger. "I just got back from my Pre-Op visit with Dr. Jonas for that liposuction procedure next week. It seems that my HIV test was positive. I know damned well that I didn't get it on my own, which leaves only one explanation; you gave it to me. I'll ask you one last time, Todd. If you value your life, don't lie to me. Who the hell was she?"

Todd felt sick to his stomach. He needed to go to the restroom, but he dared not move. Was Shelly crazy? How could she think that he'd had an affair? Did she really have AIDS? Had she infected him? The bitch must have fooled around on him! He felt a surge of anger that made him indignantly ask the last question of his life.

"I didn't fool around, and I didn't give you AIDS, but if you've got it, I'm guessing that I should be the one to ask who you fucked?"

The blast reverberated in their upscale kitchen. Suddenly Todd was on the floor with blood flowing freely from his groin. Shelly stared at her husband, then at the gun still in her hand. Numbly, she walked to the telephone mounted on the kitchen wall and dialed 911.

CHAPTER 2

Detective Lacy Fuller signed off on her report at 6:07 PM. She was already planning her evening: eat at the café nearby, go to Charis bookstore, then leisurely walk home and settle in for the night with whatever reading material she had bought. The unseasonably cool July temperatures in Atlanta would have made it an excellent evening for a long run, but after her long week, all she could think about was relaxing. Lately she had begun to feel older than her 37 years.

Stretching, she looked out the window beside her desk and raked a pale hand through her almost shoulder-length onyx hair, wondering just how long she would let it grow. She'd worn it cropped just shy of her ears most of her adult life. After making the move to the homicide department the previous year, she'd decided to try looking a little less like a police officer in case the opportunity for an undercover assignment presented itself. Unfortunately, the longer hair had been of little value toward her make-over. She still had piercing blue eyes that constantly scoured her surroundings in search of a potential threat and, though only 5'4" and 118 pounds, she walked with the 'cop-blend' of arrogance and caution. If it walks like a duck … she thought. A smile was forming at the edges of her mouth at the prospect of an evening with no chores when voices from the hallway distracted her from her thoughts. She looked up to see Captain Sumlin making a beeline toward her with her partner, Chet Avery, in tow. Chet didn't look happy. Sumlin never looked happy.

With a frown, the Captain stopped a few feet from her and crossed his arms in a challenging pose. Lacy knew the Captain well enough to know that when he approached her with defensive posturing, it was usually to assign her some bullshit case to which she would most certainly vocalize her displeasure.

Looking at the two men in front of her, she marveled again at their differences. Captain Sumlin was in his late fifties and still had the rock-hard physique that his military and FBI careers had governed. He made everything seem urgent through his rash mannerisms and constantly worried expression. The gray stubble on his face alerted people that his closely cropped hair would also be gray if not for the advent of hair dye for men. He was neither handsome nor uncomely. His suits were always crisp, and he had well manicured nails.

Chet Avery, on the other hand, was a quite handsome man who stood at least half a foot taller than the Captain, who was around 5'8" with his man-heels on. Chet's sandy hair had begun to thin and his waistline to expand at the same slow pace. Unlike the Captain, Chet was laid back, moved slowly yet deliberately, and usually wore a lazy yet genuine smile. Chet wasn't smiling now.

Captain Sumlin rubbed his hand over his whiskers and sighed. "Detective Fuller, we've got an attempted homicide that I need you and Avery to cover. The victim's name is Todd Stevens. He's been taken to Brookshire Medical Center."

Lacy felt her good mood sour instantly. She tried in vain to keep the naturally hostile tone from her voice when she spoke. "Captain, with all due respect, there hasn't been a homicide yet. You said yourself it's an *attempted* homicide."

Sumlin spoke, his lips still drawn down at the corners. "Actually, Fuller, the patient is going to be DOA. I got word from the EMT's a couple of minutes ago. So by the time you get down to Brookshire, it'll be a homicide. Besides, this is going to be a high profile case, and I need my best detectives. You see, the perp is Shelly *Farnsworth* Stevens." Seeing the startled look on their faces, he added, "Yes, *that* Farnsworth. She's being brought in now. She confessed, by the way."

Lacy wondered how anyone could talk while they were frowning. Catching herself studying the Captain's mouth, she forced her eyes to meet his before speaking.

"It seems like an open and shut case. If we know who shot him, and we know he's a DOA, we will be able to close the case tonight. We'll interview the Stevens woman when she gets to the jail, go to the hospital, then to the crime scene. Then, it'll be midnight." Lacy's stare hardened as thoughts of her leisurely evening at home faded. She looked at her partner and guessed that he, too, was unhappy that he would miss another dinner with his wife and child.

An emotion passed over Captain Sumlin's face that Lacy couldn't read. She waited impatiently until he spoke again.

"Okay, I guess you'll find out soon enough. It isn't actually Todd Steven's homicide that you'll be investigating. You'll be looking into Shelly's future homicide."

Both detectives stared at him blankly. Things were going from weird to weirder, Lacy thought. She waited for a moment before she spoke as she tried to assimilate the information she'd just heard.

"If Mrs. Stevens is still alive, how in the hell does it warrant putting two homicide detectives on the case? Besides, how do we investigate a *future* homicide? Who in the hell has ESP around here, Captain?"

Sumlin closed his eyes and took a deep breath. Lacy wondered if he was chiding himself inwardly for being such a spineless slave to politics.

"Here's the deal. Shelly is a Farnsworth, as in *Judge* Farnsworth's niece."

Both Lacy and Chet nodded.

"In case you ever wondered how influential Judge Farnsworth is, I received a call from the Chief *before* the call came through from the emergency medical technicians. Apparently, Shelly found out earlier today that her HIV test was positive, and she went ballistic. She accused Todd of murder for giving her the disease and shot him. I guess seeing her husband bleeding to death must have brought her back to her senses. She started feeling guilty for shooting him and realized that he'd seemed genuinely surprised by her accusations. She called her uncle, Judge Farnsworth, who's insisting that a homicide investigation be conducted to locate the woman who transmitted the virus to Todd Stevens without his knowledge. He wants us to find her and charge her with two counts of attempted homicide."

Lacy, with her pale skin and dark hair, looked like the perfect Halloween ghost standing there with her eyes wide and her mouth in a small O.

"Jesus Christ, Captain! That's the most ridiculous thing I've ever heard! How in the hell can you give in to these people just because of who they are?"

Sumlin shook his head. "I know you don't give a shit about power or authority, Lacy. For instance, I'm directing you to go to Brookshire and here you are, arguing with me six ways to Sunday! Sometimes you've just got to work with people, especially if they're capable of putting food on your table."

Lacy wondered if the Captain was threatening her, but decided that he didn't have the balls. He knew how much she hated playing politics. Still, it was a direct order, and she couldn't refuse.

Lacy looked over at Chet, who was still quietly glowering. "Can we at least wait until tomorrow to type up the preliminary report?" Lacy asked through clenched teeth.

Captain Sumlin attempted a smile through his almost permanent frown as he nodded. The result was a ridiculous grimace that Lacy thought made him look constipated. The detectives walked away before he could add anything further.

On the way to the parking lot, Lacy had a thought that almost made her smile. The evening might not be a total waste if she got to see that cute Dr. West again!

CHAPTER 3

Dr. Sharon West entered the staff lounge in the Brookshire Medical Center's Emergency Room and asked herself again why she had become a physician. This night had been pure hell with ten more hours before she was free to go. Pouring herself a cup of strong coffee, she shrugged out of her lab coat and slumped into an uncomfortable, dark purple chair. Ever the smartass, she wondered if the harder-than-concrete, visually alarming furniture scheme was intended to keep the staff from getting too comfortable and taking long breaks. She could envision that little weasel of a CEO, Thad Brock, reclined back in his well-padded leather recliner flipping through his latest edition of an office furniture magazine, pointedly ignoring any item in which the description indicated comfort.

She looked across the room at the image of herself in the mirror. She couldn't remember the last time she'd been free of the dark circles that underlined her hazel eyes. When she pulled her blonde hair back as she did on the days she worked, the darkness was even more pronounced, giving her that half-raccoon look. She was thankful for her olive skin that helped camouflage her exhaustion. Rubbing the back of her neck, she forced her thoughts to the two patients who had contributed to her hellacious night. As if by a divine orchestration, the door to the lounge was opened by the charge nurse, Maria Ortiz.

"Here are the folders you asked for, Dr. West. Labs and x-rays are in there now."

Taking the proffered files, Dr. West thanked Maria and watched her bustle out the door. Sighing, she opened the first of the two folders.

Room 21: Sophia Tippens. Patient is a white female, 71 years of age, who presents with intense abdominal pain. Currently undergoing radiation therapy for brain cancer, the patient is taking hydrocodone for pain management and prednisone. Mrs. Tippens is neither ambulatory nor lucid. Next of kin: daughter, worried that her mother's pain could stem from an enema she had given her that morning. There had been no evacuation of the contents of the enema.

Laboratory results were all within normal limits, effectively negating pancreatitis or appendicitis. Radiology films showed a hole within the small intestine. Prednisone, necessary for the intracranial swelling from the tumor as well as the radiation therapy itself, had made the tissues thin. The introduction of an enema had likely caused the delicate intestine to rupture. Surgery to repair the tear would be a risky, brief prolongation of the short life Mrs. Tippens had left. Sharon was now going to have to tell the already guilt-laden daughter that her fears were reality. An extraordinarily lousy day in the life of the young lady: the day she unwittingly became her mother's executioner.

Gingerly closing the folder, as if delicacy could somehow overturn the severity of the situation, she placed the second folder atop the first and opened the cover. Room 22: George Kilpatrick. Patient is a white male, widowed,

64 years of age, who presents with nausea. Patient is obviously agitated at being brought to the hospital at the insistence of, once again, his daughter. He is currently taking blood pressure medication and vitamins daily. Mr. Kilpatrick is both ambulatory and lucid. Remembering the sheen of perspiration and the unhealthy pallor of his skin, Sharon quickly skimmed to the laboratory results: elevated cardiac enzymes indicative of an acute myocardial infarction. The EKG printout echoed the lab findings.

Had his daughter not insisted on taking the cranky man to the ER when she did in all likelihood she would soon have been without the comfort of either parent.

Closing the chart, she thought, one daughter: the slayer, one daughter: the savior. Suddenly the cheap, uncomfortable chairs appeared insignificant. Despite the warnings of endless self-help books, human nature seemed to demand that we indeed "sweat the small stuff." Coffee too cold, parking space too far away, uncomfortable chairs, or any number of shallow complaints that mankind made daily. Sharon assumed that Mrs. Tippens' poor, well-meaning daughter would trade her predicament for a lifetime of endless trivial annoyances in a heartbeat. Sharon vowed to appreciate the little things in her life that made it great and rose to face the patients in rooms 21 and 22.

As she was putting her lab coat back on, her trauma pager sounded. She opened the door and briskly strode toward the nursing station in time to hear the details: white male, gunshot wound to the groin, estimated time of arrival - five minutes. She would ask Maria to page the on-call cardiologist and surgeon to consult with Mr. Kilpatrick and Mrs. Tippens since she'd be busy with the trauma. She thought if she could avoid breaking the news of the intestinal rupture to Mrs. Tippens and her daughter, that would be one bullet dodged, much unlike her incoming patient.

CHAPTER 4

Sharon approached the charge nurse. "Maria? Could you page the surgeon and cardiologist on call for rooms 21 and 22? It looks like I may be detained with the trauma."

Maria Ortiz frowned slightly and pointed to trauma room 1. "They're here already, Dr. West, and I don't think you'll be detained at all. I think they're waiting for you to pronounce the time of death. But yes, I'd be glad to make those calls."

Puzzled, Dr. West bounded toward the trauma room and noticed two paramedics who looked vaguely familiar leaning against the wall. They quickly straightened to an uncomfortably erect stance when Sharon approached.

Sharon looked at each of the EMT's badges and won them over when she spoke. "Good afternoon, Tim, William. Am I to understand that there's really *no* trauma after all?"

The taller of the two, William, spoke. "Yes, Doctor. I'm sorry about that, but I was told by my superior to phone it in as a 911 trauma even though the guy was dead at the scene of the incident. I didn't put in the call until we were just outside in the ambulance bay. I didn't want to bother you any sooner than I had to. I mean, he was dead.

We tried CPR for several minutes and then, when the cops got there, the wife started saying something about him having AIDS and getting her sick and all. Anyhow, Tim and I had gotten blood all over us in spite of our usual precautions because there was a pool of it around the guy. I mentioned the fact that we'd had an exposure to my boss and he said to talk to you about getting some sort of pills."

Sharon knew that within two hours of being exposed to HIV, people can begin a regimen of prophylactic anti-viral medication which greatly reduced their chances of becoming infected with the disease. Looking at these two young men with rust-colored smudges from head to toe, Sharon realized that time was of the essence. Anti-viral medication wasn't without possible side-effects, so policy dictated that the source of the exposure have an HIV test prior to dispensation of drugs to the one exposed. She needed to pronounce the body soon and collect a blood sample if she had any hope of meeting the two-hour window. She nodded to the young paramedics and entered the trauma room.

On the table lay the bloody body of a once attractive male with an almost confused expression on his face. Death must have come soon for him. Putting her stethoscope to his chest, she verified the lack of a heartbeat. Although she presumed that the 911 call had been placed immediately after the shooting occurred, she would still need to estimate a time of death.

Rigor mortis typically began anywhere between one and six hours after death. Since the smaller muscles were affected first, Sharon tried to manipulate the man's fingers. They were not yet completely stiff. She then placed her hand upon the arm of the victim and found that it was only slightly cool. Raising the arm slightly, she noticed the mottled appearance of the skin on the underside which was indicative of beginning stage livor mortis. If the livor mortis progressed, the entire undersurface would have been uniformly plum-colored from the pooling of the body fluids after death. Considering these three pieces of information together, Sharon estimated that the man had been dead for less than one hour. Maria entered the room carrying the newly created chart for the victim and placed it upon the instrument tray.

Appraising the body, Maria frowned and said, "I made those calls, Dr. West. Dr. Amaya is here already, so he's taking care of the MI patient. Dr. Cabrerra will be in within the hour to take Mrs. Tippens to surgery. About this one; they said his wife did it."

Sharon had no clue as to the details of the shooting and at this moment couldn't have cared less. First and foremost was to get a sample of blood so that the lab could do a stat HIV test and she could begin to treat the paramedics. Those were lives she could, in theory, still do something about.

"I'll need a scalpel and two 10 ml red top vacutainers to collect a sample for an HIV test," she said.

Without question, Maria ventured to the orderly cabinets and brought Sharon the requested items.

It was impossible to draw blood using the traditional methods if a person had been dead long enough for their blood to congeal, as was the case here. Sharon took the scalpel and made a vertical incision along the forearm of the man, carefully extracting a three inch portion of his radial artery with the hemostats that Maria had instinctively positioned close at hand. Squeezing the clotted blood from the now flaccid artery, Sharon initialed the tube and asked Maria to make sure it was labeled with the patient's name and medical record number. She then placed the small severed vessel back into the incision she had made since there would be an autopsy and all pieces of anatomy must be accounted for.

She wasn't certain if this was proper protocol, but it was a workable solution. It would have taken too much precious time to have researched the policy for this case. She asked Maria to order a stat HIV test and focused her attention on the lifeless body as Maria exited the room.

Sharon picked up the chart and learned that the victim's name was Todd Stevens and he had indeed been shot by his wife because he had given her AIDS. She recorded her estimated time of death as well as the time that she had actually pronounced the body. Knowing that she still needed to talk to Mrs. Tippens and her daughter, Sharon turned and left the trauma room.

Pausing outside, she hoped to regain enough composure to handle the impending discussion with the Tippens family. The eager, anxious faces of Tim and William, the EMTs, met her as soon as she closed the door. She said, "Guys, you'll need to go through Admissions so that we can draw some blood for baseline labs. If you'll go to the nurses' station and explain the situation, they can get you registered and taken care of in just a few minutes."

She watched as the two men walked uncertainly to the registration desk of the ER. They had both been here countless times, swaggering through the doors, yet their uncertain gaits spoke volumes. They were caregivers, not used to seeking assistance. She closed her eyes and began to fabricate plausible explanations for Mrs. Tippens' ruptured intestine that didn't include an enema. Still lost in her thoughts, she jumped a bit at the mention of her name.

"Dr. West? I don't know if you remember me or not, but—"

"Hi, Detective Fuller. Of course I remember you. What brings you here?"

Even as the words came from her mouth, Sharon knew how ridiculous they must sound. Of course the homicide detective was here for Mr. Stevens, the homicide victim.

"Uh, this is my partner, Detective Chet Avery. He and I are here to discuss a patient of yours, Todd Stevens. I understand he was brought in here after the shooting?"

"Yes, he was. Unfortunately, he was a DOA. There isn't much that I can tell you since all I did was pronounce him dead. I ordered an HIV test on him since the paramedics were exposed to his blood and apparently, according to his wife, he has AIDS."

Lacy sighed, disgusted with this 'so-called' case already. "Well, it does seem that way if you believe his wife. We'll need to take a look at the body and also talk to you for a few minutes if you have time."

Sharon nodded and extracted a pen and prescription pad from her jacket pocket. Scribbling down four numbers, she tore the page off and handed it to Lacy. "Absolutely. Mr. Stevens is inside this room. You'll find a recent incision on his right arm. I did that collecting a blood sample. I may be awhile; I've got two paramedics and a couple of critical patients to check on. Here's the code for the staff lounge. I'd love to tell you that you'll be more comfortable in there, but I try not to lie. At least you'll have relative peace and quiet so you two can discuss the case. Help yourself to the coffee if you'd like. The lounge is just down this hallway, the last door on the left. I'll be with you as soon as I can."

Lacy and Chet thanked her and entered the trauma room as Sharon approached the nurses' station. She perused the list of patients waiting to be seen: a thirty-six-year-old with vaginal bleeding; a nine-year-old with a rash and sore throat; an eighty-year-old who had fallen; and a twenty-year-old with a migraine. She could pop in on Mrs. Tippens and probably do an initial examination on one or two of the other patients while the HIV test was being completed.

The door to Mrs. Tippens' room was slightly ajar. Sharon tapped gently and entered. She was met with one pair of tired, frightened eyes and one blank stare.

In a soft voice she said, "Well, I've looked over the x-rays we took. There seems to be an intestinal rupture, so I've called in a surgeon. I've brought the consent forms which will need to be signed."

Instantly, Selma Tippens, the "bad" daughter, hung her head shamefully and began to quietly sob.

"It's because of the enema, isn't it? I knew it. I gave it to her because she had a CT scan yesterday, and they warned me that the barium she had to drink for the test could cause constipation. I didn't want her to be constipated. I had no idea this could happen. God help me."

Sharon found herself beside Selma, her hand working small circular motions on the grieving woman's shoulder. She wanted to explain that the untreatable cancer would shortly be robbing the life from Selma's mother anyhow, yet she knew that to voice that sentiment would be giving credence to the young woman's guilt complex. 'Yes, your mother would soon be dying, perhaps not as soon as now, thanks to you' was definitely not a message that she wanted to convey.

"Where are we?" asked the small voice from the gurney.

Sharon had to compose herself before she spoke.

"Mrs. Tippens? You're in a hospital. You have a problem with your intestine, and you'll probably need surgery."

Selma Tippens interjected immediately, "She told me, you know, before the cancer spread to her brain, that she didn't want another major surgery. Ever. Isn't there something else you can do?"

Since Selma had obviously educated herself about her mother's illness, Sharon decided to be forthright. "You could always elect not to have surgery, but the intestinal bacteria have already spilled out into the abdominal cavity. She would probably only live for a few days at the most, and I'm afraid there would be substantial pain involved. On the other hand, if she did have surgery, the infection could possibly be controlled and she could live a bit longer."

In a shaky voice, Mrs. Tippens said, "I want to live. I'm not ready to die yet. I'll have the surgery."

Selma began crying loudly, saying over and over that it was all her fault.

Mrs. Tippens spoke, the once prominent quaver no longer present. "Honey, what are you doing? Nothing is your fault. You're the best daughter anyone could ever have. Stop blaming yourself. Doctor? Would you make sure that she knows that my being sick is not her fault? Ever since I can remember, she's had this guilt complex. One time I asked if she felt guilty after a big earthquake killed so many people in China. She just looked at me like I was crazy, but I said, 'Well, I guess *that* was your fault, too."

Amazing, thought Sharon. The lucidity of the woman's remarks sent a chill up her spine. Here was a woman who didn't remember where she was after having spent the last several hours inside an emergency room, yet she remembered details from a conversation many years before. The human brain was a fascinating and intricate machine.

Trying to sound convincing, Sharon said, "Your mother's right, Selma. This is not your fault. Cancer is an often unbeatable enemy."

Just then, a tap came from behind them and Dr. Javier Cabrerra entered the room.

"Good evening, Dr. West, Mrs. Tippens." He nodded at Selma. "If you'll please excuse us, I need to touch base with Dr. West for a moment."

Heading toward the door without making physical contact, Dr. Cabrerra made his exit. Sharon thought about the course in bedside manner that she'd been required to take in medical school and cynically mused that it must not have been required for this surgeon. She excused herself and stepped outside.

"Sharon, what are we doing here? The woman's tissues are going to be paper thin. It would take a miracle for her to survive the surgery! She's been on prednisone for six months. Do you really think it's worth it to do surgery?"

Seething, Sharon managed to barely suppress her anger. "Of course it's worth it. We can explain just how dangerous the surgery will be and that she may not pull through. Otherwise, it'll help the family by giving them a few extra days to come to terms with losing her."

Dr. Cabrerra took a deep breath before speaking. "I just don't want them to have any grand illusions about this. I read her chart; you know as well as I that it's a matter of time before she dies. Do you realize it's already been six hours since the enema was administered? Do you know how quickly E. Coli can replicate in six hours? She's probably septic already. We're talking a massive infection that I just don't see how we can contain."

Through an angry stare, Sharon said, "Yes, I'm fully aware of that information. Do you realize, Doctor, that by taking this attitude, you're one step away from shunning your Hippocratic oath? If it were your mother lying on that table, would you want her last remaining hours spent with a raging infection and excruciating pain or would you rather take your chances that she pulled through surgery and was allowed to die more peacefully?"

Sharon hoped that the surgeon would recall the cases of abdominal sepsis that he'd encountered throughout the years.

With a nod, Dr. Cabrerra conceded, "I'll take care of having the consent signed and reserve an OR room."

With that, the doctor turned and went back inside the patient's room. Maria Ortiz approached Sharon with a perplexed look.

"Dr. West? The stat HIV test is back on Mr. Stevens. It was negative."

"Are you sure?" asked Sharon.

"Yes, Doctor. The lab even repeated it since they had apparently been told it would be positive. They're in the process of running the test on an instrument now rather than simply relying on the results of the rapid test kit. They said the repeat testing takes about 45 minutes. What are we going to do about treating the paramedics?"

What indeed, Sharon wondered. There was no sense in administering any medication if the source of their exposure was HIV negative. Still, the rapid test kits lacked the extreme sensitivity that the slower instrument possessed. It would be seriously pushing the two hour time frame, but Sharon decided to postpone her decision of treatment until the second set of results came back.

"Please explain the situation to the paramedics and tell them that we'll know something definitive within the hour."

With a nod, the nurse was off again. Sharon walked over to room 24 and picked up the chart from the plastic bin outside. Ah, yes, the eighty-year-old woman who had fallen. She tapped and opened the door.

"Mrs. Sides? Hi, I'm Doctor West. You've taken a fall?"

"Oh, yes, honey, it was awful. It seemed to happen in slow motion, but there was nothing I could do about it. I landed on my chest and stomach. I'm really sore, and it hurts like the blue blazes!"

Blue blazes. That was a phrase that Sharon hadn't heard since she moved from Alabama several years before.

"I bet it does. I'm going to have them bring a portable x-ray machine in here so you don't have to get up. I'll order something for your pain and come back to see you after the x-rays are developed, okay?"

"Okay. Just don't forget. I don't think I can sleep with this pain."

"I promise you, Mrs. Sides, I definitely won't forget. I'll be back soon."

Walking back toward the nurses' station, Sharon thought how sad it was that the poor little woman thought that she'd be forgotten. Was she accustomed to being forgotten by society in general or just by physicians? Sharon wrote the orders for x-rays and morphine and handed them to the patient's nurse before going to the next room and scanning the chart.

Room 25: Jeremy Tyler. Patient is a nine-year-old male complaining of a sore throat. Mother says he has an "awful looking rash" on his chest, which is why she brought him to the ER. No known drug allergies. Sharon's first thoughts were that she'd be dealing with either a streptococcal infection or possibly a tick-borne illness. Tapping gently on the door, she entered the room.

A small, bookish boy sat wrapped in the hospital-issued gown looking gaunt and tired. His parents sat nearby with worried expressions.

"Jeremy? Hi, I'm Dr. West. You must be Mr. and Mrs. Tyler. It's nice to meet you. How long has Jeremy had these symptoms?"

It was Mrs. Tyler who spoke first. "He's had a sore throat for several days now. He hasn't been eating much or sleeping well the last few days. Anyhow, this afternoon he wanted ice cream, so I bought him a cone while we were out shopping. It was chocolate, his favorite, and he just let it melt all over him and his clothes. When we got home, I had him take his shirt off, and that's when I saw the God-awful rash on his chest and back. As soon as I saw it, I brought him down here."

Sharon focused her attention on Jeremy. Meekly, the boy opened his gown to reveal several brownish splotches. A feeling of nausea overcame Sharon as she mentally noted that this wasn't a case of simple infection or a virus from a tick bite.

Trying to keep the alarm from her voice, Sharon asked, "Jeremy? How long have you had this rash?"

"I don't know. A month I guess." The young boy fidgeted as he answered.

"Can you open your mouth for me so I can check your throat?" Sharon asked in her most soothing voice.

Shining her light inside his mouth, she was dismayed to see several white patches indicative of thrush. So, this poor child had a terrible yeast infection in his mouth as well as lesions on his body that looked like Kaposi's sarcoma. Each of these symptoms were indicative of a weakened immune system, however Kaposi's was a common symptom of AIDS. If she were the betting kind, Sharon thought sadly, she would wager that she was looking at her first case of juvenile HIV.

"Jeremy, I'm going to need to draw some blood from you so that we can do a few tests. I'm also going to need to talk to you about some of your activities over the past few years."

The boy looked at his parents before he answered. "Okay."

Mrs. Tyler looked worried, Mr. Tyler looked sleepy. Sharon knew that after her first few questions into his son's life, he would likely be wide awake. Maybe it would be better to do this without his parents in the room. Children seemed to be more forthright about certain things when their parents weren't around, especially of a sexual nature. She reached over and pressed the nurse call button on the side of the bed. When the tinny voice asked if it could help her, Sharon requested that Maria Ortiz be sent to room 25.

"Could you guys step outside for a few minutes when the nurse comes in so we can complete the examination? If you'd like to go to the vending area to get a drink, I'll come get you when we're through."

When the door opened and Maria stepped in, Mr. and Mrs. Tyler rose in unison and left. Pointing to Jeremy's open chart, Sharon said, "These are the tests we'll need to run, Maria. If you want to get the supplies, I just have a few questions for Jeremy."

Maria scanned the orders and briefly closed her eyes, no doubt bothered by the necessity of an HIV test on a nine-year-old child. She mumbled that she'd be back and quickly left the room.

Turning her full attention on the boy, Sharon smiled what she hoped would pass as a carefree greeting.

"I'm just going to ask you a few questions, Jeremy. It's important that you tell me the truth about everything. You won't get in trouble, no matter what you tell me. Do you understand?"

The child looked scared. "Yes, Ma'am. I mean, Doctor."

Palpating Jeremy's neck and axillary region for swollen lymph nodes, Sharon softly asked, "Have you ever gotten stuck with a needle when you weren't inside a hospital? Like maybe one of your friends had a needle and you somehow got stuck by it?"

"No."

Warming her stethoscope in her hand, she asked, "Okay. Do you kind of know what sex is?"

Blushing, he nodded in assent. Reason number five million that Sharon was glad she didn't have children; nine-year-olds knew what sex was.

"Have you ever had sex or done things with another person of the sexual nature?"

"No." The boy began squirming awkwardly on the table.

Sensing that her eye contact may have been adding to his discomfort, Sharon averted her glance and began listening to his heart. "It's okay if you have, Jeremy. I really need to know if you have."

"I just held a girl's hand once. That's all. Honest."

Stepping back slightly, Sharon smiled at him. She hoped she could mask the concern she felt. "Okay, Jeremy, I believe you. Do you know what a blood transfusion is?"

Brightening, as if happy to be able to answer yes for a change, Jeremy said, "Yes, Ma'am! I had one after my bike wreck. The handle bars hit me in the stomach and busted something, so I had to have an operation. I got somebody else's blood, and Dad got mad because they had to operate before he could give me his blood. Want to see my scar?"

Dad would get a hell of a lot madder if a blood transfusion had infected his son with HIV, Sharon thought. She wondered how she could have missed seeing evidence of a major surgery until the boy reopened his gown. The angry splotches demanded full attention, yet she looked down and saw the scar left over from an apparent splenectomy.

Sharon said, "Wow. That's pretty impressive. I don't have any scars that big on me. You must be a pretty brave guy."

Blushing again, Jeremy smiled as he closed his gown. Maria chose that moment to enter the room with a tray of blood collection equipment and placed it on the bed next to the small boy. She expertly tied the tourniquet and drew three tubes of blood. Jeremy didn't even flinch. He really was a brave little guy.

"Well, Jeremy, I'm going to get your parents now. Would you like a soda or something?" Sharon asked.

"No, Ma'am. It burns my mouth and throat."

Sharon remembered the thrush and mentally chided herself for being inconsiderate. "Okay. I'll be in to see you in a little while after the results of your tests come back." She patted Jeremy on the shoulder and left the room with Maria shadowing her closely.

As soon as they were out of hearing distance, Maria asked, "What makes you think AIDS?"

"You didn't see the yeast in his throat or the *rash* which looks like Kaposi's," Sharon said, handing Maria a dollar bill. "I don't think a sports drink would burn his throat, so if you'd get him one when you retrieve his parents, I'd be happy. Well, okay, not happy; a child appears to have AIDS and the most likely explanation seems to be linked to a blood transfusion. So, no, happy isn't the right word. But I would appreciate it. Also, could you page me when the results come back on this one? I'm going to check on the other two patients before I talk to the detectives. Let's make sure we order the automated HIV test for this little guy, okay?"

"Sure, Doctor West. I'll send it to the lab now."

Thirty minutes later, the patient with the migraine was on a morphine-phenergan drip and was feeling much better. A positive pregnancy test on the patient with vaginal bleeding indicated a possible miscarriage, so Sharon paged the Ob/Gyn on-call. Mrs. Tippens was in surgery. Mr. Kilpatrick had been admitted to the coronary intensive care unit for observation. And finally, the automated test for HIV had come back negative on Todd Stevens. Sharon had given the EMTs the option to take the prophylactic drugs just in case and both had chosen to do so since the wife had been adamant that the victim had AIDS. With fifteen minutes left before she would get the results of Jeremy's HIV test, Sharon decided it would be a good time to talk to the detectives.

CHAPTER 5

Lacy paced the lounge like a caged tiger. Chet, on the other hand, sat in a purple chair which he'd leaned against the wall, reading an automotive magazine and sipping a cup of coffee.

Annoyed by her partner's apparent comfort, Lacy snapped at him. "How in the hell can you sit in those damned uncomfortable Barney chairs?"

"Lace, you never cease to amaze me. I didn't know that you even knew who Barney was!" He did gather from the venomous way she spoke the name that she did *not* love the TV dinosaur.

"Just because I don't have kids doesn't mean I live my life in a vacuum, Avery."

He shrugged and went back to reading while Lacy resumed her pacing. A few minutes later, a visibly depressed Dr. West entered the lounge. Chet rose immediately, and Lacy stopped dead in her tracks when she saw Sharon. Damn, she thought, Dr. West was a very attractive woman, even wearing scrubs and a lab coat!

Sharon leaned against the wall and said, "Hi, Detectives. I'm sorry you've had to wait so long. I've probably got about fifteen minutes before my pager goes off. It's usually a zoo around here, but today has been really bad."

Lacy looked at the attractive blonde, noticing the dark circles beneath her eyes and the crow's feet at the outer corners. She was probably about 5'6, which made her a couple of inches taller than Lacy herself. Lacy had remembered how genuinely kind she'd seemed the first time that they had met. When was that? Six months ago? Wow, and Dr. West had remembered her name! Shit. Avery was talking. She had zoned out again.

"—so Detective Fuller will be the lead on this case." With a smile, Avery looked from Dr. West to Lacy and sat once again.

Sharon and Lacy followed his lead and sat as well. Lacy, who sat perched on the edge of the hard seat as if ready to pounce on some unsuspecting prey, opened her pad to begin taking notes.

"Dr. West? Has anyone given you the history on Todd Stevens yet? I mean, why his wife shot him, why he was brought here as if he wasn't already dead, stuff like that?" Lacy asked.

"Well, I know that his wife shot him because she thought he had AIDS. It turns out that he didn't. Because this is an ongoing investigation, I'm sure that you'll need to send a sample to the State Crime Lab for verification. We tested by two different methods, though, and both results were negative. The paramedics who were exposed both decided to take the prophylactic treatment since the particulars of the case are a bit strange."

"Huh. I wonder why she thought he had AIDS?" Lacy was thinking aloud again and was so focused on her own question to herself that she missed the question Sharon asked.

"I don't know why the paramedics brought him here as a trauma when he was actually dead at the scene. Do you?"

Avery cleared his throat when it became obvious that Lacy wasn't going to answer.

"Todd Stevens' wife is Judge Farnsworth's niece and Ivan Farnsworth's daughter. My guess is that nothing about this case is going to be routine."

Lacy chose that moment to rejoin the conversation. "If the husband was dead on arrival and HIV negative, I guess we really only need a copy of his medical record for tonight. The crime scene techs will probably drop by later to get a sample for the State lab, like you said. Oh, and I'd like to pick up his personal belongings too while we're here."

Sharon nodded. "Detective Avery? If you'd be so kind as to go to the registration desk and ask for Maria, she'll give you Mr. Stevens' bag."

"Sure thing, Doctor. Thank you for all of your help." Avery extended his hand toward Dr. West.

"You're both welcome. I'm sorry you had to wait so long for so little information."

Lacy watched Avery leave the room. Believing that she knew what was about to be discussed, she attempted to hold the questions at bay by focusing on the current case.

"Oh, I think that finding out tonight that the husband didn't have AIDS is a tremendous amount of information. If we'd had to wait for the State to send in the results, it would have been weeks," Lacy said as she closed her notebook.

"Well, that's good to know. So, how is your friend, Nancy?"

Man. No beating around the bush for Dr. West, just as Lacy had suspected. Lacy thought back to that night, six months ago, and began replaying the events in her mind. She'd gotten a call at work from her lover, Nancy, saying that she was going to kill herself. Lacy had rushed home to find Nancy lying on the couch bleeding from both wrists. She had applied pressure bandages and taken her to Brookshire Medical Center, where she had first met Dr. West. The system mandated that any suicide attempts be kept in the mental health ward for some pre-governed laughably short period of time. Nancy was out in a week.

Dr. West had recommended that Lacy move out while Nancy was away. She had said, "Your partner feels that your work is more important to you than she is. My brother is a police officer, and I know how important it is for you to have all of your faculties about you on the job. You don't need this kind of a relationship. You should get out while you have the chance." That evening, Lacy had packed up her things and moved in with her friend James until she found an apartment.

Clearing her throat, Lacy said, "Well, as it turns out, she didn't really love me after all. That was one of the reasons that she was so pissed off at me all the time. She felt like I was beneath her or something. Anyhow, every time I would work late on a case, she would brood over how I treated her like shit, and she stayed with me even though she didn't love me. I think she was mostly angry with herself and took it out on me. Now, she's dating some woman who works at a bank. Nice, regular hours and no calls in the middle of the night. I'm sure Nancy is happier."

"Well. I'm glad that situation worked out as well as it did. Are you okay with it?" Sharon asked.

"Yeah. It's funny, but I didn't love her either. She was so selfish and whiney. I've been wondering for the last six months what I was thinking when I moved in with her."

The shrill beeps of Dr. West's pager caused them both to start. The message, from Maria, was "911-25" since it was a numerical text only beeper. That meant that Jeremy, the patient in room 25, needed attention worthy of a 911 call. Sharon assumed the HIV test was positive.

Looking deflated, Sharon said, "I'm glad you're doing okay. I've got to check on this patient. The official report of the medical record for Mr. Stevens will be ready in 72 hours. I'll request a copy of it and you can pick it up. I'm off the next three days, but I'll be back again on Monday. I'm sorry to have to rush off like this."

"No problem, Dr. West. I just have one more thing I need to say. Thank you for the advice, you know, about Nancy. I *am* much happier and more alert at work. You were right. I appreciated your taking the time to talk to me that night. People don't usually give me advice. I guess my reputation as a hothead scares them off."

With a wink, Sharon said, "Well, you're certainly welcome, and I didn't know you were a hothead or I may have kept my mouth shut, too! Good night, Detective Fuller."

Lacy saw a tired smile play on the corners of Dr. West's mouth before she turned to leave the lounge. Lacy followed her, thinking how that was the first time in either encounter that she'd even seen a hint of a smile on the doctor's face. Yet, the crow's feet and little laugh lines around her mouth indicated that she must be making up for her sobriety at work by laughing hardily somewhere else. She enjoyed the fact that Dr. West had winked at her, although she knew it was the "playful" wink rather than the "flirtatious" wink. Still, she loved winks.

Lacy had also noted the absence of a ring on the Doctor's left hand. Was she single? Actually, there was a lack of rings on either hand. Maybe there was no deeper significance to it than she chose not to wear jewelry to work. She spotted Avery leaned against the wall near the exit, holding a small purple bag. What was it with this place and purple?

Chet spoke as Lacy approached him. "Hey, Lace. Are you ready to go downtown and question the newly widowed Mrs. Stevens?"

"Yeah, but why don't you go home? You've got a wife and kid to see. I'll handle the interview."

"Well, um, I was just thinking, um—"

"Damn, Avery! Spit it out! I'm not made of fucking porcelain!"

Chet averted his eyes as he spoke. "Well, you know, you aren't the nicest interviewer we've got, and it *is* an interview with a Farnsworth."

"Who just so happens to be a murderer! I'm so sick of hearing the name Farnsworth that I could scream. Besides, I'm not a total dumbass. I know when to be nice and, contrary to popular opinion, I actually can be!"

Watching her stalk off to their car, Avery decided that he would never have come up with the analogy of Lacy being made of porcelain. Sure, her skin was probably the color of a porcelain doll, but those delicate dolls said "Mama" whereas Lacy said "Mother Fucker." Uh-oh, he thought. Lacy was standing beside the driver's door. She always wanted to drive when she was angry. He distinctly remembered having driven them here in a sensible manner. He dug into his pockets and handed her the keys. Moments later, he was belted in for dear life as they made the warp-speed trip back to the department in silence.

CHAPTER 6

By the time Lacy and Chet walked into the department, he was having a massive anxiety attack and thinking of increasing his life insurance, but she was in a decidedly better mood. He guessed it was worth the near death experience to have her not be mad anymore. He hated it when women got mad and hated it even more when they were sad. Reaching their desks, Lacy began perusing the stack of mail and phone messages while Chet made a quick call to his wife, Monica. By the time he had hung up, Lacy had sorted his phone messages, too. Nah, she wasn't still mad.

"So, Lace. Any ideas?" he asked, somewhat cautiously.

"Yeah. I'll be bad cop, you be good cop."

"Well, that's not very original," he said. Lacy swatted him with a police apparel magazine she'd gotten in the stack of mail.

"Yeah, I know," she said. "Okay, I was thinking; what if Mrs. Stevens knew how she contracted HIV, knew that it had nothing to do with her husband, and figured that she'd get off scot-free since A) she's the Judge's niece, B) who would convict a distraught woman for shooting her husband if she thought he'd given her AIDS? and C) she has the means to hire a good enough lawyer to get her some kind of medical pardon because of her condition?"

"Well, what would her motive have been? She wouldn't need the money from life insurance." He knew that his treacherous ride from the hospital had left him with life insurance on his mind. He also knew that she couldn't have collected anyway if she had murdered the policy holder.

"Maybe she was just sick of him. You know, it happens," Lacy said, nonchalantly.

"Jesus, Lacy, do me a favor and honor me with warning if you ever start to tire of me as a partner!"

Lacy smiled at him. "Okay. Ready to get this show on the road?"

"You bet, but I get to be good cop."

Lacy rolled her eyes in mock disappointment as she agreed.

Lacy and Chet entered the interrogation room to find a subdued Shelly Stevens wearing standard issue prison-wear that was at least two sizes too large. She was actually an attractive woman: platinum blonde hair in a stylish, shoulder-length cut, a healthy looking tan evenly coating her skin, and absolutely gorgeous blue eyes. Next to Shelly Stevens stood an unnaturally pale, tall, thin man wearing an obviously expensive suit. Apparently, this egret-looking man was her lawyer. Lacy thought that if the designer of the aforementioned suit could see it draping off egret-boy he would surely sue whoever allowed him to purchase it. Chet, having already playfully but firmly established his role as the lead interrogator, stepped forward and offered his hand to Shelly Stevens.

"Mrs. Stevens? Hi. I am Detective Chet Avery and this is Detective Lacy Fuller."

Lacy nodded at Mrs. Stevens and then pierced Ichabod Crane, Jr. with her stare.

Ever the socialite regardless of the dire consequences, Shelly offered, "This is my lawyer, Martin Strausser. It is a pleasure to meet you, Detectives."

In a nasal voice even more absurd than the manner in which he filled his suit, Martin Strausser said, "Good evening, Chad, Lacy."

"Um, it's Chet," Chet volunteered.

"Ah, yes, of course," said the egret with absolutely no trace of sincerity in his tone.

"Mrs. Stevens, Detective Fuller and I have been assigned to work your case. I'd like to get your permission to tape this interview."

"Yes, of course."

Turning the tape recorder on, Chet stated the names of all parties in attendance, the time and the date.

"When you were arrested, were you read your Miranda rights?" he asked.

She answered, "Yes."

"As a matter of policy, I will be reading your Miranda rights again and ask that you sign this form stating that you were read your rights both at the time you were arrested as well as now." Chet then began reading from an index card he had retrieved from his inside pocket.

As soon as he had finished, Shelly Stevens took the proffered pen and paper and signed her name.

Chet said, "I must tell you that the charges you were booked under, attempted homicide, have been upgraded to homicide. Your husband didn't make it. Do you fully understand—"

The egret spoke. "Now wait just a minute, Chad. I don't want you to get too far in over your head, here. You *do* realize that this is Judge Farnsworth's niece?"

"Uh, yes sir, I do. She is also Todd Stevens' wife who confessed to shooting Mr. Stevens earlier this evening; the same Mr. Stevens who's now deceased."

Looking offended, Martin Strausser said, "Surely, Son, you'll agree that the poor woman was mentally anguished. After all she had done for him, to think that he would give her that faggot's disease? He deserved to be shot!"

Chet noticed Lacy bristle at the slander and was extra glad that he was the lead interrogator. Quickly, before Lacy could interrupt, he said, "Well, actually, the preliminary HIV test on Mr. Stevens has come back negative."

Shelly Stevens gasped. "Is that true?"

Martin Strausser didn't give Chet the opportunity to answer. "Now just hold on there, Shelly. I'm sure the police or the hospital or whoever tested that sample made a mistake. Of course he had the disease, and he gave it to you. Nobody in their right mind would dispute that." The lawyer's beady eyes were fixed like lasers on Chet.

Again, Shelly asked, "Seriously, is it true? If he didn't have AIDS, then how did I get it? Oh, my God; I shot him!"

Shelly Stevens began softly crying, looking fragile and deflated.

"Now see what you've done, Chad?" said the egret, shaking his head in courtroom showmanship disappointment.

Speaking slowly and forcefully, Lacy said, "His name is Chet. C-H-E-T. Not Chad, C-H-A-D."

The egret opened his mouth to once again feign apology, but promptly shut it once he saw the look in Lacy's eyes. She directed her glare at Shelly, who was watching the display intently and sniffling in an utterly unladylike manner.

Lacy said, "I think if I were you, I'd get another attorney. If this guy can't remember someone's name when it's only four letters and he was told twice, he damned sure isn't going to give you adequate representation in the court room!"

Egret stuck his chest out and took a step toward Lacy. "Now wait just a minute, Miss Fuller. I don't think you have a firm understanding on just what consequences your verbal onslaught may lead to. I'm personal friends with the Chief of Police as well as Captain Sumlin, and I can assure you, they *will* hear about this."

Chet could feel the tension from Lacy's anger toward the lawyer as soon as he'd referred to her as "Miss" rather than acknowledging her title of detective. Her voice was thick with sarcasm when she said, "Well, guess what? You won't even have to call your buddy Captain Sumlin because he's watching this whole scenario through that mirrored glass over there."

Martin Strausser began to blush and was suddenly transformed from egret to pissed-off pink flamingo. Even his hands turned pink with anger.

With forced bravado, he said, "I'll see to it that Judge Farnsworth himself hears about this little incident."

"Oh yeah? Well, I might just beat you to the punch. I might just decide that it's in the best interest of your client to have an attorney who can remember names. After all, it would be a shame to have a conviction overturned because of incompetent representation."

The flamingo's face was now the color of a Halloween devil costume, and his mouth was drawn into a harsh pucker that Lacy thought looked rather rectal in comparison.

Shelly Stevens had regained some of her composure. "Martin, why don't you step outside for a while and cool off? I'll call you back in when you're needed."

"I'm afraid that isn't a good idea, Mrs. Stevens."

"I'm afraid that I don't care what you're afraid of, Martin. I'm paying for your services, and you will do as you're told. Is that clear?"

Looking as though he'd just smelled an outhouse, and yet redder than ever, Martin Strausser said, "Very well. I'll be outside the door if you need me." He turned to pick up his briefcase, and Lacy couldn't resist one final jab.

"Oh, Mr. Schnausser?"

"It's Strausser!" A large vein erupted from the lawyer's forehead as he angrily walked to the door. His countenance indicated that he was fully aware that he'd been played. To make matters worse, he couldn't even slam the door as he left since it was a pneumatic closing system designed to shut quietly. Watching the door ease gently closed with a soft click, Lacy smiled inwardly; another battle won.

"God, what a shit he is. He's been our family's attorney since forever. Well, actually, before him it was his father, but they're one in the same. I'm sorry for his behavior, Detectives." Shelly looked at Lacy, and the women both smiled at each other.

Chet had to hand it to Lacy. Few people could best a lawyer that quickly, and the fact that Captain Sumlin actually *was* in the next room watching and had yet to pull Lacy from the interview meant that he felt she was still towing the line. The two women seemed to have bonded somehow, so Chet reversed his earlier plan, deciding that Lacy should take the lead.

Chet spoke. "Mrs. Stevens? Detective Fuller here has some questions to ask you."

Lacy raised an eyebrow as she looked at Chet, who was smiling at her sheepishly.

The exchange apparently wasn't lost on Shelly Stevens. "Let me guess. He thought you'd piss me off because you have an attitude. Now, he's probably thinking that you and I are peas in a pod, so it's okay for you to do the talking. Is that about right?"

Chet cleared his throat and said, "Guilty as charged."

Shelly laughed for a moment. "It's okay. I get that all the time. I'm so used to it that I often make a game of it. It's kid gloves and eggshells if you're a Farnsworth."

Lacy sat directly across from Shelly. She said, without the slightest trace of sarcasm, "Well, I'm glad you're so easy to deal with. I do need to tell you, however, that you probably should have counsel present when we talk to you since you're being charged in the death of your husband."

"No. You'll be taping everything still, I presume?"

Lacy answered, "Yes."

"Then, no, I'd prefer not to have Martin in my presence. I confess that I did shoot my husband. Since his being shot caused him to die, I'm responsible. End of story." Shelly's eyes moistened again, and Chet handed her his handkerchief.

Lacy almost felt pity for the woman, which seemed ridiculous. "How long have you known you had the AIDS virus?"

"I just found out today. I had a follow-up appointment with my doctor."

"What's your doctor's name?" Lacy asked, opening her notepad.

"Dr. Jonas, down on East 3rd Street. He was just doing a routine checkup because I'm due, well, *was* due to have liposuction performed on my thighs next week. I had donated my own blood, even though I didn't think that I'd actually need to be transfused. Still, there's always a chance. Also, I heard about there being a blood shortage, and I decided that if I needed blood, I shouldn't get any of the blood that's in short supply for a damned elective surgery. I remember, when I got pregnant, I had complications and wound up losing the baby and almost dying myself. If it hadn't been for the people who had donated blood back then, I wouldn't have made it. So, I donated my own blood. Did you know that if you donate your own blood, they still do all of the testing they do on the general supply of blood, even though it's illegal for anyone but you to get the unit?"

"No, actually, I didn't. So, the HIV test that came back positive was from the blood center? Maybe they made a mistake," Lacy volunteered.

"No. That's what Dr. Jonas thought, too, until he got the notification that I had tested positive again with the second unit. He said that sometimes you can have the virus for years before you get sick."

Staring at the healthy looking woman, Lacy asked, "So, are you sick?"

"Not yet, but I am HIV positive. Dr. Jonas said he had no clue when I might have been infected. Todd and I have been married for twenty years. We got married during our first year of college. Todd was pretty smart, but not scholarship material, and his family didn't have much money, so things were always tough for him. I got tired of him having to work three jobs, so I pretended to be pregnant and he married me."

Mild-mannered Chet came to life. "You tricked him into marrying you?"

Laughing, Shelly said, "Oh, God, no. I tricked my family into thinking I was pregnant so that they would give their blessing on my marrying someone beneath me in social stature. Anyhow, then I just told them that I had lost the baby and, meanwhile, they paid for mine and Todd's education, apartment, groceries; well, everything.

Sometimes it doesn't suck to be a Farnsworth. Still, I always wondered if my previous lie wasn't why our baby died during childbirth."

"So why did you assume you got HIV from Todd?" asked Lacy.

"I've never fooled around on Todd. He is, was, boring but sweet. He'd been mortified when I told him about the fake pregnancy. I liked that about him. I thought that was a good indicator of the type of person he was. I loved him, and I believe in monogamy. Plus, I've been taking an anti-depressant most of my adult life, and it affects my sex drive. Todd and I hardly ever had sex, so I thought he might have needed something that I wasn't giving him." Shelly looked pensively at an imaginary spot on the table in front of her after she spoke.

After jotting something down in her pad, Lacy asked, "Have you ever injected drugs?"

"No. I never would, either. I live as clean a life as I can, try to keep up my looks, take a variety of exercise classes, have psychotherapy twice a week, and still battle depression in spite of all that and the medicine."

Lacy made intense eye contact with Shelly Stevens and continued. "So, you have no idea whatsoever how or when you became infected with HIV?"

"No. I mean, I guess that if you can have it for years and years before you get sick, I could have gotten it from the guys that I dated before Todd. That was back in the early 1980's. If that isn't the case, then I just don't know."

Lacy furrowed her eyebrows and waited a moment before speaking. Convinced that the woman was telling the truth, she finally said, "Well, I think you'd be best served hiring a private investigator to research how you became infected rather than depending exclusively on Detective Avery and me. We're already pretty busy and, since you're obviously not dead yet, I'm afraid we'd be able to spend only a limited amount of time on your case since we're homicide detectives. We'll need a complete description of the events that took place once your husband got home today, but I'm going to insist that your attorney be present for that."

Shelly agreed. "I will hire an investigator but I'd also feel better if you did whatever you could on the side. Don't go out of your way, and please don't let anybody push you around because of who I am. Still, I'd like to know how I got AIDS."

"I would, too," said Lacy, and she meant it. She studied the woman sitting across from her and saw a fat tear slowly roll down her cheek and splash on the table.

"I'm really sorry about Todd," Shelly said in a chillingly quiet voice.

The egret was allowed to enter once again and remained quiet for the remainder of the proceedings. Shelly discussed at length the events of earlier in the day, her feelings of betrayal and anger over Todd's lie. Lacy requested the names of all of the men whom Shelly had slept with in the years prior to marrying Todd Stevens. The list was overwhelming. Young Shelly must have been definitely looking for something. It was hard to fathom that boring, nice-guy Todd could have ended a virtual sexual spree.

When Shelly wrote the last name, she sighed and handed the paper to Lacy, who quickly tallied up the numbers. Eighteen names!

"Huh. Is this *all*?" Lacy asked, not bothering to hide her sarcasm.

With a smile, Shelly nodded her head in affirmation before directing Martin to wait outside once again. This time, there was no objection as he stiffly walked to the door.

Shelly nervously looked around the room. Finally, she spoke. "Detective Fuller? I have a favor to ask of you."

Suspiciously, Lacy eyed Chet, who nonchalantly shrugged. Sure, he could shrug; an inmate wasn't asking a favor of *him* while the Captain looked on.

Finally, Lacy said, "Go ahead."

With a sad smile, Shelly said, "You remind me of me, which has something to do with the request I'm going to make of you. You see, I don't have many friends because I never know if someone is *pretending* to like me because of what they can get from me or not. I think that's one of the reasons I married Todd. I knew he loved me in his own way for *me*, not because of who I am. Anyhow, the friends that I do have, those with whom I socialize, are basically all in my economic stratum."

Lacy raised her right eyebrow and said, "I hate to interrupt, Mrs. Stevens, but there are laws in place, and I can't befriend an inmate."

"Just hear me out, please, Detective. I'm not asking you to be my friend. I do think, however, under different circumstances, that we could have been. No, you see, the friends that I do have are pretty superficial. I know you probably think that I am, too, because of the face-lifts and liposuction. I mainly try to look my best so that I'll feel better about myself, not because of any false pride or vanity. Anyhow, back to the point. We, I, have a cat. I've paid for him to be groomed and boarded at the vet for a month. I was wondering if you could try to find someone to adopt him?"

That wasn't the request that Lacy had imagined the woman would ask of her, though she wasn't entirely certain what she thought it might have been. Cautiously, yet somewhat relieved, she asked, "So your friends won't take him, even for a little while?"

"No, they just tolerate him and don't believe people should allow animals to live indoors. They even refuse to sit when they come by the house because of all the white fur on the furniture. He can't help shedding. He could stay at the cat clinic, but I'm afraid he'll go nuts if he has to stay in a cage. I'm sure someone who works there would adopt him but they all have multiple pets and he'd do well to be an only cat. I just don't have anyone else I feel I can trust to handle this."

Lacy said, "Okay. I'll ask around."

"Just one more thing," Shelly said, "Do you think you could go by and visit him at the vet's office?"

A hint of the annoyance that she was feeling crept out in Lacy's reply. "Okay. I'll try to visit the cat and find a home for it. Will there be anything else?"

"No. If you'll just give me a pen and paper, I'll jot down the address of the vet's office, and I'll have Martin call to tell them that you'll be by for some visits."

Lacy noticed that her one visit to see the cat had suddenly become plural. With a perturbed look, she said, "I'll have to clear it with my superiors."

"I sure hope it won't be a problem. I can't even send him to live with my parents because my father is allergic to cats. Oh, I'll need to approve whoever you find to keep him." With that, she tore the sheet from the pad and handed it to Lacy. With a sigh, she said, "Can we wrap this up? I'm really tired."

Before either detective could respond, the door to the interrogation room opened and Captain Sumlin appeared. As he motioned her to follow him, Shelly Stevens said goodnight to the detectives. As the door closed, Chet began to laugh softly.

"Shut up, CHAD, just shut up!" Lacy snarled.

CHAPTER 7

Lacy arrived at her midtown apartment at 11:00, hungry and tired. She poured herself a glass of milk and made a quick peanut butter and jelly sandwich before even taking her loafers off. The flashing red light on her answering machine annoyed her. Setting her milk down, she pressed the play button and dropped into her recliner. The first message was someone selling aluminum siding. Didn't these people have a brain? She lived in a loft apartment; what in the hell would she need with aluminum siding? She vowed to call the dumbass back the next morning and give her a piece of her mind.

The second message was from her friend James, asking if her blood pressure had returned to normal yet. "I knew an aluminum siding salesperson would piss you off royally. That was my sister, by the way. Remember, I told you she'd be in town this weekend? We were wondering if you could join us for dinner tomorrow. Just give me a call." The little shit! Lacy was somewhat accustomed to his phone antics, but he'd never before drafted the aid of an accomplice. Consequently, she was always able to tell it was him regardless of the goofy accent or voice he used. Two hang-up calls made her wish she had caller ID so she could call them back and hang up on them.

Through with the sandwich, but by no means sated, Lacy trolled the cupboards for something salty to eat. Half a family-ized bag of chips later, she made a mental note to jog an extra couple of miles this weekend. Scanning her music collection, she extracted a Sara McLachlan CD and began playing it softly. Removing her shoes, she once again settled into the recliner.

As she closed her eyes, she thought about Shelly Stevens and the strange case she'd been handed. Oddly enough, after having met the woman, Lacy wasn't nearly as pissed off about the assignment. Well, maybe the part about finding a home for the cat and going to visit it. How in the hell had that happened?

She took a notepad from the coffee table and began jotting down notes.

- How long until someone becomes symptomatic after being exposed to HIV? (Ask Dr. West)
- Multiple sex partners in early 80's. Were they all from the Atlanta area? (Ask Shelly)
- Interview the 18 guys. (Avery to help)
- Do a walk-through of the Stevens' place.
- Visit the cat. (Ask Shelly cat's name)

Yawning, she took the empty milk glass and rinsed it out before heading to the bathroom to brush her teeth and go to bed.

Chet pulled into the driveway of his house and was happy to see the light softly glowing in the living room. Monica had waited up for him again. She was so good to him.

Entering the hallway, he heard her bare feet softly padding towards him. He was still smiling about his good fortune in finding a woman like her when she rounded the corner and melded into his body for a long hug.

"I made beef stew for dinner. It turned out pretty good, too," she said.

"It always does, Hon."

Pulling away from him, she gave him a quick kiss and headed toward the kitchen while he shrugged out of his suit coat, then removed his gun and locked it safely away. He then followed his wife toward the kitchen.

"Tea?"

"Water, but I'll get it."

"No, sit down and eat your salad. I'll get it."

He sat and asked how her day had been. Placing a glass of water and the plate of stew in front of him, she told him all about her day.

"So, C.J. kept out of trouble?" he asked.

C.J., or Chet Jr., was currently proving to be a candidate for the most terrible of the children going through their terrible two's in history.

"He did. You know what they say, miracles do happen. Now, tell me about your day."

"Ivan Farnsworth's daughter killed her husband. Shot him when he came in from work. Lacy and I were assigned to the case."

"I'd say you've increased your percentage of solved cases yet again if you already know who did it."

"Yeah, I wish. She confessed alright, but that's only part of the case. It seems she tested positive for AIDS, thought he'd given it to her, and shot him. The kicker is, his HIV test was negative. So our job will be to investigate how Mrs. Stevens got the virus. The Atlanta PD puts two homicide detectives on this case because she's a Farnsworth. Sometimes I feel as cynical as Lacy. We'd definitely not be doing this if it were just your average citizen."

"No, you wouldn't. Believe me, though, if you ever become as cynical as Lacy, I might just have to shoot you!"

They laughed at the absurdity of the statement. Monica had never even touched a gun in her life. Chet had only recently gotten her to start carrying pepper spray.

Finishing the stew, Chet said, "That was great. Now, what do you say we go to bed and try *not* to make another little C.J.?"

During the first few months of C.J.'s life, Chet would always ask if she wanted to go upstairs and try to make another little C.J. After the too-brief period of the infant's docility, however, they now focused on not having a second child because CJ was definitely all they could handle for now.

"That sounds great to me. After you shower."

"After I shower," he agreed, loosening his tie.

At 7:00, Sharon West was walking towards her locker when she heard an overhead page announcing that she had a phone call. As she approached the nurses' station, the receptionist, who was on another line, mouthed *line 3* and smiled.

Sharon smiled back and held the receiver to her ear. "Hello, this is Doctor West."

"Dr. West? Sorry to bother you. This is Detective Fuller. I remembered you saying that you wouldn't be working again until Monday, and I had a couple of quick questions that I was hoping you could answer."

"I'll be glad to if I can."

"I've been trying to figure out how Mrs. Stevens contracted HIV. She swears that she didn't cheat on her husband and has never injected street drugs. Other than sex or drug use, what are some of the other potential modes of transmission?"

"Well, those are actually two of the most common. For healthcare workers and those who are caring for infected persons, the introduction of blood or body fluids through open wounds or needle sticks constitutes a plausible way to contract the disease. In the case of the average person, like Mrs. Stevens, it would seem that any incident which could potentially cause an exposure would stand out in their mind. Like, say for instance, she assisted someone after an accident or something and got blood from an infected person in her mouth, eyes, or an open wound. If she's being truthful with you, she would have probably mentioned that as a possibility. If she wasn't thinking clearly yesterday, and I don't imagine she was, you may want to ask if she recalls any such incident. Also, ask if she's ever had an unexplained cut or gash. Since she's a somewhat well known person, if she ever bumped into someone on the street and came away with a cut, it could have been done on purpose by someone with a vendetta against her uncle.

That's pretty far-fetched, like something from a mystery novel, but I'm just thinking of any possibilities I can. There's also a slight possibility of disease transmission from a blood transfusion. For a while, before the laboratory tests to detect the presence of the antibody were developed, some people became infected through receiving blood transfusions. Now, transfusion-induced cases of HIV are almost unheard of."

This conversation was making the hairs on Lacy's forearms stand up as a result of the chill bumps that had arisen when the doctor had begun tossing out possibilities. With a shudder, she asked, "She mentioned having had multiple sex partners about twenty years ago. Could she have contracted the virus from one of them?"

"That's extremely doubtful if she just recently learned she has the virus. Typically, there can be a period of several years in a healthy individual before any symptoms occur, but twenty years is excessive," Sharon explained.

"So, if you were the detective instead of me, you wouldn't interview her previous sex partners just yet?"

"If I were the detective, I would submit a list of those men's names to the CDC's reportable disease department along with whatever court order you might need. If any of those men were diagnosed with having HIV, their names would have been turned over to the CDC by their physician. It might save you some time."

"Okay, thanks. I'll do that. Well, I guess that's all for now. I'll probably come by on Monday to pick up the records for Todd Stevens."

Still concerned about her nine-year-old patient with thrush and her suspicions about his contracting HIV through a blood transfusion, Sharon had a thought.

"Detective Fuller? Do you know if Mrs. Stevens ever had a blood transfusion?"

"Yes, she has. I don't know when, though. Why? I thought you said that people don't get HIV from transfusions anymore?"

"They almost never do. Still, on rare occasion, a person will donate blood within a few days of being exposed to the virus themselves. During the period of time while they're forming antibodies to the virus, the test could be negative. It's a long shot, but so is contraction of HIV from a partner twenty years ago."

"Okay. Well, I'll ask when she was transfused. Thank you again, Dr. West."

"You're welcome. If you have anymore questions, feel free to call me. Oh, let me give you my home number in case you uncover something over the weekend and have a question."

Stunned, Lacy took down the doctor's home number as well as her cell number and sat staring at the paper long after she'd hung up the phone.

As Sharon drove home, she was feeling unsettled by the bizarre night she'd just spent. There were usually some strange cases that came into a downtown emergency room during the wee hours of the morning, but her previous shift had far more than average. Could there in fact be two persons who contracted HIV from getting a blood transfusion who had crossed her path within the course of a few hours? That seemed entirely too coincidental. More likely, the woman had actually been unfaithful to her husband at least once which led to her contraction of the virus. Still, it would be interesting to find out when the Stevens woman was transfused.

She had learned that Jeremy's bike accident had occurred when he was five. If Shelly Stevens had gotten a blood transfusion during that time frame, perhaps there had been a test kit that had somehow failed to properly detect positive results. That scenario was unlikely because of QC testing. Having worked in a hospital laboratory while she was in medical school, Sharon knew that all test kits were checked at least daily to ensure proper performance. This process, called quality control or QC, was a required part of any laboratory testing. In addition to the patient samples, a known negative and a known positive specimen were tested. If there had been a problem with the test kit, it would surely have been detected during the quality control process. She would have to think about this further over the weekend, but for now her brain was just too exhausted.

Pulling her British racing green Jaguar XJ8L into the driveway, she noticed that her father's pickup wasn't there. He'd probably taken their dog, Penny, for a short trip. Sharon had moved back into her parents' home when her mother had become ill a few years before. After her mother died, Sharon stayed on. She always laughed inwardly when she thought about how embarrassed she used to get, being in college at Auburn University and living at home with her parents. When she'd moved to Atlanta to go to medical school, her parents moved to the Atlanta area as well. Soon thereafter, her brother applied for a job with several police departments in the metro-Atlanta area and joined them when he was hired by Gwinnett County. Theirs was a close-knit family. Now that she was in her late 30's and by all means probably *should* be embarrassed to still be living at home, she wasn't.

Four happy felines greeted her when she opened the front door. Putting her gym bag down, Sharon sat on the floor in the hallway and let the kitties ease her tension through their demonstration of unconditional love. Animals, she thought, seemed to have a built-in gloom barometer. When their owners were sad, they became extra attentive and cuddly. During the first months after her mother's death, neither Sharon nor her father had an animal-free lap for any length of time. She couldn't fathom a life without animals. They truly were one of God's sweetest gifts.

Reluctantly, she stood and headed toward the kitchen with felines in tow. Giving them their morning treats, she scanned a note from her father saying that he and Penny had gone to the post office. As she headed toward her basement apartment, Sharon picked up her gym bag and made her way to the spare refrigerator in the laundry room. Taking out a cold beer, she drank more than half of it in one long swill. She sat down at her computer and opened her word processor to begin writing poetry.

Yes, kitties, doggies, beer, and poetry: her own personal prescription for easing the hectic, disappointing events of another night at work. The only thing missing from this scenario for the morning was Penny, who would be home soon.

Within minutes, she was well into a poem about losing someone and survivor guilt. Cozy, her only non-black kitty, a gray Maine Coon, had positioned himself at her feet. Ella, her only female, had lain upon the monitor. Salem and Coal, short for Charcoal, her two biggest cats, had decided to cohabitate her lap as she sat cross-legged and typed. By the time she heard the front door open upstairs heralding the arrival of her father and Penny, both legs were completely asleep beneath the combined 33 pound weight of her boys.

Lacy walked toward her desk with a spring in her step. She felt as though she'd just unleashed a multitude of endorphins, the same feeling she got when she ran several miles. She had looked in the phone book to see if Dr. West's number was listed; it wasn't. She had both that number *and* the doctor's cell phone number. Could that be a subtle hint?

Chet was already sitting at his desk, eating a biscuit.

"Good morning, Chet. How are you doing?"

Chet looked understandably confused by Lacy's good mood since she was obviously not a morning person.

"Hey, Lace. What's up?"

"Well, I talked to Dr. West, and she said it would be highly unusual for someone to come down with HIV after twenty years. In other words, Shelly Stevens probably didn't get AIDS from one of her many partners before her marriage."

"When did you talk to Dr. West?"

"This morning right before I left for work. Anyhow, she said that it would be easier to get a court order and submit the names to the CDC to see if we can find a past partner who has HIV than to hunt down these guys one by one and ask them. Makes sense to me."

Chet felt himself blush as the realization hit him. It wasn't the information per se that Lacy had gleaned from Dr. West that had put the spring in her step; it was the fact that she'd had a conversation with the doctor. He wondered if Dr. West had recommended they analyze dog shit if Lacy would still be standing here saying it made sense to her. He figured she would.

"Okay, so do you want me to get the order?" he asked.

"Sure, that would be great. I need to talk to Shelly Stevens again. Dr. West thinks that she might have gotten the disease from a blood transfusion."

Lacy was beginning to quote Dr. West the way his wife always quoted some afternoon talk show doctor. He found it amusing.

"Want to know what I think? I think she did have an affair and lied to us," he said.

"I don't think so." Lacy's eyebrows furrowed at Chet's suggestion.

"Why? I mean, if she shot her husband presumably because she was mad at him for possibly having an affair, what makes you think she would tell us of her indiscretions?"

"It's just a feeling I have, that's all. Her eyes, I guess. She sure didn't look like she was being anything but truthful."

Chet normally was a true believer in Lacy's feelings. More times than he could clearly recall, she had busted a case wide open with nothing more than a hunch. Still, he wondered about this time. After all, Lacy hadn't been seeing anyone for several months, and the Stevens lady did have amazing eyes. Annoyed with himself for thinking those thoughts, he decided not to push the point any further.

Clearing his throat, he said, "Okay. Well, I'll go over to the courthouse and see about getting those papers. Want me to track you down when I get back?"

"Yeah, then we'll head on over to the CDC building. I should be through talking to Mrs. Stevens by the time you get done."

Police headquarters was four blocks from the jail in which Shelly Stevens was being held. In spite of the Atlanta summer heat, Lacy decided to walk. The aroma of Krispy Kreme donuts filled the air and Lacy caught herself breathing deeply. She was debating whether or not to buy Chet a couple of donuts on her way back from interviewing Shelly Stevens when her attention was drawn to the other side of the street.

Two teenagers were poking around in the tall grass across the street with a stick and laughing. Their laughter had an evil sound to it that made Lacy suspicious. As she eased across the street, she heard a small voice asking to be left alone.

The teens were like vultures on the trail of a mortally wounded animal. Lacy unholstered her gun as quietly as possible, but one of the boys turned and saw her.

"Freeze! Police!" she yelled.

Both boys began running with Lacy in hot pursuit, calling for backup on her handheld. She was gaining rapidly on the boys, who didn't have the common sense to split up. They ran to the top of an embankment, and Lacy was so close, she could hear them panting. Pathetic out of shape thugs, she thought. One of the boys tripped and fell over on a large concrete slab sticking up from the ground and began whining and holding his ankle. Lacy gave him a swift kick as she ran by, hardly breaking her stride. The boy yelped. Lacy grabbed the other punk and threw him to the ground.

In a voice unaffected by the brisk run, Lacy asked, "What part of 'freeze' don't you understand?" Cuffing him while he was down, she pulled him to his feet and half dragged him back to where the other boy was still lying and holding his ankle. Lacy saw three uniformed officers heading in her direction. Looking down the embankment, she noticed two officers standing over the person the boys had been accosting.

"You kicked me!" The hoodlum had the audacity to sound offended.

"You ran from me."

"Detective Fuller, are you alright?" asked one of the officers.

"Yes, I'm fine. You can take these sacks of shit and book them. I'll be over within the hour to make my statement."

As Lacy walked back down the embankment, she heard the whiner telling the officers that she had kicked him. She smiled when she heard the young officer's response. "You're lucky she didn't do worse."

Approaching the abandoned lot with knee-high grass, Lacy saw the officers talking to a homeless old man. Lacy knew he was in that grassy area and knew also that she was supposed to run him off, but instead she would sometimes buy him lunch. His name was Homer.

"Hey, guys. Thanks for responding so fast. Hi, Homer. What happened? You've got blood on you."

"Yes, Ma'am. Those boys said I disgusted them and that I was an animal because I live out on the street. Then they just started kicking me. Thank God you came along when you did. I kept telling them I didn't want any trouble, but they just kept on."

Lacy was doubly glad she had kicked the one asshole and secretly wished she could have somehow done the same to the other. The shrill sound of an approaching ambulance brought her thoughts back to the present.

"Homer? You're going to need to have that gash on your head looked at. I'll make sure that nothing happens to your stuff while you're gone. When you come back from the hospital, you're going to need to give us a statement about what happened to you. After that, I'll buy you some lunch. Okay?"

"I don't want to go to the hospital, Miss Lacy. Folks always look at me funny there." Homer studied the ground as he spoke.

It took a tremendous effort on her part not to ask if folks didn't look at him funny as he wandered around the streets with a shopping cart and a long coat on in the summer.

"I know, Homer. I just think you might need stitches, and I worry about you getting an infection. Just let them take a look at you. Will you do that for me?"

"Okay, Miss Lacy," he softly agreed.

Aware that the two uniformed officers were standing there, mouths agape, Lacy watched the ambulance slow down and stop. She knew the officers were puzzled that she would let anyone get by with calling her *Miss Lacy* and decided that the soft feminine side of her needed to go into hiding once more before her reputation as a bad-ass took a beating.

Wiping the sweat from her brow, she exclaimed, "It's hot as a bitch out here. I've got work to do. I've got to interview a husband-killer before I come in and give my statement. I'll get there when I can."

Looking at the elderly man sitting quietly in the grass, Lacy reminded the officers to take care of his shopping cart and directed the paramedics to be nice to him. Oh, what the hell. The day was young. She still had plenty of time to be an asshole and regain some of her status as a bitch.

"Take care, Homer. One of these officers is going to bring you back after you get checked out at the hospital."

Still sweaty from the chase, Lacy went to the ladies restroom as soon as she entered the jail to get a cool, wet paper towel. After wiping down her forehead and neck, she felt better. Once she got back to the department, she would change out of her sweaty oxford shirt and chinos and into the spare set she kept in her locker. She stopped to get a Diet Coke from the vending machine before she approached the control booth and asked the deputy to bring Mrs. Stevens out.

"I'll send for her. How about room three?" the deputy said.

"Room three works. I'll go on in, if that's okay."

"Yeah, that's fine, Detective. I'll buzz it open."

Lacy walked down the dimly lit hallway and paused in front of the door to the interrogation room. When she heard a click and a hum indicating that it was now unlocked, she opened the door. Although it wasn't the same room in which she'd interviewed Mrs. Stevens the previous night, it looked identical. At the center of the room was an old, battered table probably handed down from an area high school cafeteria. Four folding metal chairs sat around the table looking as though they hadn't been cleaned in years. Lacy made her usual mental note to remain standing. The door at the opposite side of the room clicked and opened. In walked Shelly Stevens and a large female deputy.

Shelly smiled at Lacy. The deputy grunted.

"You know what button to push when you get done, right?" The deputy's question came out in grunt form.

"Yes, I do. It shouldn't take too long."

The deputy left, shaking her head from side to side.

"What's up with her?" asked Lacy before she could stop herself.

"Oh, I've already had *several* visitors this morning. Mother and Father, Uncle Leon, my weasel attorney, and now you. She said she was definitely *not* getting paid to be my personal escort. It makes me wish I could have more visitors, you know?"

Lacy did know.

"You mentioned last night that you had received a blood transfusion in the past. When and where was that?"

"After I gave birth to my son on April 19, 1999, at Hillsborough Medical Center. A mother never forgets her child's birthday or when he dies. His was one in the same," Shelly said sadly.

"Have you ever given medical assistance to anyone who was bleeding? Like, say, after an accident?"

"No. The most heroic thing I've ever done was call 911 for a lady on I-75 who had a flat tire."

Lacy persisted. "How about ever receiving a cut that you didn't know how you got? Or bumping into someone in a crowd and coming away with a cut?"

"I don't think so. Why? Do you think I got AIDS from something like that? I think it was probably one of my past boyfriends; some of them were pretty sleazy. For the most part, I just dated them to piss my family off."

"I talked to a doctor about this, and she said that twenty years was probably too long ago for you to have been infected with HIV and still be healthy. Were all of the guys on the list from around here?"

"Yes. Most of them I dated in high school, and they were a couple of years older than me. But, yeah, they were all local boys."

"Okay. Well, I ran into a little problem on the way over here, so I'm going to have to cut this shorter than I had planned to. Maybe I'll come back by later on, just to piss off the deputy. Oh, yeah, I'm planning on going to visit the cat today. What's his name?"

Smiling warmly, Shelly said, "Snowpuff"

"What in the hell kind of name is Snowpuff?" Maybe the lady was crazy after all, thought Lacy.

"Right after I got home from the hospital after the miscarriage, Todd brought home this little ball of white fur. He's a Persian, and Todd thought that having something to take care of would help me with the depression I was feeling. He was right, too. Anyhow, Todd suggested naming him Snow, but I liked the name Puff."

"Puff?" Lacy asked puzzled.

"Remember those old Dick and Jane books when we were little? Their kitty's name was Puff. I always wanted a Puff. Those kids always seemed so happy and carefree, I wanted to be them. Anyhow, as a sort of joke, we named him Snowpuff."

Lacy watched as tears filled the other woman's eyes.

"I'm sorry. I don't mean to cry."

"That's okay. I'd cry too if I had named my cat Snowpuff!" Lacy joked.

Pressing the button to summon the unfriendly deputy, Lacy smiled at Shelly Stevens. When the door opened, the scowl on the deputy's face helped Lacy make up her mind. She would definitely return that afternoon just to annoy the unpleasant woman.

"Okay, Mrs. Stevens. I'll be back later," Lacy said enthusiastically.

Walking back to the police department, Lacy couldn't help but think about that damned name: Snowpuff. She tried saying it quietly aloud just to see if she could without feeling an unpleasant expression overtake her face. She was unsuccessful. Each time she said the name she felt herself making a 'what the fuck?' face. She'd just have to ask for the cat by the owner's name instead.

"Hey, Lace. I hear you had some excitement," Chet mumbled through a mouthful of cinnamon roll.

"You remember Homer, right? Well, two dumbass little maggots were beating him up in the lot right across from headquarters."

"Now, Lacy, what would your mother say about you calling those boys maggots?"

"Well, Avery, believe it or not, we've actually had that discussion before. She said they aren't maggots, they're poor misguided souls. I said we could compromise; they're souls who were misguided down the pathway to maggotry."

Chet laughed. "Leave it to you to put things into perspective. I got the court order for the list of names in record time. I think that sidestepping the red tape might be the only thing I actually like about this case."

"Well, since I've got to give my statement and hang around here until they bring Homer back, why don't you run that over to the CDC by yourself? At least we could say we were doing something productive. Meanwhile, I'll call the hospital where Mrs. Stevens received that blood and see if they can track down the donor."

"Sure. I can do that. I'll catch up with you later on," he agreed.

By the time Avery returned from the CDC, Lacy had accomplished everything on her list except actually talking to someone from the Hillsborough Medical Center. She'd given her statement, denied kicking anyone, but maybe remembered being tripped up by something lying on the ground, and bought Homer a nice big lunch of fried chicken, mashed potatoes, sweetened iced tea, and corn-bread. She had left him with a twenty dollar bill and told him she'd be by to check on him later on. When the phone rang, she was glad to hear that it was someone from the Hillsborough Medical Center.

"Detective Fuller? Hi, my name is Jane Stewart. I'm the transfusion services director at Hillsborough Medical Center. I understand you have a question about a patient who was transfused here a few years ago?"

"Yes. Actually, I was wondering if there was any way that you could locate whoever donated the unit of blood she received? It seems that she's come down with HIV, and there are some questions about how she contracted the virus. She did recall having a transfusion about four years ago."

"Four years? That was before we began using a com-puter program for our Blood Bank Department. I can cer-tainly get the information for you, but it might take a few hours. I'll need the patient's name, an approximate date of the transfusion, and a signed consent form. I'll fax the form to you. It'll need to be signed by the patient before we can release her records."

"Okay, her name is Shelly Stevens, and she was trans-fused on April 19, 1999."

"Oh, dear; I just read about her in the newspaper this morning. I'm sure it won't take too long to get that infor-mation for you since you gave me an exact date. All I'll be able to give you will be the unique identifier of the unit she received and the name of the blood center from which we got the blood. I'm afraid you'll have to contact the blood donor center directly."

"Okay. That will be a tremendous help. You can call me back at this same number until around five this evening."

"Oh, heavens, I leave at three, so I'll definitely call you back sooner than that."

"Thank you for your time, Ms. Stewart."

"You're welcome, Detective."

After giving the woman her fax number, she called her friend James back while she was still in her telephone mode.

"Tolbert Landscaping, this is James."

"Hey, Kiddo. It's me. When and where for dinner?"

"Hey, Lace! I was thinking Einstein's at around 7:30."

Einstein's was a restaurant in midtown Atlanta that served excellent food, but the real reason to go was the ambiance. For most months of the year, patio dining was available. Frequented by gay and straight alike, it was the place to take someone from out of town to give them a memorable experience.

"Count me in. How long is Maggie in town?"

"Just until Sunday night. I can't wait for you two to meet."

Lacy thought about James and his sister, Margaret. They had always been close. He was forever talking about her. Lacy was excited to finally be meeting her.

"Me either, but I've got to run. I'll see you tonight," she said.

After ending her call with James, she went to the fax machine and removed the consent form from Hillsborough Medical Center. She quickly made the short trip once more to the detention center and obtained Shelly's signature. The phone on Lacy's desk rang just as she was returning from the fax machine.

"Homicide, Detective Fuller."

"Hi, Detective Fuller. This is Jane Stewart. I've got the information for you regarding the transfusions that Mrs.

Stevens received. It turns out she was given three units of blood, all from the Metropolis Blood Center. If you've got a pen and paper handy, I'll give you the numbers of the units of blood and the telephone number for Metropolis."

"Yes, I'm ready."

After writing down the information and hanging up the phone, Lacy looked across her desk to see Chet smiling broadly and extracting a report from his typewriter. While the rest of the world was using computers, Chet was using a typewriter that was at least as old as he was.

"*Voila*! Care to take a look-see? I've typed up a preliminary on this case since you handled the Munson case yesterday."

Proudly handing the paper over to Lacy, Chet leaned back in his chair and yawned. Lacy didn't even have to scan the report before noticing that he'd typed, "Detective Fukker and I" instead of "Detective Fuller and I." Looking down at her keyboard, she noted the side-by-side proximity of the l and the k keys.

"Okay, *Chad*. I'm not Detective Fukker. How about I type up the reports from now on? I appreciate what you were trying to do, but I think I can handle it from here."

Snatching the report from Lacy's hands, Chet looked like a scolded child.

"Aw, man! How did that happen?"

Ignoring him, Lacy glanced at the clock. She had a great deal to do before her dinner engagement.

"What do you say we knock off early today? I know Monica would be happy if you came home early, and I've got a few things to do. I'm just going to make a call to this blood donor center, retype the report, and head out. It's okay with me if you want to go."

"No, Lace. I'll wait until you're done. Say, did you really kick that guy earlier?"

"Yep."

"I knew it!" Chuckling to himself, he stood and stretched.

Chet wandered away, leaving Lacy to wonder who he had suckered into betting with him that she hadn't kicked that punk. It must have been someone new to the department. Oh well, maybe he'd win enough that he could take Monica out to dinner.

Picking up the receiver, Lacy dialed the number for the blood center and got some automated system that gave her entirely too many options. Finally, the option to stay on the line to be connected to the operator was mentioned.

"Metropolis Blood Center, this is Miriam. How may I direct your call?"

"Hello, Miriam. My name is Detective Lacy Fuller with the Atlanta Police Department. I need to speak to someone about finding out the identity of some blood donors from four years ago."

"That's classified information, Ma'am," the woman said snidely.

"Yes, I know. I'm prepared to obtain whatever legal paperwork you require, but first I need to talk to someone to find out what information I need."

"Well, we don't disclose the names of our donors."

"Okay. How about this. I'm an officer of the law, and you're a switchboard operator. Why don't you do your job and connect me with someone in charge, and I'll do my job and detect what's necessary for me to do to find out the identity of your donors?"

"Just a minute," the woman said, irritably.

The minute dragged out into six. Chet came back with a ten dollar bill in his hand. Lacy was about to ask him who he had suckered to win the money when a voice came on the line.

"Hello? This is Dr. Stephenson. How may I help you?"

"Yes, Dr. Stephenson. This is Detective Lacy Fuller with the Atlanta Police Department. I need to find out the identity of the donors for three units of blood collected in 1999. We have a person who tested HIV positive who claims that she hasn't had any other means of exposure to the AIDS virus other than these transfusions four years ago. I have the numbers of the units."

"Okay. I'll need a court order for the information. If you'd like to give me the unit numbers, I'll compile the data for you and have it available by early Monday. By then, you should have your paperwork in order. I'm ready whenever you are for those unit numbers."

Lacy read off the list of numbers that she'd been given and thanked the doctor for her help. She quickly typed Chet's report on her computer and handed it to him to sign off. He did so happily and went to submit the report to the Captain. When Chet returned, they clocked out and walked to the parking lot together.

"Tell Monica I said hello, and give CJ a hug for me."

"Will do. Have a great weekend, Lace."

"You, too."

She opened the door of her car, a 1991 black Alfa Romeo Spider convertible, and was assaulted by a blast of hot air. Thank God the Spider's air conditioner worked well. That had always been her dream car and, now that she owned it, she just prayed that it didn't need any major service. Parts and labor for that particular car were damned expensive! Cranking it, she turned on the CD player to listen to Patty Loveless, one of her favorite performers. By the time she arrived at Powell's Cat Clinic, she was in a good mood. Then she remembered the name: Snowpuff.

The clinic was actually a white wooden house. Walking through the front door, Lacy wondered how this could be an animal clinic. The décor was something out of an interior design magazine. Rich colors and Queen Anne furnishings created an ambiance that Lacy was sure would soothe the owners, if not the cats. Scented candles were placed in sconces, giving the air a subdued floral aroma while peaceful music softly played overhead. The setting would have been a virtual oasis but for a screaming plastic box and the *grown* woman knelt with her face at the front cooing ridiculously.

"May I help you?" a young receptionist asked as she entered the room.

"Yes, I'm Detective Lacy Fuller. I've come to visit Shelly Stevens' cat."

"Oh, Snowpuff! What a little darling he is. It's such a shame about Shelly and Todd. I wonder what's going to happen to Snowpuff now? Are you going to take him?"

"Huh? No, not me, but I'll try to find someone to," Lacy said absentmindedly, still staring at the woman ridiculing herself on the floor.

"If you'll follow me, I'll let Dr. Powell know you're here."

Lacy followed the woman into an examination room that had an expensive settee and lush Oriental rugs on the floor. Noticing the numerous scratches on the woman's arm, Lacy hoped none were from Snowpuff. The human scratching post exited the room. From the back of the building, Lacy heard a cat screaming bloody murder. Again, she hoped the source wasn't Snowpuff.

After a couple of minutes, the door opened and an attractive, petite, blonde woman carrying an enormous white cat entered.

"You must be Lacy Fuller. I'm Elizabeth Powell, and this is Snowpuff."

"It's nice to meet you."

Lacy watched as the woman lovingly put the cat down on the examination table and stroked his head. The cat looked pissed.

"It was just tragic to hear about Shelly and Todd. They always seemed so happy. If there's anything I can do to help Shelly, I'd be glad to do it. You know, I thought it was a bit odd that she would want to board Snowpuff. I'm sure it must have been a misunderstanding. She usually donates a good bit of money to our orphan fund, you know. Well, I'll leave you two to get acquainted. Remember, if there's anything I can do, just let me know."

Lacy and the cat watched the woman leave the room. When the door shut, the cat turned his focus on Lacy.

"Well, hello there, big cat." Lacy eased toward the cat and stared at him. To her surprise, he walked toward her and rammed his head against her hand. She tentatively began scratching underneath his chin and heard a sputtering purr come from the still pissed off looking face. Huh. Maybe he actually liked this. Maybe that was just his face; maybe this was Lacy in cat form. She smiled at that image, and Snowpuff rammed against her again. She decided to sit on the settee because her feet were killing her, probably from chasing those assholes in her loafers, she thought.

As she sat down, she noticed the cat staring at her. After a moment, he jumped from the examination table and walked over to Lacy. He began rubbing against her navy blue pants and purring again. Finally, he jumped onto her lap, turned two complete circles, and lay down. Lacy started petting him again and thought that he did seem to be a sweet cat. After thirty minutes, she decided that she'd better get on the road. She still had to visit Shelly Stevens before the cranky deputy left for the day and then go home and get ready for dinner with James.

Sticking her head out of the front door, she spied the receptionist.

"I think I'm ready for the cat to go back now. I've got to be going."

"Absolutely, I'll just tell Dr. Powell. Unless you've changed your mind and want to adopt him after all?"

Shaking her head, Lacy said, "No," and closed the door. The cat sat on the settee still staring at her. Cats liked to stare, Lacy gathered. She sat beside him and surveyed the white fur that now coated her pants.

After a moment, the rear door opened and in walked Dr. Powell.

"Isn't he a dear?"

"Yeah, he seems affectionate."

When Dr. Powell reached over to take Snowpuff, he wrapped his front legs around Lacy's right forearm, but didn't scratch her.

"It looks like he doesn't want you to leave. You remind me of Shelly. Maybe you remind him of her, too. He doesn't like being caged. I hope someone finds a good home for him soon."

Feeling a surprising twinge of guilt, Lacy pried Snowpuff's legs from around her arm. Once he was in the custody of Dr. Powell, Snowpuff emitted a tiny, mournful meow.

"I'm going to do my best to find a good home for him," Lacy offered in utter sincerity.

It wasn't until she was driving back toward the jail that Lacy realized what Dr. Powell had implied. If Shelly Stevens had paid for Snowpuff to be boarded *before* she shot her husband, then a solid case for premeditation could be made. If, however, she had paid a grooming fee and made a donation to the orphaned kitty fund, there would be no proving that the murder wasn't committed in a state of temporary insanity.

Pulling into the detention center parking lot, Lacy thought about what she would tell Shelly Stevens. It would be completely unprofessional, not to mention unethical, for her to inform the woman of the possible premeditation issue, but somehow Lacy actually liked Shelly. She decided she'd play it by ear.

This time, when the unfriendly deputy deposited Mrs. Stevens into the interrogation room, she didn't speak a word; however, the disgusted face was still in place. Lacy smiled at her for the hell of it. She glared in response and turned to leave.

"Well, I see I've just completed her day in a cheery fashion," Lacy said with a smile.

"She's a piece of work. Did you go see Snowpuff? How's he doing? Isn't he terrific?"

"Yeah, he's sweet. He's doing fine. I think he likes me. Does he always look pissed off? I mean, he's pretty, but I've seen cats before that don't look as annoyed as he does."

"That's because of his little smushed face. He can't help but look annoyed. You'll know if he really is mad because his little ears slick back. God, I miss him."

"I can see why. Well, we're going to have a list of information on the people who donated the blood you received on Monday morning. Also, we've submitted the list of names of your ex-boyfriends to the CDC to determine if any have been reported as having HIV. That's about the extent of what we achieved today."

"Thank you for believing me about not fooling around on Todd. I mean, I know it would be easy for you to just think that I was feeding you a line of bullshit, but I really never was unfaithful. I'm not used to people believing in me. You did, and it means a great deal to me."

Lacy's mind was made up.

"Do you remember when you paid for Snowpuff to be groomed and boarded?"

"Yes."

"No, you don't. You probably remember paying for Snowpuff to be groomed and giving a charitable donation to the orphan fund. You should tell your egret-lawyer to go to Dr. Powell's office and pay for Snowpuff's boarding."

"I've already paid for that."

"No, I don't believe that you have. If you had already paid for boarding, then an argument could be made that you knew you were going to shoot your husband and subsequently be arrested. The fact that you arranged for lengthy boarding of your cat could constitute premeditation, Mrs. Stevens."

Finally understanding, Shelly smiled and offered, "You know, you're right. I'll have Martin take over the check for boarding this evening. Hey, when do you think you'll go back and see Snowpuff?"

So Shelly Stevens wasn't the sharpest thing in the world, but she was still likeable and strangely persuasive.

"Yeah, be sure you do. I've got to run, but I'll probably go by and visit Snowpuff tomorrow or Sunday, if they're open."

"They aren't open on Sunday, but if you'll tell Dr. Powell what time you think you'll be by, she'll meet you there, I'm sure. She's sweet that way, and it's not just because of who I am."

"Okay. Well, try to have a good weekend."

"You, too. Thanks again."

Lacy summoned the deputy, who looked decidedly more irritable than earlier, no doubt feeling as though she were Shelly Stevens' personal attendant. She led the prisoner from the room, and Lacy left via the opposite door.

CHAPTER 8

*Waking from a long nap, Sharon West wandered up-*stairs to brew a pot of dark roast coffee. She needed to at least clean the bathrooms and kitchen before her brother and sister-in-law came over for their weekly visit. She remembered how her mother would thoroughly clean the whole house anytime they were going to have visitors. In contrast, all Sharon did was make the essentials somewhat more presentable. While the coffee noisily brewed, Sharon swept the kitchen. Coal lunged at the broom and eventually attacked it so thoroughly that the very act of moving the broom was a chore beneath the weight of the seventeen pound kitty. So much for sweeping the floor! At least, she thought, her family was accustomed to the messy environ.

Their "family nights" were always a wonderful ending to her week. Next Friday, in honor of their mother, they were going to have a fish fry in the back yard. It was going to be fun if Sharon could manage to learn how to actually fry the fish. That had always been her mother's job while Sharon made the homemade tartar sauce using sweet Vidalia onions, dill pickles, and mayonnaise.

Stirring her cream and sugar into her coffee, Sharon sat at the kitchen table and scrolled down the list of missed calls on her phone. The only call she would return was from her friend, Dr. Jessica Pope. She and Jessie had worked in the hospital laboratory together while they were in medical school. Jessie had fallen in love with the pathology rotation and decided to go into that field. Now working for another local hospital, Jessie and Sharon only managed to meet a couple of times a month at most.

While Sharon couldn't fathom a life of death and autopsies, Jessie seemed totally in her element. Sharon envied her that. While emergency medicine was exciting and challenging, Sharon never seemed fully contented. Maybe, she thought, it would be different if she could follow-up on all of her patients. As it was, she felt like the middle-man in an assembly line. Sure, she could find out about Mrs. Tippens on Monday when she got to work, but Jeremy was admitted to a children's hospital, and she may never know what became of him. She did inform the parents that she would contact the facility where he was transfused and obtain some information on the donor of the unit of blood he received. She remembered the stunned, angry faces on both parents when she had told them their son had HIV. It seemed as though the stages of grief were all hitting the couple at one moment rather that progressively. She hoped she remembered to tell Detective Fuller about this case on Monday.

Thinking about Lacy Fuller distracted Sharon from continuing the absent petting of Salem, now seated on the kitchen table directly in front of her. A forceful meow caused her hand to go on auto-pilot and scratch the big cat behind his ears. Lacy was a strange person. She seemed so tightly wound that Sharon wondered what she would be like away from work and not in the middle of a 'my girlfriend tried to kill herself' drama or a homicide/future homicide investigation. She thought she could sense an inherent goodness in the woman in spite of her aloof yet stern demeanor. After working the morning crosswords and the word jumble, Sharon dialed Jessie's work number.

"Dr. Pope speaking."

"Hey, Jess!"

"Sharon? You're up early. It's only 5:30 and the sun is still up. What gives?"

"Trying to clean up the house for when Jon and Jean come over. The felines have decided to make that a near impossibility, so I thought I'd check in with you. How are things going?"

"Not too bad. Gary and the kids are going camping this weekend, so I was wondering if you'd like to have supper tomorrow night?"

"That sounds great. What time were you thinking?"

"How about I pick you up around six or so?"

"I'll be ready. Oh, I'd better let you go. Coal has abandoned the broom, so I'm going to try to finish sweeping before he reclaims his prize."

As Sharon reached for the broom, Coal got a running start and pounced upon the straw enemy. Sharon smiled at her silly cat.

Lacy pulled up to her apartment and found a parking space on the side of the road. Parallel parking with ease, she pulled her little car into the spot and hopped out. Going upstairs, she heard the awful beat of too-loud music coming from down the hallway of the seventh floor. Lacy didn't know many of her neighbors, especially those on the lower floors. She decided it was time to make a new acquaintance.

Knocking on the door, she identified herself as a police officer. When the door was opened, a greasy-haired teenager with a goatee stared at her through bleary, bloodshot eyes.

"I'm with the police department. Your music is too loud." Lacy flashed her badge briefly in front of the teen's face.

"Says who?" His words ran together, forming a slurry language all his own: dopeheadese.

"Says anyone who has ears within a two mile radius as well as the law. Turn it down, buddy," she said.

"You gonna make me?"

Lacy hated defiant little drugged up shits like this guy. She decided to call in the report and let someone else handle it.

"Nah. Don't worry about it," she said, giving a little nonchalant shrug. As the door shut, she could hear the guy laughing hysterically, no doubt thinking that he'd just pushed around a cop. Jogging the remaining flights of stairs, Lacy opened her door and made a quick call to the narcotics division.

"Hey, Lou. It's Lacy. There's a guy here in my building blasting music. His musical tastes suck, so I decided to ask him to turn the volume down. When he opened the door, the house reeked of marijuana; hell, I half expected Cheech or Chong to stumble up to the door behind him! Just thought I'd pass the info on. He's in apartment 713 of the Amber Haus apartments."

"Thanks, Lacy. We'll be right over," he said.

Lacy hoped that the little shit would at least give the name of his supplier and make it worth Lou's time going there. Looking through her closet, she pulled out a pair of faded jeans, a cropped white t-shirt, and a pair of brown loafers. She would probably never win any fashion awards, but at least she would be comfortable. After a quick shower, she jogged down the stairs and paused briefly to speak to a couple of uniformed officers standing vigil outside reefer-boy's apartment. She decided to walk over to Einstein's since it was only a few blocks away and her loafers were so well worn.

James, Maggie, and Thomas, James' partner of ten years, were all seated and waving to her when she arrived. With an enormous full pitcher of beer in front of them, the golden liquid in their glasses and their goofy smiles indicated that they had been here long before 7:30.

James gave her a bear hug, Thomas hugged her more daintily, and before James could introduce Margaret, she, too, had hugged Lacy.

"You must be Lacy. I've heard so much about you from James. He just loves you to death! I'm Maggie."

"I gathered," Lacy said in her typical monotone voice.

After exchanging a glance with her brother, James and Maggie both burst into beer-induced laughter.

"So, you really are as terse as James said you were." Maggie laughed.

"You said I was terse?" Lacy cast an accusatory glance at her oblivious friend.

Smiling, James said, "Well, it beats cranky, or surly, or almost any other descriptions I could use for you."

Lacy decided that she definitely liked James better when he wasn't drinking. Sure, maybe he thought all kinds of shit about her, but he generally kept it to himself when he was sober.

"I hope like hell you have a designated driver among the bunch of you because my terse, surly, cranky ass sure won't be offering to drive y'all home."

Laughing, all except Lacy, they sat down once again.

Still not fazed by Lacy's annoyance, James said, "We've already ordered. We knew you'd be on time, and

I knew you'd get the cheeseburger with sweet potato fries and a Diet Coke. Want some beer?"

"No. Nor do I want to drive you home."

God, she must be PMS'ing because she was feeling unusually edgy.

Thomas raised his beer and said, "Non-alcoholic. Say hello to your designated driver."

Relief washed over Lacy, and she began to somehow feel less cranky. She studied the similarities between James and Maggie: both blonde and blue-eyed with mischievous faces. She then looked over at Thomas, who was the epitome of tall, dark, and handsome. His quiet reserve was somehow a perfect match for James, and she was glad they had found one another. After the food arrived, she was feeling little of her previous irritability. She thought about making an apology, but decided against it. Anyone who knew her knew that she suffered from social anxiety. Even meeting friends whom she liked in restaurants that she enjoyed could sometimes cause her to become tense.

Lacy noticed Maggie staring at her intently. Finally, Maggie spoke. "So, James says that you're a detective. How did you decide to go into police work?"

"Originally, when James and I met, I was in pre-law at Georgia State University. I decided to minor in something that would be an easy way to up my GPA, so I took a criminology course. I enjoyed it much more than I had any political science course that I had taken, so I decided to major in criminal justice. From there, I joined the Atlanta PD, and now I'm a detective."

All of the facts, neatly, tersely presented. Lacy conceded that maybe she was all of the aforementioned identifiers that James had labeled her with.

"Wow. I just don't think I could do it. I'm a social worker, and it's hard enough dealing with the things I see on a daily basis," Maggie said.

Before any further discussion began, Lacy's pager went off. Excusing herself, she left the dining patio and stepped a few feet down the sidewalk before calling the number listed on her pager.

"This is Detective Lacy Fuller."

"Lacy? This is Lou. Listen, that little druggie punk you told us about? What a pain in the ass!"

"Well, shit, Lou! I'm sorry if I've ruined your evening by passing along a druggie to the narcotics squad!" she said.

"No, not that, Lacy. Damn, chill out. No, you were right. There was a meth lab set up in the apartment and shitloads of marijuana, crack; hell, you name it! We look like fucking heroes! No, the reason he's a pain in the ass is that he demanded to speak to his lawyer. It seems you've met this lawyer guy before, a Martin Strausser?"

"Yeah, I've met that egret-bastard."

"Well, he didn't seem favorably impressed with you either, Lacy. This kid's mother works for Judge Farnsworth. I just wanted you to know about the lawyer thing since he seems to have some vendetta against you."

"Thanks, Lou. I don't need to come down there, do I?"

"No, we've already booked him. I'm thinking the little punk will sing like a bird because of the bad press on his mother and her position with the esteemed Judge and all." Lou sounded happy.

"She should get bad press with a meth lab in her home. Jesus, that's in my building! If that thing had blown up, lots of innocent people would have been harmed!" Lacy said.

"No, it's not her apartment; it belongs to the son."

"He's, what, fifteen? How can he own an apartment?"

"Try twenty-two."

"He must be making some potent anti-aging drugs along with meth in that little lab of his. Well, thanks for the update."

Hanging up the phone and feeling less than sociable again, Lacy walked back up to the table and put a twenty dollar bill down.

"Sorry to break up the party, guys, but I've got to head back downtown."

"Aw, Lacy, we were just getting started. We were going to go out clubbing. We thought you could dance with Maggie." James was making sad puppy-dog eyes at her.

Knowing somehow that James had been attempting to fix her up with Maggie, Lacy wondered if that was the reason for her previous bad mood. He was always talking about how well the two of them would "hit it off," and now he had them dancing together. No way. She knew better than to ever get involved with a good friend's sister.

Trying to sound convincing, Lacy said, "That would have been great. Maybe tomorrow? Anyhow, I've got to go. It was a pleasure meeting you. Sorry I was irritable earlier. It's been a long week."

Kissing cheeks and hugging, they vowed to try again the next night. As Lacy walked away, she hoped she could think up a plausible excuse for not meeting them the next evening. As it turned out, she wouldn't have to lie twice.

On her way back to her apartment, Lacy remembered that she hadn't checked on Homer as she had promised. It was only a few minutes after eight, so she decided to go when she got home. She remembered the first time she'd met him, maybe three or four years ago. He'd been standing at a busy intersection holding a sign that said "Will work for money." Lacy had immediately thought that most people would work for money since that *was* the general idea. Most signs held by the homeless read "Will work for food." She had stopped and introduced herself to the small, aged black man in worn overalls.

"So, what kind of work will you do?" she had asked.

"Just about anything I can, Ma'am. What is it you need done?" His voice was a satiny baritone.

"I don't need anything done. I'm a police officer. I should be directing you to move along," she had said.

"Yes, Ma'am. I'll just be going, then."

"Wait. I said I *should* be telling you to move; I didn't say that I was telling you to move. How long has it been since you've eaten?"

"I had me some biscuits this morning. One of the restaurants will give us their leftovers if we come there before the lunch crowd shows up."

Lacy handed him a ten dollar bill and he again asked what she needed done.

"Nothing; I'm just giving this to you so you'll have some money to eat with."

"God bless you," he said as he pulled out a sizeable wad of money and added Lacy's ten to the pile. Feeling used, Lacy asked about all of the money.

"Well, Ma'am, I'm taking this money over to the Humane Society. They have a real good one here, you know? They try not to kill any little animals unless they just have to. Anyhow, that's my job. I do whatever odds and ends that folks need done, then I keep me back a little for myself, but most of it I take down to help the little animals out seein' as how they can't help themselves."

Lacy remembered clearly the lump that she'd gotten in her throat when he said that.

"You mean you work for the animals, essentially?" she had asked.

Smiling proudly, Homer had said, "Yes, Ma'am. I had a dog back when I was somebody. She was just the sweetest little thing. After my wife, Essie, died, she was the only thing that kept me going. I quit my job to take care of my wife. After she passed on I found out that I had let her life insurance policy lapse, and I hadn't realized that, so we ran out of money pretty soon. The landlord was real nice and let us stay there for a few months while I tried to find a job. My little dog was getting up there in years, and she passed away three months to the day after my wife had. After that, well, I guess I just kind of went crazy with depression. I was afraid I'd be evicted, so I moved out on my own. I reckon it would be mighty embarrassing to be evicted. I was just glad he let me and Rosie, that was my dog, stay as long as he did.

A couple of months later, I took the landlord fifty dollars that I had earned by sawing up downed trees since he'd lost so much money on me. He wouldn't take it. In fact, he cried. A big old strapping guy, and he just cried. He asked if I wanted to move back in, but by then I was used to living on the streets and didn't want to take advantage of his kindness, so I said no. I took the money to the Humane Society and gave it to them, in memory of Rosie. Since then, I've given them $947.50 in her memory."

Lacy felt humbled. She looked at this little man who could have spent that money on himself, but chose instead to help orphaned animals. She thought about him saying, "God bless you" after she had given him the money. She knew that if she were homeless, she might say that line, but it would quickly be followed by "Because He sure hasn't blessed me!" She remembered thinking that this encounter had been a good one for her spiritual growth. Now, every time she saw Homer, she would try to remember to ask how much money he'd earned for Rosie. Last year, for Christmas, she'd given him a ledger and a pen so he could better keep up with his transactions. He'd been touched by her gift. Before that, he'd written down the information on fast food napkins or receipts. He was a gentle soul. She felt a sudden surge of anger at the two young, white punks who had been hurting him earlier.

Approaching her apartment complex, she dashed inside just long enough to grab her keys. She never kept her car keys on her house key ring, just in case someone stole her car. She figured it would be easy enough for them to find out to whom the vehicle belonged. It would be bad enough to have someone break into her home, much less waltz in with her key. With a happiness she couldn't describe, she bounded down the stairs two at a time to see her friend, Homer. God bless you, too, Homer, and maybe, just maybe, I can help Him.

Pulling her Spider into a parking space at the police department, Lacy hopped out and headed directly over to Homer's place. As she was crossing the street, she heard his familiar voice humming something melodious and soothing.

"Homer? It's me, Lacy."

"Well, Miss Lacy. I knew you'd come by."

"How's the head?"

"Well, it's still there, but it does hurt a bit."

"Have you eaten dinner?"

"No, Ma'am. Have you?"

"Net yet. How about we go to the Varsity and get a couple of burgers and some fries?" she asked, knowing that Homer loved hamburgers.

"Well, I don't know if I feel up to walking all that far, Miss Lacy. I'm sorry."

"We aren't going to walk; I'm going to drive us. Just stay put and I'll get my car."

"Okay. Well, that does sound good."

As Lacy turned away from him, she wondered what it meant that she had rather spend a Friday night with Homer than dancing with James' sister.

CHAPTER 9

The alarm clock was set for 8 am, but Lacy was awakened long before that by a call from Captain Sumlin.

"Lacy? Listen, I know it isn't your turn to take a case, but aren't you and Avery just working on a couple of cold cases and the Farnsworth thing?"

"Yes, we wrapped up the Munson case on Thursday. Why, what's up?" she asked groggily.

"We've got a floater in the Hooch."

Lacy was like most officers; she hated bodies that had been found floating in water. The smell alone was bad enough, but the bloated appearance of the skin was enough to sicken her for weeks, especially when the body of water was the Chattahoochee. She remembered when she was in college rafting down that dirty river. Now, all she could think of when she heard the mention of the river was the four or five bodies that she'd seen pulled from there.

"Have you called Avery?" she asked.

"No, I called you first. Anyhow, a couple of kids fishing smelled something bad and went to investigate the origin of the odor. They found a hand sticking up from the water just like in that movie *Deliverance*, they said. These are six-year-old kids; what in the hell are they doing seeing *Deliverance* anyway?"

"What are they doing by themselves fishing at this hour is what I want to know," Lacy muttered.

"I don't know, Lacy. I think they live in that trailer park, River's Edge, and they had gone before their parents knew it. When they found the body, they ran home and told their mother. She's the one who called us."

"So, you want me to call Avery?"

"Yes. They're in unit number 17. There are already a couple of uniformed officers on the scene as well as someone from the medical examiner's office."

"Alright," Lacy grumbled.

In spite of herself, Lacy was happy to have a case that was both current and the victim was actually dead. Sumlin was right about her and Chet having only cold cases to work. That was the problem with having the highest number of solved cases in the department; you were assigned cases that were several years old, then expected to solve the crimes.

Lacy had always wondered if she and Chet weren't handed those cases to bring their numbers down closer to the other detectives. She knew some of the detectives had complained to the Captain about how their number of closed cases looked bad compared to the tag team of Fuller and Avery. She also knew the Captain was too big of a weenie to tell them, as she would have, to start solving more of their cases if they wanted to close the gap.

After quickly calling Avery and filling him in, she called and awakened a hung-over sounding James. He was, predictably, unhappy that she and Maggie would miss another opportunity to dance together. Lacy feigned her most sincere apology and hung the phone up. Feeling relieved, she took a quick shower and left, purposefully, without eating breakfast.

Pulling into the River's Edge trailer park, Lacy was surprised to see that the units were well kept. Frowning as she heard gravel being flung into the side of her car, she silently chastised herself for having brought her own vehicle instead of a patrol car. Pulling beside an Atlanta PD car, she quickly got out and walked toward unit 17.

Knocking on the door, she was immediately met by a nervous looking woman with wild red hair.

"Good morning, Ma'am. I'm Detective Lacy Fuller of the Atlanta Police Department. I understand that you placed a 911 call this morning?"

"Yes. My boys had gone fishing, and they found a dead body. God, it could have been them! I've been telling them all morning that they should never leave home without me or their papa going with them. Maybe you can talk some sense into them. They never seem to listen to us. Oh, where are my manners? Come on inside."

Stepping into the trailer, Lacy noticed that the inside of the trailer looked much worse than the outside. The carpet was worn in a pathway toward the kitchen, and the furniture looked to be several years old. At either end of a sofa looking like twin bookends sat two red-haired children with big, scared eyes. The center of the sofa sagged as if under the weight of an obese ghost.

"Detective, this is Josh and Jimmy. Boys, this is the detective who will tell you just how bad it is to leave home without either your papa or me knowing."

The boys' heads drooped downward, and their faces flushed. Lacy hoped that Avery would arrive soon. He was much better at dealing with kids than she was.

"I understand that you found a dead body?" Lacy asked as she removed her notepad.

No response from either bookend.

"Boys, answer when you're spoken to. I'm sorry, Detective."

Lacy was about to try again when a sharp knock indicated another visitor. Sighing with relief when she saw Avery enter, she quickly looked at the box of Krispy Kreme doughnuts in his hand.

"Good morning, Ma'am. I'm detective Chet Avery with the Atlanta PD. Hey, fellas. I thought since cops liked doughnuts so much, and since you two are honorary policemen for the day, I'd stop buy and pick up some breakfast," Chet said, nodding his hello to Lacy.

"Can we please, Mom?" asked the bookend on the left side of the sofa. Both boys were looking at Chet as though he were their idol.

"Yes, Jimmy. Remember to say 'thank you' to the nice detective."

"Thank you." With that, grubby little hands went into the box, further reminding Lacy why she never wanted children.

"Lacy, want one?"

"No, thanks."

Lacy wondered how in the hell those kids could eat so soon after seeing and smelling a dead body. She knew that it would be late evening before she'd have any pangs of hunger whatsoever. Well, maybe since they only saw the arm, like in *Deliverance*.

"What were you guys using for bait?" asked Chet, his mouth full of doughnut.

This time, the right bookend spoke. "Earthworms. We found 'em this morning."

"You know what I always use? I use chicken livers. It's grosser than earthworms, but I usually have better luck, especially with the catfish!" Chet said, enthusiastically.

Lacy fidgeted noticeably while the male bonding discussion ensued and was relieved when Officer Steve Spitz entered the trailer.

"Steve, do you think you could show me to the scene while Avery finishes up here?" she asked him immediately.

"Sure, Detective Fuller. It's about a half-mile down the road."

The guys were still talking about rods and reels and well on their way to depleting the box of doughnuts when Lacy slinked out of the trailer trying to avoid the disappointed look on the face of the mother. Well, hell, how was she supposed to lecture the kids when they wouldn't even talk to her?

By the time Lacy and Officer Spitz reached the little pathway leading from the road to the river, Lacy could smell the ruthless odor of death. As they walked down the steep trail, the stench became overpowering. No doubt, the crime scene people had moved the body out of the water.

Sure enough, as they came to the clearing, they saw a bloated torso lying among what Lacy knew was entirely too many officers. Granted, the body had obviously been dead for several days, but still the officers should have made some effort to cordon off the area better than they had. Even if there was little evidence left to preserve, at least there were appearances to keep up if and when the media arrived.

Fighting the urge to make a smart remark, Lacy inched closer and looked at the remains of the floater. Only then did she realize the body was missing the head. No wonder Captain Sumlin had put her and Avery on this case. This was the second decapitated body found in the area this month. He was undoubtedly worried about the prospects of a serial killer, as was she. Still, the first case had gone to Detectives Rogers and Weaver. She wondered why, since this may well be related, Detectives Tweedle-Dumb and Tweedle-Dumber hadn't gotten this call?

Taking out her pen and pad, Lacy scribbled a couple of notes to herself.

1. Get the folder on the previous decap victim
2. See if autopsy can be done ASAP in case serial killer
3. Remember to run an extra mile today
4. Visit Snowpuff

Closing her pad, she thought that it would be a long day.

It was noon before she and Chet got back to the department. She'd called ahead to ask for a copy of the case file on the first decapitation. As soon as she got to her desk, she dialed Captain Sumlin's home phone number.

"Hello?" he answered.

"Captain? This is Lacy. You're aware that the body discovered this morning was missing a head, right?"

"Yes, Lacy, I'm aware of that."

"Why didn't you call Rogers and Weaver? Don't you think this case may be related to the one they're working already?"

"Because it's been three weeks since the last victim was found, and so far we haven't even got an identity on the body."

After a few minutes of discussion with the Captain, Lacy hung up and looked over at Chet. She had to admire her partner. She would never in a million years have thought about making those two boys honorary cops for the day or bringing doughnuts. He had four pages of notes from the boys, and not all of them were restricted to the discovery of the body.

"So, you asked the boys about unusual cars or people around the area?" Lacy asked.

Looking much like the cat that had eaten the proverbial canary, Avery nodded an affirmative.

"Okay, Chet, what did you get?"

"The boys said that they sneak down to the lake all the time. They said that on Wednesday, there was an old *Smokey and the Bandit* car parked along the road for a long time in early morning. They said that the driver was a white guy, about their father's age, with big muscles and hairy as Chewbacca."

"Okay, so these kids watch entirely too many movies. Other than that, you're saying that they might have seen the killer?"

"I'm just saying that it's possible. The ME puts the time of death as probably being on Tuesday, the kids saw the car early Wednesday; it could be. They said the car was black, just like in the movie, and looked to be the same model. I think the number of black Trans-Ams from the seventies that are still running would be an easy enough detail to find out."

"True. Good work, Chet. Why don't you get the DMV on that while I check the other victim's chart and look for similarities between the two cases?"

"Lacy? Why do you think we got this case instead of Weaver and Rogers?"

"Because we kick ass and they kiss ass," she joked.

Lacy walked toward the records room, leaving Chet to make his call to the DMV. She filled out the required form to remove the copy of the chart and went back to the solitude of her desk. Chet was nowhere in sight. He'd probably gone to the vending machine to feed his sweet tooth. Sitting down, she opened the file and saw a smaller, less bloated headless victim.

"Victim is a John Doe. NCIC reports no match on the fingerprints. Attached are the findings from the autopsy."

And James thought she was terse! At least she was terse and thorough, unlike Detective Weaver.

The ME had determined that the head had been removed by a knife akin to the common kitchen boning knife. From the description of the sever wound and the volume of blood found inside the lungs, it hadn't been a quick or painless death. There were no identifying marks on the body, such as piercings, tattoos, or birthmarks. The body had been found in a heavily wooded area within five miles of the location in which the second body had turned up. Two teenagers had stumbled upon the body while they were in the woods drinking beer. They had waited until they sobered up to call the police, but hadn't had the foresight to dispose of their empty beer cans. In Weaver's short synopsis, there was more about the beer cans and the underage drinkers than the victim. Lacy thought, shit, you'd think that Rogers and Weaver were investigating the teenagers rather than a headless body. Type of beer, amount consumed by each teen, even photos of the beer cans scattered about in the cleared area of the woods. Great work, Detectives!

Remembering that the state of Georgia put fingerprints on their driver's licenses, Lacy extracted a copy of the victim's print. She would give this to Avery so that he could send it along to the DMV as well. Maybe they'd get lucky and the victim would have prints on file with the DMV if he'd lived in Georgia for a few years, even if they weren't on file with NCIC. This was something that Rogers and Weaver should have thought of. Still, it was worth a gamble.

Looking at the clock, Lacy decided to take a break and visit Snowpuff. After that, maybe she'd go for her jog, then come back to the department. Chet could stay until the information came back from the DMV, then go home if he wanted to.

It was 5:30 when Lacy arrived at the department again. The visit with Snowpuff had lasted longer than she'd expected. The jog, on the other hand, had been much shorter than she'd hoped. Somehow, she just wasn't up for the occasion. She decided she'd blame the humidity. She was surprised to find Avery still sitting at his desk.

"Still here, Chet?" she asked.

"Yeah. We got a match on the fingerprints for both victims. They were brothers."

"Already? Why didn't you call me?"

"I knew you were going to be running and that you'd be back here at some point. I just decided to wait for you. Sumlin is impressed. I think our names will be mud with Rogers and Weaver."

"Well, we can't help it that they're dumbasses. How did you manage to get the prints from today's body so fast?"

"I just went over and made a quick copy of them. I figured since my friend at the DMV would be looking up one set of prints, he may as well look up two."

"I'm surprised they had started the autopsy. They didn't seem too gung-ho when I asked them to rush it."

"They hadn't. I took along a printing kit."

Lacy remembered that Chet's first job as a law officer had been with the Sheriff's Department of a nearby county in the gun license division. Consequently, he could print with the best of them.

"Will that hold up? In court, I mean?" she questioned.

"Nah, but it did make the ME's office get their butts in gear since the two victims are brothers. There isn't much doubt now that the cases are related. They're set to start the autopsy within the hour and will be sending over an official printing of the victim tomorrow afternoon."

"So, are we going to do the next of kin notification on the first victim or are the D-Team?"

Since Chet objected to her calling Weavers and Rogers Tweedle-Dumb and Tweedle-Dumber, she called them the D-Team for the Dumbass Team. Oddly, he didn't seem to mind that.

"The Captain hasn't called me back yet about that. It wouldn't break my heart if they did the notification."

"Mine either," agreed Lacy.

True to form, Dr. Jessie Pope pulled up outside Sharon's house at 6:00 sharp. As Sharon got into the late model minivan, she noticed that Jessie seemed to have lost weight since the last time she'd seen her.

"Hey. Have you been on a diet? You look thinner."

"No. I have lost a few pounds, though."

"Are you sick?"

"No, I just haven't been as hungry as normal. I feel okay, though. Speaking of food, what are you in the mood for?"

"You choose. I'm not picky, as you well know." Sharon laughed.

After deciding on Thai food, the two ladies were seated at a booth in the quaintly dim restaurant. Quickly making their selections, the talking began.

"So, Jess, is there anything wrong? You just seem, I don't know, quiet."

"No. I'm okay. Just tired, I guess. How about with you? Are you seeing anyone yet?"

"Nope. How's work?" Sharon asked, hoping to avoid Jessie's inquisition into her dating life.

"Let's just say I never need to worry about job security; people die all the time."

"Yeah, I know what you mean. God, this past week, I diagnosed a case of HIV in a nine-year-old child. I think he may have gotten it from a transfusion. I'm waiting to hear back from the blood center about the status of his donor," Sharon said sadly.

"Really? We've had a couple of HIV cases recently that were suspicious. One I remember quiet clearly. It was a little old lady in her seventies. She denied any of the classic modes of transmission except for a blood transfusion. We checked with the donor center, and her donor was called in for testing. The donor tested HIV negative, so we still don't know how she got the virus."

"What donor center did you call?"

"I don't know. I only know about the case because I happened to sit-in on the Transfusion Committee meeting for one of the other pathologists. I can find out, if you'd like for me to. Aren't there only a couple in the area, though?"

"Yeah, I guess so. So, you remember that one; what was the other case?"

"Oh. A nurse got stuck by a needle after she'd given a patient a shot for pain. You know how, when there's an employee exposure, blood is drawn from both the source of the exposure as well as the employee? Well, the source was a young sickle cell anemia patient, 21 years old, who has received multiple transfusions. She tested positive for HIV, so the nurse was started on anti-viral therapy."

"So, if she's a sickle cell patient, she probably gets transfused frequently. Were all of her donors called in for an HIV test?"

"Yes, but it really wasn't as tedious as it sounds. She has a rare phenotype and multiple antibodies. It seems she only has a couple of regular donors even though she's transfused frequently. They alternate donating bi-monthly and have always tested negative for HIV."

"That's just so weird. What do you think is happening?" Sharon asked, more to herself than to Jessie.

"I don't know. It is strange, though. It doesn't appear that these people have actually gotten HIV from their blood transfusions, yet there doesn't seem to be any obvious source of exposure to the virus."

"Have you talked to the Infectious Disease doctors to see if there are more cases?"

"No, I rarely see any of the ID docs. Actually, I haven't given it much thought lately and probably wouldn't have even mentioned it if you hadn't brought up the topic," Jessie said, putting her fork down beside her plate.

"Would you mind checking with the ID docs and letting me know?" Sharon asked.

"Not at all. You seem to be obsessing over this."

"You'd obsess, too, if you'd seen that nine-year-old with full blown AIDS."

"That's what I keep telling you. It's better to work with those you never get to know."

"I'm not doing autopsies and tissue examinations for my living, Jess. It'll never happen."

Still wondering about the frail appearance of her friend, Sharon decided to forgo ordering dessert. The very thinness of Jessie made her feel the need to diet even more strongly than usual.

Monday morning, Sharon called the blood center to inquire about the HIV status of Jeremy's donor. She was told that the donor had tested negative. Once again, Sharon found herself left with a strange feeling of foreboding. She made a mental note to check in with the Infectious Disease doctors for her hospital to ask if they'd seen any other cases of unexplained HIV contraction lately, just as she'd asked Jessie to do at her facility. She decided to go into work early so that she could retrieve Todd Stevens' medical record for Detective Fuller and also hopefully catch one of the ID doctors.

It was 4:45 when she walked into the Brookshire Medical Center. Making a bee line for the office of Dr. Haverty, her favorite ID doctor, she was relieved to find that he was still there for the day. His grey hair was an unruly mop framing a haggard face. Sharon wondered if he intentionally tried to look like a mad scientist.

"Noah? Hi. I was going to see if you had a couple of minutes to talk to me about a patient I saw the other day."

"Sure. Have a seat."

Sharon glanced around the cluttered office and sat in the only available chair.

"How's the family?" she asked.

Sharon always tried to keep names at bay because she wasn't great at remembering them. She thought his wife's name was Tonya, but had no recollection of his son's name.

"They're fine. They're off in Michigan visiting Tonya's folks. That's one of the reasons I'm still here; the house isn't the same when they're gone. How's your dad?"

"Good, thanks. He said we should have more tomatoes before too long. I'll be sure to bring you a few."

"Great. Those things the grocery stores try to pass off as tomatoes these days are frightful, really."

"Yes, they are. Oh, the case I wanted to talk to you about was a nine-year-old child who contracted HIV. I think I was pretty thorough in my medical history check, but it seems that the only plausible way for him to have gotten the virus was via transfusion. The odd thing is, I called the blood center, and his donor has tested negative for HIV. Also, I talked to a friend of mine who said there were a couple of similar cases at her hospital where the most likely source of HIV exposure was from a transfusion. Again, the donors were all regular donors who've since tested negative repeatedly. I was wondering if you had any other cases similar to this or if maybe in your research you knew of some new means of viral transmission?"

"Hmm. You asked the child about sexual practices and IV drug use, I'm sure."

More a statement than a question, Sharon still nodded in affirmative that she had.

"I've had three cases lately that were questionable, according to the patients, though none were quite as strikingly blatant as your nine-year-old. These were all middle aged individuals who denied having unprotected sex and drug abuse. Still, two of the three admitted to having been with someone sexually within the past few years whom they knew little or nothing about, you know, one night stands, but swore they used condoms. They didn't even recall the women's names, which negated follow up testing of the women.

We chalked it up to their previous sexual encounters, but something didn't feel right to me at the time. I think it's because a great deal of the time that condoms fail to work properly it's because the user fails to properly apply them. Both of these men were married and late thirties, early forties. They struck me as being capable of knowing how to use a condom. Still, there's the chance of tearing with a condom. Have you ever seen a condom manufacturing plant?"

"No, I can't say that I have," Sharon said, suppressing the image of Noah in a condom factory.

"Well, I've seen them on television. They put those little suckers through one hell of a workout. They stretch them to an unrealistically enormous size and check for tears. Though unlikely, there's a minute occurrence of tearing. I guess I'm just saying that I was never truly convinced that these guys got their disease from their sexual encounters."

"Did you ask if they had ever received a blood transfusion?"

"Of course. Both men had, and we did check the transfusion service to see if their donors could be traced and checked for the virus. As in your case, the tests were negative."

"What about the third patient?"

"Well, she kept trying to blame a dentist or a doctor for her infection. Kept repeating over and over that she was a virgin and had never used drugs. She seemed to be a religious fanatic, plain Jane woman; wore no makeup. Anyhow, it was against her religion to receive a blood transfusion, so that didn't pan out either. We don't know what to make of her case. I'm sorry I can't be of more help than this."

"No, you've been great. I have this feeling that something strange is happening. I just can't quite put a finger on it."

"I know what you mean. It's a feeling I have, too, especially after hearing about your pediatric patient," Noah said with a frown.

"Well, I've got to run. I've got to pick up a chart from Medial Records before I start work. Thanks for your time, Noah. Give my best to your family."

"You, too. Take care."

So far, between her Thursday night patient, Todd Stevens' wife, Jessie's two patients, and now Noah's three patients, it did seem that something was awry. She decided to talk to Detective Fuller about it when she came by to pick up the chart on the Stevens homicide.

Lacy checked her watch. It was only 5:20, still too early for Dr. West to be on duty. It had been as she and Chet had expected; Detectives Rogers and Weaver had pretended to be enraged over their lack of notification of the second homicide victim on Saturday. Lacy knew that the actual source of their ire was the quick identification of both victims that Avery had uncovered in a matter of a couple of hours. Captain Sumlin had played innocent on the knowledge that the second victim had also been decapitated, citing the heavy workload already undertaken by the D-team as the reason he'd called in Lacy and Chet. He'd also slyly passed the case over to Lacy and Chet under the guise of their lighter case load.

As a result, she and Chet had spent the entire day interviewing the family, friends, and co-workers of the two deceased, decapitated men. Chet had gone home a few minutes earlier so that he could spend some quality time with his family. Lacy thought she might visit Snowpuff before going over to the hospital since it was too hot to run. Plus, she was starting to miss the friendly white cat with the silly name despite herself.

Pulling into the veterinarian's parking lot, Lacy had the thought that maybe she would ask Dr. West if she wanted a cat. As she entered the building, she was greeted by the same receptionist she'd seen the first time she came to visit. Lacy was pleased to see that some of the previous scratches on the woman's arms were healing. She was also reminded that she'd been glad to learn that Snowpuff hadn't been the origin of the scratches.

"Ah, Detective. If you'd like, I can take Snowpuff into Dr. Powell's office for your visit. All of our rooms are in use. I'm sure she wouldn't mind."

"Okay. So, how's he doing?" Lacy asked, following the receptionist to Dr. Powell's office.

"Truthfully? He seems depressed. He didn't eat this morning, and he hasn't purred when I petted him all day. Here we go. If you want to have a seat, I'll just be a second."

Sitting in the veterinarian's office, Lacy found herself feeling sorry for the cat. She thought about the many oft-forgotten victims of horrible crimes, such as the children and pets. It was a shame that human nature so routinely dictated that rash actions prevailed over the well-being of all involved. She heard the door open and saw the receptionist lugging Snowpuff in.

"Here we are. Stay as long as you'd like. I'm sure he'll be happy for the company."

Feeling bolder about the intricacies of relating to felines after her last two visits, Lacy decided she'd try to pick the big cat up. Scooping his behemoth body up, she tried to hold him in the manner she'd seen the receptionist and Dr. Powell doing. Both she and the receptionist were amazed to see that Snowpuff began ramming his head gently into Lacy's face and purring audibly.

"Well, he hasn't purred for anyone all day. Looks like you've got a little buddy."

"Looks like," agreed Lacy.

"You can just press this intercom button when you're finished with your visit. I'll come back and get him."

"Thanks."

After the door was closed and Lacy had sat, she returned her attention to the furry cat who had now curled himself into a contented ball in her lap. He was still purring as though his life depended on it. Yes, Dr. West would be a good owner for this guy.

Pressing the button, Lacy waited for the receptionist to return. It was a matter of seconds before the door was opened.

"Well, that was a short visit!" The young receptionist's face looked somewhat disappointed.

"Oh, I'm not through. I just thought that maybe you could bring him some food and water in here. Maybe he'll eat for me since he seems to like me," Lacy said.

Smiling once again, the woman left to retrieve some food. After returning with a plate of something tan and stinky and a small bowl of water, the receptionist left. Snowpuff began eating voraciously, purring all the while. How could he do that? Lacy thought that maybe she'd try humming while she ate later, just to see if humans could do that, too. When the plate was licked clean and he'd lapped some water, Snowpuff once again resumed his position on Lacy's lap and began licking his left front paw. Taking the paw, he gingerly wiped his mouth. Repeating the action time and again, he eventually stopped, presumably when he felt he was clean. He then reached over and licked Lacy's arm. She smiled down at the still-purring cat.

Lacy and the cat had dozed off, so the sound of the office door opening startled them both. It was Dr. Powell. Shit, what time was it?

"Detective Fuller? I'm glad you came to visit Snowpuff. I understand he's becoming quite attached to you. We're getting ready to close. Have you thought of adopting Snow yourself?"

Huh. Snow? Why hadn't Lacy thought to call him that before? Wasn't that the name Todd wanted to give the cat? Well, she'd have to remember not to abbreviate the name to Snow when she was talking to Shelly. Oh, shit, she'd been asked a question.

"Uh, actually, I was going to ask a doctor I know who works for Brookshire to consider adopting him."

Nicely done, she thought. Avoid the question by giving an acceptable alternative answer.

"Well, I sure hope he likes this guy as well as he likes you," Dr. Powell said.

"Actually, it's a lady, and I'm sure he will."

Reluctantly handing Snowpuff to the doctor, Lacy made her exit. Looking down at her watch, she was surprised that it was already 7:30. She could make it to Brookshire by 8:00 if she drove straight over. If, however, she ran by home and freshened up a bit, she could still be there by 8:30. She decided that the second option sounded better.

Entering the emergency department of Brookshire Medical Center, Lacy realized that it had taken far longer to get cleaned up than she'd estimated. She should sign up for one of those time management seminars the department offered. Walking toward the reception area, she identified herself and asked to see Dr. West. After being told to have a seat in the waiting room, Lacy walked over to the area in time to see a child vomit. Hearing a couple of other patients sneezing and hacking, she decided not to sit. She also thought she'd have to take her third shower of the day as soon as she got home.

After what seemed like hours, which was actually only a matter of ten minutes, she heard her name paged overhead to the reception desk. As she walked up, she saw Dr. West standing there, smiling.

"Hi, Detective Fuller. I've got the chart you requested, but I was wondering if you had a few minutes to talk?" Sharon asked.

"Sure. Do you think I could wait in the staff lounge again? The people out here are sick."

Laughing, Sharon said, "Well, it *is* an emergency room. Do you remember the code?"

"Yeah," answered Lacy.

"Great. Have you eaten dinner yet? I was just about to order a pizza if you'd like to join me. If you think you can wait that long, I should be ready to take a break by the time it arrives. What do you like on yours?"

"Cheese. Yeah, I'd like that. I actually expected to have a bit of a wait."

"Great. I'll just order now and send you back with the Stevens chart. I'll be in to join you as soon as I can."

Taking the folder from Dr. West, Lacy felt an electrical shock sensation as she brushed against the doctor's hand. Wow; it had been so long since she'd felt that particular sensation that she'd forgotten how nice it was. She walked toward the staff lounge feeling equally euphoric over "the touch" as she did the fact that the doctor had wanted to talk to her *over dinner*! Mentally chiding herself to not make a mountain of a molehill, Lacy entered the four digit code and once more entered Barney's lair. She'd noticed while she waited for Dr. West earlier that several of the nurses also wore scrubs of the same deep purple color.

Sitting on the uncomfortable chair, Lacy opened the folder and was greeted with samples of Dr. West's handwriting. Small, legible, precise cursive seemed to flow over the pages. She read the entire file in a matter of minutes. She knew that since the autopsy had been performed by the medical examiner's office, there wouldn't be a copy of the report in this chart. She decided to re-read the file, just so she could study Dr. West's handwriting. God! She was becoming infatuated with someone who was probably out of her league as well as more than likely straight; how pathetic.

When she heard the door open, she looked up to see Dr. West carrying a huge pizza box and once more smiling. That was two smiles she'd been the recipient of within the past thirty minutes. It made her feel warm inside.

"I've asked one of my colleagues to cover for me, so I've probably got a good forty-five minutes, unless the trauma beeper sounds."

With that, Sharon placed both the pizza and the potentially intrusive pager on the table. Walking to the refrigerator, she pulled out a two-liter bottle of Diet Coke.

"Is this okay with you? If you'd rather have something else, I can run down to the vending area."

"No, actually, that's my beverage of choice."

"Great," Sharon said.

After pouring two drinks, Sharon returned to the cabinets to get some disposable plates and napkins as well. Once she had finished, she sat directly across from Lacy and removed two slices of pizza for each of them.

"I always get cheese pizza, too. The other ingredients have so much sodium that I bloat up like a piglet if I eat them," Sharon said.

Lacy had a hard time imagining Dr. West as a piglet, but the casual, self-effacing talk seemed to make her feel more comfortable. Feeling that she needed to add something, Lacy finally said, "Yeah, me, too."

"That was sweet of you to agree with the whole bloating thing Lacy but your total body fat is probably half of mine," Sharon said through a smile. "I've been thinking a lot about Todd Stevens' wife and the ambiguous way she seems to have contracted HIV. Did you remember to ask when she was transfused?"

"Yeah, it was four years ago." Lacy took a bite of pizza.

"Well, I saw a patient the other night; actually, it was the same night they brought in Mr. Stevens. He was a nine-year-old who had symptoms of HIV, so I had him tested. It turns out he's also positive. He also received a blood transfusion four years ago. I'm pretty sure he hasn't had another potential exposure to HIV. I even had his parents tested in case he was born with the disease. They were both negative."

"Really? Well, I think that Shelly Stevens is telling the truth about not having used drugs or slept around. Do you think she could have gotten the disease from a surgery? She's had several of them, mostly cosmetic procedures."

Thinking about a surgical link between Jeremy and Shelly, Sharon paused before replying.

"Well, I guess if an autoclave wasn't working properly and failed to sterilize the instruments between patients, it might be possible. Surgery isn't my forte, so I'd have to ask around. I was also going to mention that a friend of mine who works for Stranton Hospital said that she'd recently uncovered a couple of cases similar to mine, whereby the positive HIV status of her patient was discovered, and there were no obvious explanations for their being infected. In each case, the patients had received a blood transfusion, but I didn't ask about surgery. I'll give her a call, though. Also, I checked with one of the infectious disease doctors about unusual cases of AIDS recently. He had three cases that came to mind, two of whom had been transfused."

"I'm inclined to discount the transfusion possibility because I contacted the blood center where the units that Shelly Stevens received had come from, and none of the donors had HIV," Lacy said, taking another bite of pizza.

"Yes, the donor for my nine-year-old patient was also negative. I checked, too. Surgery, huh? Well, I'll check around," agreed Sharon.

"I appreciate your help with this case," Lacy said as she dabbed at the corner of her mouth with her paper napkin.

"I appreciate that you seem to be truly investigating the origin of the Stevens woman's infection. Would you do that if it weren't for her family name?"

"Yes, but I would never have been given the chance to."

"That's what I thought. You know, AIDS isn't necessarily a death sentence, especially for those who have the means to obtain the medication cocktails." Sharon took her first bite of pizza.

The women sat and ate quietly for a few minutes. It was Sharon who broke the silence.

"I was thinking that maybe there was someone in the testing department at the blood center who was neglecting to report positive HIV tests. If that were the case, these donors would still be allowed to donate blood, and that would be a plausible explanation for their continued HIV negative status. The only problem with that is that the same employee would have to perform all of the repeat testing on these donors. Still, we need to find out if the same blood center collected all of the units of blood in question. Now that you mention surgery, though, that makes it a bit more complicated. I'm pretty sure that if surgery is the common denominator, not all of the operations occurred in the same facility. I don't know; I get this feeling that there's something illicit happening that's causing people to contract HIV, and I think we're only just scratching the surface."

"Well, I'm in it for the long haul. I've been given strict orders that I'm to *detect* the source of Shelly Farnsworth Stevens' HIV infection or else," Lacy said determinedly.

"Good. I'll help out any way I can. We should get together later this week to see if either of us has gleaned any useful information."

Lacy tried to suppress the smile that she inwardly felt.

"How about Friday?" Lacy quickly asked.

"Oh, I always have a date on Friday. It's a standing thing."

Noticing the abrupt stiffness and irritated frown that overtook Detective Fuller, Sharon thought that she must have said something offensive. She'd never had a lesbian friend before; maybe they thought that straight women were afraid they were coming on to them or something and that made them extra-sensitive. Whatever it was, Lacy's countenance had definitely changed.

Sharon explained, "My brother and sister-in-law come over every Friday evening. Actually, this Friday might be a good time for us to get together because we're having a fish fry in memory of my Mother. I'd love it if you'd come. I'm sure we'll have a chance to talk about it then."

Looking less edgy, Lacy asked for the address of Dr. West's house and also asked if she could bring someone.

"Sure. It should start around 7:00 or so. Also, I'd like it if you'd call me Sharon rather than Dr. West. Is it okay if I call you Lacy?"

Lacy nodded and watched as Dr. West, Sharon, wrote down her address and drew a little map to get to her house. Feeling bold and daring, she decided to ask the big question.

"Sharon? Have you ever thought about getting a cat?"

"I have. In fact, I thought about it so much that I got some. I have four kitties. Oh, and a little dog. Why?"

"Oh. I guess you wouldn't want another one then. I'm trying to find a home for Shelly Stevens' cat."

"Why don't you take him?" asked Sharon.

"I've never had a cat."

"Well, haven't you ever heard the expression 'there's a first time for everything?'" Sharon said, playfully.

Wondering if the statement were a double entendre,

Lacy couldn't quite force herself to acknowledge the question.

"Seriously, there's nothing to it. All you've got to do is provide them with food, fresh water, a clean litter box, and, *voila*! Instant companionship," Sharon said with a smile.

"I hadn't given it much thought." Lacy took the directions from Sharon's hand.

"Well, do. I'll try to give you a call in the middle of the week to bring you to speed on what I learn about these questionable cases and possible surgeries. I should probably go back to work. Thank you for your time."

"No, I should thank you. How much do I owe you for the pizza?"

"Nothing. I enjoyed the company. It was the first meal I've eaten in this room that I didn't bemoan the damned uncomfortable chairs. I feel as if I should pay you!"

Laughing, both women left the lounge.

Tuesday night, Lacy went by to visit Snowpuff and decided to take him home with her on a temporary basis, just until she found him a suitable home. She'd stocked up on small, expensive cans of cat food and purchased a couple of litter pans. He'd slept curled around her head, purring her to sleep, both Tuesday and Wednesday night. He seemed happy. She also had to admit, it was nice having someone to come home to.

Wednesday afternoon, she'd asked Homer if he'd be interested in going to the fish-fry with her on Friday. She'd been surprised by his enthusiastic reply. She was still working on a way to tactfully tell him he needed to shower. She was also thinking about going to a department store and picking up a new outfit for him. She hoped he didn't insist on wearing that damned long coat.

By Thursday afternoon, Lacy and Chet had solved

the decapitation homicides. It turned out to be far less enthralling than a serial killer. Instead, the perpetrator, who drove a 1974 black Pontiac Trans Am, had first met the two brothers at a bar. He'd been waiting to play pool when the brothers finished. Apparently, the siblings lacked enough talent in the pool playing department that the perpetrator, one David Liese, had begun making rude remarks. After several beers, he'd eventually pissed the brothers off enough that they beat the shit out of him. The police had been called but charges hadn't been pressed because Mr. Liese had fled the scene by then. The bartender said he didn't want to make trouble for two of his most frequent patrons, so a police report had been filed and stowed away. David Liese was a six foot two mountain of a man with a full beard. He did, in fact, look like Chewbacca. Lacy once again had to applaud the work of her partner for uncovering the information that led to the arrest of the killer. They'd been assigned to a new case, the premature demise of a local drug pusher, and Lacy wondered what had happened with the little punk she'd turned over to Lou.

Sharon called Thursday evening to say that she'd been in touch with her friend, some doctor at some other hospital, and most of the patients had indeed had surgery. She'd also informed Lacy that if the cases of HIV were being contracted through improperly autoclaved utensils, it would be due to an unlikely case of malfunctioning equipment throughout the city at various hospitals. Lacy had since learned that an autoclave was a sterilizing device for re-usable medical equipment. She had also learned that this theory seemed even less probable than the transfusion theory. Sharon had asked Lacy to try to obtain a list of employees at both of the area blood suppliers, which she had already done earlier that day.

On her way home from work on Thursday, Lacy stopped by Homer's abandoned lot to find out what size clothes he wore and hint about the bath. As it turned out, he'd already given thought to the bath issue and had paid his five dollars to sleep at one of the local shelters that night. That way, he explained, he could shower the next morning before leaving. She obtained his shirt, slacks, and shoe size and went home.

Entering her apartment, she was immediately greeted by a talkative Snowpuff.

"Hey, Big Guy. Did you miss me? Are you ready for your dinner?" she asked.

First fixing Snowpuff a plate of fishy stuff from a can, then fixing herself her usual peanut butter and jelly sandwich with a glass of milk, Lacy retreated to her recliner after pressing the play button on her answering machine.

Thinking about Friday night and Dr. West caused her to totally ignore whatever messages she'd just played. By the time she realized that, she was half through with her sandwich. As she turned to get her milk glass, she saw a large, white face ensconced in the glass.

"Hey!" she shrieked.

The ears went back, but the head didn't lift out of the glass.

"Shit. Well, I guess cats do like milk. Come on, I'll put that in a bowl for you. I'd hate to have to take you to the animal ER with your head stuck in a glass, if they even have animal ERs," Lacy said, crankily.

With that, she took the milk and poured it into a saucer for Snow, who intently followed her every move and happily began lapping at the treat. Pouring a fresh glass of milk for herself, Lacy sat down and finished her dinner while studying her newly acquired lactose-loving house guest.

CHAPTER 10

Sharon stood at the large brick grill her father had built years before watching the flames rise high and drinking her second beer. She thought she remembered that the oil in the enormous pan needed to bubble before she began immersing the battered fish and shrimp into it. It hadn't yet gotten that hot. Jon and her father were sitting next to each other on the white plastic chairs her mother had bought for occasions such as these. She knew that Jean was in the kitchen making the tartar sauce. She wondered why Detective Fuller hadn't shown up yet. Hoping she hadn't changed her mind, Sharon finished off the beer.

She'd been unhappy when Lacy had asked if she could bring a friend along with her since she was hoping to have some time with the detective alone to learn more about her. She'd also prepared her family that two lesbians would be coming and that they weren't to make any remarks or stare. When she heard a door slamming in their driveway, she began wondering who Lacy would bring. Her last girlfriend, or at least the one whom Sharon had met in the emergency room, was fairly attractive but also totally self-centered and crazy. She hoped in this case Detective Fuller had done better for herself. Looking up, she was surprised to see the detective holding onto the arm of a thin, elderly black man. Was this her friend?

Lacy walked through the fence toward the back of the house. Dr. West had told her to go around back, so here she was. Homer was smiling from ear to ear.

"Miss Lacy? I smell happiness," he said.

"Well, Homer, you *should* smell fish since we're late."

Watching Dr. West approach, Lacy felt as if someone had sucker punched her. God, she was pretty! She was also more voluptuous in jeans than in scrubs.

"Hi, Lacy. I'm glad you two could make it," Sharon said with a smile.

"Hi, Sharon. This is my friend, Homer Files."

Shaking Homer's hand, then Lacy's hand, Sharon noticed how visibly relaxed and happy the detective looked. She also noticed for the first time that Lacy was quite beautiful. Remembering her manners, Sharon began the introductions.

"This is my brother, Jon, and my father, Jay. My sister-in-law, Jean, is in the house. She should be out soon. I've got to check the fish. Help yourself to the drinks in the cooler. There's beer, Coke, wine coolers, and water. If you want anything else, we've probably got it."

Turning toward the brick pit in the back yard, Sharon stopped long enough to extract a beer from the cooler. She noticed that Lacy had also come to the cooler and picked up a beer as well.

Hoping she'd be followed, Sharon walked toward the pit. Sure enough, Lacy was shadowing her. Glancing over her shoulder, Sharon saw Jon opening a Coke for Homer and pulling forward another plastic chair for him to sit in.

"Sharon? I hope you don't mind my bringing Homer."

"Of course not, why would I mind?"

"I don't know. He's homeless, but he's my friend. He's a good person, and I remembered him telling me that he and his wife had fish cookouts during the summer, so I thought he might enjoy coming. His wife died."

"Well, I'm sure we'll enjoy his company."

Sharon watched Lacy gingerly sip her beer. Half expecting her to make a face, Sharon volunteered, "Really, we have all sorts of liquor in the house and a slew of mixers. I'm sure we could fix you whatever you'd like."

Raising her eyebrow as if puzzled, Lacy replied, "I like beer. That's usually what I order when I go out. But, thanks."

Noticing that the oil had finally begun bubbling gently, Sharon dropped several pieces of breaded red snapper into the pan, quickly followed by some shrimp and hushpuppy batter. She'd never known a beer-sipper before. She, herself, swigged the brew with gusto.

The back porch door opened, and Jean came out with Penny following close beside her. As they approached the men, Penny began barking and wagging her curled tail at the sight of a stranger.

Homer's face lit up. "Hello there, puppy! Aren't you cute? What's your name?"

Jon answered, "Her name is Penny. She isn't a vicious dog, but she'll bark her little head off until you pet her."

That was all the okay Homer needed. Standing, he walked over to where Jean and Penny stood and thrust forward his hand.

"Good evening, Ma'am. My name is Homer Files. You must be Miss Jean?"

"Yes, I am. It's nice to meet you, Homer."

"And you must be Miss Penny? It's a pleasure to meet you."

With that, Homer bent down toward the dog and she rolled over onto her back.

Lacy looked at Homer's smile and was thankful that she'd invited him. Looking around the back yard, she was taken aback by the amount of land. From the front of the house, it wasn't obvious that there was this kind of spread behind. The house itself was an average, brick middle-income family home. She was somewhat surprised. Didn't doctors live in bigger, newer houses?

There was a small garden on the left side of the yard that Homer, Jay, and Penny were walking toward. Jon and Jean had moved inside to a screened-in back porch where they appeared to be setting the table. A sudden burst of cursing brought her back to the present in time to see a pissed off looking Sharon shoving a pair of barbeque tongs in her direction.

"I just got shit on by a bird! I've got to go shower and change. Son-of-a-bitch! Would you mind finishing this up? I'll send Jean out to help you."

"I'm not sure I know how to tell when fish is done," Lacy said, concerned about ruining the dinner.

"Didn't you say that Homer used to have fish cook-outs? Maybe he can help. I just know that I've got to get cleaned up immediately," Sharon said irritably.

Lacy called Homer over, who was all too pleased to help. Jay and Penny followed along as Lacy retrieved the white plastic chairs.

Going inside the house, Sharon stuck her head into the screened in porch to ask Jean to help with the fish frying if she was needed. Glancing down toward the grill pit, it was obvious that Homer had everything under control.

Jon sidled up to Sharon and said, "That's just about the nicest lesbian I've ever met."

Sharon nodded and said, "Yeah, Lacy seems to be a real gem."

"I wasn't talking about her, I was talking about Homer. You said two lesbians were coming for dinner. I've got to admit, though, I wouldn't have pegged him as a lesbian."

Sharon swatted playfully at her brother's arm and affectionately called him a smartass when their banter was interrupted by Lacy's voice.

"Um, Homer asked if y'all had some paper towels and a plate to put the fish on. He said the first batch is about ready to come out."

Lacy stood outside on the landing, talking to the siblings through the screen wire.

"Yes, of course. Jean? Jean, this is Detective Lacy Fuller. Lacy, this is Jean. She can get you the paper towels and stuff. Come on inside."

With that, Sharon walked off as Lacy opened the French door and came inside. After shaking Jean's hand, she wandered toward the indoor opening to the porch.

"What's up with Sharon? She just sort of ran through here in a hurry," Jon asked.

"A bird dropped off a little present for her, on her head," Lacy said drolly.

Laughing until tears came to his eyes, Jon finally had to sit down.

"That's funny as shit!" he said.

"Literally." Lacy delivered excellent one-liners in her monotone voice.

Laughing harder after Lacy's input, Jon said, "Well, at least the little bird didn't shit in the frying pan. If I know my sister, we would have had to throw everything away and start over."

Jean appeared with a roll of paper towels and a cookie sheet.

"Here you go. This should do. If y'all need anything else, just let us know."

Thanking her, Lacy walked out of the house and down the steps wishing she had a brother or a sister. Or a girlfriend.

By the time Homer had removed the second batch of fish from the pan, Sharon had returned looking far less annoyed. She still had wet hair and had opted for cut off shorts that accentuated the muscles in her legs. Hopefully, Lacy asked if she was also a runner.

"Me? No way. Why?"

"Because you've got such well defined muscles in your calves."

"Oh. No, I hardly even walk my little dog but I do develop muscles fast. A couple of months ago, I decided to take an aerobics class, but I quit when my calves began looking like Popeye's forearms. Unfortunately, it didn't seem to be burning any fat. I think my calves are a residual from that fiasco."

Although Sharon looked a little heavier than Lacy remembered from the emergency room encounter several months ago, she didn't look as though she needed to lose any weight. Lacy was just about to tell her that when she noticed both Homer and Jay studying them. Feeling lecherous, Lacy ventured closer to Homer and asked if she could help him do anything.

"Yes, Ma'am. You can help us take the food on up. We're ready to eat!"

Dinner was filled with nonstop easy talk and much laughter. Stories were told from all the members of the West family who, in turn, asked Lacy and Homer to recount some of their precious memories. Penny got several bites of snapper and a couple of shrimp from both Homer and Jay, after both men made sure there were no bones in the morsels.

After everyone was finished with dinner, Sharon offered dessert. "We've got homemade vanilla ice cream, apple pie, and watermelon for dessert. Anybody ready for it now, or do we want to wait?"

Groans and declinations were voiced around the table as everyone agreed dessert would have to wait.

Lacy asked Sharon if she needed help cleaning up the kitchen and was elated when the doctor agreed. Arms loaded with dirty dishes, Lacy followed Sharon to the closed kitchen door where both women looked helplessly at the handle. Thankfully, Jon was also coming behind them holding the catsup bottle.

"Need a hand, ladies?" he asked as he opened the door.

"Thanks, Jon." As Sharon walked into the kitchen, she seemed to be overtaken by some bizarre act of ventriloquism in which she was channeling a total idiot's voice.

"How are my itty, bitty, witty, kitty cats? Are they still pissed at their Momma? Let's not be pissed off at Momma, okay? I brought you some fishy-wishy."

Lacy looked at the kitchen table to see the source of her moronic talk and spied four large, miffed cats. She remembered what Shelly Stevens had said about Snowpuff being pissed off when he slicked his ears back. Seven out of eight ears were slicked back. She imagined that Snow would be annoyed, too, if she talked that way to him.

"They hate to be cooped up," Sharon explained.

Looking at the other end of the kitchen, Lacy noticed that the door was open. It seemed that Dr. West's version of her cats being "cooped up" meant that the den and screened porch were off limits. From her estimate, that left in excess of 2000 square feet for them to mill around in.

Lacy put the dishes on the counter near the sink and wandered back over to the cats. Putting her hand forward for them to sniff, she remembered Snowpuff ramming against her hands. These didn't do that. Of course, Snow may not have done it either if Lacy's hands had smelled like seafood. Instead, all four of them inched closer to Lacy, sniffing at first the air and finally her fingers directly. She began to pet them.

"What are their names?"

Bringing over a Styrofoam plate filled with fish and placing it in the center of the table, Sharon pointed to each kitty as she shared their names.

"This is Cozy, and this is Charcoal. They were litter mates. This is Salem. I found him wandering around the hospital parking lot after they had just paved it. He was just a baby, starving to death, and he had ear mites and asphalt from the paving in his little ears. You'd never know that he started out so puny to look at him now. And this is little Ella, my only female. Well, other than Penny."

As Sharon rinsed off the plates, Lacy wandered around the kitchen staring at the framed poetry on the walls. All of the poems were initialed with SLW.

"Did you write these poems?" she asked.

Turning to look at Lacy, Sharon answered with a sweet smile. "Yes. I would never have framed my own stuff and hung it around my house, but I'd always make Momma a copy of my happy poetry. Every time I came over, I'd notice that she had hung another of my works on the wall. For Christmas a few years back, I reprinted them on pastel paper that matched the kitchen color scheme and framed them for her. Now that I live here again, I don't want to take them down because they remind me of her every day. I can't believe it's been three years since she passed away," Sharon said solemnly.

Unable to think of anything sage or comforting to say to Sharon, Lacy simply asked, "Some of your happy poetry? It's not all happy?"

"No. Actually, I had a friend once tell me that I wrote three kinds of poems; sad, sadder, and suicidal. After that, I tried to lighten up a bit. It must have worked because Momma never had hung any of my sad poems on the wall. What about you? Do you have any hobbies?"

"I like to run. My first girlfriend got me into jogging and I try to run at least three days a week. I like photography, too. I've started taking online continuing education courses and learning more and more about different elements of photography. One of my other girlfriends used to always make a big fuss over my photos. Sometimes I like to read, when I have the time," Lacy said enthusiastically.

Abruptly switching topics, Sharon said, "That's great. It's important to have hobbies. Hey, did you get a chance to contact the donor centers about a list of employees?"

"Yeah, they're getting together a list of employees for the past ten years. They also have photos of the employees if we need them. The list should be ready to be picked up early next week."

"Good. I've given this matter a great deal of thought. I believe that someone working for the blood center is somehow behind all of this. Either that or it's all just one giant, unlikely coincidence. I'm not real sure what a list of names will tell us, but I guess it's a starting point. Maybe we could find out who performed the HIV testing on the days that the donors involved in the suspicious cases were tested. If it's the same person, we might get an answer."

Lacy thought that her experience taught her that anything this convoluted never had that easy of a solution, but decided to keep her pessimism to herself.

"That would be nice," she heard herself agreeing.

"Wouldn't it, though? I also thought that someone may be injecting the virus into the bags of blood, you know, after they've been donated," Sharon said.

"Shit! You mean, like, who?"

"I don't know. Someone at the blood center, I guess. I forgot to call Jessie, my friend over at Stranton, to ask which supplier their blood comes from. If it's a different supplier than ours, we could try cross-referencing the names on the lists you'll get next week. Otherwise, we may need to check into courier services that deliver the blood to the hospitals or maybe even hospital personnel. I know it isn't uncommon for those in the medical profession to work at another hospital to supplement their income. God, this is exhausting just to think about. How do you do this for a living?"

"It's usually somewhat fun, in a morbid, challenging way. This case is different, though. It reminds me of the time that somebody put cyanide or something in over the counter pain capsules," Lacy said.

"I was thinking that same thing the other day. Would you excuse me for a few minutes?"

"Sure."

Watching Sharon leave the kitchen, she heard four thuds and turned in time to see a little processional of kitties following their owner. Having a shadow was something that Lacy was just starting to get used to with Snowpuff. Suddenly alone in the kitchen, Lacy began reading some of the poetry. As she read, she noticed that she was moved by each piece. Dr. West certainly had a way with words. As she finished the third poem, Sharon and the cats come back into the room.

"These are really good. Have you ever thought of getting them published?"

"I did send in a few for consideration once, but it's difficult to get single author poetry published. I had a couple of offers for inclusion into quarterly poetry magazines, but there were rights waivers that had to be signed, and I didn't want to lose any of my stuff. Besides, most of them are pretty dark and foreboding. I've got a stack of at least a hundred. If you'll notice, five are hanging. The other ninety-five are kind of downers."

"I'd love to read them all sometime."

"Really? Well, maybe next week you could bring by some of your photography and I can look at that while you read my poetry."

"Name a day."

Cringing inwardly, Lacy hoped she hadn't just sounded as desperate as she'd felt. Moving toward the kitchen table, she began petting the two large, black cats. Charcoal and Salem? Yes, that was right.

"How about Saturday or Sunday?" Sharon said.

Hmm, thought Lacy. Her weekend was free.

"Either day works for me unless a new case comes in."

Watching Lacy pet the two cats, Sharon remembered the cat that Lacy had been trying to place.

"Hey, whatever happened with the Stevens woman's cat?"

"I took it home with me until I can find it a good home," Lacy said evasively.

"Want me to post the information on the board at work? There are quite a few listings for houses and vehicles, and every so often there's a pet, too. The pets usually get adopted quickly."

Lacy brusquely said, "No. I'll take care of it. Thanks."

Sharon turned away from Lacy so that the detective couldn't see the smile on her face. Lacy was already attached to the little cat. That was good. They both needed a friend. Suddenly thinking about herself, Sharon realized that she, too, needed a friend. Jessie was the only person she ever did anything with. She was sort of feeling that Lacy was a friend, which was silly since they didn't know each other well. Still, all friendships began somewhere.

Sharon picked up Cozy and began kissing his head. After a moment, she spoke. "Okay, how about next Saturday afternoon, a picnic in Piedmont Park?"

"Great. I live within walking distance. If you'd like to meet me at my apartment, you'd have an easier time finding parking."

"It's a date."

Lacy wondered if it was a date or a *date*? She decided to try not to get her hopes up. She usually prided herself on having a reliable 'gaydar' and nothing about Dr. Sharon West gave her any indication that the woman was a lesbian.

After rejoining the others in the den, Lacy was amused to see that the three men were half watching a baseball game and half telling stories. Jean was cross-stitching what seemed to be a headless bear sitting next to blocks with *ABC*'s on them. Sharon sat on a loveseat and patted the space beside her. Looking around, Lacy noticed that the invitation was unnecessary since there was nowhere else to sit, except the floor. Before she could sit, one of the large black cats hopped onto the cushion. With a well-practiced hand, Sharon swept the feline into her lap and said, "Hurry up before someone else beats you to the spot again."

Lacy noticed that whichever cat was in Sharon's lap seemed unaccustomed to being moved and was somewhat displeased about the turn of events, as evidenced by the flat ears. The cat propelled itself off his owner's lap and began bathing a paw. Sharon just laughed.

Listening to the two old men talk, Lacy was glad she hadn't grown up in as small of a town as apparently both of them had. They mentioned names like "Rusty Hobbs" who apparently had red hair and freckles, "Stinky Ottman" who bathed on Sunday whether he needed it or not, and "Stubby Witt" who had lost an arm in a saw milling accident. Remembering James' description of her, she felt certain she would have been "Crotchety Fuller" or something equally as unflattering.

When the time came to leave, everyone hugged Lacy and Homer. Sharon said she'd call Lacy later in the week. Lacy quickly wrote down her home number for the doctor. As they walked to the car, Homer stopped just shy of the passenger side and hugged Lacy.

"Thank you so much, Miss Lacy. I haven't had this much fun in a long time."

"You're welcome, Homer. Neither have I."

After almost falling into the little car and eventually managing to buckle his seat belt, Homer said, "That's the first time anyone's hugged me since Essie died," as a tear slid down his cheek.

CHAPTER 11

Chris Frazier poured himself a glass of orange juice and grabbed his daily arsenal of newspapers before moving onto the balcony. He'd stayed out in the sun too long yesterday, and consequently the stench of sautéed aloe vera from his body blended with the fishy saltwater smell of the air and created an offensive combination. Settling into the comfortable patio chair, he once again admired the view from his oceanfront condominium. The sun had been up long enough that the early morning shell gatherers had retreated, giving way to those eager to wade into the water, many carrying a gaudy plastic raft along with them.

After taking a sip of the orange juice, he picked up the San Francisco paper and began scanning the headlines. After about ten minutes, he decided there was nothing of interest, so he reached for the *Atlanta Journal*. He'd always enjoyed living in Atlanta, more so than Frisco, so he usually read this paper more thoroughly.

Stopping to read an entire story about a suicide jumper who held up traffic on I-75 for three hours on Tuesday, he found himself annoyed because the police had managed to talk the guy down from the overpass. He paused when he saw a photograph of Shelly Stevens and thought that she was pretty in a haggard looking way. He guessed that killing one's spouse could do that to a person. He thought about his wife. Casting his eyes away from the paper and once more to the vast aqua expanse, Chris remembered when his life had first begun to unravel.

He'd married his high school sweetheart, Justine, after college, and they had two little girls, Kristy and Susie. They bought a starter house with an actual white picket fence, drove American cars, and had a dog; the American dream. Everything was ideal until his brother, Craig, was diagnosed with HIV. Chris had been devastated. He hated the way Justine had reacted when she heard that Craig had AIDS and hated even more the way she filled the girls' heads with so many narrow-minded phobias. When Craig breathed his last breath, Chris had been the sole person in the room. Everyone else was afraid that they would "catch AIDS" from being in close proximity.

It was after this that Chris' verbal onslaught of his wife had begun. He could never forgive her for the way in which she treated Craig, and she could never forgive him for all the vicious arguments they'd had over the subject. He still remembered coming in from work that day in August to find his three girls gone. Hell, she'd even taken the dog! He'd not heard from her since, and it would be coming up on one year pretty soon. Granted, he'd moved, but if she really wanted to find him, she could.

Feeling suddenly hot and itchy, he decided not to think about his past anymore for the time being. Looking back down at the paper, he learned that Mrs. Stevens had apparently shot her husband because she believed that he'd infected her with HIV. According to her lawyer, the husband didn't have the disease after all. In fact, nobody seemed to know how Mrs. Stevens had gotten the virus.

The lawyer argued that his client was innocent of murder because she'd temporarily become insane upon learning of her illness. Chris thought that anyone would be capable of murder given the right motivation. He guessed that being infected with an incurable disease would constitute the right motivation in many people's book. He carefully took the Metro section of the paper and placed it in a chair beside him. A sudden feeling of excitement overtook him. Maybe things were finally starting to happen after all!

Deciding that the news story warranted a celebration, he walked inside and made a bee line for the liquor cabinet. Extracting his favorite coconut rum, he put a generous splash into his juice and stirred it gently. Looking into the mirror, he was still somewhat taken aback by his appearance. He'd lost a great deal of weight during the past year and had become quite thin for the first time in his life. He'd also made other changes, such as dying his hair blond rather than its natural black, wearing contacts rather than glasses, and getting a deep, even suntan, all in an effort to render himself incognito. He had to admit, it was a smashing success. In fact, he now looked eerily like Craig had when he'd still been healthy. Raising a glass to the mirror, he toasted the image before him and uttered two simple words, "To patience."

CHAPTER 12

Lacy awoke on Saturday feeling happier than she had in a long time. Snow was still curled around her head and began purring loudly when she stretched her legs. Slowly, the white cat stood and stretched as well before ambling down onto the side of the bed and looking at Lacy. While most people enjoyed the weekends, lately Lacy had begun to abhor them. She felt somewhat useless just hanging around doing nothing instead of trying to solve a crime. Somehow, she thought, this weekend might be different. She would run, start cleaning her apartment for when Dr. West came over next Saturday, and maybe even work on her online photography class. Reaching over to pet Snow, she decided that it may well prove to be a good weekend after all.

After feeding Snow a half can of food, scooping the litter boxes, and drinking a protein shake, Lacy donned her running gear and began stretching. After a ten minute stretching routine, she headed out and down the stairs. On her way to Piedmont Park she found herself humming. She decided that Dr. Sharon West was good medicine.

As she ran, she noticed all of the couples and families having picnics on the grass. She saw a few people throwing Frisbees for their dogs, several fellow runners, some skaters, and even a few bicyclists. Though the day was early, it was still quite hot. Still, Lacy felt immune to the heat today and ran six miles easily. The only thought she had about any of her cases was to briefly wonder if there might be some kind of new mode of transmission for HIV. She stopped by a local restaurant and bought some lunch before returning home. Jogging up the stairs just in time to hear her phone ring, Lacy opened her door and heard James' voice.

"— might want to go out tonight. If you do, give me a call on the cell phone. We've got a lawn in Buckhead to do, but after that, we're free. Talk to you later. Bye."

He was still probably pissed off at her for not going dancing with his sister. She really did like James, so she should call him back. Snow was sprawled out on her sofa asleep. Cats sure did like to sleep. Catching herself creeping by the couch, Lacy rolled her eyes at her behavior. If James' voice hadn't awakened the cat, then surely she wouldn't either. Removing her jerk chicken sandwich from the bag, she noticed that apparently the smell woke the cat. Cats liked to eat, too. Removing the other half of the can of food from the refrigerator, Lacy thought she might need to find out how much cats are supposed to eat a day. She could only imagine how annoyed Shelly Stevens would be if her little Snowpuff became huge — a Snowdrift! Maybe she should find that out pretty soon before Shelly began scheduling kitty liposuction procedures for the cat.

Sharon was brewing a pot of coffee and absently humming when Penny waddled through the kitchen, breaking her trance. After lapping up some water, the little dog walked over and licked Sharon on her foot. Smiling, she bent down to pet Penny and was besieged by jealous cats. Where had they all come from? Taking turns so that nobody would be left out, Sharon alternated strokes until her coffee pot began making gurgling sounds.

"Sorry, guys. Momma's got to get caffeinated now."

After pouring herself a mug of French Roast, she retreated to the sun room and sat in a wicker rocker. She thought about how much fun the previous night had been and how someone as standoffish as Lacy could have befriended someone as unassuming as Homer. However it had happened, she was glad it did. Everyone needed to know someone as gentle as Homer. She thought about what her mother had always said about 'angels among us' and wondered if Homer was that. Had he been introduced into Lacy's life to give her something good and solid to cling to? She felt a poem stir in the back of her head and quickly jotted down a few ideas before returning her thoughts to Lacy.

Dark hair, ivory skin, pretty pale eyes. Nice athletic figure. Beneath that strong façade, Sharon thought she could detect an innate insecurity. Did she identify with Homer somehow on that level? Sharon liked to work puzzles of any type, and Lacy was beginning to feel like a puzzle. Remembering how her mother could meet someone in the grocery store and within five minutes tell you all about their lives, Sharon wished that she had that kind of skill where people were concerned. She always thought that, by her asking a series of questions, someone would probably feel as though they were being interrogated. Still, she decided that she was going to delve a bit into Lacy's persona.

Chet and Monica took C.J. shopping for some new clothes. In the course of thirty minutes, the child had managed to annoy most everyone in the store. He'd pitched at least three temper tantrums, slung a pair of sandals across the floor, and pulled several shirts off their hangers. Chet had finally taken him outside when the glares from the other shoppers had become too much.

Their pediatrician had said that C.J. would outgrow this, but Chet didn't think it could possibly be soon enough. Chet also thought about Monica, at home with this type of behavior day-in and day-out. Had she demanded a wage for her time, Chet knew he could never in a million years pay it. Still, she needed a bonus. He thought he might see if his parents could keep C.J. tonight so he could take her out for a relaxing, child-free evening. Removing his cell phone, he called his parents and set his plan in motion. By the time he'd ended the call, he looked up to see Monica lugging four large sacks and smiling from ear to ear.

"Honey? We saved *twenty* percent with our mystery coupon! That's the highest amount, you know."

"Wow, that's great. C.J.'s been fine since I brought him outside."

"He hates shopping. Like father, like son." Monica smiled at him.

Feigning hurt feelings, Chet said, "I don't recall ever pitching a fit. So, I was thinking that you and I could go see Kayla Taylor in concert tonight. An evening of jazz classics under the stars with your favorite singer and a bottle of wine. What do you think?"

"We don't have a sitter." She sighed.

"Wanna bet? Mom and Dad agreed."

"God, I love you."

"I love you, too."

CHAPTER 13

Monday morning, Lacy arrived before Chet and began reviewing the particulars of the case they'd been assigned last Thursday. A drug dealer, known to sell to kids still in elementary school, had been shot repeatedly. Lacy found a separate folder with the autopsy results and quickly scanned the findings. There had been "at least twenty shots" with a .38 caliber pistol, most of them non-lethal. Death had been slow to come. Identification had been made by fingerprinting the victim, William Lanier, a.k.a. T-Bone. Lacy jotted down a few notes:

1. Check MO violent overkill, .38 weapon
2. Locate/interview next of kin
3. Check with Lou about pothead in my building
4. Check with blood centers about lists of employees
5. Ask Dr. West if there might be a new mode of disease transmission
6. Get oil changed in Spider

Deciding that she may well catch Lou at his desk in spite of the early hour, she thought it would be good to start the day off by being able to cross something off her list.

The call was answered on the first ring. "Narcotics."

"Lou? It's Lacy Fuller. What the hell were you doing, sitting on the phone?"

"Hey, Lace! I've got to hand it to you; we've had a successful week thanks to that little pencil-necked pothead you delivered us. He's been spewing names left and right."

"Glad to hear it. So, what deal did we cut him?" Lacy asked.

Sighing, the narcotics officer waited a beat before answering. "Oh, he'll walk. He's going to be under house arrest on the condition that he vacate his apartment and move back in with mommy. I guess that's better than nothing."

"Yeah, actually it's good. I've always thought my apartment complex had a low level of pestilence. His departure will keep it that way."

"Oh, yeah, remember that lawyer guy, Strausser? What did you do to him?" Lou sounded puzzled.

"Shelly Stevens' lawyer?" Lacy asked.

"Yeah. And this little pothead's lawyer."

"I haven't even seen him in a week or so, why?" Now it was Lacy who sounded puzzled.

"Because he was singing your praises the other day. It was quite the 180 from his past remarks about you. I just figured something was up."

"Not that I'm aware of. It probably means I screwed something up procedurally, and he's thinking he can get the Stevens woman off on a technicality. Thanks for the heads-up. I'll check into it. See you later, Lou."

Lacy wondered what in the hell the egret was up to. Checking off item #3 on her list proved to be countered by the addition of an item #7.

7. See Shelly Stevens and ask about Egret

Sitting there wondering where she might have strayed, Lacy smelled rather than heard Chet's approach. Inhaling deeply, she turned to face her partner. "You smell good. What is it?"

"Thanks. It's Drakkar Noir. I probably slaughtered the pronunciation."

"I'd never know; I didn't take Latin," Lacy said with a straight face.

"It's French," Chet replied.

"No shit!" Lacy turned to face her partner with a small smirk. The ear-to-ear grin on Chet's face convinced Lacy that this would be a good day. Chet always seemed a bit down on Mondays, but today was different.

"Why the good mood, Avery?"

"Because I don't have Monica's job. Do you think it's wrong of me to be happy to escape? It makes me feel like an asshole."

"No. They don't call it the terrible two's for nothing. I'd want to escape, too."

"That's not saying much, Lace. Still, I feel bad about it. Hey, want a candy bar?"

Afraid of what smartassed remark would come out, like maybe 'you don't feel too bad for a candy bar,' Lacy just shook her head. As she watched him wander off down the hall she hoped that C.J. grew out of this monstrous phase soon. She then thought about her dead drug dealer. He'd apparently never outgrown the stage where inappropriate behavior reigns superior to ethics. Once again, she was thankful she would never have a child. There were just too many variables on how they turned out, too much left to luck, society, and genetics. Plus, they were gross when they slobbered.

"What's the face for?" Chet asked, returning with a king-sized candy bar.

Caught thinking unkind thoughts about children, Lacy quickly recovered by saying, "Wondering how in the hell you can eat that shit for breakfast, that's all."

"So, what's on the agenda for today?" he asked.

Lacy showed him her list. He volunteered to call the blood center while she checked the national database for homicides similar to that of the pusher.

It became clear to Lacy after an hour perusing the database that most crimes in which overkill to the extent of twenty bullet wounds occurred had already been solved. In the majority of the cases, domestic issues seemed to be the underlying theme. Both love and hatred hinged upon the common ground of extreme passion. Lacy thought that the Egret would realize that and try to make something of the fact that Shelly Stevens had only shot Todd one time. Maybe there was some credence to that theory. Often people had no concept of just how dangerous firearms could be. Potentially, it only takes one shot from the tiniest of guns to commit homicide. Thinking of the Egret reminded Lacy that she needed to see Shelly after checking in with Avery.

"Metropolis Blood Center said that they have the information ready for us. I didn't actually get a real person at Community Blood Center, but I left a message," Chet said, interrupting her thoughts.

"Okay. Well, I'm going to give you the identification numbers for a couple of units of blood. Would you check and see if you can find out which employee did the HIV testing on those units while you're there?"

"Sure. What are you going to be doing?" he asked.

"I've got to see Shelly Stevens. Apparently, her asshole lawyer has suddenly decided he *likes* me, so I want to know what gives."

"Do you think we screwed something up?" Chet's brows furrowed.

"That's my bet, but I just don't see what it could have been."

"Well, let's meet up later then. I'll probably grab lunch while I'm out. There's a good Tex-Mex place close to Metropolis. I just can't drive by there without going in and getting a burrito. Want me to bring you something?"

"That place with all the pinto beans? The Tex-ico?"

"That's the one! Stupid name, though. Makes you think about a gas station," Chet said, shaking his head and chuckling.

"That's because it *is* a gas station! God, no, I don't want anything from there. How in the hell can you eat that and not be propelled to the moon?"

Laughing hardily now, Chet grabbed his jacket and headed toward the exit.

Lacy decided that since Chet was going to be having a virtual bean-fest for lunch, it would behoove her to come up with plans which would require they use separate vehicles for the remainder of the day.

On her way to the detention center, Lacy stopped by to check on Homer, but he wasn't there. He was probably somewhere earning money for the animals. At least he wasn't getting kicked by a couple of punks, she hoped. Pulling her pad from her back pocket, she added to her to-do list to check on those punks, too. Determinedly, she vowed silently to personally see to it that they served the maximum amount of time. Dejectedly, she then wondered how she would pull that off since she didn't have any friends in high places.

Entering the detention center, Lacy had to check her gun, per policy. She always hated doing that because she felt a naked vulnerability that reminded her of when she was a little kid. She was escorted to an interview room and was just beginning to pace when Shelly Stevens was brought in.

"Hey, how're you doing?" Lacy asked with genuine concern.

"I'm doing much better now that I found out you took in Snowpuff. Thank you."

"Yeah, well, I'm still trying to find him a home. He wasn't eating much at the vet's, and they said he was becoming depressed. I meant to come by and tell you myself."

"That's okay. Is he eating now?" Shelly asked hopefully.

"Oh, yeah. He seems to be happy, too. He curls up around my head when I sleep."

Through tears, Shelly said lovingly, "He always did that with Todd. It used to make me jealous, you know? He'd sit in my lap all the time, but he never did that tiara thing with my head."

Lacy thought it had been much cuter for the cat to curl around her head before she heard it referred to as 'that tiara thing'.

"I need to ask you a question. I can't promise that it'll be off the record, but I'll try to keep it that way," Lacy stated flatly.

"Okay," Shelly answered.

"It seems that your lawyer has taken a sudden liking to me. Do you have any idea why?"

Laughing, Shelly said, "Yes. It's because I told him you brought it to my attention that if I'd paid to have Snowpuff boarded before I shot Todd, it could be considered premeditation."

Breathing a sigh of relief, Lacy said, "Oh. I thought I must have screwed something up with the investigation."

"How could you screw up something when I've admitted that I shot Todd?"

"I don't know. It didn't seem logical, but since we, your lawyer and I, had gotten off on such rotten terms, I was a bit worried that he suddenly seemed to have a good opinion of me. He's not going to say anything about that, is he? I mean, it was unethical for me to tell you that and would probably constitute grounds for a mistrial."

"No way. You saved him from a great embarrassment if the prosecutor had uncovered the information after he'd overlooked it. I guarantee that nothing will be said, Detective."

"I read in the paper that you're going to plea temporary insanity. Do you know yet when the trial will start?"

"Probably in a couple of weeks. Martin is trying to postpone it as long as possible so that maybe some of the media frenzy will have died down by then. What do you think? I mean, about the temporary insanity plea?"

"I think you seem genuinely sorry that you killed your husband. I also think that most people experience anger when they're diagnosed with a terminal disease, especially one with the social stigma of AIDS. I've seen numerous instances where anger overrode sanity. It makes sense to me for you to do that," Lacy responded.

"Thank you. I've been feeling bad about it." Shelly started picking at a fingernail with a worried look.

"Um, Mrs. Stevens? I don't think you should be talking to me about this."

"Oh. You said it was off the record. Was that just when you thought you were in trouble?" Shelly's tone was flat.

"No. Well, yes. I mean, you sounded like you were about to admit that it was premeditated to me, and if that's the case, I don't need to hear it. I'm not being an asshole, really. In fact, remember when I suggested you hire a private investigator? Well, I definitely think you should hire someone to look into suspicious cases of HIV in Georgia during the past five or ten years."

"Really? I'm not the only one?" Shelly asked, incredulously.

"I'm just giving you an anonymous tip. God, I hope like hell these rooms aren't bugged. And don't tell your attorney that it came from me!" Lacy said.

"Thank you, Detective Fuller. You seem to be going out of your way to help me. Is there something I can do for you?"

Lacy was taken aback. Was she talking about money? What in the hell kind of cop did that woman think she was? Granted, she'd broken a couple of laws, but she could never be bought. Just then, she had a thought.

"Well, actually, I have a friend who was assaulted by a couple of young punks. He's homeless and black; they're middle-class white kids. I'm afraid their sentence won't reflect the harm that they caused my friend. Strictly off-the-record, do you think your uncle could do anything to maybe ensure that their punishment is suiting their crime? Just maybe push for the maximum sentence?" Lacy asked.

"Whew! You scared me for a minute there. You looked like you were fixing to punch me out for insinuating you might be on the take!" Shelly said with a smile.

"I was. Then I remembered Homer, my friend." Lacy returned the smile.

"I'm sure if I mention it to my uncle, it'll be handled to your liking. It'll also be strictly off-the-record. Not even Martin will know."

"Thanks. His name is Homer Files. That was what I was doing when I said I got sidetracked on the way to see you a couple of weeks ago. I was chasing down those punks. You'd like Homer; he gives almost all of his money to the Humane Society. In fact, he likes animals more than he cares about his own comfort and well being."

"I'll speak to my uncle about this today. Is there anything else?" Shelly asked.

"No. In fact, I can't believe that I'm asking a favor of you. I never, ever do this. Not just with inmates, but with anyone."

"I believe you. Homer must be a pretty special man."

"He is. Well, I'm going to go now. I'll take a couple of pictures of Snowpuff and bring them to you the next time I come by."

"No, please don't. I'm afraid that looking at him would just be a constant reminder of what I did to Todd. Thank you anyway. Detective? Martin isn't all bad: he really can keep his mouth shut. Nobody will ever know that you told me about the boarding fee." Shelly winked at Lacy, then added, "Be careful out there."

Lacy mused over why Shelly Stevens had told her to be careful. She hadn't had anyone tell her that for many, many years. It would have felt nice if it hadn't had such an ominous ring to it.

Lacy beat Chet back to the department, so she decided to give Dr. West a call at her home to ask about the possibility of a new mode of viral transmission.

"Hello?"

"Sharon? Hey. It's Lacy. Do you have a minute?"

"Sure. What's up?"

"Well, I was just wondering if maybe there's a new mode of transmission for HIV that people don't realize yet. What do you think?"

"I wouldn't realize it yet either, if that's the case! Seriously, I guess it's possible. Did the donor center stuff not pan out?"

"Chet isn't back yet. He could only get the people from Metropolis Blood Center, not Community Blood Center."

"Well, I checked with Jessie, my friend I was telling you about? Her hospital also only uses blood from Metropolis, so that may be the common link."

"What about the new mode of transmission theory? I mean, I remember people freaking out because they thought they could get AIDS from being bitten by a mosquito," Lacy asked.

"No, not a mosquito. I don't know, really. That would be something you'd need to discuss with someone from the CDC or the Global Infectious Diseases Health Initiative."

"What if they think I'm a dumbass?"

"Why would they think that?" Sharon wondered aloud.

"I don't know. I just don't want anyone thinking that about me."

"Would you like me to go with you?" offered Sharon.

"You'd do that?"

"Sure. I work Tuesday, Wednesday, and Thursday of this week from seven at night until seven the next morning, but if you scheduled the meeting accordingly, I'd be glad to go."

"Okay. Why don't I call them now and try to set up an appointment?"

"Call me back and let me know, will you?"

"Sure. Bye, Sharon." Lacy was surprised that doctor's first name was finally starting to easily come from her mouth.

After scheduling an appointment the following day at noon with the people from Metropolis, Lacy had figured out a legitimate means of ensuring that she and Chet took separate vehicles that afternoon. As if on cue, Chet walked in looking a bit bloated, but happy.

"How was lunch?" Lacy asked.

"Great. I had two burritos, and I'm stuffed."

"You're exploding," Lacy said, disgustedly.

Sitting in his chair and leaning it as far back as it would go, Chet sighed and looked content.

Lacy looked at Chet and said, "I was thinking about going around and asking some of my sources about T-Bone."

"Steak?" Chet asked, lazily.

"Jesus, Chet, haven't you even read the folder on Thursday's case?"

"Yeah, on Friday. It didn't mention anything about steak in it."

"It's not steak, it's the victim's alias," Lacy said irritably.

"The victim didn't have a name until the autopsy was performed, which wasn't until *after* Friday, much less an alias." Chet looked annoyed.

Knowing that she'd been unnecessarily cranky with Chet, presumably because he'd eaten pinto beans for lunch, Lacy decided she could dole out a rare apology.

"Sorry."

"It's okay."

After a silent lull of about two minutes, Lacy decided it was safe to resume conversation.

"So, I was going to ask around and see if I could find out about this T-Bone guy. Lou said he hadn't been in a gang that he was aware of, so I'd just kind of like to know who he did hang out with. I was thinking if you felt like it, you could try to track down the parents."

"Why don't I come with you?" Chet offered.

Thankful she'd already given thought to a response for anything he might ask, she said, "Because you know my informants are more informative if I go alone."

"Hmm. Okay, but I still don't like it: you being all alone among people like that."

"I've got my vest, I've got my gun; I'll be fine. I'm going now."

"Okay. Be careful," Chet said softly.

As she walked out of the building, Lacy had a strange sense of déjà vu. Chet had spoken the same words that Shelly Stevens had said a mere hour earlier. She decided that she'd try to be extra careful for the remainder of the day.

CHAPTER 14

In just a matter of a half hour, Lacy learned that T-Bone hung out almost exclusively with a guy called 'Shroom'. In a mere matter of twenty dollars, Lacy learned Shroom's real name and address. Chet had never understood how Lacy could come away with so much information, and Lacy would never tell anyone of her preferred technique. It was actually quite simple; Lacy didn't care what law these folks were breaking at the time as long as it had no direct bearing on her case and nobody was being harmed. She was a homicide detective not a member of the vice squad.

She had established these unwritten ground rules with about forty of the city's less upstanding citizens, including prostitutes and petty thieves. In fact, the guy she'd gotten Shroom's name and address from hadn't even bothered to stop smoking his joint when Lacy approached. She knew, also, that he trusted that she wouldn't call the Narcs on him so much that he would continue to hang out in that same spot for the remainder of the day with his little baggie of marijuana concealed someplace on his person.

Chet wouldn't have been happy with her at that moment. Chet would *really* not be happy if he knew where she was going next. Lacy had a brief thought to postpone the visit until a day when perhaps nobody told her to be careful, like any one of her previous several thousand.

Even as she drove to the complex, she kept having visions of the females in horror movies always doing stupid things and getting killed. Still, she drove on. If this day were projected onto the big screen, the audience would be groaning and telling her to turn around, no doubt.

Pulling into a No Parking zone, Lacy got out of her car and looked around. She felt a bit like a carnival exhibit as she saw all of the interested, hostile eyes directed toward her. Walking up a narrow staircase to the third floor, she looked around to make sure nobody was lurking in the shadows to hurt her. A roach scurried past her feet and retreated into a small crevice in the wall. Well, at least it wasn't a rat.

Approaching the door to Apartment 31, Lacy was greeted by a beautiful little girl with ebony skin, ponytails, and curious brown eyes. She was holding a dirty stuffed animal tightly against her left side as she watched Lacy approach.

"Mama said to tell you she's not at home," the little girl said loudly.

"Do you live in this apartment?" asked Lacy.

"Yes, and Mama does, too, 'cept she's not at home."

"I'm actually here to see your brother." Lacy guessed that this was Shroom's sister.

"Shroom? I'll go get him. He's in there with Mama."

Watching the little girl reach up for the door handle, Lacy wondered who Mother Shroom thought was going to be coming by that she wanted to avoid so badly she asked her daughter to keep a vigil and lie. When the little hand finally twisted the knob and the door opened, the girl stuck her head inside and yelled for Shroom.

Expecting a bad-assed gang member type, Lacy was surprised when a heavy set young man with a pleasant face and glasses came to the door.

"Shh, Cicely. Mama's sleeping."

"Okay, but this lady said to call you."

Only then did Shroom look up at Lacy. There was a fleeting look of fright and surrender in his eyes, but no malice.

Softly, the young man said, "Okay, Bitsy. You go sit with Mama for a while in case she needs something. I'm just gonna be right out here if you need me."

In a voice still too loud, Cicely yelled back, "Okay, Shroom. I'm gonna take care of Mama, just like you do!"

Watching the little girl in pigtails determinedly walking inside the apartment, Lacy noticed a small smile at the corners of Shroom's mouth. All evidence of the smile was gone when he turned to face Lacy.

"Mama's got kidney disease. She's pretty sick. We thought you were a social worker. I missed several days of school last year, and the truancy officer with the school sent a social worker over. I don't know why; I mean, I passed all of my courses. She's come by once and was scheduled to come back by this week to talk to Mama. You aren't her, so who are you? Police?"

"Yes, I'm Detective Lacy Fuller with the homicide division. Do you have a real name?" Lacy knew his real name, thanks to her informant, but she wanted to ascertain how forthright the man would be with her.

"Tyrone. This must be about T-Bone."

"You got it. What are you guys, part of a food gang? Am I going to be looking for a Spud next?"

Smiling a bit at the joke, Tyrone asked, "Do you want to sit on the ground?"

Remembering the roach, Lacy opted to stand as Tyrone leaned against the wall. He looked tired.

"I need to know if you have any idea who killed your friend."

"Look, yes, he was my friend. He'd always taken up for me in school and helped me earn money so I could get Mama some medical treatment. The thing is, if I tell you anything I know and somebody comes after me, Mama and Cicely won't have anybody at all. I just can't do that."

Lacy continued, "Well, don't you think his murder had something to do with his selling drugs? Did you sell drugs, too? So maybe someone is already coming after you. You mentioned he *helped* you earn money. Was that by selling drugs to little kids?"

"I never sold drugs to the kids. T-Bone moved here after elementary school. I told him I couldn't sell there because the teachers would know me but really I just couldn't sell to kids. I always think about how much I would hate it if someone tried to get Bitsy into drugs. Anyhow, we didn't go to any of the other schools."

"Well, that was big of you," said Lacy, her voice an equal mixture of sarcasm and disgust.

"Look, I know it's wrong. I just kept telling myself that if they didn't buy the stuff from me, they'd get it somewhere. T-Bone, he liked the money for what all he could buy; cars, stereos, clothes, women, you name it. I just wanted the money so Mama could have dialysis at a better place. When you're poor and you go to these free clinics, it sometimes takes hours for you just to be called back into the room to be dialyzed. Mama didn't feel like sitting there for so many hours. I'm not trying to excuse my behavior; I'm just telling it like it is."

"Okay. Well, there are a shitload of other ways to earn money, and most of them are legal. I'll try to help you out if you'll just give me something to work with."

Lacy noticed a look of resignation cross the young man's face. "He got a call on his cell phone the night before he was shot. The caller just said that he 'wasn't going down because of T-Bone's big mouth' and hung up. T-Bone didn't know what he was talking about, so he called me to see if I'd been talking to someone. He said he didn't recognize the voice, that it wasn't his supplier. That's all I know, really. Is there any way you could not mention coming here?"

"Yeah, if we'd found his cell phone, we would have subpoenaed the call log anyhow, but we didn't. I guess nobody has to know that if you have his number. Do you?"

Before he could answer, Lacy saw a slow movement from the corner of her eye and turned in time to see the barrel of a pistol being raised. Without thinking, she flung herself in front of Tyrone just before she heard the deafening roar of the gun and felt the impact. The force of the bullet caused both Lacy and Tyrone to fall down. Through the most intense pain of her life, Lacy chambered a bullet in case the shooter came forward. Instead, she heard the thuds of footsteps running down the stairwell.

The door to Apartment 31 opened, and Cicely stood there crying.

"Shroom! Are you okay? Mama said what if they shot you like they did T-Bone?"

"I'm fine, Bitsy. Could you call 911?"

"Is the lady hurt?" asked the little girl.

Lacy growled through clenched teeth, "Yes, the lady's hurt! Call 911 and tell them that there's a police officer down. Tyrone? Hell, you call 911, you're okay!"

"Yeah! I can take care of the lady while you call," the little girl chimed in.

Tyrone stood and walked into the house as Cicely circled Lacy and stared at her through teary eyes. Without a word, she handed Lacy her little stuffed whatever-the-hell it was and sat beside her. She took Lacy's hand in one of hers and began sucking the thumb on her other hand. Lacy was disgusted at the thought of lying on the roachy surface and wished she felt like standing, but she didn't. Only then did she realize how tightly she'd been holding the small hand. The little girl reminded Lacy of herself at that age before she'd been exposed to the harsh realities of the world. Yes, Cicely definitely could take care of the lady, she thought, as she closed her eyes.

CHAPTER 15

After what seemed like an eternity, a uniformed officer bounded up the stairwell and ran to Lacy's side. His was a face she didn't recognize. He looked happy, a fact which instantly pissed Lacy off in spite of her pain. Still, he was here, and he was armed, so hopefully no more harm could come to her, so she decided to play nice.

"You must have been in the neighborhood," Lacy said.

"Affirmative. Did you know you parked illegally?" the officer asked.

"Did you know I don't give a shit? Some asshole just shot me!" Lacy groused, the pain seeming to intensify.

"We heard the shot, and I looked up in time to see a man running out of the building. My partner is in pursuit."

"Good," Lacy muttered weakly.

The officer whose tag read Stancil was leaned over Lacy and sweating. She watched a particularly fat drop of sweat on his chin fall down on her face.

"Jesus, Stancil, move before you drown me!"

"You must be Detective Fuller. It's a pleasure to meet you."

The young officer leaned back with a grin and extended his hand. Groaning, Lacy removed her hand from over her stomach and gave a brief, firm shake.

He said, "You're something of an idol among the officers around here. I've seen pictures of you and heard stories about you since I started with the force in 2000. It's a damned good thing you were wearing your vest."

"I always wear my vest," she replied.

"Then it's a damned good thing the perp didn't have armor penetrating ammo or decide to go for a head shot."

Finally, thought Lacy, someone who was even more gloom and doom than she was. At that moment, sirens could be heard in the distance, and Cicely looked at Lacy with big eyes.

"Po-lice!" the little girl said excitedly.

Tyrone came out from the open door to the apartment looking upset and said to Lacy, "Momma says her chest is hurting real bad. She thinks it's her heart because she was so afraid I'd been shot."

"Well, the ambulance will be here soon," Lacy grunted.

At that moment, Stancil looked at Lacy as if she were missing more than a few brain cells. He then bellowed, "That's your ambulance!"

"Don't need one."

"Yes, you do," Officer Stancil countered.

"No, I don't," Lacy said.

Feeling like one of two small children arguing over something inane finally pissed Lacy off enough that she sat up, still holding onto Cicely's hand.

"Okay, Stancil. Here's the deal. I'm bruised and feel like shit, but the lady inside that apartment is possibly having a heart attack."

"We can call another ambulance for her."

"We don't need to." Lacy stared at him until he grumbled something and walked away.

After he left, Cicely yelled over the now deafening sirens, "That man sure did sweat a lot."

"Yes, he did," Lacy agreed.

About that time, a barrage of uniformed people charged up the stairs. Before one of the EMT's even began to squat in front of Lacy, she waved him toward the apartment and told him there was a possible heart attack inside. Judging from the concerned yet calm expression on the little girl's face, Lacy assumed that her mother being sick was something she was all too accustomed to.

After arguing with several other officers about going to the hospital, Lacy finally convinced them to let her call Dr. West.

A cheery sounding Sharon answered the phone on the second ring.

"Sharon? This is Lacy. I've been shot. Well, not shot, I mean, I was hit, but I'm wearing my vest."

"Oh, my God! Are you okay? Do you want me to meet you at the hospital?"

"I'm not going to the hospital."

"Not going to the hospital? That's crazy!" Sharon said incredulously.

"Not if you'll come over to my apartment and check me out. If you still think then that I need to go to the ER, I will. I promise."

"You're stubborn as hell. If I say no, you're still going home, aren't you?"

"Yes," answered Lacy, truthfully.

"Okay, I'll be there. I just need to get a quick shower," said Sharon, disgustedly.

"Thank you. Do you need directions?"

"No, you gave them to me earlier in the week, remember?"

"No, but I'll see you in a bit."

Hanging up the phone, Lacy heard a familiar voice booming up the stairwell and looked over just in time to see a visibly upset Chet running toward her.

"Lacy? Are you okay?" he asked.

"Yeah, Chet. I'm fine. Maybe you could give me a lift home?"

"Home? You've got to be kidding me." With a disgusted sigh, Chet continued, "Yeah, I was going over to T-Bone's mother's house when I heard an officer down call. After hearing the location, I felt all relieved because that couldn't possibly have been you. Then I thought, hell, I don't even know where she is, so maybe it is her. I called dispatch, and after a few minutes they returned that it *was* you. I told you to be careful!"

"Well, shit, Chet, it's not like I was running around asking to be shot! I was doing my job, and I'm always careful at work."

"No, Lacy. Careful at work would be bringing your partner along with you when you go to places like this so maybe you wouldn't get shot," he said, angrily.

Primed to argue the point a bit more because it seemed to be making her feel better, Lacy was about to open her mouth when she heard a commotion from within the apartment. Turning slightly so she could see, she noticed the EMT's bringing out a large woman with Tyrone in step just behind them.

"Listen, Bitsy. I'm going to ride to the hospital with Mama. I'll take you next door to Ms. Allen's," Tyrone said.

"I don't want to go to Ms. Allen's. I want to ride in the ambulance, too," she whined.

At that moment, the large lady reached her hand out to the little girl and spoke up.

"Bitsy? I know you want to come along, but only one person can ride in the ambulance with me. If you'll just go next door, I promise I'll make it up to you."

"Okay, Mama. Can't I go with the lady who was shot? She's going home."

"No, Bitsy. We don't know the lady well enough to impose on her. Besides, she's hurt."

"I could take care of her! Just like Shroom and me do you!"

"No, Bitsy. We still don't know her well enough."

"But Ms. Allen fusses at me all the time."

Tyrone knocked on the door to Apartment 32 and waited in silence.

"Ms. Allen went away," Cicely said, happily.

"Why didn't you tell us that earlier, Bitsy?" asked Tyrone.

"You didn't ask. Can I go with the lady, pleeease?"

Lacy thought about the little girl whose only family was getting ready to be swept away in an ambulance and whose mother was so desperately ill. She then looked down at the teddy-something that the little girl had offered her after she'd been shot. Finally, she realized that the little girl was still holding her hand as well as stretching so that she could hold her mother's hand, too, and her mind was made up.

"It's okay, Ms. Stewart. If you'll let her come home with me, she really does take good care of folks. At this point, unless you have another alternative to Ms. Allen, it's either Social Services or me."

Tyrone interjected, "It's probably okay, Mama. After all, she offered and she did take a bullet for me."

Looking at the impatient faces of paramedics and at the suddenly hopeful face on her daughter, the woman once more spoke. "Thank you. My name is Velma, by the way. If you're sure it wouldn't be an imposition on your family—"

"My family is just me and a cat."

"Mama! She has a kitty! Does it look like Sylvester?" Cicely asked.

"Sylvester is her stuffed toy cat that you've got. Okay, I'll have Tyrone give you a call when we find something out. Thank you so much. God bless you for all you've done for this family."

Hearing those words made Lacy think of Homer. She didn't think she'd been blessed since that first time she'd met him. As they watched the lady being taken down the stairwell, Tyrone obtained Lacy's phone number from Chet, who was still looking acutely mystified. After thanking Lacy for taking his bullet, giving his mother her ambulance, and looking after Bitsy, Tyrone ran down the stairwell.

Chet helped Lacy to her feet and was able to persuade the other officers that he'd take Lacy's statement this evening at her home. He then accompanied Cicely into the apartment to pack an overnight bag. The apartment was immaculate. A stack of Trigonometry books were stacked upon the kitchen table alongside a slightly smaller stack of medical bills.

When they came back out, Cicely was excited because she was going to get to ride in a "real live po-lice car" while Chet trailed behind her lugging two large gym bags and looking slightly amused.

After loading Lacy into the back of the Crown Victoria, Chet opened the front door for Cicely to get in. Only then did he notice she was scooting in next to Lacy, and *Lacy* was holding her hand out to the little girl! He wondered if he was somehow dreaming. As he got inside the car, he looked back at the 'shut-up, Chet' expression on Lacy's face and realized that this wasn't a dream.

"Chet? You know Homer? Do you think we could stop by and see if he'd come over and stay with me tonight?" Lacy asked.

"Lacy, with all due respect, he's an indigent."

Looking once more at the face in his rear view mirror, Chet quickly decided not to argue with her about this.

"Okay, sure, Lace. I can stay, too, if you need me."

"Thanks, Chet."

They drove in silence for a while until Lacy felt Cicely simultaneously tugging at her shoulder and stretching up to Lacy's ear.

"He pooted. He's supposed to say 'scuse me. That's what Mama says," she volunteered, still a decibel or two above acceptable library talking levels.

"He had pinto beans for lunch," Lacy said in his defense.

"I had pintos for supper last night!" Cicely shouted.

Great, thought Lacy. She was trapped inside the combustion mobile. Looking into the rear view mirror, she noticed Chet was grinning, no doubt enjoying her predicament.

Fifteen minutes later, they pulled over to Homer's lot, and Lacy rolled her window down.

"Homer?" she called softly.

A few seconds later, she heard some shuffling and saw the little man coming out wearing a big smile and the clothes she'd bought him for the fish fry.

"Hello, Miss Lacy! I was just thinking about you. Actually, I've been thinking about you something power-ful all day. How are you? And who's that pretty little lady you've got there?"

"Well, I've been shot. I'm fine; it hit my vest. Still, I was wondering if you'd stay with me tonight in case I need help."

"I'll be there!" said the small, shrill voice.

"Yes, of course you will, but Homer can drive, and you won't be old enough for another couple of years will you?" asked Lacy.

Looking happy that Lacy apparently thought she was much, much older than her four years, Cicely beamed at Homer.

"Hi. I'm Bitsy. I'm gonna take care of the lady, but you can drive."

"It's a pleasure to meet you, Miss Bitsy. As far as the driving, well—"

"You'd be glad to, won't you, Homer?" offered Lacy.

Lacy hoped that he could read between the lines and would drop the subject before revealing that he didn't have a current license, otherwise the child might once again feel that her caretaking responsibility was being usurped.

"Yes, Ma'am; I reckon I would. Let me just get a few things and I'll be ready to go."

"Does that man live in the woods?" asked Cicely.

"Yes, he does. He's a special man." Lacy answered.

"If I live in the woods, will I be special, too?"

"Honey, you don't need to live in the woods to be special," Lacy said with a smile.

Lacy noticed that Chet's mouth was literally hanging open. She guessed he was confused by the seemingly strange bond she'd developed with this little girl.

"Okay, Miss Lacy, I'm ready to go," said Homer, lugging a giant trash sack behind him.

CHAPTER 16

Chet had his arm protectively over Lacy's shoulder as they walked toward her apartment. Lacy was still cradling the little dirty stuffed thing that she'd learned was supposed to be a cat. Cicely was holding both Lacy's and Homer's hands. It was quite an image that Sharon saw as the foursome approached her, effectively interrupting her pacing in front of Lacy's apartment.

"What took you so long?"

"I had to take care of a few things," she said, weakly.

She winced as she pulled her key ring from her pocket and handed it to Sharon.

After unlocking the door and three deadbolts under Lacy's instruction, the little group entered the apartment.

A talkative Snowpuff entered the room at that precise moment and froze instantly upon seeing the other people.

"Look! It's the kitty! Can I pet it? It's even prettier than Sylvester. What's its name? Is it a boy or a girl?" Cicely shrieked.

With ears at half-mast, Snow turned and sauntered toward the living room. By the time they made it into the same room, the only sign of Snow was a large, white tail sticking out from beneath the sofa. When

Cicely spoke again, even the tail retreated beneath the furniture.

Lacy said, "He's a boy. I don't know how much he likes people; I've only had him for a week. I'm going to sit in the recliner now."

Sharon said, "Oh, no, you're not! You and I are going into your bedroom, and I'm going to check your injury."

With a sigh, Lacy said, "Okay. Make yourselves at home. Bitsy, you're welcome to pet the cat if he'll let you, but don't chase him. His name is Snowpuff."

"Hee hee. That's a funny name. Snowpuff. I won't chase the Snowpuff."

With that solemn vow, Lacy slowly led Sharon to the bedroom thinking that this was really not what she had in mind when she thought of her and Sharon in the bedroom together.

Closing the door behind them, Sharon requested that she take off her shirt and vest. Yes, this definitely wasn't what she had in mind, thought Lacy. Normally that request from an attractive woman would have brought forth a slew of sensuous feelings. All Lacy could manage to think at the moment was that it was going to hurt like hell taking off her clothes.

"Do you need some help?" Sharon offered.

"Maybe; I don't know."

Without waiting for a reply, Sharon crossed the room and began unbuttoning Lacy's shirt. For the first time, Lacy realized that her shirt, which was one of her favorites, had been trashed. She wondered if Land's End still made that style? She'd have to check. Shit, that hurt.

"You'll have to give me instructions on the vest," said Sharon, with a puzzled look.

"It fastens on the side. You'll see it when I raise my arms," she said, dreading the pain that would cause.

"Oh. Okay. Yeah. There we go," Sharon said as she unfastened the vest.

When the pressure of the vest was relieved, Lacy almost fainted from the immediate flush of pain. Sharon caught her and helped her sit on the bed.

"Here. Why don't you lie down for me? I can check you out better that way."

Putting her arm around Lacy's back, Sharon eased her down on the bed and began examining her stomach.

"Well, I don't see anything too alarming here. You've already got a gigantic hematoma, and you'll probably have bruising for several weeks. How did you get shot?"

Lacy recounted the events leading up to the shooting incident as Sharon applied some sort of ointment to her bruises.

Sharon began explaining what she was doing. "This is a cream based of homeopathic herbs. It'll help with the bruising. I'm going to prescribe a mild pain pill. I don't want to give you anything too strong because I want you to be able to assess the level of your pain. If it worsens, you'll need to go to the ER. I wish you would just go to the ER now and let them check you out with a CT scan, but I know you won't. Thank goodness you were wearing your vest; otherwise, Snowpuff would have been orphaned twice. By the way, who would name their cat Snowpuff?"

"Shelly and Todd Stevens, apparently. I call him Snow," Lacy said.

"I'll call him Snow, too. I like that. He's a handsome little guy. If you'll tell me what shirt you'd like to wear and where to locate it, I'll help you change. Or, would you like to shower first? I brought a couple of pain pills to tide you over until you get the prescription filled. If you take two now, you'll probably feel more like bathing in about twenty minutes."

Remembering the roach that had crawled across the floor and how her face had lain upon that same floor, Lacy opted for the shower first. She shuddered at the thought of how painful showering would be.

"Let me get you a cup of water to take the pills with and tell the others what the plan is. I'll be right back," Sharon said, turning to leave.

As Sharon left the room, Lacy lay there thinking how lucky she was. Typically, she did pay attention to motion at her periphery, but not as much when she was interviewing someone. Had she not been asked twice that day to be careful, she wondered if she would have even noticed the small movement in time to save Tyrone's life. More than that, she thought how lucky she was to have the diverse group of people in the next room here with her, caring for her. Hearing the door open once more, Lacy looked at Sharon and managed a smile.

"Here we go. Take these, and I'll sit here with you for a bit until they start to work. Then, if you need me to, I'll be happy to help you get cleaned up," Sharon offered.

"Thank you. There were roaches on the floor I fell on when I got shot. I hate roaches." Lacy shuddered.

"I think everyone hates roaches. By the way, Snow has come out and is sitting on Homer's lap. The little girl is petting him carefully, and Chet is taking care of dinner before he gets your prescription filled."

"Huh. What did I have that he found to make dinner with?"

"Well, actually, he's ordering pizzas," Sharon said with a smile.

CHAPTER 17

After the bathing ordeal was completed, Lacy had to admit that in spite of it all, she did feel much better. It was strange having someone bathe her body for her. Once again, any lustful thoughts were held at bay because of the intense pain. Sharon was right; the pills she'd given her were mild, but they did seem to take some of the bite out of the pain. Sliding Lacy's moccasins onto her feet for her, Sharon stood and took Lacy's face in her hands and just stared at her. Lacy was feeling weird by this somewhat intimate act, but dared not squirm lest the moment be broken. Finally, Sharon spoke.

"I'm glad you're okay. It scared me that you might have been hurt severely. Let's go get some pizza."

Releasing Lacy's face, Sharon took her by the hand instead and led her toward the doorway. Lacy wasn't thinking about pizza at all. Instead, she was wondering what had just happened between them.

Entering the living room, they found all three people and Snow sitting on the sofa eating pizza.

"Don't feed the cat pizza! I don't even know if cats can have pizza," Lacy groused.

"They can, as long as it's only cheese pizza and they just have a bite or two," Sharon offered.

Homer and Cicely looked less mortified by Sharon's response, so she decided to introduce herself once she got Lacy settled into her recliner.

"I don't believe we've been properly introduced. I'm Dr. Sharon West."

The little girl extended a greasy hand and said through a mouthful of food, "I'm Bitsy. If you're a doctor, can you make Mama better?"

"I don't know. We'll have to see," replied Sharon.

After saying hello to Homer and Chet, Sharon went into the kitchen and put two slices of pizza on a plate for Lacy. Looking into the refrigerator, she only saw one beverage selection—Diet Coke. Taking a can out, she headed toward Lacy, who now had a contented looking Snow on her lap bathing and purring.

"Here you go. Where's Snow's food kept?" Sharon asked.

"In the cabinet closest to the refrigerator."

"I'll put some food down and maybe you can eat in peace."

As she had predicted, the moment the top of the can was popped, Snowpuff made a mad dash for the kitchen. He'd apparently decided that his fear of strangers was no match for his appetite as he began sniffing Sharon's jeans, waiting for the food to be delivered in front of him. Once Snow was taken care of, Sharon got a couple of slices of pizza and a Diet Coke for herself and went to the living room. Both Chet and Homer offered to let her have their seats, but Sharon declined and flopped down on the floor in a much practiced manner.

When dinner was over, Chet began taking Lacy's statement while she gently stroked the cat, who had resumed his vigil in her lap. Homer and Cicely were in the corner of the room making themselves palates of old blankets and quilts. Everyone looked uneasily at one another when the phone rang, wondering if it was going to be news of Velma Stewart's condition.

Chet rose and answered on the third ring. "Oh, hi, Lou. This is Avery. Yeah, she's fine. Sore as hell but the medicine seems to be working. In fact, she's not as cranky as usual, so I'm going to try to bribe the doctor into writing her a lifetime prescription of it. Oh? Really! Lives here? Oh. Well, are you going to go there? Good. Do you want to tell her yourself? Oh, okay. Hey, thanks for calling. Alright, see you tomorrow."

After hanging up the phone, Chet looked around at the others, then shared the news he had just learned.

"That was Lou, the Narcotics Division Captain. It seems that the guy who took the shot at you has revealed some pertinent information. He said that some guy who we had arrested on drug charges last week had told him that T-Bone was the one ratting everybody out to the police. According to Lou, this is some little punk who lived in your apartment complex that you turned over to the narcs, Lace. Lou said he was under house arrest because he had turned in so many dealers' names. Today's shooter said that he didn't kill T-Bone, but only because somebody beat him to it. He thinks he could find out who did it if we agree to get him in the witness protection program. That's not likely to happen. Lou and his squad are getting ready to arrest that guy you fingered now and take him back into custody."

"Son-of-a-bitch!" Lacy said, suddenly aware of the glacial stares coming from all three adults and the giggling of Cicely. "Sorry. Yeah, I called Lou on him last week. Well, that's good. He was probably giving out all of those names to us so freely because he was planning to stay in business, and he wanted to eliminate the competition.

What better way to do it than to blame somebody else for being the rat? Oh, yeah, what was that about me being less cranky?"

"Just a joke, Lace. That's all. You're still just as cranky as ever! I'm going back to the department and turn in your statement, then head on home if you don't need me to stay. Your prescription is on the kitchen counter. I'm glad you're feeling better. It was nice meeting all of you. Thanks for looking after my partner. I'll call and check on you in the morning, Lace."

"No, you'll see me in the morning. I'm not sick, Chet. I'll be at work."

"Dr. West? Maybe you can talk some sense into her," Chet sighed.

As Sharon walked Chet to the door, she told him that Lacy's discomfort the following morning would likely change her mind quickly. Closing the door behind her, she heard the telephone ring and answered it.

"Hello, this is Tyrone Stewart. May I speak with Detective Fuller, please?"

"Sure, just a moment."

Handing the cordless phone to Lacy, Sharon sat on the arm of the recliner and began to pet Snow.

"Detective Fuller? How's Cicely doing?" Tyrone asked.

"She's fine. How's your mother?"

"Well, it wasn't a heart attack. They think it was angina which could someday lead to a heart attack, so they want to keep her a couple of days and monitor her. What are we going to do about Bitsy?"

"Maybe I'll bring her by the hospital tomorrow on my way to work. If you need to spend more evenings and nights there, I can let her stay with me in the evenings. We can play it by ear. Why don't you talk to her?"

"Okay. Thank you again," he said.

"You're welcome. Bitsy? The phone's for you."

Skipping toward the phone, Bitsy's volume once more crept into the far too loud range. Lacy closed her eyes, Snow slicked his ears down, Sharon stood and put some distance between her and the loud talk, and Homer just chuckled.

"She's got a real live cat! His name is Snowpuff! He lets me pet him. He ate some of my pizza. He can only have cheese pizza. I get to sleep on the floor tonight with Homer. Homer lives in the woods! How's Mama? Okay, Shroom. I'll see you tomorrow. Bye-bye."

Handing the phone back to Lacy, Cicely patted Snow's head, then scampered back over to hers and Homer's matching palates. Noticing that Lacy looked a bit tired, Sharon asked if there was anything she could do for her before leaving.

"No, not before leaving. But do you think you could pick me up for the meeting with the Global Health Initiative people tomorrow? I don't think I'll feel like driving. I'm probably not going to work tomorrow after all."

"I don't think you'll feel up to making the meeting. Why don't we postpone?" Sharon suggested.

"Really, I'm sure I'll feel like being driven to a meeting. I'll probably come home afterwards, but I think I'll feel like going," Lacy said stubbornly.

"I guess I should take heart in the fact that you're willing to stay at home until a noon meeting rather than show up at work in the morning like you told Chet you would. I'll give you a ring before I come over. Meanwhile, if you feel worse in the night, call me; I can be over in fifteen minutes."

"Okay. Thanks again, Sharon."

"It's my pleasure. I'll get Homer to lock up after I leave. Do you want some help getting in bed?"

"Yes, I think I'd like that very much. I didn't realize until earlier just how sore my stomach muscles are or how much of a part they played in simply lying down."

Taking Snowpuff from Lacy's lap, Sharon kissed him on the head before putting him on the floor. With a tenderness that Lacy found sweet beyond words, Sharon helped her stand and walked with her toward the bed. After covering her and bringing her a glass of water and her pain pills, Sharon bent down and kissed her on the forehead. She then turned off the light and left.

Lacy felt Snow hop upon the bed, then curl around her head, purring softly. She heard Sharon talking to Homer, then heard Cicely scream goodnight. With a smile, she fell quickly asleep.

CHAPTER *18*

Lacy awoke to the smell of coffee and happy chatter in the next room. Snow slowly sidled down from around her head and waited to be petted. Reaching over to him, she realized how sore she was; this was going to be a long day. A quick knock on her door made her wonder which of her house guests was going to be paying her a visit.

"Come in," she said.

Instead of Bitsy or Homer, in walked Chet with a Diet Coke and a bag from a local bakery.

"Here you go, Lace, your favorite beverage and a cheese bagel with cream cheese."

"Thanks, Chet."

"How do you feel?" he asked, his brows knitted in concern.

"Like a possum after it's been hit by fifty or so semi trucks."

"Well, that's an appetizing image for you. I brought over the list of employees from the Metropolis Blood Center. Don't you have a laptop?"

"Yeah, why?"

"Because I also got you a user name and password so you can access the databases from home since that's where you're going to stay for the next couple of days."

"When did you do that?" she asked.

"Last night when I dropped off your statement," Chet replied. "I'm telling you, that Shelly Stevens has some major influence. The Captain would probably give you your own Ferrari if it had anything to do with this case."

"Thanks, Chet. I think I will stay home most of the day, but Sharon and I are going to the Health Department at noon. We're going to ask about unusual occurrences of HIV contraction and the possibility of a new mode of transmission. I can work on the names you brought me and not feel so idle. Thanks. You're a sweet man," Lacy said with a smile.

"You're sweet, too. I know it's only because of the pain meds that you're sharing your feelings. I think I like the medicated Lacy. I think it's great what you did yesterday. When I mentioned you taking a bullet for Tyrone, little Bitsy's eyes lit up. She thinks you're Superwoman." Chet paused, then added, "And I think you're pretty damned close."

"Thanks, Chet," Lacy replied.

The uncomfortable silence between them was interrupted when Snow took the opportunity to rub against Chet's black slacks, leaving behind a streak of white hair before once again moving toward Lacy's hand.

"Thank goodness for tape, huh?" Chet chuckled.

"Yeah, my whole place is coated in a layer of fur. It looks like one of those swinger's pads from the sixties."

"Yeah, that's you; a hip party animal!"

"It's been an adjustment." Lacy laughed. "The other night a weird noise woke me up. I grabbed my gun and started easing toward the door to check out the sound, although it had seemed to come from the bedroom. As I was walking past the dresser, I stepped on something slimy. When I turned on the light, I thought it was a big dead white mouse. It scared the shit out of me! You know what it was? It was a hairball! Sharon said Snow will keep getting them unless I brush him daily and feed him anti-hairball treats."

"I think that qualifies as too much information. You know, a side-effect of your pain medication must be excessive talking. Listen, kiddo, I've got to run. Let me get you the folder and your laptop," Chet offered as he turned to leave.

Cicely and Homer came into the bedroom after Chet left. Cicely asked if she could crawl up in the bed and pet Snow. After plugging in Lacy's computer, Homer went back into the living room to watch television. Lacy worked on the database with Cicely and Snow snoozing beside her until Sharon called to say she was on her way.

After the tedious process of helping Lacy dress, Sharon helped her to her car. They pulled into the parking lot of the Global Infectious Disease Health Initiative with a mere two minutes to spare.

Entering the building, Sharon identified herself and Lacy to the receptionist, who led them to a meeting room. Sharon helped Lacy sit down, then sat beside her. After a couple of minutes of mindless chatter, the door opened and a stern looking, well-dressed black woman entered the room.

"Good afternoon, ladies. I'm Dr. Pounds."

"I'm Dr. West," Sharon responded, "and this is Detective Fuller. Thank you for agreeing to meet with us this soon."

"It's no problem at all. My whole life seems to consist of meetings, so one more didn't hurt in the grand scheme of things. Now, what exactly can I do for you?"

"We're investigating a few suspicious cases of HIV infection and discovered the CDC had uncovered others," Sharon explained. "We were wondering if you had any ideas about those that might apply to the current cases."

Dr. Pounds paused before answering, pulling a file from her desk drawer. "Yes and no," she replied. "There have actually been eight reported cases of HIV infection already this year that we've been unable to identify a causative factor for. That's two more than for the entire 2002 for Georgia and 2003 is only half over. Prior to 2002, we had only one or two suspicious cases per annum." She waited a beat before adding, somewhat defensively, "Unfortunately, no, we don't have any ideas what's going on now."

Lacy, who had been uncharacteristically quiet to this point, could hold her tongue no longer. "You don't have any ideas? Don't you guys investigate these things?"

Dr. Pounds glared at Lacy and said, "Yes, Detective, of course we do. Each of the individuals completed a detailed fifteen page questionnaire about their lifestyle which we ran through one of our most sophisticated computer programs. The highest probability for a match came with the fact that they had all been transfused; however, all of the donors have subsequently had non-reactive HIV tests."

"So you just let it drop with that?" asked Lacy.

"We do what we can with the budget we have." Dr. Pounds sighed, resignedly. "In a perfect world, we'd still be on this hot and heavy. Instead, we've had to bench the investigation temporarily. Remember, we don't just deal with HIV. We've had SARS, West-Nile virus, Mad Cow Disease, and a host of other infectious diseases that we've also had to investigate."

Sharon interjected, "Have you given any thought to the possibility of a new mode of transmission?"

"We have, but we've concluded it highly unlikely with such a small number of cases."

"What about the prospect of someone tampering with the blood supply or surgical instruments?" asked Sharon.

"Again, we couldn't attribute the transmissions to anything specific."

Lacy asked, "What about somebody putting the virus in food?"

"No. HIV is actually quite a delicate virus. It isn't capable of sustaining life outside a host for long. We're talking minutes here. If this were a series of suspicious cases of Hepatitis, I'd say the answer to that question could be yes or at least maybe. Not HIV, though."

"What about in, like, ground beef or something with blood in it? Wouldn't that blood be like a host?" Lacy persisted.

"No. Bovine blood couldn't sustain the human AIDS virus. It just doesn't work across species."

Suddenly feeling tired and deflated, Lacy asked, "Could we have a copy of your list of cases along with the questionnaires? I'll have a warrant faxed over tomorrow if necessary.

"That won't be required," Dr. Pounds said. "I'll have my secretary make a copy before you leave. I'm assuming that all of this concern is because of the Stevens case. I read that she didn't know how she had contracted the virus," Dr. Pounds added pensively.

Sharon responded, "Mrs. Stevens' case is the one that alerted Detective Fuller to this situation. I had just seen a case of a young child with unexplained HIV, then a colleague mentioned she'd seen a couple of cases as well. It just seemed too coincidental that within the course of a few weeks we would see this many seemingly unconnected cases."

"Oh, I'm afraid there probably is a connection." Dr. Pounds sighed. "We just haven't found it yet. Truthfully, I'll be glad to hand the information over to someone who can devote more time to it"

Thanking the doctor for her time, Sharon stood and watched as Lacy eased her way to a standing position. Slowly, the two women began walking toward the parking lot. When they reached the car, Sharon opened the passenger door and helped Lacy into the seat. Seeing the sheen of sweat across Lacy's forehead made Sharon ask about the level of pain she was in.

"It hurts like hell," Lacy winced. She hated to admit the meeting had taken a lot out of her. "I should've taken some of those pills before I came, but I didn't want to be loopy."

"That'll be the first order of business when you get home, then. Do you need me to stop and get you anything on the way? Groceries, magazines, lunch?" Sharon asked.

"Lunch wouldn't be bad if you're sure you have the time. Maybe we could just take it back to my place. I left my cell phone at home today. Can I borrow yours to see if Homer and Cicely are still there? If they are, we'll need to pick something up for them, too," Lacy added.

"Sure." Digging the phone from her purse, Sharon thought that if they kept minimizing the size of telephones, it would become impossible to locate them at all.

Lacy dialed the number and waited until her own voice on the answering machine picked up. Turning the phone off, she handed it back over to Sharon.

"I guess they've gone. Tyrone said this morning that he was going to pick Cicely up and take her home for a while. He said he'd drop Homer off at his house; wait until he sees Homer's house! He's going to wonder what the hell he was thinking allowing his sister to spend the night with a wounded police officer and a vagrant."

"I've got to admit, I was wondering what you were thinking when you took her in," Sharon said, casting a sideways glance in Lacy's direction.

"Yeah, you, Chet, and probably everybody else in the world. Maybe I'll tell you about it over lunch. Speaking of, what would you like?"

"It doesn't matter to me. You're the injured party; you pick." Sharon smiled.

After stopping to get fried chicken salads, they went back to find Lacy's apartment empty.

"Why don't I fix the table and you take your pain pills," Sharon offered.

"Would you help me change clothes first? The waist on these pants is hurting my stomach."

"Sure. I can relate; my waist band is bothering me and I wasn't even shot," Sharon commiserated.

Walking by the sofa, Lacy picked up a note written by Homer. He said he'd be in his spot all day if she needed him. He thanked her for letting him shower and closed by saying that he hoped she was feeling better. Cicely added a largely illegible post script and drew what Lacy assumed was Lacy as Superwoman. It looked nothing like Lacy. In fact, it looked nothing like Superwoman. Sharon had found Snowpuff and was petting his head and smiling. Once the clothes changing ordeal was completed, Lacy took her pain pills and sat at the table in the breakfast nook. She remembered when she had bought the table thinking how great it would be to have a glass table. She had since learned that glass tables were fingerprint magnets.

She sat there and looked at what must have been Cicely's prints. Such tiny little fingertips. She saw larger ones that were probably hers and larger ones still that were Chet's or Homer's. Only then did she spy a print that looked different from the others; it was a paw print! Son of a bitch! She wouldn't allow cats on her table. She'd have to have a word with Snow, the little shit, as soon as Sharon left. Gross. Sharon did let cats on her table. How in the hell could a medical doctor schooled in germ management allow a cat on the kitchen table? With those little grubby paws that had waded through the litter box only moments before? She watched silently as Sharon washed the dish cloth with antibacterial soap and wiped the table off several times before drying it at last with a paper towel. Well, she guessed that if you cleaned the table off that thoroughly, cats could get up there. Looking through the glass, she saw Snow's two big blue eyes staring at her. He seemed to be giving her an 'eat shit' look. Did cats know what you were thinking about them?

"Lacy? Are they?" Sharon's voice startled her.

"Huh? Are they what?"

"Clean or dirty?"

"What?" Lacy asked.

"The dishes in the dishwasher. God, where do you go sometimes?" Sharon asked.

"Clean. I was just thinking about cats." *And germs, and feline ESP, and litter box feet...*

"Why don't you go ahead and start eating while I feed Snow. I'll be there in a sec."

Still watching Snow through the table, Lacy noted that his ears twitched when the can of food was opened. He then began sniffing the air, no doubt deciding from his lack of motion that the fried chicken smelled much better than what was going to be dished out in the kitchen.

"Kitty, kitty, kitty, Snow? Here, kitty kitty," Sharon cooed.

Oh, God, not the cat talk again. Fortunately, Snow was having no part of it either. Lacy watched as Sharon rounded the corner and sat at the table in apparent resignation.

"You can't make kitties do anything. I guess you're figuring that out by now."

"I guess," Lacy replied.

"Okay, so are you ready to tell me the story behind your bringing home that little girl yesterday?"

Sharon had asked in such a happy manner, Lacy almost decided against telling her.

With a sigh, she began. "My father abused my mother. It had gone on since before they were even married. I was always puzzled how anyone could marry someone who beat them. He got to where he even stopped apologizing for the beatings. One day when I was six, he came in from work late and shoved me. He'd never laid a hand on me before that day, neither in violence nor in affection. Mother slapped him and told him to leave me alone. He did, too. After he beat the shit out of my mother, he left the house and neither of us have seen or heard from him since.

My mother had to be hospitalized in ICU for a week, and I was too young to even visit her. She had no friends and had become estranged from her family because they hated my father, so off to Social Services I went. I spent a total of three weeks with a foster family, and it was just as bad as living with my father. They kept telling me that it was my fault that my father left and filling my head with all sorts of shit. They were quite skilled at verbal and physical abuse. I couldn't believe that the State was paying them to take care of me.

Don't get me wrong; I know there are several good homes out there, far more than bad ones. Also, it's the only option for situations like I was in. Yesterday, it seemed that there was at least one more option. I just kept thinking about how those three weeks completely changed who I was and how I felt about myself afterwards. I actually did feel like his leaving was my fault.

To make matters worse, I was glad that he wasn't still around beating my mother. She didn't see it the same way, though. She had some crazy co-dependency thing going on with him, and she went into a deep depression for several months. Cicely had been so sweet, sitting there wanting to hold my hand, giving me that dirty stuffed animal, wanting to take care of her mother, and sucking her thumb. I guess I thought it would be a shame if such a sweet disposition got tainted so early on. I know next to nothing about caring for a child; that's why I had Chet pick Homer up on the way."

"Homer has a child?" asked Sharon.

"I don't think so. Why?"

"I don't get it. If Homer doesn't have a child, why did you have Chet get him?"

"Oh, because I figured that even if he didn't have children, at his age, he's bound to have been around some at one time or another."

"So, whatever happened to your mother?" Sharon asked, frowning.

"She's still around. She lives in south Georgia. We talk about once a week. She's disappointed that I'm a cop, disappointed that I'm a lesbian, disappointed that I don't live closer, presumably because a weekly phone call isn't enough to vent all of her disappointments. Each week she says she's 'stumbled upon' some new program that can help change my sexual orientation. It's obvious she's researching the hell out of the topic. I mean, nobody just stumbles across that much information."

"I'm sorry to hear that. Really, I think the story of your life has made me lose my appetite," Sharon said, pushing her salad away.

"I didn't mean for that to happen," Lacy said.

"No, it's okay. I'll take it to work with me. That's really sad, Lacy. Have you talked to anyone about it?"

"Like who? A shrink? Nope, and I won't, either," Lacy said irritably.

"Hey, cats love fried chicken. Can I give Snow a bite of mine?" Sharon asked, trying to lighten the mood.

"Yes, but not on the table or the counters," Lacy demanded.

Sharon gasped. "Oh, God, you must think I'm a boor! I should have warned you the other day about my kitties getting on the table. I just don't have the heart to fuss at them. They look so hurt. Instead, I just clean the kitchen thoroughly at meal times."

"Snow never looks hurt. He just looks pissed off," Lacy observed.

Lacy watched as Sharon lured Snow into the kitchen by holding down a piece of the chicken so that he could smell it, then slowly backing down the hallway, and she thought how painful that would be for her to attempt at this moment. She looked down at her plate and noticed that she hadn't touched her lunch either. Sharon rounded the corner still looking upset by the story that Lacy had told her, and it made Lacy sorry she'd shared that bit of her past. In fact, she'd never spoken about it to anyone before. She had, however, gone to the foster couple's house as a rookie on the force and put the fear of God in them, if such animals actually feared God.

Extending her hand toward Lacy, Sharon said, "Come on, Sweetie. Let's get you settled in before I leave. I'd stay for awhile, but I didn't sleep well last night, so I thought

I'd try to sneak in a little nap before work. I'll refrigerate your salad. You might have to share another piece of the chicken with Snow later on. He really liked it."

As Sharon helped her rise, Lacy realized that she felt a bit woozy from the medicine. Sharon helped her into her bed and brought her the cordless phone as requested.

"Oh. How are we going to do the deadbolt thing? Last night, Homer was here to lock them after me, but today it's just you," Sharon asked.

"Look in the second drawer from the stove. There's a key ring in there that has a copy of all of the keys to the apartment. Why don't you take it with you when you go? I've got my set and won't need the spare set before I see you again."

"Okay. I don't usually go anywhere on the days that I work, so if you need me, I'll either be at home or at work. Please don't hesitate to call. Your body has taken a pretty bad trauma, and you don't need to try to do too much."

After kissing Lacy's forehead, Sharon left and let herself out of the apartment leaving a tired, sore, yet somewhat happy Lacy in her wake.

CHAPTER *19*

Driving back to her home, Sharon thought about the story of Lacy's childhood. No wonder she was so stand-offish! Life had dealt her a bitter hand, but she was making the best of it. That probably explained why she befriended Homer; he was an underdog as she had once been. Sharon thought back on her own life and how idealistic it had been. She always felt thankful for what she'd been given, even more so after hearing tales of dysfunctional families. Her family had never had much money when she was growing up, but there was so much love and happiness that she considered herself the richest girl in the world.

She missed her mother today, even more than usual. She thought there was something about an injured Lacy that reminded her of her mother when she was unsuccessfully battling cancer. Maybe it was the similarity between the two strong, proud women who suddenly found themselves asking for and needing help.

When she had put Lacy to bed the night before, she'd kissed her forehead without even thinking about it. It felt so natural, almost like it had felt kissing her mother. She'd worried about it most of the previous night, thereby causing her to lose sleep. She hoped Lacy didn't think it was anything sexual. She hadn't seemed to take it that way. She certainly hadn't seemed to take the bath or the changing of clothes as an overture, either. Today when she'd kissed her on the head she'd been motivated by that sad story. What Sharon had really wanted to do was hold her and tell her that she would never again feel that kind of solitude. How could she feel so close to someone in such a short period?

Lacy lay in bed thinking about Sharon kissing her on her head. What was up with that? She wondered if she should read anything into those actions. Thinking back, she recalled having seen her kiss Snow on the head, too. Maybe it was that simple; to Sharon, Lacy was a cat! Hmm. Well, that might not be such a bad thing. The lady seemed to be crazy about cats. The telephone ringing startled her.

"Hello?"

"Lace? Hey, it's Chet. How are you feeling?"

"Better. Like maybe only about twenty semi trucks hit me."

"Is Dr. West still there?"

"No."

"Well, I was calling to tell you that you'd be proud of me," Chet said, sounding like a little boy.

"Oh yeah? Did you solve the T-Bone case?" she asked.

"Nope. We did get his cell phone log, so it's just a matter of time, I'm sure. Guess again."

"You figured out the HIV thing?"

"No, that's your baby. Guess again."

"Jesus Christ, Avery, by the time I guess a million wrong things I'll be so pissed off at you saying 'guess again' that I wouldn't be proud of you no matter what you'd done!" Lacy groused.

"Oh, so you *are* feeling better. I thought you were just appeasing me, but I hear a bit of that spunk creeping back into your voice. Well, you wouldn't have guessed it in a million years anyhow," Chet said.

"Then why the hell did you keep saying for me to guess?"

"I don't know. I thought you were having fun guessing."

"Am I ever going to get the opportunity to be proud of you or not?" Lacy asked. She looked at Snowpuff and noticed his ears were slicked back. Chet was even annoying the cat with his little guessing game.

"Okay, okay. Well, your favorite Homicide detectives, the D Team, solved one of their cases today," Chet said.

"Did you help them? If you did, no, I'm not proud of you, Chet."

"No, I didn't help them. I put a 'Congratulations' card on their desks with a doggie bone inside," he chuckled.

"No way."

"Way."

"No shit? Well, you're right, Avery. I am proud of you. How did you sign it?"

"Well, actually, I didn't sign it. I chickened out."

"That's probably just as well. Nobody would suspect you of having done that. It's a damned good thing I'm off or my ass would be in Sumlin's office explaining myself."

"Well, I'm going to let you go. Anything you need me to do for you?" he asked.

"No, thanks."

Hanging up the phone, she laughed a bit about the joke Chet had played on the D Team. Laughing proved to be painful. She heard determined scratching coming from the next room. Oh, hell, she hadn't scooped the litter box, and *that* would really hurt! Maybe it could wait until later.

As she powered up her laptop, Lacy opened the folder from Metropolis Blood Center. They had not only provided her with a list of the individuals who had been employed there during the past ten years, but also a copy of their photos as they appeared on their badges. Earlier, she'd begun pulling them up in NCIC alphabetically and had only gotten to the C's. She'd learned nothing exciting from her exercise except that they had an employee with several outstanding traffic violations in North Carolina who was listed as 'Route Driver I'. So much for an extensive background check, she had thought. She decided that she might alter her method somewhat since, at that rate, it would take days to look up these people.

Flipping through the photos one by one, she slowly began making a separate pile. She always prided herself on her ability to read people by just looking at them. Usually, it was something in their eyes. She attributed it to having a father whose countenance changed from average, to hostile, to angry, and then to downright evil on an almost daily basis. By the time she reached the end of the pile, she guessed she had about twenty employees isolated instead of the several hundred whom she had begun with. She logged onto the national database and began entering the names of the employees.

By 4:00, she was getting sleepy and beginning to tire of her task. She was only to the N's. She decided that she'd go through the P's before she quit for the day. When she entered Alfred Owenby into the database, her heart skipped a beat. Alfred Owenby, missing since 1994, yet here was his photograph stating that he'd been a Component Preparation Tech between the years of 1995-1999. That was definitely interesting. Looking at the photograph, Lacy saw the reason she had set him aside; crazed eyes.

Feeling a sudden surge of energy, she abruptly reached over to call Chet, and a stab of pain reminded her of the reason she had stayed home today. Leaning back onto her pillow, she waited out the worst of the pain. After a few minutes, she decided to slowly try again, but Chet didn't answer his phone. He was probably getting a candy bar.

She wondered if she had unrestricted access into the databases and set about the task of finding out. Within minutes, she had the last three addresses and phone numbers for Alfred Owenby. She noticed that none of the information matched what Metropolis had on file for Mr. Owenby. Dialing the most recent first, she learned that the number had been disconnected. As she dialed the second number, she found herself wondering what she would say if the phone was answered, which, of course it was on the third ring since she was unprepared.

"Hello?" a woman's voice said.

"Hi. Could I speak with Alfred Owenby please?"

"Alfred Owenby? What about him?" There was desperation in the voice; bingo.

"Does Mr. Owenby live there, Ma'am?" Lacy asked.

"Yes. No. I mean, he's been missing since 1994. Who is this?"

"This is Detective Lacy Fuller with the Atlanta Police Department. Who am I speaking with?"

"This is Norma Owenby, Al's wife. Have you found him?"

"I'm not sure, Ma'am. We've uncovered some information that an Alfred Owenby worked at the Metropolis Blood Center between the years of 1995 and 1999."

"A blood center? Al didn't know anything about blood. There must be some mistake. Al worked with sheet metal; he was a fabrication manager."

Scanning the photograph once more, then looking at the database information, Lacy noticed that the man in the photograph looked to be in his twenties whereas Alfred Owenby was listed as fifty-five.

"How old is your husband?" she asked.

"Fifty-five. Have you found him?"

"I'm not sure, Ma'am. I'll need you to come down to the station later this week to look at the photograph of the man who claims to be Alfred Owenby."

"Later this week? Are you serious? Do you know how long I've been waiting to hear something about Al?" the woman said, her voice sounding close to tears.

"I understand, and I'm truly sorry, but my shift is almost over and—"

"So leave the picture with somebody else! I can be there in a half hour," she pleaded.

"Actually, I'm working from home today, so I'm not at the precinct."

"Well, can't you go there? You called me, remember?" asked the woman.

Thinking out her possibilities, Lacy thought she could fax the photo or scan it and email it to Chet with little hassle.

"Okay. I'll send a copy of the photograph to the precinct. It's the location on Ponce de Leon. When you get there, ask for Detective Avery in Homicide."

"Homicide? Oh, God, no."

"Ma'am? I'm not saying there's been a homicide. I'm just saying that I'll send the information over to Detective Avery who happens to work in the Homicide Division."

"Oh. Okay. Thank you. I'll be there in thirty minutes."

Shit, she thought. She'd handled that very badly. Poor Chet. She'd owe him big time for sending some distraught woman over at 5:00. Big time, as in doughnuts every morning for a month. Oh, well, what are partners for? After placing the warning call to Chet, she scanned the photo and emailed it to him. It would have been less work to have just faxed the information, but the quality of the photo was poor enough as it was.

After painfully scooping the litter buckets and returning to her bed, the phone rang.

"Hello?"

"Hey, Lace. According to the wife, that isn't Alfred Owenby. How did you do that? There were at least a thousand names in that folder I gave you this morning," Chet said.

"I looked at the photographs and narrowed the search down. Shit. So, it's not him. Well, unfortunately, that doesn't help us much because he was obviously using an alias. Do you think you could swing by Metropolis tomorrow and pick up the full personnel file on him? I'll call ahead and let them know you're coming. It should still be covered under our previous subpoena."

"No, I don't think it will. We requested a *list* of employees, not their personnel files. I'll go by first thing and pick up the subpoena, then I'll head on over there. Damn, Lacy! Even shot and at home in bed, you still kick ass!" Chet said, admiringly.

"Thanks, Chet. I'm not really shot."

"Well, almost shot then. Need anything?"

"No, thanks. As it stands, I'm staying home again tomorrow. Maybe you could bring over more paperwork, and I'll have something constructive to do."

"Will do. See you tomorrow."

Lacy hung the phone up and decided that she wanted her salad. Gingerly getting out of bed, she thought that, although they may not have zeroed in on the person responsible for the HIV cases, they had uncovered someone who was committing identity fraud at the very least. In cases where there was a missing person and identity theft, often there was a homicide lurking in the background.

CHAPTER 20

Lacy's doorbell rang at 6:35 the following morning.
After slowly getting out of bed and leaving a much annoyed Snow because their routine of him being petted before she had arisen had been disturbed, Lacy looked through the peep hole to see Chet with wet hair. As soon as she opened the door, Chet barged into her apartment holding a newspaper.

"Did you see this?" he asked.

"What is 'this'?"

"It's the front page of today's *Atlanta Journal.*"

"I don't subscribe to a paper, and I was still sleeping, so no."

"Well, here. Look at it." He shoved the paper toward Lacy.

Lacy thought that Chet was being unusually brusque and knew there had to be a good reason for it. Looking at the headline, she understood why. In at least forty point bold font was the headline: Baffling AIDS Epidemic Hits Atlanta. Oh, shit. Scanning the article, she learned that Shelly Stevens had wasted no time in hiring a private investigator who had, in turn, wasted no time in opening a huge can of worms.

"Why do you seem pissed off at me?" Lacy asked.

"I don't know, Lacy, you tell me. It just seems a bit odd to me that you seem to be chumming around with the Stevens woman and now this hits the newspapers."

"You think I told her?" Lacy tried to sound offended.

"The thought did cross my mind."

Wondering how well she'd be able to lie and act at this hour of the morning and with no forewarning, Lacy recalled how she had in fact hinted to Shelly Stevens about there being more than one case of unexplained HIV. She also seemed to recall suggesting the woman hire a PI. From the information presented in the article, the PI had apparently detected almost as much information as Lacy had in a lot less time.

"Maybe she just figured that if she got HIV and nobody could figure out how, that there were others," Lacy said, now trying to sound nonchalant.

"Maybe you told her. Dammit, Lacy, I know you don't always play by the books, but this is going to bring the scrutiny of the world on us, you know."

"I didn't do anything!" A small lie; she hadn't actually *done* anything, merely *said* something.

"Sumlin called me this morning and asked if I thought you'd had anything to do with this. I told him no, but I'm still not sure. He's scheduled a press conference for 8:00 this morning. This story is already being covered on the news and the radio. People are calling in a panic. It's just awful, Lace."

"Okay. Let me get dressed," she said.

"Get dressed? No, I didn't mean for you to come to work today. I just needed to find out if you had anything to do with this."

Lacy felt a pang of guilt course through her and decided to confess, sort of.

"I might have mentioned to her that Dr. West had a case the same night Shelly shot her husband where a little kid had AIDS and there didn't seem to be any explanation."

"Aw, Lacy! I knew it," Chet said, running his hand through his damp hair.

"Well, hell, Chet, I didn't call her up and give her or her PI a list of names or even tell them how many there were or anything! I haven't talked to her since Monday when I went to see why her lawyer was suddenly singing my praises. So, whatever is in that article, the PI must have uncovered by herself. Besides, don't you think that the public has a right to know about this?" Lacy asked, seething.

"Yes, but later; like maybe when we've figured out something. As it stands, the public will be demanding that we find out what's going on and wondering why it's taking so long. There isn't any way that we won't come out of this smelling like poop."

"I guess. I didn't mean to cause any trouble. Is Sumlin pissed?"

"No, because apparently Judge Farnsworth is quite happy."

"Why in the hell would anyone be happy about an AIDS epidemic?" Lacy asked.

"Because, I guess, with fear and panic running amok, the likelihood of his niece being convicted and sentenced to anything major has just lessened significantly."

Chet always got so damned articulate when he was annoyed. He also rarely increased his use of curse words, unlike Lacy. Hell, he had even said 'poop' for 'shit'. Opposites attract in police partners as well, she thought.

"I'm sorry, Chet."

"I know. I know you wouldn't have done anything improper on purpose if you'd known there would be this kind of backlash," he said, softening a bit.

"No, I don't want to be under a magnifying glass any more than you do. Maybe we've hit on something with this Owenby guy. Will you still bring me the file?"

"You bet I will. I'll bring it by even sooner now that our progress will be assessed by everybody in the country. I better get going. I'm not mad, Lace, and I won't tell Sumlin or anybody else that you maybe planted that seed in the Stevens woman's head."

"Thanks, Chet."

After Chet left, Lacy turned around to find Snow looking sympathetically at her. That was ridiculous, she thought. He had the same expression as he did when he was pissed or being petted or anything else. Or did he? When she sat on the sofa, he hopped up and crawled in her lap. Okay, maybe he did look sympathetic after all.

Reaching for the remote control, she flipped from country music videos over to the local early edition news. Just as Chet had said, there was a picture of Shelly Stevens in the corner as the newscaster hyped the fears of the general public. This was a 'complete mystery to police and health officials' with 'no apparent end in sight.' Groaning, Lacy watched as they introduced Martin Strausser, the egret bastard, who was standing beside a homely woman even taller and thinner than he was; a female egret. Egrets of a feather stick together, Lacy mused.

The woman was identified as the private investigator who had 'blown the case wide open,' according to egret. Her findings would 'substantiate his client's innocence' once the public gave thought to the possibility that the same thing could have happened to them. Egretette spoke, saying it was a 'there but for the grace of God go I' occurrence. Lacy had just about had enough of this shit. Just because there was an 'epidemic' of unexplained cases of HIV didn't mean that Shelly Stevens was innocent. She'd still shot her husband to death. Chet was right; the police department was going to look bad even though they had made decent progress considering the bizarre nature of the case, the fact that Shelly Stevens wasn't dead, and the fact that they had only been investigating for a couple of weeks. Deciding that she'd be of more use downtown, Lacy turned off the television and scooted Snow off her lap.

Pulling her shirt off, she stood in front of the mirror and looked at the enormous bruise on her torso. She looked like a skinny eggplant. Smiling at her sudden thought that she would have fit in with T-Bone and Shroom, Lacy heard the phone ring and all humor faded. It was probably Sumlin.

"Hello?" she asked tentatively.

"Lacy? It's Sharon. Have you seen the news?"

"Oh, yeah. I've also seen the paper."

"I didn't tell anyone. I don't know who might have leaked the story, but it wasn't me," Sharon said, obviously upset.

"I know; it was me," Lacy confessed.

"What? Why?"

"I don't know, it just sort of came out when I was talking to Shelly Stevens. I had no idea that anything would go this far, especially this fast. I was just trying to make her feel better," Lacy said.

There was a palpable silence before Sharon blurted, "You should know better than to let your hormones get the best of you, Detective. I'm disappointed in you."

Feeling as if she'd just been slapped, Lacy began in a slow, calm voice.

"First off, I'm not sexually attracted to Shelly Stevens. She's not my type. Second, would you or your associates have acted on these suspicious cases if I hadn't been hounding you for information? I think not. You heard the lady at the Health Initiative place say that the investigation had been temporarily tabled. Last, I'm sorry to have disappointed you, Doctor West. You can join the club, I presume. I manage to disappoint just about everyone who knows me. If you have no further complaints with me, I'm going to hang up."

"Oh, Lacy. God, I'm sorry. I really am," Sharon apologized. "I don't know what came over me. I guess it just bothered me that you had fallen for a felon this time around. You're right; I would have done nothing further. I guess I'm also frustrated because this is causing a panic among the public. We had at least twenty calls between 6:00 and 7:00 asking about HIV testing. It's not your fault, though, and I never should have made reference to your sexual orientation. I'm not disappointed in you if you promise you aren't falling for the Stevens woman."

"I'm not. People who are that concerned with their appearance are too shallow for me. Besides, she named her cat Snowpuff. How stupid is that?" Lacy said.

"Does this mean you're not upset with me?" Sharon asked softly.

"I'm not upset with you. How about you?"

"Mad at you? No, not mad or disappointed. I'm just tired and frustrated. I didn't mean to say I was disappointed in you. I wish I could take it back. In fact, I've actually got a little get-well present for you. I was going to see if maybe I could stop by on my way home for a few minutes," Sharon asked.

"Sure, but I might be in the shower. If you knock and there's no answer, just let yourself in."

"Okay. See you in a bit."

Still unsettled from her earlier anger at Sharon, Lacy finished undressing and was looking forward to a nice, warm shower. Maybe Sharon would feel bad enough that she'd bring over some breakfast. She wasn't quite sure why hearing that she had disappointed Sharon would make her feel this badly. She generally didn't care what people thought of her. Maybe Sharon was becoming a closer friend than she was used to having.

CHAPTER 21

Lacy purposefully took an extra lengthy shower, taking time to let the warm water massage her knotted muscles. She wondered if somehow, subconsciously, she wasn't deliberately allowing Sharon time to enter her apartment with her own key. That would be a nice feeling, even if she was still a bit miffed at the doctor. She noticed a few gray strands while she was blowing her hair dry and wondered if it was time to start coloring her hair. Wrapping herself in her favorite terry robe, she walked out of the bathroom and was surprised at the difference in temperature. She'd apparently taken a warmer shower than usual. She smiled when she heard cat-talk coming from the kitchen: Sharon was here.

"Sharon?" Lacy called out as she walked into the living room.

"In here, Lacy. I'll be out in a minute."

Sitting in her recliner, Lacy noticed for the first time that she did so without either flinching or grunting from pain. That was good. She spied a cheerfully wrapped present with her name scrawled in Sharon's characteristically tiny writing. Too big for a CD, maybe it was a book. It was probably poetry or something, she thought.

LEE KELLY

"I brought you by a selection of bagels. They're in the kitchen. Would you like a Diet Coke?" Sharon asked.

"Sure. Thanks. What flavors of bagels did you get?"

"Cheese, French toast, plain, everything, and chocolate," Sharon replied as she went to the kitchen to get a Diet Coke for Lacy.

Lacy requested a cheese bagel and, moments later, Snow and Sharon entered the room. Snow hopped up on the arm of the recliner as Sharon set the Coke upon a coaster within Lacy's reach and handed her the cheese bagel. She then bent over and picked up the present.

"I got this a couple of days ago. I hope you like it."

Lacy set the bagel down on her lap and gingerly opened the package as Sharon hovered over her. Lacy wanted to ask the woman to sit down; she hated people standing over her. Looking up at Sharon, she saw the almost child-like exuberance on her face and decided not to make her sit down. Removing the last of the tape, Lacy uncovered a book about cats.

"I thought, since you've never had a kitty before, you might enjoy learning about them. I've got this book, and it has information about their characteristics, body language, care, well, just everything you could imagine needing to know. I hope you like it," Sharon said.

"I'm sure I'll learn a lot. Thank you."

Sharon knelt in front of Lacy and reached out to pet Snow, who was avidly sniffing the wrapping paper.

"He probably smells my kitties on the paper," Sharon said as she looked back to meet Lacy's gaze. "I just wanted to apologize again for saying those things to you this morning. This whole thing is so weird; I just don't know what to do."

Lacy watched as Sharon took the book from her and set it on the coffee table. She then took Lacy's hand in

194

hers and held it tightly. Lacy felt at that moment that she could forgive the woman for anything.

"It's okay. I probably wouldn't have reacted like I did if Chet hadn't just chewed my ass out moments earlier," Lacy said.

"So, have you got any new leads on this case? Uh-oh," Sharon said with a frown.

Lacy followed Sharon's eyes to a happy Snow who had abandoned paper sniffing and was licking the cheese bagel seated in Lacy's lap.

"Oh, shit, Snow!" Lacy said with surprisingly little annoyance.

Reluctantly, Lacy allowed Sharon to remove her hand and watched as Sharon stood, her joints creaking in protest. She picked up Snow and gently set him on the floor. She then took the bagel from Lacy's hand and headed toward the kitchen. A moment later, she returned with the bagel.

"I don't eat after cats. It's okay; I'll just have another flavor," Lacy said matter-of-factly.

"Oh, no, I had gotten two of each kind. I threw the one he licked in the trash. Would you like for me to toast it for you?"

"Nah, this is fine. I'd like some cream cheese if you could bring it for me."

"Sure. Snow will probably like it, too."

Watching Sharon return to the kitchen, Lacy thought it was odd that it had felt so natural to ask her for the cream cheese. She'd rarely in her life asked anyone to bring her anything, and consequently it typically felt strange to do so. In this case, it had felt all too natural.

"Here you go," Sharon said with a smile.

Taking the knife and cream cheese container, Lacy noticed that Snow was eyeing her avidly. After smearing a thin layer on each side of the bagel, she put a small glob of the cheese on the cover of one of her running magazines and set it on the floor for the cat. He did seem to enjoy the treat. Lacy took her first bite of bagel and spoke with her mouth full.

"We might have a break in the case."

"Really? Can you tell me about it?"

Swallowing, she reached for the can of Diet Coke.

"I probably shouldn't, but I can't see how it could hurt anything at this point. Do you remember how we subpoenaed the list of employees for Metropolis Blood Center?"

Sharon nodded in affirmation.

"Well, it turns out the name of one of the employees whose application and photograph shows a male in his late twenties is really a fifty-something-year-old guy who has been missing for several years," Lacy said.

"Maybe two people have the same name?" Sharon offered.

"The social security numbers match, too. No, it's definitely at the least a case of identity theft. Maybe we'll get lucky and it'll be more than just that."

"What did he do at Metropolis?" asked Sharon.

"He was something called a *component tech,* and he worked there during the years that the suspicious units were donated."

"That might just make sense. Remember I told you that I had worked in a hospital laboratory while I was in med school?"

Lacy didn't, but nodded as if she did anyway.

"My favorite department to work in was the Blood Bank. We had a donor center in-house for people who wanted to donate their own blood for surgery or for those who were donating for a friend having surgery at our facility. We didn't do any component separating, but I still know a great deal about it. It actually stands to reason that someone in that position would be more capable of introducing something into a unit of blood than someone in the testing department like I had originally thought," Sharon said excitedly.

"I don't have a clue what you're talking about. Do you think you could dumb it down a bit for me so that I'd be as excited about this as you are?"

"Oh, sorry. When someone donates blood, it's removed from them and fills a large bag, thus making a unit of whole blood. The reason it's whole blood is that, in addition to containing the red blood cells, it also contains platelets, plasma, and clotting factors. At the hospital where I worked, we were only a collection facility, which is why I never did any of the component preparation. We would then ship the units to a local blood center where the unit of whole blood was divided into the separate components that I mentioned earlier."

Lacy was chewing her bagel and looking the part of a captivated student as Sharon continued.

"So, you have this unit of whole blood, and you spin it down in a centrifuge and remove the liquid portion, or the plasma. The portion that's left in the original bag is the unit of packed red blood cells. That would be what Shelly Stevens received when she said she'd had a blood transfusion.

Meanwhile, the plasma portion of the whole blood is further processed by centrifugation and separation techniques to yield plasma, platelets, and cryoprecipitate, which is rich in clotting factors. These elements of the whole blood are referred to as components. So, if this guy was a component preparation tech, he would have been the one processing the units of whole blood. In other words, he would have definitely had access to the blood.

Did you find out if he was working when the possibly tainted units were processed?"

Lacy swallowed another bite of bagel and said, "No, not yet. I just came across this information late yesterday. I still don't get why he would be any more likely of a candidate than anyone else who had access to the blood."

"Because nobody would have questioned seeing him messing around with a unit of blood since that was his job. Also, it bothered me that there didn't seem to be any way that someone could have tampered with a unit of blood without it becoming contaminated or the plastic bag obviously leaking. All hospital Blood Banks are careful to check units visually to ensure that there's no compromising of the plastic or the seals and also that there are no signs of bacterial contamination. A component tech, however, would have had access to an instrument called a sterile docking device which would allow them to add or remove something from the unit of blood in a sterile fashion, thereby minimizing any bacterial contamination risk and negating any damage to the plastic bag itself."

"So, how does this sterile device thing work?" Lacy asked.

"It would be easier to draw you a picture. Do you have any paper?"

Lacy removed her notepad from beneath a stack of magazines that she had yet to peruse and noticed that she'd written Sharon's name several times on the top sheet. Blushing, she tore the top several pages off before handing the pad and a pen over to Sharon. God, how sophomoric of her! At least she hadn't drawn little hearts with arrows through them around Sharon's name. She hoped the doctor wouldn't notice her suddenly red face. Looking over, she decided that she needn't worry. Sharon was busily drawing on the notepad. Whew. When in the hell had she written that? She seriously needed to take a few moments later in the day and evaluate her feelings toward Sharon.

"See? Lacy? Do you see what I'm talking about?" Sharon was holding the pad in front of Lacy's face.

"Huh? I'm sorry; I was trying to digest what you had told me. Could you repeat it?"

"Sure. The needle is attached to this tubing, which is attached to the unit of blood directly in the center of the bag. On either side of the bag, there are two little ports, the little p's on the drawing, which are where the nurses put the blood tubing into the bag when they're transfusing the unit. If either of these ports is punctured, it's obvious because there's a plastic sheath covering the ports that has to be torn through. Blood Bank facilities would reject any unit that arrived having the port exposed. If you were to stick a needle into the bag anywhere else, blood would leak from the puncture site. Again, the unit would be rejected by the receiving facility.

Now, after a unit has been processed, the tubing is removed by sealing it off a couple of inches above the entrance to the bag. This leaves a little neck, if you will, that one can use to gain access to the main unit if they have a sterile docking device. Maybe I'll take you and show you what I'm talking about," Sharon said, noticing the blank look on Lacy's face.

"So, using this device, someone could add something to a unit of blood and nobody would be able to tell?" Lacy asked.

"It would be possible. Some things, like bacteria or certain chemical compounds, would alter the appearance of the unit enough that it would be noticed upon visual examination by the receiving facility. Bacteria would cause the unit to darken and become bloated due to the release of carbon dioxide from the living bacteria. Many drugs would cause the red blood cells to burst apart, or hemolyze, thereby causing the unit to take on a fruit punch looking coloration which could be detected as well. With a virus, however, there would be none of that type of red flag to alert of potential tampering."

"Shit. I'm glad I mentioned this to you. In a minute I'll call Chet and have him find out if the suspicious units were ever processed when this guy was working. By the way, that's a pretty lousy drawing," Lacy teased.

Laughing, Sharon looked at her little depiction of a unit of blood.

"Yeah, well, I wouldn't have wanted Van Gogh to diagnose me if I were sick."

"Good point. Maybe I could take some photographs of all of these things you're talking about. Does your hospital have this stuff?" Lacy asked.

"Yes. I could swing by to pick you up on my way in if you could get Chet to take you home later since I work such long shifts."

"Tonight? That sounds great."

Rising from her crouch, Sharon stretched and yawned.

"Speaking of long shifts, I'd better get going so I can get some sleep before I go in tonight. Since you seem to be doing so much better, do you want me to leave your key to the front door?"

"No. I'd kind of like it if you'd keep it for a while. You know, just until I'm completely better," Lacy said.

"Well, I'll see you tonight around 6:15 or so. You've done good work on this, Detective. I think you may be onto something here."

Lacy watched as Sharon turned toward the door and bent to pet Snow one last time before leaving. She'd gotten accustomed to some form of physical contact when

Sharon left and was instantly alarmed by the sudden change. Had Sharon seen her name written all over Lacy's pad? Moving more quickly than she had in days, Lacy caught up to Sharon as she neared the door.

"Thanks for the book. I'm sure Snow will thank you, too."

Turning, Sharon smiled at her and leaned over to hug her. Lacy softly kissed her cheek and thought that this goodbye was much better. Locking the door behind Sharon, Lacy walked over to the phone to call Chet. She felt better at that moment than she had in days.

"Detective Avery speaking."

"Hey, Chet. It's your instigating partner. How's it going?"

"Not so good. There've been shitloads of phone calls this morning about the HIV thing."

"You said 'shitloads'," Lacy said, astonished.

"Yeah, I guess I did. I was just going to get the court order so I could head over to Metropolis. As soon as I get that folder, I'm going to bring it over to you."

"Great. Sharon just came by, and she thinks that this is our guy. She explained all about how his having that position could have allowed him to mess with the blood supply without arousing any suspicion. Do you think you could find out if he had access to those units of blood? Do you still have the unit numbers?"

"Sure, I've got them written down in my folder. I can do that. Would you get mad at me if I asked why the Doctor was making such an early house call?"

"It's not like that, Chet. She just brought me some breakfast and a book about cats."

"Oh, yeah. How's the little guy?" Chet asked.

"He licked my bagel."

"So, let me guess; you threw it away."

"Hell yes, I threw it away!" Lacy snapped.

"You could have just picked off the portion that he licked."

"Gross. Don't you need to get going now?"

"Yeah, I suppose so. I'll give you a call when I'm on my way over, okay?"

A few minutes later, the telephone rang. Lacy decided that it was probably neither Chet nor Sharon, so she decided to screen the call. When she heard the voice on the answering machine, she was glad she'd done so.

"Lacy? Hi. It's Mom. I've got bad news. I wanted to call to let you know that Brother Morrison has passed away. I know you always liked him, in spite of his ousting you from the church. The funeral is set for the day after tomorrow. Call me if you'd like to go, and I'll give you the information. You know how I hate to talk on these things. Well, I'll talk to you later. Bye now."

Lacy felt sadness overtake her. Not only because of Brother Morrison's passing, but also because her Mother just didn't seem to quite grasp her unusual relationship with the preacher. It wasn't as if he had *ousted* her from the congregation. She thought back on that afternoon several years before when she had approached him, at her Mother's insistence, about her homosexuality. He'd fixed her a mug of hot chocolate and sat across from her as she expressed her innermost feelings and fears. She'd been raised a Baptist and was convinced she was committing a sin by her being attracted to females.

Brother Morrison had told her that the Baptist church was probably not the place for her. Had the discussion ended there, Lacy could have understood her mother's belief that the preacher had ousted her from the congregation. Instead, Brother Morrison had kindly pointed out numerous passages from the Bible that had led him to feel that homosexuality was indeed an acceptable life-style. He'd then gone on to tell her that, although he felt she wasn't committing a sin, others in the Baptist church would disagree. He recommended a particularly under-standing Episcopal Church in a nearby town as an alterna-tive. She recalled his words, almost verbatim.

"Lacy, dear. I feel as though I'm failing you. I'll never be able to stand in front of the congregation and read to them these passages as I have you. I'd lose my job and likely never be offered another position in a Baptist church. Do I think I'm being hypocritical? Yes, I suppose. There are quite a few things with which I'm at odds with the Baptist Church on. Still, I was raised a Baptist, re-ceived my PhD in Theology from a Baptist University, and am married to a devout Baptist woman.

I could follow my heart and preach until I was blue in the face that I felt homosexuality wasn't a sin, but what would I glean? My wife would be horrified, as would the congregation. I'd never be able to sway the die-hard zeal-ot's opinion on the matter. I'm truly sorry that I'm letting you down. That's why I feel that you should attend the Saint Thomas Episcopal Church. They're far more open-minded and accepting of situations like yours. If you'd like, I can give you the name of the priest there. I'm cer-tain he could make you feel better."

Lacy recalled the smell of burning wood in the fire-place, could still see the concerned and saddened look upon the old man's face as he tried to help her. She'd never called the priest he'd recommended, nor had she sought solace at any other church. It had been enough for her that Brother Morrison hadn't felt she was sinning. She'd related the exchange word for word to her mother, who had felt that the preacher had "kicked her out of the Baptist Church." After all these years, her mother still felt that way. Lacy owed the preacher a great deal for having helped her with her feelings so many years before. She would have to make time to attend his service.

Driving home, Sharon was excited by the apparent progress that the detectives seemed to be making on the case. Lacy was really something else. She began to wonder why she felt so disappointed in Lacy when she thought that she'd been attracted to Shelly Stevens. Why should she care? Had she really, as she'd told Lacy, not wanted her to get mixed up with a felon or was it something more? She knew she felt unusually protective of the detective. She also believed that she felt an unusual bond forming with the other lady. She respected her in spite of the fact that she'd leaked the HIV information to Mrs. Stevens. Typically, Sharon wouldn't have tolerated that type of unprofessional behavior in any of her friends. In this instance, however, it seemed okay. Maybe on her first day off she'd try to diagnose what she was feeling toward Lacy.

Chet had requested the original personnel folder from Metropolis Blood Center and was patiently waiting as they xeroxed the information within to keep for themselves. While someone was busily copying the information, Dr. Stephenson herself was researching whether or not Alfred Owenby had processed any of the units in question. Chet was pacing back and forth looking at a whole slew of posters on the wall urging people to donate blood. He was just about to memorize each detail of the posters when Dr. Stephenson returned looking quite somber.

"Detective Avery? Alfred Owenby processed all of the units you asked me to check on. Here's his personnel folder. I'll personally try to put together a list of all units that Mr. Owenby processed while he worked for Metropolis. It'll take several days, but you can rest assured that I'll be thorough."

Thanking Dr. Stephenson for her time, Chet left and went by headquarters. He made a couple of copies of the information within the folder, then went to the fingerprinting department.

Fortunately, Mikah Chan, a.k.a. Mikey, was working. He was a fingerprint analysis nerd if Chet had ever seen one. Consequently, he could often be counted on to identify if not an entire print, at least a couple of usable swirls that could lead to a computerized match more often than not.

"Mikey! How's it going?" Chet said.

"Hey, Avery! How's Lacy? I heard she got pretty banged up the other day."

"Oh, she's getting better all the time. Thank God for body armor. She's working this HIV case from home. Actually, she found a suspicious character that we're hoping has something to do with this whole AIDS thing. There are a couple of problems, though. First, this guy was using a stolen identity when he was working for the blood center. Second, we've got his employment application from the blood center, but it's over five years old. This is why I'm here. Do you think you can work your magic and lift some prints from this paper?"

Mikah's eyebrows knitted together as he studied the paper.

"Five years? It would've been better if the paper wasn't a matte finish. The prints will probably be smeared. I'll try ninhydrin first on a small corner of the paper. If that doesn't work, I'll try Iodide fuming. There's no way you could get a fresher sample of the prints on, say, more porous paper?" he asked.

"I don't know. All I asked for was the personnel file. I didn't think five years was too long," Chet said.

"It wouldn't be if we were dealing with another kind of paper. This shiny surface prohibits the uptake of the oils from the prints. I'm not ruling anything out, Avery. I'm just saying you might need to try to get another sample of something that this guy touched. Preferably, more recently."

"Yeah, I know. More recent and on a more printing-friendly paper surface. I hate to ask you this, but do you think you could rush this for me? The media is having a field day with this case, and we'll need any help we can get to try to solve it ASAP," Chet said.

"Not a problem. I'll have something for you at the end of the day. I'll even run what I get through the databases for you. After all, I've seen the memo."

"What memo?"

"The memo from the Chief that says to drop everything else if we're asked to do something relating to the AIDS epidemic case. I thought there had to be a large number of people who got sick before it was called an epidemic?"

"Usually you're right. I guess now it's either a large number of people or a relative of Judge Farnsworth and a few others," Chet said disgustedly.

"How sure are you that these prints are connected to the HIV cases?"

"I'm not sure, but Lacy seems pretty certain. She's made friends with this doctor who says that it would make sense. I think she's worked in a blood center or something before," Chet said.

"Great. Well, I'll get right on this per the recent memorandum. I'll call you when I'm finished or you can come by sooner and hang out. I know how much you miss printing."

"Thanks, Mikey."

As Chet walked away, he thought about how much he would have enjoyed doing actual print development for a living. At least he wouldn't have all of the scrutiny that he'd be getting for the remainder of this case. He thought about that unpleasant turn of events during the drive to Lacy's apartment and was annoyed with her again by the time he rang her doorbell.

"Hey, Chet. Come in," Lacy said after opening the door.

"I've brought the personnel file on Alfred Owenby. Everything is a copy. The original is down in the printing division. Mikey is going to try to work his magic and see if we can ID this jerk," Chet said matter-of-factly.

"So, you're still pissed at me, huh?"

"What makes you say that?"

"Because you haven't even attempted to make small talk. You know, 'Hey, Lace. How're you feeling?' or anything like that."

"Yeah, I guess I am still a bit peeved. So, how are you feeling? You look pale."

"I always look pale."

"Yeah, but not usually this bad."

"Okay, I think I preferred the 'no small talk' Chet to the one telling me I look like shit," Lacy said.

"Lacy, you won't believe this. Our guy worked on all of the units of blood that were linked to these cases. Dr. Stephenson, the Director of Metropolis, is going to try to put together a list of all of the unit numbers that he worked on during his employment."

"Kick ass! I knew we were onto something. Now we just need to find this guy. I think I'm feeling good enough to return to work tomorrow. When did she say she would have the list completed?"

"Not for several days," he replied.

"Shit. Well, then, I guess we'll need to track down the disposition of each of the units of blood this guy processed and call people in for HIV testing."

"Oh, Lacy! I hadn't even thought of that!" Chet said with a sigh.

"Well, we've probably only seen the tip of the iceberg, unfortunately," Lacy said.

"I'm going to leave before you depress me any further. Darn it."

"So, what do you want me to do?" she asked.

"I don't know. Look through the file and do whatever you can think of. I don't know how much more I'll be able to do on the case today. There's another press conference scheduled at 1:00 that I'll have to attend. Also, I swear, it seems like the bulk of the calls from the public asking to be tested for HIV have been finding their way to my desk. Sumlin is thinking about calling in the GBI to help."

"This isn't their case!" Lacy yelped.

"No, Lacy, it isn't. Now, however, because the media has been made aware of this information sooner than I would have liked, we're going to have to try to close this case in record time. If the GBI can help us do that, more power to them," Chet said, pointedly.

Lacy knew that Chet had a good point. If she had just kept her big mouth shut, there wouldn't be the sense of urgency surrounding this case. She watched him walk toward the door, ignoring Snowpuff and actually stepping away from the cat. Lacy felt angry.

"Well, shit, Chet. Snow didn't have a damned thing to do with my leaking the information to Shelly Stevens! You could at least act like you see him or pet him! You know, psychologists would call that transference because you're transferring your anger to the cat rather than to me."

"No, Lacy, I'm not transferring any of my anger away from you. It's still present in its entirety," he retorted.

Lacy watched as Chet left her apartment and wondered if their relationship would ever be the same again. Earlier that morning, he'd seemed to have gotten over his anger toward her, but now it was back with a vengeance. She walked over and coaxed Snow to hop up onto a kitchen chair so she wouldn't have to bend as far to pet him.

"He's pretty pissed at me, Buddy. I guess I don't blame him. He didn't have to ignore you, though," she said, scratching under his chin.

Snow was purring loudly and bumping his head against Lacy's hand repeatedly.

"Well, at least you aren't mad at me. That's good."

Taking the personnel folder and a Diet Coke, Lacy headed toward the makeshift command center that she'd established on the unoccupied side of her bed. Snow took a running jump and landed on some loose papers on the bed. Before Lacy knew it, the papers and the cat had slid off the other side. She was trying not to laugh as she rounded the foot of the bed and saw the cat bathing a paw, his ears slicked down in an unhappy fashion. Lacy had noticed that cats seemed to bathe their paws when they were embarrassed. She wondered if the book that Sharon had given her would make any reference to that.

Lacy tried to coax Snow onto the bed again, only to be met with a 'no way in hell' stare. Sighing, she bent down, picked the cat up, and placed him on the bed. Shit, that hurt! She watched as Snow looked around, jerked his tail a couple of times, and jumped off. Apparently in the cat world, if it wasn't their idea to do something, it was a bad idea.

Sitting on the side of the bed, Lacy opened her can of Diet Coke and took a sip. She then leaned back against the bolster and opened the personnel file. There was a copy of the application. Lacy was no handwriting analysis expert, but she could detect the numerous hesitations that had caused little ink blobs to preside in what should have been smooth writing. She surmised that the ink blobs were present only in the information that was fabricated: name, address, references, previous employment, education, and signature. There were no hesitation blobs in the date nor were there any in the telephone numbers for his references or his home phone number. That would be where she started, then.

Logging onto her laptop, she accessed a couple of databases and looked up the telephone numbers only to find that each of the numbers had been reassigned. Lacy jotted down the information on the newly assigned owners of the numbers before digging deeper and uncovering the information for the previous owners. Not surprisingly, she found that Alfred Owenby's number wasn't actually registered to an Alfred Owenby at all. Rather, the name given was Michael Dunn. Similarly, the numbers for all of the references, even the Greater Bay Blood Center in San Francisco, were all registered to Michael Dunn.

Lacy began feeling her excitement stirring cautiously. It couldn't possibly be this easy to track down somebody who was ingenious enough to concoct such an elaborate scheme of introducing a virus into the blood supply. It was then that she noticed that two of the numbers had San Francisco area codes.

Lacy did a search on Michael Dunn and uncovered that he, like Alfred Owenby, was a missing person. She also discovered that the IRS had been busily looking for a Michael Dunn for failure to submit tax information for the year 1992. She reached for her notepad and began making the first list that she had made since the shooting.

- Find out if IRS is looking for Alfred Owenby, too
- Contact Greater Bay Blood Center and ask if Michael Dunn or Alfred Owenby worked there
- Find next of kin for Michael Dunn

Lacy decided that the first step she would take would be to contact the Greater Bay Blood Center. She thought she would need to be somewhat crafty to get the information she needed without obtaining a subpoena, which she doubted she could get unless she traveled to San Francisco.

"Greater Bay Blood Center, this is Gina. How may I direct your call?"

"I need to verify employment of an individual," Lacy said.

"Okay, hold one moment while I transfer you to Molly in Human Resources."

Lacy listened as classical music played softly in the background and noticed that the music did seem to somewhat soothe her nerves. By the time Molly picked up the phone, Lacy was so relaxed that she jumped a bit at the sound of the voice.

"GBBC, this is Molly. How may I help you?"

"Good morning, Molly. My name is Lacy Fuller, and we have a couple of applicants at the Metropolis Blood Center in Atlanta who were employed by you in the early 90's. I just need to verify employment, please."

"Absolutely. I'll need names and social security numbers," Molly said.

Lacy slowly related the information on each of the names and waited as Molly checked the information for her.

"Well, Michael Dunn was employed here, but we have no record of an Alfred Owenby. Is he claiming that he worked here?"

"Yes. The two came in together and said that they had both worked at your facility as Component Preparation Techs," Lacy lied.

"Well, Mr. Dunn was a Component Tech, but like I said, there's no record of an Alfred Owenby."

"Thank you, Molly. You've been helpful. Have a nice day."

Lacy hung up the phone before the puzzled lady asked any additional questions of her. Shit. What if this guy had done this in San Francisco, too? What if there were other cities as well? When she had told Chet that this was the tip of the iceberg, she had no idea just how true that might be. Lacy decided to attempt to get in touch with the next of kin for Michael Dunn. Pulling up the missing persons data, she found the contact number to be for the Oakland Sheriff's Department. Dialing that number, she noticed that the hairs on her arms were standing straight up. Where was that soothing classical music when she needed it?

"Oakland County Sheriff's Department. What's the nature of your call?"

"This is Detective Lacy Fuller with the Atlanta PD. I'd like to speak with someone regarding a missing person's case that dates back to 1990."

"Just a moment, Detective."

Contrary to the Greater Bay Blood Center's relaxing music, the Oakland Sheriff's Department had a monotone voice reciting crime statistics for the previous year as well as the current year to date.

"This is Tom Riker. How can I help you, Detective?"

"I'm looking into a case of possible identity theft, and I turned up the name 'Michael Dunn' as a reference for my stolen identity guy. I was going to call him and ask a few questions, but then I noticed that he, too, was on the missing persons list, along with my guy. I was wondering if you could share some information with me."

"Well, I'd like to help you, Detective, but my caller ID says you're calling from a private number. I just can't give out any information to private citizens," he said.

"I'm calling from a private number because I was shot the other day, and I'm taking a few days off at home. If you'd like to verify my credentials, I'll be glad to give you the phone number to the Atlanta PD."

"Nah. That's okay. I've actually pulled you up on my computer, verified your employment as a Detective with the Atlanta PD, and traced your home number to the one that's showing up on my screen."

Lacy was amazed by the speed with which this guy worked.

"Shit! How did you do that so fast?" she asked.

Laughing, Deputy Riker said, "Well, this *is* the Silicon Valley area. Yes, we had a missing person by the name of Michael Dunn. What Social Security number do you have for him?"

After Lacy read her nine-digit number to Deputy Riker and they verified the numbers matched, he resumed talking.

"He turned up in 1992. He washed ashore near the Bay Bridge. Not a pretty sight."

"Floaters never are. How long had he been dead?" she asked.

"Long enough to have decomposed. Had to ID him based on dental records, but it was the same guy."

"What line of business was he in?" Lacy asked.

"He was a pharmaceutical salesman."

"What would I need to send you to get a copy of the information inside his file?"

"You aren't used to working with other agencies, are you, Detective?" asked Deputy Riker.

"I guess not. What makes you say that?"

"Because I'll send you the information today and you won't need to do a thing for me. How would you like it sent? Fax, email, snail mail, or other?"

"You could email it to me?" Lacy asked.

"Sure. We scan all of our files into a word processing program. Want me to send it to you at home or at work?"

"You can send it to my work email. I've got access to the database from home. Hey, I might need to get in touch with someone from the San Francisco PD. Do you have any friends over there?" she asked.

"Sure. I used to work there. Still get together with some of the guys a couple of times a month and hang out. What's the nature of the case? Is it your other missing person?"

"Have you heard anything about an outbreak of HIV in the Atlanta area?"

"Sure. It's all over the news today," he replied.

"Well, we think someone has tampered with the blood supply and introduced the virus to victims that way. My missing person listed Michael Dunn as a reference. Michael Dunn worked for a blood center in San Francisco *after* he was reported as a missing person. I'm afraid that my guy was doing this out there before he moved to Atlanta using the Dunn guy as his alias."

"Sounds like a possibility. Want me to get in touch with some of my friends at SFPD and give them your name? Maybe ask them to do a little snooping?"

"Yeah, that'd be great. We are, as you're aware, getting eaten alive by the damned media. If you could help out, I'd appreciate it. If this guy has been out there, we can dump the mess off onto the FBI."

"I heard that! Okay, Detective. It's been a pleasure talking to you. I'll give you a call later on when I hear anything. I just sent you the email. Take care."

"Thanks. You, too."

Lacy logged onto her email and found a seventeen page document from Deputy Riker. Damn, he was fast! After opening the document and printing all seventeen pages, Lacy logged off her computer and decided she needed to call Chet. She got his voice mail, which probably meant that the press conference was still in full swing. She bet it was being televised. Clicking on the television, she confirmed her assumption. Looking ill at ease, Chet was standing behind the Chief and Captain Sumlin looking like he wished Lacy hadn't been wearing her vest when she'd been shot. She turned the volume up and heard the barrage of frantic, accusatory questions being hurled at the Chief and figured that watching that shit would slow down her progress. She turned the television off. At that very moment, her phone rang.

She decided to answer it since it couldn't be Chet or the Chief, and it probably wouldn't be her mother again.

"Hello?"

"Miss Lacy? It's Homer. I was calling to see how you're doing."

"I'm hanging in there, Homer. How are you? Where are you calling me from?"

"Doing well, thank you. I'm at that pay phone next to that car washing place on Ponce. I got a visit from a couple of officers a little while ago about those two boys who were attacking me. They said that I've got a lawyer, some guy named Strausser. I can't afford a lawyer, Miss Lacy. Is he one of those free ones?"

"No, Homer. He's not. Actually, I think he's probably one of the most expensive ones in the city," Lacy said.

"I don't know what to do, Miss Lacy. He wants to meet with me this afternoon. He must think I've got money."

Lacy smiled at that image. "No. I'm pretty sure that an

acquaintance of mine is paying for his services for you. Just do me a favor and meet with him."

"Why would a friend of yours pay for a lawyer for me? Is it that nice Dr. West?"

"No, Homer. Just between us, it's Shelly Stevens."

"That lady with AIDS?" Homer asked.

Lacy thought that if the general public were like Homer, Shelly Stevens would probably walk away from her homicide rap. She was 'that lady with AIDS' rather than 'that lady who killed her husband.' No doubt, Judge Farnsworth and the egret would be pleased.

"Yes, Homer, she is. Snow was actually her cat so I adopted him when she was incarcerated. Anyhow, she felt that she owed me a favor because of all of the work I'm doing to try to determine how she got infected with HIV. I asked her to see if she could do something to help you out. I hope that's okay."

"Well, I don't know what to say, Miss Lacy."

"Well, please don't say that I've let you down or have pissed you off. I think I've heard that enough today to last a lifetime. Chet and Sharon both told me that about this damned AIDS case."

"Let me down? Oh, no, Miss Lacy. I was thinking that it was mighty sweet of you to be so good to me. You're kind of like the daughter that I never had."

Lacy felt a lump in her throat, and her eyes began stinging. She never cried, but she was fighting fiercely with her emotions at this moment.

"Homer, that's one of the nicest things anyone has said to me in my whole life. Thank you. I needed that, especially today."

"Well, Miss Lacy, I wouldn't say it if it wasn't the God's truth. Is there anything I can do for you? Would you like to tell me about this AIDS thing?"

"You've just done more for me than you could know. You just stay safe. About this AIDS thing, how much have you heard about Shelly Stevens contracting HIV?"

"I've read that she thought her husband gave it to her, but it turns out he didn't, and that she's not sure how she got it, but maybe from a blood transfusion," Homer rambled.

"Well, that's about the gist of it. What has everyone mad at me is that Sharon had a case the other day of a child who had AIDS, and nobody knew where he'd gotten it, either, unless it was from a transfusion. I mentioned this to Shelly Stevens, and she hired a private investigator who uncovered several suspicious cases of HIV within the past few years."

"How is that a bad thing you did, Miss Lacy? It seems to me that they would be thankful that you and this investigator have begun to warn the public. Isn't AIDS sort of treatable if you catch it early?" he asked.

"Somewhat treatable, yes. Not curable, though. I think they're mad because I've caused a public panic."

"Well, Miss Lacy, they'll come around. You might have saved a few people if they find out sooner that they have AIDS and they get medicine for it. I don't think you've done a thing to be ashamed of."

"Thank you, Homer. I'll stop by to see you the first chance I get when I return to work."

"Well, it was my pleasure. Keep your chin up and take care, now."

Long after she hung the phone up, she sat there willing herself not to cry. She found that she was beginning to think of Homer as the father she'd never had, one who was kind, understanding, and supportive. Snow tentatively approached the bed and hopped up on it. He settled next to her, and she petted him, trying to remember what Sharon had said about animals. Oh, yeah, that they seemed to have a 'gloom barometer' that alerted them that their owners needed extra attention. Sure enough, Lacy slowly began composing herself as she was petting the large white cat.

She began scanning the file on Michael Dunn with her free hand. She started with the autopsy report, which was actually quite short since the body was mostly skeletal remains. Suddenly, her eyes froze when they came upon the name of his employer: Anti-Retrovirals, Inc. Oh, shit! She knew from the magazines she read that anti-retroviral medication was used in the treatment of AIDS. This guy sold medicine used to treat HIV. Somehow, there had to be a connection. The ringing of the phone startled her. She would have to remember to turn the ringer volume down if this pattern continued.

"Hello?"

"Lacy, it's Chet. Did you watch the press conference?"

"No."

"Why not? You should have been up on the damned stage like I had to be instead of sitting at home petting your cat!"

Lacy looked down at her right hand, still stroking Snow, and decided that no matter what she'd done, Chet was overreacting and she was getting pissed off.

"I wasn't *sitting here petting my cat* while you were in the hot seat. I was working. I've found out that our guy probably worked in San Francisco at a blood center, and I've got someone with the Oakland Sheriff's Department checking into suspicious cases of HIV out there. Also, it appears that our guy had a different stolen identity when he worked on the East Coast. He was one Michael Dunn, a pharmaceutical sales representative who dealt in anti-retroviral therapy, or AIDS drugs. I'm thinking that our guy and this guy might have crossed paths because of the HIV link. I resent your thinking that I'm doing nothing here, Avery. I also resent your resentment of Snow. What's the deal? What did the cat ever do to you?" she spat.

"The cat belongs to Shelly Stevens," he said.

"Do you realize how fucking immature you sound? I've said I was sorry that I shared any information with Shelly Stevens. I've said I'm sorry that there's a media frenzy about all of this. I'm not sure what else you want me to do, but if I bother you that much, then maybe you should find yourself another partner!"

"That isn't necessary," Chet said.

"Well, maybe I'll find myself another partner because I can't deal with this bullshit, Chet."

"I'm not apologizing for being mad at you," Chet said. "I will apologize for taking my anger out on Snow and for implying that you've just been sitting around all morning doing nothing. So, when is this guy from Oakland going to get back with you about the HIV cases in San Francisco?"

"As soon as he knows something, probably not until late this afternoon."

"You've done good work, as usual. If this guy has been in California, too, then we can call in the FBI and they can take-over looking incompetent for us."

"I fail to see how we look incompetent here, Chet."

"Me, too, but just ask any one of the members of the media and I'm sure that they can spell it out for you."

"Well, although you're bowling me over with your un-bridled enthusiasm to speak with me, I'm going to hang up now."

Lacy found herself wishing Homer would call her back to erase the unsettled feeling she was left with after talking to Chet. That was the problem with having a friend who was homeless; he had no home phone. Maybe she would look into getting him a cell phone. Yeah, she would put that on her to-do list for tomorrow.

CHAPTER 22

Homer watched as the big black Rolls Royce came to a stop just beside him. That was a mighty pretty car indeed, he thought. Miss Lacy must be right about the lawyer being a high priced one. The rear driver's side window slowly lowered.

"Homer Files? I'm Martin Strausser, your attorney," he said, extending his hand through the window.

Taking the bony hand in his, Homer thought the man reminded him of something, but he couldn't quite place it.

"It's a pleasure to meet you, Mr. Strausser."

"Please, call me Martin. I understand you're a close personal friend of Shelly Stevens? Any friend of Shelly's is a friend of mine."

Puzzled, Homer just smiled.

"In fact, Ms. Stevens has asked for you to come by and visit her, so we'll go there first. Afterwards, you and I will need to get together to discuss the particulars of your case. The youths are scheduled to appear in court next Thursday. If you'd like to go around, you can let yourself in on the other side."

Walking around the car, Homer thought that if he hadn't cleared this guy with Miss Lacy first, he would swear he was being abducted by the Mafia.

The two men made small talk for the few blocks to the Detention Center where Shelly Stevens was being held. Homer lagged slightly behind the lawyer as they entered first the building, then a room wherein they waited for Shelly Stevens to appear. After a few minutes, the lady herself was brought into the room.

"Hi, Homer. It's so good to see you again! Martin? If you'd be so kind as to step outside for a moment. I haven't seen Homer in so long, and we've got a good deal of catching up to do," Shelly said enthusiastically.

Without a word, the lanky man exited the room.

"With all due respect, Ms. Stevens, I don't believe I know you," Homer said.

Sitting, the blonde woman favored Homer with a tired smile and motioned for him to sit as well.

"You don't, Mr. Files. I believe that you know Detective Fuller, though. She asked if there was anything that I could do to help you out, and I was more than willing to. She's watching my little cat, you see."

"Ah, yes. Snowpuff. He's a cute little fellow. I still don't understand why Mr. Strausser is under the impression that you and I are friends."

"Because I told him that we were. Lacy asked me to do this favor for her in strict confidence, so I'm pretending that we're friends so that her name isn't brought up."

Homer still looked perplexed. "She did tell me that you were paying for my lawyer because she told you about that other case of mysterious HIV."

Shelly Stevens' mouth fell open. "She told you that? She made me swear not to tell anyone about that."

Homer chuckled as he spoke. "Well, she probably should have sworn herself to secrecy, too. It seems that she's gotten several people awfully mad at her about that."

"Who did she tell and why?" Shelly asked.

"Well, her partner, Chet, and a friend of hers. As for why, I'm just not sure."

"I guess she told you that she hinted I should hire a PI to check into suspicious cases of AIDS, too?"

"No, Ma'am. I don't believe she told me that."

"Oh. Well, she did. According to Martin, this is all over the news."

"Yes, Ma'am. It's not making the police force look any too good, either."

"How so?" asked Shelly.

"It seems that the public thinks that the police department should be doing more to find out who's responsible for these AIDS cases. That's why Miss Lacy's partner is mad at her. She's at home, shot, and—"

"Shot? Lacy's been shot?" Shelly's eyes widened in horror.

"Yes, Ma'am. She was wearing a vest, but she's awfully bruised and sore."

"But she's okay?"

"Yes, Ma'am. I reckon other than having folks mad at her, she's doing alright."

"So, her partner is mad at her?" Shelly asked, trying to follow along.

"Yes, Ma'am. I reckon it's because the public thinks that the police department isn't doing such a good job."

"I see. Well, that isn't the case at all. In fact, if it hadn't been for Lacy believing me about not being unfaithful to my husband, I don't think any of this would have ever been discovered," Shelly said.

"I told Miss Lacy that she hadn't done anything wrong, but she was sort of down in the mouth when I talked to her earlier," Homer said, shaking his head slowly.

"I bet she was! The poor thing. Well, I'll have to do something about that now, won't I?"

Homer didn't answer, but he did hope that she could do something that would get folks to stop being mad at Miss Lacy.

"I'm real sorry to hear that you're sick, Ms. Stevens," Homer offered kindly.

"Thank you, Homer. I'm real sorry that I killed my husband."

"Yes, Ma'am. I bet you are. If you ask the Lord to forgive you, He will, and you'll feel better."

"I've prayed for forgiveness, but I don't feel any better," she said numbly.

"No, Ma'am. It'll take some time. I don't think you're a malicious person at all. I reckon finding out you were sick and thinking that your husband had done it was a bit much for you. I remember when my wife was diagnosed with cancer, I was filled with anger. I was angry with God, though. I kept wondering how He could make such a sweet lady sick.

I'm ashamed to admit that I was mad at God, but I was thinking earlier today about your situation. I'm not a violent man at all, but if a human had been the reason that my wife had gotten sick, well, all that anger would have been directed at them instead of God. You can't kill God, you see. I'd like to think that I wouldn't have killed a man if he'd made my wife sick, but I don't know as to how I could say that with any assurance."

Shelly wiped a tear from her eye and reached her dry hand out to take Homer's hand in hers.

"Mr. Files, Lacy was right. You are a special man. I thank you for saying that to me. I know you would never have hurt anyone or anything, but I appreciate your trying to make me feel better. You're a gentleman in an age where few true gentlemen still exist. Lacy said that you donate most of your money to help little animals. Is that true?"

Beaming, Homer told her all about his fund and how much money he'd given to date. Shelly thought that she'd spent at least a hundred times that amount on frivolous surgeries, and the realization humbled her.

"Mr. Files? Would you consider doing a favor for me?" Shelly asked.

"Why, yes Ma'am, if I can."

"I'd like to provide you with an apartment. Lacy was worried about you getting hurt living out on the streets."

"That's mighty kind of you, Ms. Stevens, but I'll be just fine," he said.

"Well, think about the animals, Homer. What would they do if anything happened to you? They're depending on you."

Homer sat quietly for a few moments, then hung his head.

"I suppose you're right, Ms. Stevens. I guess I hadn't thought about that. I can't let you pay for an apartment for me, though. You're already paying for my lawyer. It just isn't right, Ma'am."

"Yes, it is. I've got a great deal of money, and I'm feeling pretty lousy about myself since I killed my husband. I didn't feel that great about myself before, but now the guilt just seems to be unbearable. I'd take a small amount of pleasure in helping you stay healthy so that you could help the little animals and, believe me, I'd never miss the money," she said sweetly.

"Well, I'll have to think about it. It's mighty kind of you."

"Just let me or Martin know. Speaking of Martin, I guess he can come back in now. Remember, we're old friends who go way back. I think you used to deliver my newspapers."

"Yes, Ma'am. I believe I remember that." Homer smiled.

Watching Homer slowly rise from his chair, Shelly thought herself lucky to have met Lacy and Homer despite the circumstances. She would have Martin send Lacy a get well arrangement. She would also have Martin notify her father and uncle that she needed to talk with them today. She needed to do something about the police department being berated. She knew that her uncle, the esteemed judge, would probably call a press conference. She owed that much to Lacy.

CHAPTER 23

Lacy's call from California came at 4 pm. Deputy Riker's friends at the SFPD had uncovered some useful information. Yes, there had been a greater than usual number of unexplained HIV cases in the bay area between the mid-90's and now. Unfortunately, the local health authorities had been unable to make a connection to blood transfusions, and Lacy would need to submit legal documents before the names of the HIV patients could be released. Lacy thanked Deputy Riker, who volunteered to help her in any way he could.

She decided against calling Chet to ask for the court order since he was still so mad at her. Instead, she called the Superior Court and was able to fax over the request due to the extenuating circumstances of her injury as well as the clout involved by working the Stevens AIDS case. Within moments, she received a fax in return giving her the power to sequester the necessary information which she forwarded to the CDC. She then called Dr. Pounds, her contact at the Global Health Initiative. Due to confidentiality issues, Dr. Pounds asked if she could pick up the list in person. By 5:30, she had a list of names, addresses, and telephone numbers totaling 22 suspicious HIV cases the CDC had previously investigated in San Francisco.

The telephone rang at 5:45.

"Hello?" Lacy said, tentatively.

"Lacy? It's Sharon. Quick, turn on the news."

"Which channel?"

"It doesn't matter."

Lacy scrambled for the remote and turned on the television in time to see Judge Farnsworth standing at a podium looking angry. She turned up the volume.

"-will not have the media making our police department look bad. If it hadn't been for the diligent work of Detective's Lacy Fuller and Chet Avery, I fear that this crime may have continued to go undetected."

A nasal-voiced female reporter interrupted.

"During this morning's first press conference, Shelly Stevens' own attorney attributed the detection of this baffling AIDS epidemic to the work of a private investigator. Is it not true that the investigator was more instrumental than the police department in taking notice of this case?"

The Judge roared, "No, that's absolutely not true. The police were already working this case long before my niece hired the private investigator. In fact, they began working this case on the night that Todd Stevens was shot. They've uncovered a great deal more information than the investigator has."

The same woman asked, "What information might that be, Judge Farnsworth?"

"I'm not at liberty to discuss any information with you, nor do I possess all of their findings. Suffice it to say that I couldn't be happier with the progress that the police department has made. I loathe standing here watching you all making unfounded assumptions and erroneous insinuations. You ought to be ashamed of yourselves! That's all that I'll say at this moment. Good afternoon." The Judge stormed from the podium.

Lacy wondered what had made the Judge suddenly defend the police department. She did remember this morning that egret had given egret-ette credit for uncovering the story, but she must have been feeling too bad to be pissed off. Well, maybe Chet would get his panties out of the giant wad they were in. Oh, shit. Sharon was probably still on the line.

"Sharon? Are you still there?" she asked.

"I'm here. I thought you might like to hear that. Before I called you, he was saying how you were at home recovering after a shooting incident and still working hard on the case. Your reputation is looking pretty good," she said, softly.

"I wonder what made him call a press conference?" Lacy asked.

"I don't know. Did you talk to Shelly today?" Sharon asked.

"Hell, no, I didn't talk to Shelly today! I had nothing to do with this!" Lacy snapped.

"I wasn't implying that you did. It was merely a question."

"Well, then, the answer is no."

"Okay. Are we still on for this evening?" Sharon asked.

"This evening?" Lacy asked, puzzled.

"Yes. Remember, you wanted to come by and see what a sterile docking device is?"

"Oh yeah. No, I don't think so. I've turned up a whole new set of mysteriously acquired HIV cases in San Francisco that I need to check into."

"Oh, God, you're kidding! Can you do that?" Sharon asked.

"What?"

"Check into California records?"

"I've already gotten the information from the CDC with a subpoena, so yes."

"How did you know about those? Do you think they're related?" Sharon asked.

"Yeah, I do. It seems that our guy may have worked in a blood center in San Francisco before he came to Atlanta."

"You learned all of that today from home?"

"Yeah," Lacy replied.

"Well, Lacy, the Judge is right; you are one resourceful officer."

"Thank you, I like to think so. Did you say you were working tomorrow?"

"Yes, I am. Would you like to come then instead?" Sharon offered.

"Yeah. I'm pretty sure I'm going to spend the evening calling folks in California and asking if they received a blood transfusion."

"No problem. I'll give you a call in the afternoon then." Sharon said.

Within moments of hanging up the phone, it rang again. Lacy answered only to find that it was some dipshit reporter. After several "no comments," she hung up on the woman. Almost instantly, the phone rang again. Lacy decided to let the machine answer for her. It was another reporter. Shit. Maybe she'd take it off the hook. Now how in the hell could she do that if she were going to be calling people in California? Sometimes she wondered about herself. The third time the phone rang, it was Chet. She was glad she had decided to let her answering machine pick up.

"I don't know how you did it, Lace, but I'm impressed. We look pretty good now, thanks to Judge Farnsworth.

I'm sorry I was such a jerk earlier. I'll call you again later when I get home to tell you about the fingerprint results. Take care."

The fourth call was her friend James.

"Lacy? You go, girl! I heard about you kicking ass and taking names. I bet you get a key to the city. This calls for a celebration. Give me a call."

Lacy decided to take the phone off the hook until she devised her line of questioning. At this rate, she'd never get anything done.

Two hours later, Lacy confirmed that sixteen of the eighteen people she contacted had received a blood transfusion between 1990 and 1992. A couple of them had read about the cases in Atlanta and were planning on talking to their doctors about that possibility. All were happy that finally perhaps their questions were being answered. Lacy went to the bathroom and noticed that she had a bright red ear from her extended phone usage. It was quite the contrast to the pallor of the rest of her face. As the phone rung, she thought it would probably be Chet, so she answered.

"Lacy? I'm glad I finally got through. I've been calling you for the past two hours, and I thought you'd taken the phone off the hook."

"No, actually I was on the phone with eighteen people who live in California who had gotten AIDS and nobody could figure out how. Guess what? Sixteen of them received a transfusion during the time our guy was working out there at a blood center."

"Man. I wonder if there's any end in sight," Chet sighed.

"I don't know. Okay, so tell me about the fingerprints."

"Mikey was able to uncover a complete set of right hand prints. He thinks that the suspect was holding the application still with his right hand while writing with his left. That means our guy is a leftie. He ran the prints through AFIS and got no matches."

AFIS was the Automated Fingerprint Indexing System. Lacy had hoped that they would get lucky and get a match.

"Lacy? I'm sorry I was a jerk earlier," Chet said sincerely.

"Yeah, you said that on my machine," she replied.

"I know, but I wanted to tell you again. I'll apologize to Snow the next time I see him," he teased.

Lacy smiled a bit at that image.

"It's okay, Chet. I screwed up and you reacted. Well, you overreacted. I guess if I'd been down at the station all day *instead of at home petting my cat,* I would've been pretty tightly wound, too."

"Geez, I'm sorry already! Do you still want another partner?"

"Nah, it would be my luck I'd get partnered with one of the D-Team," Lacy joked.

"Good. Hey, are you coming back tomorrow or are you going to stay there?"

"I'm not sure. I seem to be making some headway here. Why? Did Sumlin ask?"

"No, I did. I was going to offer to pick you up if you wanted me to," Chet said.

"I'm not sure. Why don't you give me a call before you leave in the morning and I'll see how I feel?"

"Okay. I guess we'll be turning this over to the FBI tomorrow."

"I suppose," Lacy said reluctantly.

"Great. The sooner we're off this case, the better. Have a good night," he said.

Hanging up the phone, Lacy was glad that Chet no longer seemed pissed off at her. It was difficult to work under such strained conditions. She realized that she hadn't fed either Snow or herself yet, and the phone rang again as she stood to do so. She didn't answer. It was her mother. She'd heard about that Judge saying 'nice things' about Lacy earlier. Had she forgotten to call her mother about Brother Morrison's funeral? She really should plan on attending. Oh, and had that Judge said something about her having been shot?

As soon as the tirade had ended and her mother hung up, after reminding her of the sacrifice she was making by talking on the answering machine, Lacy turned the ringer off and walked toward the kitchen. Snow wove between her legs, making the short trip from the bedroom about twice as long as usual. There was still some leftover pizza for Lacy and a partial can of tuna for Snow. It had been a long day, but it seemed to be ending rather well.

Putting the remainder of the tuna down for Snow, Lacy put two slices of pizza in the microwave and poured herself a glass of Diet Coke. She watched Snow's ears slick back at the beeping sound coming from the microwave and realized that she and the cat were soul mates. Each had little tolerance for anything remotely annoying. She took a bite of the pizza and immediately spit it into her napkin.

"Shit, that's hot! How in the hell can I burn my mouth on something that I only warmed up for twenty seconds?" she asked. Snow had no sage answer.

Pulling her pizza apart so that it would cool faster, she ran her tongue along the little rooftop blister inside her mouth. Son of a bitch! She did that almost every time she ate pizza. How in the hell could someone in their late thirties not learn from experience? Sighing, she decided to make a to-do list for tomorrow while her dinner cooled.

- Get Homer a cell phone
- What about giving the media the suspect's photo?

- Go to work with Dr. West to see device thing
- Hand case over to FBI

The last entry caused her to recognize the growing feeling of regret. She hated starting a case and getting this much done, only to be kicked aside by the damned Feds! Why couldn't she work the Atlanta end of the case and Deputy Riker et al work the San Francisco end? Maybe just for a couple of days, until the photo was released to the press, and they could see if any leads turned up? She'd have to ask Sumlin in the morning if that was in the realm of possibility. She doubted it, though, since he was always afraid of stepping on Federal toes. Still, she could ask.

Chet would be pissed off if they continued working the case. Normally, he enjoyed finishing what he started as well, but in this instance with the hype surrounding the case, whoever worked it would be expected to make headway at supersonic speed. Maybe she could work with the FBI on the case and Chet could handle any new cases that they were given. She couldn't wait until morning when she could call Sumlin and see where she stood on this case.

After finishing her pizza, she brushed her teeth and went to bed. Snow had already beaten her to bed and was lying on top of her pillow.

"Uh-uh! Nope, I don't think so," she said to the cat.

Picking the cat up, she gently placed him on he other side of the bed and went to turn the light off. As she reached for the light switch, she looked back only to find that he had gotten back on top of her pillow. Damn, cats were fast! They were stubborn, too. Sighing, she decided that she would just move him when she got into the bed.

"Okay, I get the pillow and you get the other side of the bed. Got it?" she said as she scooted the cat over and crawled under the covers.

She felt him pacing around next to her before he finally lay down and began purring. Yeah, that was much better, she thought. Still, she knew she would awaken with a furry white feline head wrap. In her final thoughts before sleep came, she felt happy that she'd be seeing Sharon the next day.

CHAPTER 24

Lacy awakened earlier than usual and decided to call Chet and tell him she'd be working from home another day citing continued soreness as the reason. In reality, she didn't want to see him pouting at her all day while she dogged the Captain about letting her keep working on the case. Taking her chances that he'd be in, she called Sumlin's office number.

"Homicide Division, this is Captain Sumlin."

"Hey, Captain, it's Lacy."

"Detective Fuller! Great work on the Stevens case. I was going to call you sooner, but I thought you might be resting. How are you feeling? Chet said you were better."

"I am, but I think I'll stay home and work the case for at least another day."

The pause at the other end confirmed Lacy's suspicions; the case was going to the FBI, and she would no longer be involved.

"Well, Fuller, I know how you like closure on your cases, but since you turned up the California link, we'll be turning it over to the FBI," he said bluntly.

"Don't you think we could wait a day or two? I was thinking that if we give this guy's photo from his ID badge at Metropolis to the media, we'll be able to get a real name on him. I mean, he lived in the Atlanta area for at least a couple of years. Surely somebody knows him by his birth name and not just as Alfred Owenby," Lacy pleaded.

"I've already turned his picture over to the media. In fact, they're showing it all over the early news this morning, and it's in the Atlanta paper."

"Great. So, why can't we work the case a while longer before bringing in the Feds?"

"You know why, Lacy; this case spans at least two states."

"I know. I'm the one who discovered that. All I'm asking is that we work the Atlanta cases and SFPD work the California cases. Just give me twenty-four hours, Captain."

"I can't, Lacy. We've got to do everything possible to get speedy resolution in this case. You, Chet, and a handful of detectives in San Francisco won't wield the manpower that the FBI will be able to put into this. You want to see this case solved quickly, don't you, Lacy?"

No, she thought. I want to drag my ass around while dozens more innocent people potentially fall victim to a maniac! What the hell kind of question was that? She needed to keep the annoyance out of her voice if she held any hope of being allowed to work closely with the Feds.

"Of course I do, Captain. It's just that—"

"Well, so you agree that the most expedient manner in which we can investigate this is by giving it to the FBI?" he interrupted.

"Not necessarily."

"Well, it's out of your hands now, Fuller."

"Can't I work with the FBI on this?"

"You've got plenty of cases here, Detective."

"We've almost closed the T-Bone case. That and the Stevens case are the only open ones that Chet and I have at the present time, other than the cold cases."

"Not true. Just this morning I left a new folder on Avery's desk. There was a body found in a kudzu patch off I-20."

"I want to work this case, Captain. Chet can work the kudzu killing."

"We haven't determined yet if the kudzu case is a homicide. The autopsy will be performed this afternoon," he said.

"That's all the more reason why I shouldn't be pulled from this case!"

"Alright, Lacy. I'll ask the lead agent for the FBI if you can help them out. The team is due to arrive at 8:00."

Help them out? Lacy was incredibly pissed off at the Captain. Still, that was more of a concession than he'd made yet, so she decided to play nice, as Chet always said.

"Okay. This means a lot to me, sir."

"I know. I'll see what I can do. How do you think you can help them while you're home in bed?"

"Maybe the same way that I turned up all of the other leads that I've managed to uncover while I've been at home! Besides, I'll be back tomorrow. I could even come back today if that's an issue."

"Nah, stay home. I'll run it by the Feds when they get here and call you when they leave."

"Okay. Thanks, Captain."

As she hung up the phone, Lacy wished like hell that she could go jog. Usually, a nice long run would alleviate the anger and tension she felt after less than satisfying encounters like this one. Snow hopped up on her lap and stared at her. As she petted him, she turned on the television until she found a local early newscast featuring the suspect's photograph.

The familiar young, pudgy face with dark curly hair and glasses from the Metropolis ID badge was taking up the entire screen. Beneath the photo was the title "AIDS Assassin?" Just great! What if this wasn't their guy? Lawsuit city! Oh, well, she couldn't help that. A telephone number was flashed on the screen in case 'anyone had any information as to the identity of this man,' and Lacy noticed that the number was *not* that of the Atlanta PD. The case had already been passed along to the FBI.

Lacy paced the apartment for the next two hours waiting for the Captain's 8:00 meeting to be finished so that she could learn where she stood on the investigation. When the phone rang, she answered it immediately. It was Chet.

"Lacy? What in the hell are you doing trying to stay on the Stevens case?"

"I just want to, that's all."

"Well, I don't. Got it? If you do this, you'll be strictly on your own," he said, irritably.

"I know."

"Personally, I think you're nuts for wanting this. You could walk away now and, after the Judge's glorification of you yesterday, your career would be made for life."

"I'm not interested in that, Chet. I'm not the one who has a wife and children to support. I just want to be in on the capture of this nutcase!"

"Well, it looks like you will be," he said.

"Really? Did the Captain tell you that?"

"No. He's still in his meeting. I got a call from a woman who claims that she's the guy on the news' wife. She asked to speak to you or me. I told her that we were no longer on the case, but she insisted. She wouldn't even give me her name, and she was calling from a pay phone. I took down the number and told her I'd call you."

"Huh, I wonder why she's asking for us? The phone number on TV doesn't belong to the Atlanta PD."

"I don't know, but I'm pretty sure she got our names from the press conference yesterday. Since you aren't *officially* off the case until Sumlin walks through the door in a few minutes, I decided to call you and give you her number. She said she'd only wait for thirty minutes at the pay phone. It's been five already."

After writing the number down on her notepad, Lacy thanked Chet and hung up. It was an area code that Lacy wasn't familiar with, but she didn't have the time to research where it was. On the third ring, a scared voice answered.

"Hello?"

"Good morning, Ma'am. This is Detective Lacy Fuller with the Atlanta Police Department. I understand that you called to speak with me earlier?"

"Yes, I did. I just don't know what to do. I watched the news, and they said that the picture of the man on there might be responsible for putting the AIDS virus into the blood supply. Is that true?"

"Well, that's what we're trying to determine. Could I have your name?"

"No, not yet. How sure are you that this guy was doing this?" the woman asked.

"Contaminating the blood supply? Well, until we're able to interview him, we aren't sure one way or the other. My partner said that this man is your husband?"

"Yes. He worked at blood centers in Atlanta, San Francisco and New York."

Oh, shit. New York, too? Lacy cringed at the thought.

Trying to keep the alarm out of her voice, Lacy said, "Well, it's important for us to find your husband so that we can talk to him. He might be innocent. It could be that someone is trying to set him up for this crime. Do you know where he is?"

"He probably did it," the lady said, sounding both tired and disgusted.

"Excuse me?"

"I said that he probably did it."

Lacy sat there for a moment unsure how to respond to the woman's statement.

"Ma'am? If you think your husband is capable of harming numerous innocent people, I would suggest that you not return home to him. If he even *thinks* that you've been in contact with the police, you're at great risk."

"I don't live with him. The girls and I moved out when he became so hostile. I don't know where he is."

"I'd like to help you, but I don't know what you want me to do. If you won't give me your name or your husband's name, and you won't tell me where he is, I don't know how I can be of any help to you," Lacy said, trying to keep the frustration from her voice.

"I don't know, either. Part of me wants to tell you, but I'm afraid he'll find out and do something to the girls. We have two daughters."

"I understand your concerns. I could arrange police protection for your family until he's caught."

"I'll have to think about it. I'm scared. I know he already hates me. Can I have a number where I can reach you later?"

Reluctantly, Lacy recited her cell phone number for the woman. Almost as an afterthought, she asked, "Why did you ask for my partner or me? Why not call the number on the television?"

"I'm scared of the Federal Government. I saw your partner on television yesterday, and he seemed nice, so I decided to call him. He said that he was no longer on the case, but that you were. You've been so nice to me, not at all pushy or threatening. I thought if I called the FBI, they wouldn't be so nice. They never are on television."

"You're probably right. I think it's called 'obstruction of justice' when a person neglects to give the authorities information that would be useful in solving a crime. The Feds get pretty angry about that," Lacy replied.

"I need to think about this, but I will call you back."

"Please do. I'll be waiting."

Lacy felt suddenly wired. This could very well be her ticket to staying involved in the case. *If* the woman was telling the truth, and *if* the woman called her back. Sighing, she called Chet and updated him on the outcome. She learned that Sumlin's meeting was over and that Chet had been asked by the FBI to hand in all of his information on the case. She was glad that she had a copy of almost everything at her apartment. She asked Chet if he was going to mention the call from the woman to Captain Sumlin.

"Actually, Lacy, I was just on my way out. I don't think I'll be seeing the Captain before I leave, and I'll probably be working on the road all day on this new case we got. Actually, I think I may have forgotten all about it because I'm so excited to be working this new case where I get to tramp around knee-deep in kudzu with poisonous snakes," Chet said.

Lacy knew that Chet was purposefully going to avoid Sumlin. She also knew that his evasive actions went against his ethical better judgment because he was such a straight arrow. She also knew that if Sumlin found out, he'd be royally pissed off.

"Thanks, Chet. I owe you."

"No problem. Stay out of trouble, Lacy."

"Stay out of snake dens, Chet. Bye."

Lacy resumed her pacing as she wondered when Captain Sumlin would call, if and when the mystery lady would call, and if she would be granted a role in the ongoing investigation. The front door bell startled her out of her pensive state. Looking through the peep hole, she saw a bouquet of flowers.

Opening the door, she quickly signed the receipt and retreated back into her apartment. She placed the enormous arrangement in the center of the kitchen table and quickly opened the card.

"Lacy, sorry to hear of your injury. Hope you are feeling well soon. Love to you and Snowpuff, Shelly"

Shelly Stevens? Well, that certainly was nice of her to send flowers, but Lacy sure hoped that nobody found out about it. Hell, Chet and Sharon were already so pissed off at her each time Shelly's name was mentioned that this might just send them over the edge. She hid the card in the cat book that Sharon had given her and started pacing again.

CHAPTER 25

Chris Frazier looked in anger and disbelief at his image on the television set. How had anyone figured out what he'd done? He knew it must be those damned detectives whom the Judge was lauding the previous afternoon. He also knew that it was just a matter of time before they traced his P.O. Box in Gainesville. He'd given the address to his and Justine's previous neighbor before he moved in case she wanted to find him and apologize for leaving. He knew now that he could never return to get any mail from that location so there would be no way for Justine to find him. He'd just have to find her, he thought. At least nobody had his real name.

None of this was ever supposed to happen. Just a few days before, he'd been exuberant when the mysterious HIV cases began coming to light. There had been enough fear generated by the public that he felt sure people would have become kinder and less bigoted about the disease. Now, his role in the cases had been uncovered and he was back to square one. No, he wasn't even to square one yet because he'd have to use an alias and a disguise the remainder of his life.

It was a good thing that nobody in Boca Raton had ever heard the name Chris Frazier. It was also a good thing that he'd significantly altered his appearance. Fortunately, thanks to the sizeable life insurance policy that Craig had left him the sole beneficiary of, he'd been able to dedicate a great deal of time to this cause since he no longer needed to work.

Initially, he'd thought his paranoia about being discovered had been ill founded. Still, he humored himself and lost sixty pounds, dyed his hair blond, and traded his glasses for tinted contact lenses. He'd always made it a point to criticize sun worshipers, yet he was a deep bronze color. He'd also begun taking supplements to increase muscle mass and decrease body fat. He worked out five days a week and had a firm, admirable body. He looked nothing like the pasty, chubby guy he'd once been. Hell, *he* barely recognized himself so he wasn't worried about others knowing him. He doubted even Justine could identify him.

Justine. Had she contacted the police? Had she been suspicious of him? She'd once said that he was becoming "obsessed" with public tolerance of HIV. What if she heard about that Stevens woman getting AIDS from a transfusion and knew that he had something to do with it? He thought he might need to track her down and ask a few questions.

Maybe she didn't have anything to do with it after all. Maybe it was the work of the detectives. Had he left that many clues? In retrospect, he could start to see the holes in his plan. Maybe instead of putting the virus into so many units of blood it would have been better to have just tainted a few.

He'd been uncertain that the virus would be viable in all of the units and had wanted to ensure enough cases for the public to recognize the existence of mysterious transmissions. That had been the reason for tainting 25 units at each of the three donor centers. He'd planned to work at a donor center in Florida and make it an even 100, but Craig, his brother and his source, had passed away. Now he was forced to question his prior reasoning since his plan had apparently been discovered.

He remembered telling Craig that the reason for his constantly drawing blood from him was because he was part of a team investigating a potential new anti-HIV drug. Craig had been so happy to help out, even though the imaginary drug was years away from approval and would be of no help to him. He remembered Craig saying that if he could just help one person fight off the ravages of the disease, his mission in life would be complete. Chris knew it would have disgusted Craig if he'd known the truth. Craig was such a gentle soul. Sometimes Chris felt regretful for having lied to his brother. Still, he was doing it for Craig's own benefit. Surely his brother would have been able to see that, wouldn't he?

Mixing his fourth screwdriver of the morning, Chris began wondering if there were any additional mistakes he'd made that could lead to his detection. He'd murdered a man in Savannah on his trip down and had stolen his identity. He was now Ralph Otott. He'd always hated the name Ralph and had subsequently wished that he'd had better luck in the identity theft department. He'd been Michael in San Francisco, George in New York, Alfred in Atlanta, and was now Ralph. He didn't think that the body of the real Ralph Otott had been discovered yet.

He thought about the Ford Taurus that he'd fled in on the day he left Atlanta. He'd sold it to a chop shop just outside of Gainesville because he knew some of Ralph

Otott's trace evidence was inside in spite of the thorough cleaning he'd given it. To further cover his tracks, he'd decided to buy a foreign car. As Chris Frazier, he'd always prided himself on buying only American automobiles. As Ralph Otott, however, funded by a large sum of money from Craig's life insurance policy, he'd paid cash for a new Toyota Camry and paid for two weeks in an extended stay hotel in Boca Raton.

During that time, he opened a checking and savings account as Ralph W. Otott. On the day that his checks arrived in the mail, he put a hefty down payment on a two bedroom condominium unit and moved in. He hadn't made friends with anyone while he was there. When curious neighbors or the landlord asked about him, he replied that he was a writer of historical epics. He'd hoped that this would sound boring enough to stave off further inquiries. In most instances, that had proven to be true. Not so for his immediate neighbor, a World War II veteran who wanted to read some of his material.

Not wanting to call attention to himself, he copied a dull article about the French Revolution from the Internet and showed the man a sample of his writing. The neighbor had expressed his displeasure about Frenchmen, Communists, Nazis, Democrats, and various others in a twenty minute dissertation. He hadn't asked to see anything else written by Chris after learning he was a Democrat. In fact, he'd asked little else and hardly spoken to Chris since. He did, however, stare at Chris every time he saw him. Chris wondered if the old man would recognize the slight resemblance between his now lean face and the face being broadcast on CNN. If he had anyone to worry about, it would be this old man. Or perhaps Justine. Or those detectives. Maybe these people should meet with untimely deaths, he thought.

He was becoming agitated, a feeling he had too often these days when he consumed alcohol. Justine used to accuse him of becoming paranoid when he drank. Was he being paranoid about the neighbor? After all, the man had to be at least eighty and probably had lousy eyesight. Maybe the neighbor wasn't a threat, but he would have to find out more about these detectives and try to find Justine. Maybe he'd plan a little trip up to Atlanta and check things out.

Pouring straight vodka this time, he raised his glass and saluted his image in the mirror.

"You're wrong, Justine. A paranoid person wouldn't go to Atlanta with the police and FBI looking for them."

As he swallowed the chilled liquor, he could almost hear Justine's voice in one of her typical retorts: *No, Chris, but a crazy person would.*

He hurled the glass across the room and stalked out of his condo. He needed a walk to clear his head.

CHAPTER 26

Lacy was startled by the chime of her doorbell. The first thought she had was that it was the FBI coming to access her folder on the HIV case. She quietly walked to the door and, standing on her tip-toes, looked through the eyehole. It was Sharon.

Opening the door, Lacy gingerly hugged Sharon and invited her in. Snow sidled up next to Sharon's leg and began purring audibly.

"I think he likes you," Lacy said.

Bending to pet Snow, Sharon said, "I like him, too."

After several seconds of cat talk, Lacy finally said, "Don't teach him to expect cat talk, because it'll never happen with me."

Standing, Sharon playfully said, "Oh, you're just a stick in the mud!"

"A stick in the mud who isn't going to talk cat talk. So, to what do I owe this visit?"

"I decided that I'd come by and see if you needed anything on my way home from work. I also brought you some of my poetry."

"Oh. Does this mean the picnic is off for Saturday?" Lacy asked, disappointedly.

"No, not if you're up to it. It just means that I wanted to see you. We could still go on Saturday or you could come over to my house on Friday night with the rest of the family," Sharon said.

Feeling her heart skip a beat, Lacy tried to suppress an idiotic grin; the *rest* of her family?

"I'll think about it. Did you have a good night at work?" Lacy asked, trying to compose herself.

"Yes, it was actually pretty light stuff. Let's see, I had a patient with contact dermatitis, a few nausea/vomiting cases, and various and sundry other petty illnesses. I love nights like that. Some of my colleagues hate slow nights when there aren't any baffling cases or traumas, but not me."

"Why don't you go to work at an urgent care facility then?"

"Because I enjoy the excitement of saving lives. I think I'd get pretty bored treating the minutiae that the doc-in-the-box guys see every day."

"Yeah, I guess it would be like my not wanting to give up investigating homicides. I hate murder, but there's a certain thrill involved in the investigation of the cases."

"I think that's a good analogy," Sharon said.

"Would you like to sit down?" Lacy asked.

"Yes, I would. Wow, nice flowers!"

"They are, aren't they? A friend of mine sent them," Lacy said, being deliberately vague.

"Must be a pretty close friend. They must have cost over a hundred dollars," Sharon said.

Lacy didn't want to say that it wasn't a close friend, just a wealthy one for fear that Sharon would immediately conjure up the image of Shelly Stevens and get cranky again, so she simply shrugged.

"Hey, I saw your guy on the news this morning. He looked pretty harmless," Sharon volunteered.

"Well, he isn't. Didn't you notice his eyes? He has crazy eyes. That's how I found him so fast from the long list of employees. They had submitted photos of the employees, and I narrowed the list down to about twenty people. He was one of them."

"No, I didn't even notice his eyes."

"Well, I did."

"It's a good thing, too. So, the FBI is taking over the case then?"

"I guess so," Lacy said disappointedly.

"How do you feel about that? I mean, using another analogy, remember the little boy who has HIV whom I diagnosed the other day?"

Nodding, Lacy waited for her to continue.

"I'd like to know how he's doing, but he was transferred to a pediatric hospital. In fact, every time I have a patient whom I refer to another physician, I feel the regret that I'll probably not know the progression of their disorder. I was just wondering if it was the same with you."

"Yeah, I'm pissed as hell about giving the case to the Feds. I'm trying to get them to let me work with the FBI, but my Captain hasn't called back yet to let me know where I stand."

At that moment, Lacy's cell phone rang.

"Excuse me. I need to take this call," she said excitedly.

Unfolding the phone, Lacy answered.

"Detective Fuller? Hi. I spoke with you earlier about my husband. I've decided to tell you everything I know. My name is Justine Frazier."

"Justine Frazier? Your husband's name is ..." Lacy said, scrambling for a notepad.

"Chris Frazier. He had a brother named Craig who died from AIDS. Chris was always close to his brother, and he went crazy after his death."

"When did Craig die?" Lacy was busily scribbling down the information that Justine was giving her.

"Last July."

"Some of these cases are several years old, so I don't think he suddenly lost it when his brother died," Lacy said.

"No, I guess not. He'd always seemed normal until then, though."

"In what way did he change?" Lacy asked.

"I first noticed it when he was so angry with me for not letting our daughters visit Craig when he was so sick. I didn't want them to be exposed to anything. I didn't think that they would get AIDS, but that wasn't all that Craig had. He was always coughing and had awful looking sores on his body. After Craig died, Chris accused me of being narrow minded and homophobic. Craig was gay, you see. Chris was always screaming at me saying that I didn't understand and that I was no better than they were."

"Who would 'they' be?" asked Lacy.

"I think he meant the general public. I remember the last argument we had, just before I moved out, he said that it would be okay because one day *they* would change their minds."

"Who was he referring to?"

"Well, it was another argument on the public's lack of compassion toward AIDS patients, so I assume it was in reference to that. That's why I'm pretty sure he's behind this thing."

"So you think he was trying to prove to the public that anybody can get AIDS, not just homosexuals?" Lacy asked.

"I think so. He used to take Craig to his appointments and come home angry at the people in the doctor's office because they weren't kind to his brother. He said people would actually sometimes picket the AIDS clinic with signs that it was 'God's will' and other derogatory messages about homosexuality. Craig never seemed to let it rile him; he would just look sad and tired."

"You mentioned before that Chris had worked for a blood center up in New York. Do you remember the name of it?" Lacy asked hopefully.

"Yes, it was Liberty Donor Center. Why don't you know his name if you had his photograph?" Justine asked.

"Well, when he worked in Atlanta he used the alias Alfred Owenby. When he worked in San Francisco, he used the alias Michael Dunn. Does either of those names mean anything to you?"

"No. I've never heard either of them before. Who were those people?" Justine asked uneasily.

"As of now, Mr. Owenby is listed as a 'missing person' and Mr. Dunn washed up in the San Francisco Bay in 1992."

"Oh, no. Do you think he—"

"That your husband is responsible for what happened to them? At this stage, yes, I do."

"Oh, God. He really is crazy. I used to joke around and tell him he was crazy because he would get these paranoid thoughts and say and do irrational things. I didn't actually think that he was crazy."

"Well, I'd say that if he knows where you are or that if he could find you in any way, you need to move and/or seek police protection until he's been captured."

"I'm in Mississippi. We've been here since we left him. The cost of living is lower here, and I wasn't asking for child support. I was actually afraid that he'd find me."

"Do you have relatives in the area? If you do, he could still find you pretty easily," Lacy replied.

"No, my relatives live in Louisiana. It's only about a forty minute drive to their place, so I drop the girls off with my mother on the weekend. I work the weekend shift at a hospital in Louisiana. After my shift is over on Monday morning, I take the girls back to Mississippi. I don't think he could find me."

"Well, if he staked out your mother's house, he could, especially if he picked a weekend for his surveillance."

"I hadn't thought of that," Justine said in a scared voice.

"Will you give me your phone number and address now? I can contact the authorities and arrange for protection for you."

After writing Justine's information down, Lacy advised the woman to go home and wait for her to call.

Hanging up her cell phone, Lacy noticed the puzzled expression on Sharon's face.

"I thought you were off the case," she asked.

"Well, the suspect's wife called this morning and wanted to talk to either Chet or me. Chet passed her along to me."

"Have you told your boss yet?"

"No, I'm actually waiting for him to get in touch with me."

"And you're afraid if you call him, you'll get pulled from the case, so you'll just wait until he calls. In the meantime, what are you going to do with the information?" Sharon asked.

"I'm not sure. I've got the name of the blood center in New York that he worked for. Oh, shit; I forgot to ask when he worked there. I guess I'll call the CDC and inquire about HIV cases in New York and do the same thing I did yesterday for the San Francisco cases. I'm going to do as much as possible until I'm officially removed from the case," Lacy said determinedly.

"It sounds like you've got a pretty busy day ahead of you. Will you be too busy to come to the hospital tonight?" Sharon asked.

"No. I'm going to make time for that tonight. If they try to pull me from the case, I can argue that I have technical knowledge of a possible means of blood contamination. That knowledge and the fact that Justine Frazier is willing to work with me might be my only two bargaining points for staying on this case."

"Good luck. Call me if you change your mind; otherwise, I'll be by to pick you up around 6:30," Sharon said.

"Okay. Thanks for the visit. It was a nice surprise."

"Good. I enjoyed it, too."

After a quick kiss on Lacy's cheek, Sharon left. Lacy put her hand to the spot where Sharon's lips had just been. Suddenly, a strange chewing sound brought her back to the present. Looking over to the kitchen table, she saw a contented Snow happily devouring a green leafy item in the floral arrangement.

"Aaank!" she said.

Where the hell did that sound come from? That was the sound her mother made when Lacy was young and got too close to something dangerous. Scooping the cat up and into her arms, Lacy remembered Brother Morrison's funeral. It was tomorrow, her mother had said. Sighing, Lacy resigned herself to give her mother a quick call to find out the details.

After the usual disquieting conversation with her mother, Lacy learned that the funeral was at 4 pm, which meant that she would have to leave by 1 pm to get there on time. She wondered if her ribs were up to the long drive to and from the cemetery. If Sharon wasn't working tonight, she would have asked her to take her. She might still ask her, just in case. It would certainly make the trip more pleasant.

After an hour of impatiently waiting for Sumlin to call, Lacy decided she had to do something, so she walked a few blocks away to a mobile phone store. She purchased Homer a plain phone with basic services. Maybe she could get Sharon to drive by his lot on their way to the hospital this evening. Suddenly, Lacy realized that she was beginning to count on Sharon more than she ever had another soul. The realization brought a smile to her lips.

CHAPTER 27

Captain Sumlin finally called Lacy at noon. *"Lacy? I've*
got good news. The FBI is willing to let you work with
them on this case. There'll be a task force meeting tomorrow morning at 8 am."

Relieved, Lacy said, "Thank you, Captain. I've also
got some news for you. The suspect's name is Chris
Frazier. His wife called me this morning."

Before she could continue, her boss said, "Yeah, the
FBI has already discovered his identity. Did you refer the
wife to the Feds?"

"No. She said she only wanted to deal with me."

"She doesn't have any say in the matter, Lacy," Sumlin
said forcefully.

Trying to keep the annoyance from her voice, Lacy
continued, "She said her husband worked for a blood center in New York. I was just about to get in touch with them
when you called."

"Let the FBI handle this, Lacy. They can accomplish
much more than you can in a lot less time."

Sullenly, Lacy agreed and informed the Captain that
she'd be at the meeting the next morning. Hanging up the
phone, Lacy felt strangely disappointed. Sumlin hadn't

LEE KELLY

even told her that she'd done a good job, not that she re-
lied on accolades.

Unable to think of anything more that she could
do from home on the case, Lacy sat down and opened
Sharon's large notebook of poetry. For the next hour, it
seemed that time stood still. Lacy was so engrossed in the
bittersweet words that she was moved to tears. That was
the second time in as many days that she'd felt emotional.
She knew it wasn't PMS because she'd just finished her
cycle the previous week. Still, reading the poems, many
of which were about lost love, made her feel a bit like
Homer had made her feel the previous day when he'd said
she was like the daughter he never had.

Thinking that she needed to compose herself, she
once more heard the chewing sound and had to pull the
cat away from the flowers. Taking the bouquet, she tried
putting it atop the refrigerator only to discover that there
wasn't room for the taller flowers. Next, she tried the
closet in the hall, only to be discouraged by the multitude
of crap on the floor. Finally, she decided on storing the
bouquet in the bathroom and closing the door. Great, she
thought; the first bouquet I've ever received and I have
to hide it in the bathroom to keep it away from a nosy-
assed cat! Looking over at the expression on Snow's face,
she wondered again if cats had ESP. Sighing, she sat back
down in her recliner and returned to the book of poetry.

When she finished the last of the poems, she wanted to
call Sharon and tell her how wonderful her writing was,
but she figured she would only wake her up. She'd be
able to tell her on the drive to the hospital that evening,
anyhow. The poetry made Lacy wish that she knew more
about Sharon's past. Many of the poems were about the
loss of a loved one, both due to divorce as well as death.
She knew she'd lost her mother, but had there been anyone

else special whom she had lost? Had she ever been married? It bothered Lacy that she didn't know more about this lady with whom she believed she was falling in love.

No sooner than she had that thought, she suddenly felt a strong panic overtake her. How could she be falling in love? Had she ever been *in love*? She didn't think so. She'd never said the words "I love you" to anyone. She'd cared for a few women intensely, but this was different. The way she felt about Sharon made all of the feelings she'd ever known seem trivial by comparison.

How could she have overlooked the classic signs that she was falling in love until now? She thought back over the course of the past few weeks and how their paths had intertwined, all because of Shelly Stevens. She thought of the many nights since then that she awakened thinking of Sharon and feeling as if her chest had a ten ton weight upon it. She thought about the pleasure she took in the gentleness of the affection the other woman showed her. She thought about the little charge of electricity she felt when she and Sharon touched. Last, she thought about the fact that Sharon was more than likely straight and would be mortified if she knew how Lacy truly felt.

With a sigh, she turned back to what she believed was her favorite poem in the collection. She wasn't certain, but she thought it was about a young, gay man dying from AIDS. She felt that the man in the poem had been a living person because the words were too intense to have been based solely on fiction. She would have to ask Sharon who Joseph was later this evening. She began to read the poem again, aloud.

For Joseph (1961-2001)

Each breath I take a labored chore
With each I fear there will be no more

So much undone, so much unsaid
My body longs to get out of bed.
It was not so long ago I felt
I could overcome this hand dealt
Through nutrition, exercise, and mental frame
This beastly disease I'd surely tame.
Until I so weakened from its course
That each word spoken I had to force
I lay here still, my mind runs free
Basking in what used to be.
No longer bitter, I've come to terms
With my demise as society squirms
Uncertain how to deal with those
Who ail, they feel, from a life they "chose."
Don't pity me, don't hate me
Oh, lover, don't forsake me
I feel my suffering is part of some plan
Pray help mankind to understand.
I feel, I ache, I cry, I need
I long for love and to be freed
I will see the land where honey flows
And smell the garden where goodness grows.
Remember me kind, loyal, and true
Gentle to all, hurting so few
Someday I hope to look down and see
Understanding gained because of me.

Lacy thought that she knew now why Sharon's mother hadn't hung most of the poetry on the wall; it was just too damned sad! Not only that, it seemed to suck the energy right out of Lacy. In fact, she'd just about decided to take a little nap when her phone rang.

"Hello?"

"Lacy? Hi. This is Tyrone Stewart."

"Hi. Have you abandoned the 'Shroom' handle?" she inquired.

"Yeah, I guess so," he replied.

"If you don't mind my asking, why were you called 'Shroom'?"

"T-Bone named me that because I was always so protective of Mama and Cicely. He said it was like I was a big umbrella keeping them safe."

"I guess umbrella or parasol wouldn't have been too cool as a nickname, huh?" Lacy joked.

"No, I guess not. I was just calling to let you know that Mama is home and doing fine. Cicely has been bugging me about letting her come back over to visit you and to go see Homer. Mostly, I wanted to thank you again. You didn't have to do all that you've done for us."

"You're welcome."

"I hate to ask another favor of you, but were you serious about helping me find a job?" he asked hopefully.

"Yes, I was," Lacy replied.

"I don't want what happened to T-Bone to happen to me. I've stashed some money away, enough to pay for Mama's dialysis for a while longer. Hey, why haven't you turned me over for selling drugs?" he asked.

"I was hired to track down T-Bone's killer. Granted, if I hadn't met your mother and Cicely, I would have turned you over to the Narcotics Division. As it is, nobody has asked me about you, and I've not said a word. If you can turn your life around now, you've got a chance to make something of yourself."

"Thank you, Detective," he said softly.

"I think there's a position in our vehicle service bay. You'd be washing police cars, gassing them up, cleaning the interior, that sort of thing. It pays a little above minimum wage, but the benefits are the same as I have, and they aren't too bad. If you don't mind cleaning up vomit, I'd say it's a pretty good job. You won't be making what you were selling drugs, but at least you won't get arrested," she said.

"Okay. How do I apply?"

"Can you come by the station tomorrow?"

"Yes. What time?"

"Anytime would be fine. I'll put in a good word for you. All you'll need to do is fill out an application. Oh, could you pass a drug screen?" she asked.

"Yes."

"Are you sure?"

"Yes. I told you, I don't use drugs."

"Good. Well, fill out an application, and I'll see what I can do. Give my best to your mother and Cicely."

"Thank you, Detective."

"You're welcome, Tyrone."

The phone call left Lacy feeling good about herself. She quickly called Ted Barcher in Human Resources and put in a good word for Tyrone in case she forgot to later.

Thinking that it would be good to make all of her necessary phone calls, she dialed James' number at work.

"Hey, kiddo! It's Lacy. Got a minute?"

"Well, if it isn't my little heroine! So, did you get that key to the city yet?" James asked.

"No. I probably won't, either. I don't think they give those out if you're a police officer and you do your job. It would kind of be like giving a bank teller a key to the city for depositing a check," Lacy said drolly.

"Lacy, Lacy. You're so humble. Want to go out tonight?" he asked.

"No, thanks, James. I'm still sore as shit. I want to bask in a tub filled with Epsom salt and warm, soapy water."

"Okay, well just add a glass of Chardonnay, and I'll be right over!"

"No. When I think of relaxing, I don't think of naked men."

"Me either, Honey! There's nothing relaxing about naked men!" he quipped.

"Well, this conversation is going nowhere. I'm right in the middle of this case, and things are starting to heat up, so I may be out of touch for awhile. I just didn't want you to think I'd forgotten you."

"No problem, Lace. I'm used to playing second fiddle to your career," he joked.

For the next hour, Lacy perused her closet, finding something casual yet flattering to wear tonight when she went to the hospital with Sharon. After realizing that she'd neglected to tell Chet of his role in the scenario, she left a message requesting that he pick her up from Brookshire Medical Center at 8 pm.

Like clockwork, Sharon arrived at 6:15 to drive Lacy to Brookshire. On the way, they stopped by Homer's lot and gave him the cell phone. Lacy had programmed several telephone numbers for him and was grateful. Unfortunately, he then mentioned Shelly Stevens, and the moment had soured.

"Thank you, Miss Lacy. Between you and that nice Mrs. Stevens, I just don't know what I'm going to do. She's paid for my lawyer, and now she wants to pay for me an apartment! She said it was a favor to you," Homer explained.

Lacy noticed the scowl that had come over Sharon's face and hoped like hell Homer would just shut up. That was not to be.

"She's a nice lady. Everybody uses bad judgment at times," he continued.

Hoping a typical flippant, smart-assed remark would help her situation, Lacy drolly said, "Yes, but few people's poor judgment involves homicide."

"Yes, Ma'am. I'll give you that. I was just wondering what to do. I'd hate to have someone paying for me to stay in an apartment, but she said it would make her feel better."

Lacy didn't respond. After a few moments of silence, Homer finally changed the subject.

"The trial for those two kids is next week. That lawyer, Mr. Strausser, he's a strange one," he said.

"He reminds me of an egret," Lacy said, dryly.

"Yes, Ma'am! Thank you. I've been trying to figure out what he reminded me of, and I reckon an egret is about as fitting a description as any."

Lacy slowly got out of Sharon's car and stretched. She then spent the next five minutes showing Homer how to use his cell phone.

"We've got to go now, Homer. I'll call you tomorrow. Your phone should be up and running by then. If you want to call me sooner just to check it out, feel free," Lacy said, getting into the car.

"Thank you, Miss Lacy."

As Sharon pulled the Jaguar away from the curb, Lacy was aware of the tension that existed between them. She wondered why Sharon seemed to hate Shelly Stevens so much.

"Shelly Stevens is the one who sent the flowers, isn't she?" Sharon asked, icily.

"Yes."

"Why didn't you tell me?"

"Because you and Chet always get so pissed off at me anytime her name is mentioned and I'm getting pretty sick of it!" Lacy said defensively.

"So, why do you suppose she sent you flowers?"

"Because I had been shot, that's why! I was glad, too. Nobody else bothered to send me flowers! Hell, that was the first bouquet I've ever received," Lacy said.

Suddenly, the angry expression that had been on Sharon's face was replaced by a look of sadness.

"Really?" Sharon asked.

"Really, what?" Lacy answered irritably.

"That was your first bouquet of flowers, ever?"

"Yeah," Lacy said softening a bit.

"I'm sorry. I don't know what it is about that woman. Well, she can't be all bad if she sent you flowers."

After a few minutes of silence, Lacy decided to change the subject.

"So, who's Joseph?" she asked.

"I beg your pardon?"

"In your poetry, who's Joseph?"

Looking as if she'd just been slapped, Sharon waited a moment to respond.

"He was my friend."

"What happened to him?" Lacy asked.

"He died from HIV. He was alone. I wasn't even there for him because I was in Seattle for a medical conference," Sharon said sadly.

"I'm sorry."

"Thank you. I am, too. I take it you read my poetry?"

"Yes. It was wonderful. You have quite a way with words. It took my breath away."

"Thank you. It's a great way to unwind after a long night at work."

"I'm sure it is, if you have the talent."

"Well, I'm sure your photography is your outlet. By the way, you still have to share that with me. Have you given any thought to whether or not you want to come over on Friday or have the picnic on Saturday?"

"I think it'll all depend on what the task force is doing."

"So, you're still on the case?" Sharon asked.

"It looks that way, at least for now. Oh, and tomorrow

I have to drive down to south Georgia for a funeral. My former preacher passed away. I was actually going to ask if you could possibly take me, but since you're working tonight ..."

"What time tomorrow?" Sharon asked.

"The funeral is at 4:00. I'd need to leave by 1:00."

"Sure. I can do that. I don't think you should be driving yourself after your injury. On my first day off, I try not to sleep too late anyhow. I could still have at least a four hour nap, then pick you up. I might even see if I can get Earl Callaway, he's one of the dayshift doctors, to come in early for me. I'm sure he wouldn't mind. He and his wife just had twins, and he looks for reasons to arrive early."

"If it wouldn't be too hard on you, I'd appreciate the company and the support, not to mention the chauffeuring services." With a sigh, she added, "It's getting harder and harder to deal with my mother lately."

"Well, consider it done. I do have one request, though. Let's take my car. I love your little convertible, but I'd be afraid to drive it on the interstate."

"Not a problem; yours is more comfortable anyway."

The remainder of the ride to the hospital was spent in silence

Once inside the hospital, Sharon stopped by her locker in the ER staff lounge and removed two long, white lab coats. Handing one to Lacy and donning one herself, she then led the way to the blood bank department.

A happy-faced, heavy-set blonde woman who looked to be in her early forties greeted them as they entered the room. She reminded lacy of a smiley face. Three other workers sat in front of computer monitors and instruments that were making a great deal of noise, busily working. Lacy glanced around the large room and noticed several refrigerators filled with units of blood.

"Good evening, Dr. West. What can we do for you?" the smiley asked.

"Actually, I was wondering if you had any expired units I could borrow for a demonstration on the sterile docking device."

"We should. I'll check."

As the lady wandered toward one of the large refrigerators at the back of the room, Lacy pulled her digital camera out from her small gym bag.

"It's not going to be *that* exciting, my dear," Sharon joked.

"Well, it's all new to me, and I want to make sure I understand everything there is to know about this sterile thing."

"First, then, get the name right. It is called a sterile docking device," Sharon said.

Jotting the name down on a pad that had appeared from the bag as well, Lacy showed it to Sharon to confirm the spelling.

"Yep, you got it," Sharon verified.

At that moment, the smiley returned with a unit of blood and placed it on the counter in front of Sharon.

"Here you go. Do you need some aliquot bags or a syringe?"

"Yes, a syringe would be great. Thanks."

Sharon put on a pair of medical gloves and took the large syringe from the tech, thanking her for her help. Taking that as her cue of dismissal, the woman retreated to a fourth work station and began typing on her keyboard.

Sharon took the unit of blood and held it in front of Lacy.

"Okay, take a picture of the unit of blood," she directed.

Lacy complied.

"Now, this long piece of tubing in the center that sticks out at the top? There used to be another bag attached to it.

While that other bag was still in place, the unit was spun down and the plasma portion removed, like I was telling you about the other day. We won't go back into that unless you just want to."

Lacy nodded in declination.

"Good. Okay, so remember I told you that if anyone tried to tamper with the unit in a non-sterile manner it would be evident?"

"Yes," Lacy replied.

"Okay, so that's where the sterile docking device comes in," Sharon said, pointing to a plastic instrument the size of a shoebox. "If you take the long plastic tail and lay it inside one of the grooves on the docker like this, you can take the plastic tail from these specially made syringes and place it in the groove on the other side, like this. Okay, take a picture now."

Lacy took a couple of photos of the layout.

"Now, when you press *start*, these two plastic tails are moved toward each other, and a heated copper wafer is pressed upward, thereby effectively melting the plastic. The tails are aligned and sealed together so that, when you remove the unit, it's now attached to the syringe like this."

With that, Sharon removed the unit of blood and, sure enough, there was a syringe attached where there had been none previously. Lacy took a photograph.

"So, I'm thinking that if this guy had put the HIV serum into a syringe, he could have done so by using a sterile docking device, then nobody would have been the wiser," Sharon said.

"Okay, I don't get it. How would people not notice a syringe hanging off the end of a unit of blood? Do you attach them to the units of blood anyway?"

"No. This is mainly used for transfusion of neonates since they need only a small volume of blood at a time.

So, yes, people would notice a syringe *hanging off the end of a unit of blood* if it were allowed to remain there, which it isn't."

With those words, Sharon picked up a large handheld wand that somewhat resembled pliers.

"This is a heat sealer. By putting the tubing between these two hot plates inside the mouth of the sealer, you can effectively clamp down on the tubing and seal it off. Then, you just cut the tubing at the place where you've heat sealed it using scissors. When you are finished, you have a syringe and a unit of blood. The entire process is performed in a sterile fashion."

Lacy took a couple more photos, taking great care to get Sharon in the picture. Looking around, Lacy realized that a couple of the staff members were watching. Sharon glanced at the clock on the wall and shook her head.

"It's already five of seven. I've got to get going," she said.

The lady who had gotten Sharon her little demonstration items came back and retrieved them. Sharon wished them all a good evening, and she and Lacy headed back down the hallway toward the ER.

"Thanks for explaining that. I'm going to print photos of each step and give a brief narrative below as soon as I get home," Lacy said.

"It was my pleasure. I actually miss working in the laboratory sometimes. Oh, by the way, that's a clean lab coat. I know how you feel about germs, and I just wanted you to rest assured that it's clean. I always take home my dirty coats on my last day at work and launder them over the weekend. That one is a spare coat I keep here in case I get soiled," Sharon said.

Feeling unsure what to say next, Lacy thought about Chet and wondered if he could pick her up sooner. She thought it might be worth a try to give him a call and see.

"Okay. Well, thanks again. I'm going to see if Chet can come get me now."

Removing her cell phone from a little side pocket of the bag, Lacy was surprised to find Sharon's hand covering her own.

"You can't use cell phones inside the hospital. Come inside the lounge and you can use that phone," Sharon said.

Again, electricity shot throughout Lacy's body. She actually *knew* that cell phones were no-no's in hospitals, but she had apparently forgotten. Following Sharon into the purple Barney lounge, Lacy stood speechless. She hoped she didn't look as stupid as she felt. How could one simple touch render her completely defenseless?

"Lacy? Are you okay?" asked Sharon worriedly.

"Yeah. I'm just, uh, trying to remember Chet's home number. I guess I'll try him at the station first," she lied.

"Okay. Well, I've got to go. I'll come by your place by one."

"Would you mind coming by the department instead? I'm pretty sure I'm going in tomorrow."

"That would be fine. Meanwhile, you're welcome to hang out here as long as you'd like. You know, in case you can't get Chet. Take care, Sweetie."

With a quick kiss on the cheek, Sharon was out the door. Lacy looked down and remembered the lab coat that she was wearing. She decided that she could return it to Sharon tomorrow.

Chet, as it turned out, was still at work just hanging out, he said, until his chauffer services were required. The department was a ten minute drive from the hospital, so Lacy went outside the ER and waited for him at the ambulance bay. When he pulled his car up, he looked miserable. Red splotches covered his neck and arms. Atop the red splotches was a layer of pink, chalky paste.

"What in the hell happened to you?" Lacy asked.

"Poison oak," Chet said, miserably.

"How in the hell did you get poison oak? All you've been doing is working day and night."

"Exactly. That danged kudzu case. I'm just glad I only encountered poison oak and not poisonous snakes like I had feared. Oh, we closed the T-Bone case."

"Kick ass! So, who dunnit? The same guy who tried to off 'Shroom'?"

"Another drug dealer. It turned out that the phone call that T-Bone had gotten the night before he was shot was the guy who tried to kill your buddy Tyrone. He was beaten to the punch by this guy called Wesson, and I quote, 'yo, man, like the gun, not the oil' who had called T-Bone minutes before the shooting to set up a buy. Wesson had heard that T-Bone was blabbing names to the cops and shot him hopefully before his name could be released as a drug dealer. The little punk who formerly occupied your apartment complex is now probably glad to be imprisoned. The truth has come to light that he's the one finking on the other dealers, so he's asking for special safety measures in jail."

"*Finking*?" Lacy asked, amused.

"What would you have said?"

"Not *finking*. I'm not sure what, but definitely not that. Hey, do you think you could give me a ride to work in the morning?"

"I'd be glad to. It'll be nice to have you around again, Lace. I got so desperate today; I almost had to talk to one of the D-Team."

"Damn, Avery. Have you considered counseling?"

"I said *almost*. Seriously, it'll be nice to have you back. Oh, the Captain updated me on the AIDS Assassin case. He said you turned up the New York link?"

"Well, Chris Frazier's wife turned it up for me. Have they found out how many in New York yet?"

"I don't think so. I don't know. I tried to distance myself from the Captain when he began talking about the case. He said you're staying on?"

"Yeah, I don't know in what capacity, though. I've got to leave early tomorrow to go to a funeral in south Georgia."

Pulling up to Lacy's apartment building, Chet asked if she wanted him to go up with her.

"No, thanks, Chet. And they say that chivalry is dead!"

With a smile, Chet drove away. Lacy immediately began scratching imaginary facial itches as soon as he was out of eyesight. She hated whatever trick her brain played on her when she saw anyone broken out and *she* began itching. It was the same way when she drove through smoke or dust on the road. Despite the fact that the air in her car was clean, she felt the need to hold her breath until she drove through the offending cloud.

After feeding Snow and eating a sandwich, Lacy printed the photographs of her sterile docking device lecture and wrote a bit about each step. Yawning, she went to the bathroom to brush her teeth, only to be followed by Snow, who immediately found the flowers and began nibbling. She thought she'd need to ask Sharon why the cat was eating the flowers. Picking him up, she tucked him into the crook of one arm and closed the door with the other. After placing him on the bed, she turned the lights out and crawled in beside him. Even if he did eat flowers, it was nice to have someone to come home to, she thought. She'd even been thinking the last few days about keeping him.

CHAPTER 28

Chet arrived at Lacy's apartment building at 7:45 to find her waiting outside the front entrance, pacing back and forth with a garment bag thrown over her shoulder. She opened the passenger side door and got inside the car wearing a huge smile.

"Hey, Lace. What's got you looking so happy?"

"Just glad to be back doing my thing, you know? I hated missing work all those days."

"All those days? Lacy, it was less than a week."

"Well, it felt like a damned month!"

"What's in the bag?"

"Funeral clothes. I have to go to one this afternoon, so you won't need to take me home," she replied as her smile faded.

Pulling into the parking lot, she declined his offer to let her off at the door, opting instead to walk in from the parking lot with him.

Upon entering the Homicide Department, Lacy was greeted by several people who seemed genuinely glad to see her. Even both members of the D Team congratulated her on a job well done. Damn, she should get injured in the line of work more often, she thought. As quickly as the thought came, she suppressed it with the feeling that she had somehow jinxed herself in that one moment.

She went to Captain Sumlin's office only to find that he wasn't in. Chet had already begun his first excursion to the vending machines, so Lacy stopped by her desk long enough to pick up a pen and notepad before heading over to the meeting room. She wasn't looking forward to having to work with the FBI. Still, she was glad she was back at work and glad to be allowed to stay on the case.

As she walked into the room, she immediately noticed Captain Sumlin standing next to two well-dressed men. Great, she thought. Just because they were federal agents, Sumlin was looking like their shit didn't stink! She didn't recall having ever seen that particular expression on the Captain's face before, except perhaps when he was in the presence of the Governor or the Mayor. Next, Lacy noticed the agents' smug expressions and immediately thought that perhaps she had made a poor decision by deciding to stay on. Inhaling deeply, she began walking toward the group of men. Only when she was near did the Captain notice her.

"Ah, here she is! Gentlemen, this is our star detective I've been telling you about. Lacy? Meet Agent-In-Charge Harrison Shuttles and Agent Mark Herndon."

Lacy firmly shook hands with both of the men who merely mumbled that they were glad to meet her. She noticed a prevalent look of distaste on AIC Shuttles' face.

Sumlin said, "We'll have a seat now, gentlemen and turn the floor over to you."

With that, he grabbed Lacy by the elbow and began steering her toward a table at the back of the room. Walking past the other tables, Lacy counted a total of eight people whom she assumed were FBI agents as well. At one point, she tried to free her elbow of the Captain's grasp, but he was holding on tightly. After they were safely at their table, he finally released his grip on her. She was pissed.

"Jesus Christ, Captain, I wasn't going to haul off and deck anybody!" she whispered.

"What? Oh, that. This is their ball game; we're just here as pinch-hitters if they need us."

Lacy hated that Sumlin, ever the sports fan, incorporated a seasonal sports analogy into almost every situation. She'd be so glad when summer was over so they could at least move along to a football or basketball analogy.

"I thought I was staying on the case? How's that a pinch-hitter, Captain?" Lacy asked.

The noisy shuffling of papers and the sound of AIC Shuttles clearing his throat spared Sumlin from having to waffle an explanation for the time being.

Shuttles began, "This will be the last meeting we have at the Atlanta PD. In the future, we'll convene at the Bureau headquarters in Decatur. There hasn't been anything new to report since our summation last night. Mostly, this meeting was called as a favor to Captain Sumlin who would like us to meet Detective Lacy Fuller of the Homicide Division. She's the one who discovered the particulars of this case, and she's going to assist in our investigation. We'll provide her with a packet of information, but she'll be working out of the APD office rather than at Bureau headquarters. Agent Margie Olsen has been assigned as her partner."

Lacy glanced around the room and noticed that only one pair of eyes were on her. She assumed it must be Agent Olsen. She looked mousy. With a slight nod, Lacy returned her attention to Agent Shuttles.

"The reports from New York should be in by midmorning. Detective Fuller? I'll send a copy over to you when the information arrives. Meanwhile, I'll have Agent Olsen stay with you today and catch you up on everything we've learned. If there are no questions, I think we can be on our way."

Immediately, chairs were pushed back from tables and the whole Federal team was heading for the door, with the exception of Agent Margie Olsen. Lacy turned to Sumlin to continue her tirade only to find that he was gone as well. Shit.

"Detective Fuller? Hi, I'm Margie. It's a pleasure to meet you. You've done outstanding work on this case. I'm honored to be working with you. Actually, I asked AIC Shuttles if I could be assigned to work with you."

Puzzled by the woman's humble approach, Lacy wondered if she'd been too quick to judge the FBI.

"Thank you. I'm sure we'll get along fine."

"Yes. I have a packet of information for you, but I'm sure it's mostly stuff that you know already. Heck, it's mostly stuff that you uncovered yourself!" Agent Olsen said.

"Would you like to go over to my desk? I feel more comfortable there," Lacy asked.

"Sure."

Leading the way, Lacy found a note on her desk from Chet that said he was 'gone poison ivy collecting again' and wouldn't be back until early afternoon.

"Well, it seems my partner is out working another case, so if you'd like to use his desk, that would be fine," Lacy offered.

"Great. I understand you were hit the other day. Are you feeling better?"

"Yeah, I was kind of sore for a couple of days, but I'm pretty much better now. I should be able to jog again by Saturday."

"You jog? Me, too! Where do you jog?" Agent Olsen asked, enthusiastically.

"Piedmont Park. I live nearby."

"I usually jog at the Chattahoochee Nature Center. Hey, maybe we could jog together sometime?"

"Yeah, that would be great. I'll be right back. I have to use the restroom," Lacy said.

Walking away, Lacy thought that having this chipper, talkative, adoring woman in her vicinity could either make her happy or bug the shit out of her. Agent Olsen was somewhat attractive if you were into rodents. She was about 5'6", slender and athletic, brunette hair, brown eyes, and a genuine smile. After walking around the vicinity of the restrooms for a believable amount of time, Lacy decided she should go back out and talk to Agent Olsen.

"Okay, I'm back," she said.

"Great. Hey, is this your kid?"

Looking at the photo of CJ and Monica that had been on Chet's desk, Lacy wondered how in the hell the Agent had come to the conclusion that her partner would have a photo of Lacy's child and some mystery woman on *his* desk.

"No, that's my partner's wife and son."

"He's a cutie-pie."

"Yeah, so where's the folder?" Lacy asked impatiently.

"Here it is. I'll just sit here while you read it."

Opening the folder, Lacy was surprised by the lack of data. In fact, the only document present was a two-page memo from AIC Shuttles detailing all of the facts that Lacy had uncovered. She closed the folder and looked to see a smiling Agent Olsen staring back at her.

"There's nothing new here. I know all of this."

"I'm not surprised. I figured since it had been your case, you'd be familiar with the information we'd gleaned to date," Agent Olsen said happily.

"Yes, since I *am* the one who gave you guys all of the stuff you have gleaned to date." Lacy could hear the sarcasm in her voice.

"Exactly."

Okay, so sarcasm was totally lost on the woman. Lacy sighed and rolled her shoulders to hopefully quash the knots already forming there from the tension of working so closely with a dingbat.

For several moments, neither woman said a word. Lacy was about to ask Agent Olsen if she wanted to join her federal buddies at their office when her phone rang. It was Officer Gates from the ground floor.

"Detective Fuller? Hi, this is Ron Gates. There's a gentleman here to see you. He says he's an acquaintance of Chris Frazier, you know, the AIDS guy?"

"Yes, Ron, I know who Chris Frazier is."

"He wants to see you about the case."

"Did you refer him to the FBI?" asked Lacy.

"I tried, but it was a no-go. He said he'd only talk to you and nobody else."

"Okay, well, send him up."

As Lacy hung the phone up, she noticed the blank gaze on Agent Olsen's face. Oh, for God's sake!

"There's some guy downstairs who knows Chris Frazier, and he'd like to speak with me," Lacy said, trying to hide her annoyance.

"Great!"

Again, the two women sat and stared at each other until Detective Weaver of D-Team fame ambled over to them with a handsome man in tow.

"Fuller? This guy's here to see you. Says you're expecting him."

"I am. Thanks."

Without another word, Weaver wandered off and left Lacy looking at the young man. His face looked vaguely familiar. He had blond hair, blue eyes, and a great smile. Had she been straight, she would have been smitten for sure. Agent Olsen seemed smitten.

"Hello. I'm Detective Lacy Fuller. This is Agent Margie Olsen with the FBI. How can we help you?"

"Hi. I didn't want to talk to the FBI, if that's okay. It's not like I have anything major to tell you. I mostly was upset by what I'd seen on the news and wanted to talk to someone. I heard about how good you were, Detective, when the Judge gave his press conference the other day. Is it possible we could meet in private? No offense, Ma'am." He smiled shyly at Agent Olsen.

Agent Olsen blushed and stood to leave. She said, "None taken. I'll just wait outside in the conference room for you, Lacy."

"Okay. I'll get you in a little while," Lacy said.

Watching Agent Olsen leave, Lacy was glad for the interruption. Finally, when the woman was out of eyesight, Lacy turned to the man once more.

"Okay, now it's just us. I'm sorry, I didn't get your name?"

"It's Irving B. Kriell. My friends call me IB."

Shaking his hand, Lacy realized that he was even stronger than he looked.

"Would you like to sit down?" she offered.

"Yes, that would be nice."

As they sat in unison, Lacy noticed the deep tan that the man had. Skin cancer waiting to happen, she thought.

"So, you say you knew Chris Frazier?"

"Yes. Actually, I was great friends with his brother, Craig. He and I always hung out together."

Ah. That's probably why he looked familiar. If he was gay, she had more than likely seen him at one of the clubs in the city in her bar scene days.

"What exactly was the nature of your *relationship* with Craig Frazier?"

"He and I were friends, not lovers, Detective," Mr. Kriell said.

"I didn't mean to imply that I thought any differently. It was merely a starting point in the interview," she said calmly.

"I guess it's a touchy subject for me. The reason I came by is that I was thinking that sometimes Chris calls me when he's going to be in town. He usually doesn't stay with me, but I always know which hotel he's in. I guess I just wanted to let you know that in case he comes back to Atlanta. I could give you a call. That is, unless you're already about to catch him."

"I don't think so. He seems to have dropped off the face of the earth after his brother passed away," Lacy said.

"I like that you said 'passed away' instead of died. It just seems, I don't know, more reverent. You would have liked Craig. He was a wonderful guy."

"How about Chris?" she asked.

"Oh, he adored Craig."

"No, I mean, was he a wonderful guy?"

"I always liked him. He was supportive of Craig, especially when he came down with HIV. Chris was always there, taking care of him, even to the very end. Did you know that the last few weeks Craig didn't even know who Chris was?" Mr. Kriell asked.

"No. I don't know much about them at all. We've only just recently discovered his true identity."

"Well, I knew them both well. I was shocked, but not surprised, that Chris was doing this thing with the blood supply. Do you know what I mean?"

"I think so. That's the same thing that his wife said."

"You've talked to Justine?"

"Yes. She called yesterday," Lacy replied.

"Do you know where she is?" he asked.

"Yes, but I can't divulge that information."

"I wasn't asking for it. I was just going to tell you that Chris is still in love with her. Maybe you could use her as a decoy to flush him out of his hole?"

"Spoken like a true cop. What line of business are you in, Mr. Kriell?"

Removing a business card from his wallet, Lacy read that he was an Interior Designer.

Mr. Kriell said, "Heavens, not police work. I could never be a police officer! I just turn to jelly at the first sign of danger. No, leave me with my settees and armoires and I'm happy."

Lacy attempted to hand him back the card, but he shook his head.

"No, please, you keep it. If you need to reach me for any reason, my cell phone number is listed on it."

"Okay." Lacy tucked the card into the front pocket of her shirt.

"What do you think of my plan about using Justine as a decoy?"

"I think that the FBI might use decoys, but I don't. I never endanger a citizen in the pursuit of justice."

Looking deflated, Irving sighed.

"I guess you're right. I just want him to be caught quickly. Craig would have been so disappointed in him."

"Do you have any idea why he would be doing this?"

"Oh, absolutely. Craig got HIV from a transfusion of Factor VIII. He was a hemophiliac, you see. He was also gay. So, when he would go to the treatment centers, he was met with indifference at the best and disgust at the worst. Chris always felt that people assumed that Craig had gotten HIV from homosexual sex and treated him

poorly because of their bigotry. Every time someone
would imply that Craig had gotten what he deserved, it
would piss Chris off real bad. It got to where I would
take him to his appointments because Chris would always
leave the building in such a foul mood that it upset Craig."
I.B. Kriell paused and wiped a tear from his eye.

"Did he ever vocalize any of his plans to you?"

"No. I only know that he was upset with people because of their bigotry. Like I said, I was mainly Craig's
friend. I should be going now. I've got an appointment
that I can't afford to miss. I'll get in touch with you if
Chris calls me."

"I appreciate that, Mr. Kriell. Thank you for stopping
in. Let me give you my card. It has my work and cell
numbers on it, in case you need to reach me."

"It was my pleasure. I'll definitely be in touch if I hear
from him."

Watching the man walk away, Lacy couldn't help
but think that she had seen him before. Remembering
Agent Olsen, Lacy rose from her desk and went to get
her. Approaching the conference room, she heard singing;
off-key singing, and there wasn't even a radio. This was
going to be a long morning, she thought.

CHAPTER 29

Lacy had begun to think that 1:00 would never come. As it turned out, the documents hadn't been sent over from the cases in New York so Agent Olsen had sat at Chet's desk and prattled incessantly about the particulars of the case. She wondered what it said about her that she'd rather attend a funeral than have to continue listening to the agent. Finally, Lacy politely told Agent Olsen that she'd be leaving early to attend a funeral.

"Oh, no! Was it somebody you knew?"

Lacy wanted to say, *No, dumbass, I try to attend at least one funeral a week at random. That's how I get my kicks!* but decided against it.

"Yes. He was my preacher once."

"Oh. Well, that's nice."

Fighting the urge to ask what was nice about a preacher dying, Lacy excused herself to get a Diet Coke. When she returned, she was happy to see that Agent Olsen had packed up her stuff and appeared to be ready to leave.

"I'm going now. If you get back in time tonight, we usually have a summary meeting at around 8 pm if you'd like to come," Margie Olsen said cheerfully.

"Thanks. I probably won't be back by then. I'll be in touch with you tomorrow, though," Lacy said.

"Okay. Well, have a great day!" the agent said happily.

Yeah, funeral service attendance usually does make for a *great* day, Lacy wryly thought. Watching the younger woman exit the room, Lacy wondered if the FBI didn't have IQ qualifications for the position of Federal Agent. She knew that there were all sorts of physical examinations that had to be passed. She also knew that a college degree was a necessity. Still, Agent Olsen was an airhead.

By the time Sharon picked her up from the front of the building, Lacy had changed into a black dress and black sandals.

"You sure look pretty!" Sharon said, smiling warmly.

"Thanks. You, too," Lacy mumbled softly.

"Do you have directions?"

"Yes. We'll need to take I-85 South."

Sharon pulled onto the street and headed toward the interstate. She was surprised by the lack of traffic. Turning down the volume on her stereo, she asked Lacy if she wanted to change CD's.

"No. I have this one, in fact. I love Sarah Maclachlan. I just listened to this CD the other day."

Sharon smiled and said, "I bet you're one of those people who keep their CDs in the appropriate cases, aren't you?"

"Excuse me?" Lacy asked.

"Well, there are some people who just stuff their CD in any old case, and there are others who take care to always match the disc to the case."

"Which are you?" Lacy asked.

"Let's just say, this CD was in a Kathy Mattea case," Sharon confessed.

"I knew there was a reason we got along so well; opposites attract," Lacy commented.

The women laughed and sat in a comfortable silence for several minutes before Lacy said, "It's going to be a long drive. Why don't you tell me the story of your life?"

"Okay. What do you want to know?" Sharon asked.

"Well, everything. Basically, all I know is that you're a physician who has a nice family and loves cats and dogs."

"Okay. I was born in Alabama. I was a tomboy growing up. I used to wade through muddy creeks and go fishing all the time. Now, I wouldn't be caught dead doing stuff like that. I wanted to be a veterinarian until I found out that you had to put animals to sleep. That's when I decided I wanted to be a doctor, or a 'people vet,' as I called them. I had asked around and found out that doctors didn't have to euthanize their clients. Um, we owned horses. I used to ride at night a lot. I thought it was cooler for the horses, and it was just more pleasant. Are you sure you want to hear all of this?" Sharon asked.

"I asked, didn't I?" Lacy replied.

"Okay, but don't say I didn't warn you. I never missed a day of school until I was in tenth grade when I got mononucleosis. I had to miss two weeks, and it really bothered me. I graduated near the top of my class in high school and went to Auburn where I received my BS in Biology, again near the top of my class. I was accepted into Mercer's School of Medicine, and my family moved over here with me. We still have land in Alabama. We used to talk about moving back someday, but that probably won't happen. I married my high school sweetheart when I graduated from Auburn."

Lacy felt her stomach sink. Sharon was straight.

"What happened to your husband?" Lacy asked, feigning only mild interest.

"We just grew apart, you know? He was lazy, and I'd always overlooked that. Momma had some health issues, and Daddy was already in his seventies, so I assumed that Brian, that was my husband, would do things around their house to help them out. Well, he didn't. I was either working or in school more than eighty hours each week, and he only worked part-time. After I graduated, he started going out and staying late with friends while I worked. Eventually, we came to a mutual decision that we weren't in love with each other, and I filed for a divorce."

"Had you ever been in love with him?" Lacy asked.

"Funny you should ask that. Actually, no, I never was. I loved him because he liked cats, and he was sweet and witty. But I was never in love with him. It was never like it is in songs or in the movies. I'm not even sure that feeling really exists. How about you? Have you ever been in love?" Sharon asked.

"I'm not sure, but I think I've only loved, not been in love," Lacy replied.

"Forever is a pretty long time to want to stay with somebody. The next time I agree to commit, it'll be because I'm madly in love, not just because it seems like the next logical step to take in life," Sharon said.

Lacy wanted to ask if she thought that she could ever love a woman, but decided against bringing the subject up for fear of scaring Sharon off. She decided that she'd rather stay friends with Sharon and have her love unrequited than to risk losing her altogether.

"That sounds like a good plan. What's your proudest moment?" Lacy asked.

"That's an easy one. When I was five, I jumped in our lake and saved a drowning kitten."

"Wow, that's impressive. Was it yours?"

"Sort of. We lived on a farm and had a few feral cats that appeared and took up residence in our barn. One gave birth to a litter of kittens. It was one of those kittens. The neatest thing is that, eventually, after saving that one and taming him, the others began letting me pet them. Even the adults who had never let anyone near them. It was a gratifying experience. That's when I started thinking about being a vet. How about you?" Sharon asked, seeming to be enjoying the game.

"Running a marathon."

"My God! Isn't that, like, fifty miles?" Sharon asked, mouth agape.

"No, it's only 26.2 miles."

"Oh, well, *only* 26.2 miles. You ran the whole thing?"

"Yeah. That was just a couple of years ago. I was going to do it again last year, but I was working a case, and it broke wide open the day before. It was nice to know that I could run for that distance," Lacy responded.

"Well, I'm impressed. If someone told me that it would save all of the little animals in the world if I ran a marathon, I would sure give it a try, but there's no way I could do it."

Lacy was thinking that Sharon used animal references the same way that Captain Sumlin used sports ones, yet it didn't irritate her. At that moment, Sharon's purse began ringing loudly.

"Oh, that's my cell phone. Would you mind fishing it out for me please? I can never manage to find it before it stops ringing," Sharon said.

"Sure."

Unzipping Sharon's purse, Lacy felt as if she were trespassing or something. She'd never pillaged another woman's purse before. Still, it was by open invitation. Removing perhaps the smallest phone she'd ever seen, Lacy handed it to Sharon and put the purse back on the floor in front of her.

"Hello? Hey Jess! Are you at work? Oh. What's the matter? Oh, no, not Boop! That's terrible! When will you know? Is there anything I can do? God, that's just awful!"

Lacy was trying not to eavesdrop by looking out the window and listening to the music, but it was just no use. Sharon's voice had gotten far louder than usual, and Lacy couldn't tune her out. Apparently, something terrible had happened to someone named Boop. Lacy's mind conjured up an image of a cartoon character and wondered what had happened that seemed to be upsetting Sharon so much. She continued listening to the one-sided conversation.

"So that's the reason for the weight loss? I see. Well, there are some pretty good treatments out there. When will the biopsy results be in? Yeah, I know. Well, just let me know if there's anything at all that you need. Well, take care. I'll give you a call tomorrow."

Sharon's expression looked grim as she handed the phone back to Lacy.

"That was my friend, Jessie. You remember, the doctor I told you about who had also seen some unexplained cases of HIV at her hospital?" Sharon asked.

Nodding, Lacy returned the micro-phone to the inside of the purse. The continued silence caused Lacy to realize that Sharon couldn't see a nod if she was paying attention to the road in front of her, so she responded with an audible, "Yeah."

"Well, the last time I saw her she'd lost a bunch of weight. She said she hadn't been on a diet. Anyhow, they think she has BOOP."

"Boop is a thing, not a person?" Lacy asked confused.

"Oh, sorry. Yes, it's a pulmonary disease that can be difficult both to diagnose and treat."

"It's got a ridiculous name. You'd think that it would have a more serious name if it's such an awful condition."

"Oh, it's an acronym for bronchiolitis obliterans orga-nizing pneumonia."

Lacy sat there and thought she'd be royally pissed off if she were to get gravely ill from something that was nick-named BOOP. Other diseases at least were given the dig-nity of being named something dire-sounding. No matter how you said it, BOOP syndrome, BOOP disease, BOOP whatever, there was just no making it sound serious.

"Well, I'm sorry to hear that," Lacy volunteered.

"Thank you. I am, too," Sharon said softly.

As they rode along in silence, Lacy focused on the song playing on the car stereo. Sarah was singing about being in love with someone and not being able to share her feelings in her angelic voice with haunting musical accompaniment. How apropos, she thought, wondering what would happen if and when she told Sharon that she was falling in love with her.

The remainder of the drive was filled with small talk and little more. Lacy decided not to try returning to the game of 'let's get to know each other better' because it was obvious that Sharon was worried for her friend.

Giving Sharon detailed directions that she'd printed from the Internet, the two women found the church with no trouble at all. They had to park out in a field several hundred yards from the church because of all of the cars in the parking lot. Sharon wondered how that many peo-ple would fit in that small of a building.

Lacy and Sharon entered the little church with twenty minutes to spare before the service began. Sharon had to admit, she would never have guessed that there would have been this much room on the inside from the out-ward appearance. She assumed that was yet another example of the old adage about not judging a book by its cover. Lacy spotted her mother at the precise instant that her mother saw her. With a sigh, she said to Sharon, "Here we go!"

Sharon saw the woman, who looked like a gray-headed, heavier; angrier version of Lacy, walking determinedly toward them with furrowed brows. Coming to a stop before them, Mrs. Fuller said, "Lacy! I can't believe that you would have the audacity to bring *her* to the service!"

Lacy stood with mouth agape, and Sharon looked puzzled.

"Honestly, after Brother Morrison banished you from the church for your ways. What would he think about this?" her mother glared at Sharon.

Lacy was dumbfounded. Her mother must have assumed that Sharon was her partner. As Lacy struggled to find the right words, Sharon quickly responded.

"Mrs. Fuller? I don't believe we've met. I'm Dr. Sharon West. Are you under the impression that Lacy and I are lovers?"

"Shhh. Keep your voice down! What if someone overhears?"

Looking quite angry, Sharon responded. "Lacy and I are *friends,* but even if I were her lover, what would that matter? She's here out of respect for the preacher, and I'm here to give her support. Do you even know why Lacy stopped going to church?"

"I wish you'd keep your voice down, young lady. Yes, I do; Brother Morrison told her she was living in sin and that church wasn't the place for her."

"After all of these years, you still believe that's what he said?" Sharon asked, incredulously. "No, the preacher told her that the *Baptist* church wouldn't be the best fit for her and recommended a different denomination. He also told her that, in his opinion, her lifestyle was acceptable."

"Well, I never! I won't have you coming in here defaming Brother Morrison like that on this of all days!" Mrs. Fuller said, putting her hand over her chest.

"Defaming Brother Morrison? I'd bet you everything that I own that he would prefer Lacy coming here with twenty of her past lovers than to have you standing here acting like an ignorant jackass!" Sharon said angrily.

Breathing in a gasp of feigned or perhaps actual shock, Mrs. Fuller turned her gaze to Lacy and asked, "You've had twenty ... girlfriends?"

"No, Mom, I haven't. She's just saying-" Lacy tried to explain.

Her mother interrupted by turning her attention to Sharon.

"Listen, I don't know who you think you are-"

"I don't *think* that I'm anyone. I *know* that I'm Lacy's friend and, from what I've seen today, I'm wondering if I'm the closest thing to family that she has!"

"How dare you!" Mrs. Fuller looked stricken.

"No, how dare *you*! You gave birth to this woman, gave her a suboptimal childhood, and now stand here condemning her! Do you not realize what a beautiful person she is or are you so damned hell bent on finding fault with her that you can't see the true person standing before you? What happened to the woman who risked her life to keep her daughter out of harm's way from a mean, drunken man? The same woman who spent a week in the Intensive Care Unit because her husband pushed her daughter?" Sharon whispered angrily.

"I don't have to take anymore of this! Lacy, I'm disappointed in you," Mrs. Fuller said, staring at an unsuspecting Lacy.

"Disappointed in her?" Sharon interjected. "Well, normally when I meet a member of a friend's family, I like to say that it was a pleasure to meet them. In this case, I'm *disappointed* to have made your acquaintance. Come on, Lacy, let's sit down."

Slowly, Lacy followed Sharon to a seat at the back of the church and toward the end of a pew. After the women sat down, Sharon took Lacy's hand in hers and spoke.

"I'm sorry, Lacy. I shouldn't have gone off on your mother like that. It's just that she was so rude! You didn't tell me she was going to be like that."

"I had no idea that she'd jump to the conclusion that we were lovers," Lacy said, still stunned by the way that Sharon had verbally defended her to her mother.

"Wasn't she the one who called you and told you about his passing?"

"Yeah."

"So, why was she disappointed to see you here?" Sharon asked.

"I told you, she's disappointed in everything I do. In this instance, I guess she was disappointed to see me here with you," Lacy quietly said.

"Well, it just pisses me off. It reminds me of when I take Salem to the vet's office. If Dr. Powell isn't there, whoever is filling in for her always fusses about his weight. They always say he's fat and needs to go on a diet. I always have to tell them about when I found him and he was starving to death. Now, if I don't have food out for the kitties all the time, when I do put some down, he gorges until he throws up. I think he's so scared of starving again. So, no, it isn't wrong that he's overweight, and a diet is not the answer!" Sharon said passionately.

Lacy wondered what the hell a fat cat had to do with anything. In spite of herself, she couldn't suppress a "Huh?"

"Well, your mother seemed upset that I was here with you even though she doesn't know me from Adam!"

"Well, that certainly clarifies the matter," said Lacy, sarcastically.

"Oh, Lacy. I'm sorry. I usually don't lose my cool like that. You don't know how many times I'll have a child or an elderly person come into the ER with symptoms that have persisted for weeks, even months. I have to bite my tongue to keep from asking their caretakers why they haven't sought medical attention sooner. I always do, though. I never cross that line at work, but I do at the vet's office, and I did today. I guess when it's something I love, I just can't keep my thoughts to myself. Would you like me to apologize to your mother?" Sharon asked.

Lacy was glad that the organ music began. It would provide her with a reason not to answer Sharon for a while. Had Sharon just said that she loved her? Actually, she wasn't sure what Sharon had just said and didn't think she'd ever get the obese cat connection to her mother. Lacy looked down and noticed that Sharon was still holding her hand. At that moment, in spite of the scene with her mother and the fact of Brother Morrison's passing, Lacy's heart was surprisingly happy.

CHAPTER 30

The funeral was actually an uplifting experience for all in attendance, except perhaps Lacy's mother, who spent the whole service looking annoyed and moving her lips. Lacy knew from experience that she wasn't listening to the words spoken by the young preacher. Instead, she was replaying in her mind the argument she and Sharon had been involved in. She was probably reconstructing her words with all of the clever comebacks one always thinks of a little too late. By the time the service was over, Lacy felt certain her mother would have edited the argument such that Sharon fled from the church in tears.

As the choir began singing what Lacy recognized would be the last hymn, she began wondering what would happen with her mother and Sharon at the conclusion of the service. At that moment, Sharon gently squeezed her hand as though she knew Lacy's thoughts.

True to Southern Baptist funereal form, *Amazing Grace* was the last song performed by the choir. The tiny, blue-haired organist played something dismal sounding as Brother Morrison's wife and family slowly walked to the rear of the building. Lacy decided that she should probably make a CD of some of her favorite songs to have played at her funeral, lest she be subjected to the selections of others.

Sharon had let go of her hand as people began passing their pew and amazingly, Lacy found that she was glad. Although this small town wasn't the one in which she'd been born and raised, she had no doubt that anyone who knew her mother and would sit still long enough knew of her "sinful sexual preference." She remembered all the years of politely correcting her mother that it wasn't a *preference* because it wasn't a choice. She then tried to recall the last time her mother had made her feel as if she was anything other than a disappointment. She realized for the first time that there had been no such day since her father left. The realization brought tears to her eyes. Shit, she thought. Tears for the third time in as many days. Maybe she was menopausal?

"Lacy? I will if you'd like me to, even though I'm not sorry. Oh, God, you're crying! Is it because of what I said?"

Lacy realized that Sharon must have been having quite a long one-sided conversation while she'd been lost in thought.

"Huh?" Lacy asked.

"I'll be glad to apologize to her, you know. Especially if it's making you cry."

"To my mother?"

"Yes, that's what we've been talking about."

Lacy hated to break it to Sharon, but *they* hadn't been talking; Sharon had.

"No, I don't want you to do that. I think she deserved it. What's more, I don't think I would have ever said those things to her because I'm not sure I even realized it myself. I'm glad you said it for me."

"So you *are* crying because of what I said," Sharon said, looking miserable.

"Well, I mean yes and no. I'm mostly sad because it occurred to me that she's never acted proud of me."

"It's her loss, Honey," Sharon said in a soft whisper and pulled an unusually wooden Lacy toward her for an embrace. After a moment, Sharon released her and rose from the pew. Scanning around to see if anyone was looking and/or scowling, Lacy also stood and was glad that nobody seemed left in the chapel except for the organist and them. As they made their way out the open doors at the back of the chapel, Lacy noticed that the funeral procession was already underway. How long had they lagged behind after the service had ended? Oh, well, she hadn't planned on attending the burial anyhow, but she would have liked the opportunity to give Mrs. Morrison her condolences.

"Maybe she's blind," said Sharon.

"Who's blind?"

"I said *maybe* she is."

"And I said who?" Lacy asked again.

"The organist."

Wondering if this was going to be another remark from left-field like a fat Salem, Lacy chided herself for using a sports analogy. Yes, Sumlin would have been proud.

"Okay, I'll bite. Why would she be blind?" Lacy asked.

"Because she's just launched into another hymn, and there's nobody left in there."

"Does there always have to be a medical condition with you doctors? Maybe she just likes to play," Lacy said irritably.

"Maybe," Sharon agreed.

Lacy watched as the last of the cars pulled out in the long processional and remembered her grandmother's funeral several years before. There had been a large number of cars in attendance for her funeral, too, which had always puzzled Lacy. She'd never even met the woman who had disowned her daughter, Lacy's mother, when she chose to marry Lacy's father, so the funeral had been anything but a sad experience. Mostly, Lacy remembered wondering how someone so callous could have amassed that many friends. Lacy wondered who all would go to her funeral. Well, it would probably be attended by a slew of police officers. Other than that, she could count the number of true friends she had on one, well maybe two, hands.

Deciding that she needed to rein in her thoughts and begin paying more attention, Lacy focused on her surroundings. The first thing she noticed was that Sharon was no longer beside her. The second thing she noticed was that dreary organ music no longer filled the little church. The third thing she noticed was Sharon leaned over talking to the little blue-haired organist.

Debating whether or not she should wander into the chapel and interrupt, Lacy decided to hang back. A moment later, two young men in overalls and baseball caps entered the chapel. They wiped their feet on the little mat inside the entrance and quickly removed their caps. Both were probably mid-twenties and clean-cut guys with sweet faces and dark tans. Was she the only person in the whole damned world who had ever heard of skin cancer?

In a Southern voice, one of the young men spoke.

"Um, we're here for the flowers, Ma'am. Can we just go on in and pick them up?"

"Oh, I don't work here. I think that would be fine, though. The only person I've seen who's still here from the church is the organist, and the processional is underway."

"Thank you. We'll just go on in and start lugging them out to the van."

Lacy watched the two men walk down the aisle and begin gathering the arrangements. She stepped aside to let them pass and noticed Sharon helping blue-hair from the organ loft. Slowly, the two women made their way toward Lacy.

"Lacy? I'd like for you to meet Mae Burns. Ms. Burns? This is Lacy Fuller."

"Oh? Are you Deborah's daughter?" the little blue-haired woman asked in a sweet voice.

"Yes, Ma'am," Lacy answered uncomfortably.

"So, you are the detective?"

"Yes, Ma'am."

"Well, I know she's real proud of you, dear."

"Really?" asked Lacy with a mixture of hope and skepticism in her voice.

"Lord, yes, child! She thinks you can move mountains. Why, just the other day she was upset about something, and she said, if you were here, it wouldn't have happened. Now, what was it that had happened?" Ms. Burns asked herself.

Lacy stood there in shock while Sharon hovered near-by with a sickened look on her face. Mae Burns continued desperately to try to remember more of the circumstances surrounding the story she'd just recounted. After a min-ute, she apparently gave up.

"It's awful getting old. You can't hear, can't see, can't walk, and can't remember things. Well, not recent things anyhow. At least I can still glory in the day when I wake up and smell the sweet shrubs coming through the bed-room window."

Sharon cleared her throat and spoke.

"You've got sweet shrubs? God, I love the smell of sweet shrubs! I haven't seen any of those since we lived in Alabama. Maybe I could go smell them when we take you home."

Noticing the slightly puzzled expression on Lacy's face, Sharon added, "I've offered Ms. Burns a ride home.

Her son is the preacher who performed the service, and he's gone to the cemetery. We've just got to write him a little note."

Lacy nodded and watched as Sharon picked up a tithing envelope, fumbled through her purse, took out a twenty dollar bill and a pen, and handed the pen and envelope to Ms. Burns.

"Oh. Could you write it please? My hands are so arthritic, I can't do much writing anymore. I should have mentioned that a minute ago when I was listing the things I can't do well at my age. Lordy, the list would be endless," she said with a good-natured laugh.

While Sharon put the money inside the envelope, Lacy asked, "Don't you think your son will get worried if he comes back and you're not here?"

"Well, honey, that's why we're leaving him a note."

"Yeah, but if it's not your handwriting, how will he know it's not foul play?"

Chuckling a bit to herself, Ms. Burns said, "Well, if I did write the note, I don't believe he could read it anyhow. I write like those doctors write. Besides, this is small-town south Georgia, honey. I get rides home from church all the time. I'm sure he won't be worried."

Sighing, Lacy wanted to belabor the issue, but decided against it. Looking down at the pale, fragile, gnarled hands, Lacy wondered how she had played the organ at all, much less as well as she had. She wondered if it would be politically correct to ask, but decided against it.

Lacy sat in the back seat so that Ms. Burns could ride in the front and, within five minutes of their departure from the church, they arrived at Ms. Burns' home. It was an absolutely gorgeous wooden house painted pale yellow. There was a giant oak tree in the front yard and a wrap-around porch with two swings and several rocking chairs which added an extra air of welcome to the place. Lacy thought it would be nice to just stretch out on one of the swings and take a nap after the emotionally draining morning. She felt a sudden throbbing from the area where she'd been shot and was again thankful that Sharon had driven her.

After taking Ms. Burns up on the offer to have some lemonade and cookies, Sharon and Lacy found themselves delighted to be sitting on the porch, enjoying the woman's hospitality. The cookies were big, soft tea cookies with just a slight hint of a lemon flavor, and the lemonade contained just enough pulp to convince Lacy that it was the real stuff. Lacy wondered if this was what she'd missed by not having the storybook grandmother. She wanted to ask Ms. Burns again about the stuff that her mother said about her, but decided not to. She'd just try to ask her mother herself if an ideal opportunity presented itself.

After about an hour, Sharon and Lacy excused themselves and thanked the woman for her generosity. After they made a quick detour around the house to see the sweet shrubs, Lacy agreed with Sharon that it was as heavenly a scent as she'd ever smelled. As soon as they got into the car, Sharon started apologizing again.

"Oh, Lacy, I'm so sorry I jumped all over your mother like that! I guess I was wrong about the way she feels toward you. I need to apologize to her."

"No, really you don't. She was out of line, as usual. I'll probably call her tomorrow and have a long talk with her to try to clear the air. I just can't believe she says nice stuff about me to people. Hell, she's never said anything nice to me to my face. Hey, you didn't put Ms. Burns up to saying that, did you?" Lacy asked warily.

Sharon looked astonished.

"No. Do you realize how absurd that sounded, Lacy?"

"Yeah, actually I do. Even as it was coming out, I knew it was a dumb thing to say."

"Well, not dumb, but maybe paranoid."

"Yeah, I don't know. It just seemed too surreal that she would have anything nice to say about me, that's all."

"Well, maybe I'll send her an 'I'm sorry' card," Sharon said.

"Yeah, the 'I'm sorry' section is right there between the 'best wishes' and 'new baby' cards in the store," Lacy said, dryly.

Playfully, Sharon said, "Smartass! There are such cards, I've seen them."

"If you say so."

"Aside from the thing with your momma, this has been a nice afternoon. I mean, I've kind of felt like shit about going off on your mother. It's been an underlying theme, actually. Also the fact that we were at a funeral was sad."

"Aside from that, Mrs. Lincoln, how did you enjoy the play?" Lacy quipped.

"You really are a smartass, you know."

"I never denied it," Lacy agreed.

Lacy helped navigate them back to the interstate, then a comfortable silence fell between the women. Lacy closed her eyes and listened to the soft music playing on the CD player. In a few minutes, she had dozed off.

Sharon looked over to find Lacy asleep. Taking care not to hit any of the yellow reflectors between lanes for fear she would awaken her friend, Sharon tried to assuage herself of the guilt she felt for being rude to Lacy's mother by thinking of pleasant things and getting lost in the music. In a matter of minutes, she felt much better. She really had enjoyed the time spent with Lacy.

CHAPTER 31

Chris Frazier had watched the news at the bar in his posh hotel. Fortunately, he'd been the sole customer. At $9.00 a drink, he could understand why. The bartender had barely even looked at him, so fear of discovery wasn't a major issue even when his photograph was shown on the television. He watched as the bartender looked from the television to the lone customer at the bar with no sense of recognition whatsoever when he ordered his second Tom Collins.

Chris asked for the sound to be turned up when an unfamiliar face came on the screen. The man was identified as FBI Agent Mark Herndon, the second in command on the task force looking for Chris Frazier. He was a bit of a sullen looking man, probably pissed off he wasn't the first in command. Well, they'd never in a million years catch him, so the fellow didn't know how lucky he was that he wouldn't be the one taking the fall for the failure of the FBI.

Agent Herndon said that, to date, there had been 'roughly fifty' cases of HIV from the tainting of the blood supply. He assured the public that they were 'close on the trail' of the man responsible. *I'm right here, you inept jerk!* thought Chris. A young woman came to the bar and sat close to him. She ordered a glass of white wine, and Chris noticed that the bartender was much more accommodating and talkative with her. He also noticed that she kept looking over at him. Fighting a momentary panic, he finally turned to face the woman. Now would be a good time to borrow the identity of his good friend Irving B. Kriell.

"Hi. I'm Irving."

The woman smiled, and the bartender raised an eyebrow and ambled off to the other end of the bar.

"I'm Samantha. It's a pleasure to meet you. Are you in town for the convention?"

"What convention would that be?"

"The American Dental Association?"

"No, I'm not a dentist."

"You look like one. Or maybe a doctor. You don't look like an Irving."

"I know. I was disappointed myself when I got that name."

The lady laughed and offered to buy Chris another drink.

"Shouldn't I be the one asking to buy you a drink?"

"Well, you didn't so I thought I'd take matters into my own hands."

"I'm officially asking; may I buy you another glass of wine?"

"I'd be delighted," she giggled.

Three drinks later, the woman asked in what Chris assumed was her sexiest voice if he'd like to join her in her room.

"Oh, I'd love to, but I'm married."

"You don't look married."

"Well, some things aren't as they seem. I don't look married, and I don't look like an Irving, but I did enjoy the company, Samantha."

Pouting, she bid him a good night.

As he walked away, he realized just how much he enjoyed hearing women talk and laugh. Maybe he could find Justine and make her love him again. If not, he guessed he'd just have to move on and find someone else. The thought angered him. If his name and face hadn't been all over television, she would surely have been able to forgive him for his breakdown after losing Craig. Now, she might believe all the things that were being said about him and have a problem with that.

Not that it wasn't all true, he ceded. Still, he wasn't sure if she could forgive him for the part he'd played in infecting so many people with HIV even if it was for a good reason. If it hadn't been for that damned nosy female detective, none of this shit would have ever happened. He would see to it that she paid with her life for her intervention.

Feeling much better after thinking of possible ways to murder the detective during the long elevator ride to his floor, he debated about renting a movie. After perusing the options, he decided that sleep would be a better alternative. He wasn't sure whether he would make his move against the detective the next day or not. Either way, he felt that getting a good nights sleep would be of the essence. Yes, some day real soon was going to be a big day for him.

CHAPTER 32

Friday morning, Lacy awoke feeling a mix of happiness and despair. Snow slinked from his perch above her head down beside her body and promptly stepped on her left breast.

"Shit, Snow! For God's sake, you've got all of this space to tromp about ... why do you insist on targeting my boobs?" she grumbled.

Purring and dancing, Snow didn't respond. Lacy shoved his feet off her breast, and he meowed loudly as she stood. Snow followed her into the kitchen. After fixing him a plate of canned food, Lacy opened a Diet Coke and called Chet to tell him that she thought she felt like driving herself to work this morning.

After hanging up the phone, Lacy decided that she should put in a load of laundry before she took her shower. Checking her pockets, she was happy to discover a twenty dollar bill she hadn't recalled stuffing into her shirt. She also came across Irving Kriell's card. Placing both the card and the money on the coffee table, she started the wash cycle.

She thought about what she was going to say to her mother during the long shower. As she was toweling off, she still had no clue how to broach the subject. Hopefully by this evening when she made the call she would have decided upon what to say. While she was looking through her closet for something to wear, her cell phone rang.

"Hello?" she answered.

"Detective Fuller? Good morning. This is Agent Herndon with the FBI. Did you talk to an Irving Kriell yesterday?"

"Yes. Why?"

"He just notified us that Chris Frazier is coming to town this morning to clear his stuff out of a storage building. He said he tried the station for you and couldn't get you. Agent Olsen will meet you at the storage building. One of you two can pretend to be the employee there. I'm guessing he's going to be closing out his account today, if he's going to be getting his stuff out of storage. Good work, Detective! We've got the bastard!"

"Great. I'll need the address of the building," Lacy said excitedly.

"Oh, right. Okay, it's 975 Sultan Circle."

Lacy scribbled the address on a notepad she always kept on her bedside table.

"Got it. Will you guys be there?"

"Oh, yeah. We'll be behind the building so you may not see us. Agent Olsen will meet you at the actual storage unit, number 135. If she beats you there, which she probably will, she'll go ahead inside, so just knock twice and she'll let you in."

"Great. Thanks, Agent Herndon."

After hanging up the telephone, Lacy decided that the FBI wasn't as annoying as she'd initially thought. Suddenly, the clothing that she selected for the day took the back seat. She was off to catch a madman; how exciting was that? Quickly pulling on a pair of khakis, putting on her vest and a polo shirt, and slipping on a pair of hiking boots, Lacy tore the piece of paper with the address on it from the pad and headed toward the living room.

As she powered up her laptop, she thought that she'd probably be able to find the location easily enough. Still, she had begun to rely on getting detailed driving directions online. It was a great feature. Within moments, she was impatiently waiting for the printout. Without even shutting her computer off or saying bye to Snow, she was out the door.

Homer Files woke up and looked into the early morning Atlanta sky. Bright oranges and reds intermingled with deep blue to create one of the most splendid sunrises he'd seen in a long time. What was it that his Mama used to say? Oh, yes, 'Red in the morning, sailors take warning. Red at night, sailors delight.' He guessed he was glad that he wasn't a sailor.

Stretching, he thought about how much he enjoyed waking outside in his sleeping bag when the weather was moderate like this. He thought about all of the changes that would occur if he took Ms. Stevens up on her offer of an apartment. Most of them, he had to admit, would be for the better. In fact, waking up to a morning like this one in the outdoors was probably the only thing he would miss. He wondered if he could get a little dog if he lived in an apartment. He bet he could. Maybe he would get a cat, too, to keep the dog company. Yes, indeed, that might just be alright, he happily thought.

Suddenly, an image of Lacy came to his mind. Homer was a 'man of visions'. His mother had been and her mother before her. It was a 'gift,' according to his Mama. In Homer's visions, which he only had when something terrible was about to occur, he would see the person's face in a blurred image. Generally, within the course of the day, the person whose image had come to him would have an accident. This image of Lacy now was even stronger than the one he'd had on the day she'd been shot.

Whenever he had a vision, he would try to contact the person and warn them, even though they usually thought he was crazy. Still, it was worth them thinking he was nuts if he could help save them from a tragedy. He'd have to walk over to a phone booth and call Lacy, he thought. Then he remembered the cell phone that she'd given him the day before. Going to his backpack, he pulled it out and looked at it for a moment. Spotting a small green button, he pressed it, hoping it was the power. Lacy had gone over some of the details of the phone the previous day, but he wasn't sure how much of the information he had retained.

Relieved, he noticed that the face of the phone lit up. He sat back down and thought hard to recall how to use the 'phone book' feature. Pressing a couple of buttons, he was happy to see Lacy's name. He then pressed a button below the word 'details' and saw that there were three listings for Lacy. He decided to try her at home first. He pressed the button that he hoped would select the number and found that the little phone began dialing the number by itself. Lord have mercy! This little phone sure was a smart thing.

Lacy's recorded voice came on the line, and Homer decided to leave her a message to call him in case she was in the shower or something.

"Miss Lacy? This is Homer. I'm using my new phone you got me. I sure do like it. I was wondering if I could get you to call me back just as soon as you can. I've got something that I need to tell you. It's real important. Well, thank you now. I'll talk to you soon. Bye."

He pressed a button that ended the call, then went through the whole process again after selecting her cell phone number. He left a similar message on her voice mail, then set about calling her work number.

Chet walked into the department to find a woman he didn't know sitting at his desk. Remembering that Lacy was going to have an FBI shadow, he assumed this was her. Clearing his throat as he approached, he extended his hand.

"Good morning. I'm Detective Chet Avery."

"You've just got the cutest little boy ever!" she said.

Noticing the photograph of Monica and CJ on his desk, Chet thanked the woman, then asked her name.

"Oh, I'm such an idiot! My name is Agent Margie Olsen. I'm with the FBI."

"It's a pleasure to meet you, Agent Olsen. Lacy will be in later on. She's usually here a bit after me anyhow, but she's probably still moving in slow motion thanks to her injury last week. Could I possibly ask you to wait at her desk until she arrives?"

"Oh, sure. What did you do to your face?"

"My face? Oh, that's poison oak. It's looking much better now. In fact, I had almost forgotten about it until you said that," Chet said, suddenly itchy.

Moving her stuff over to Lacy's desk, Agent Olsen asked if she could use Lacy's computer.

"I don't see why not. Lace uses password protection for all of her confidential files, though, so I don't know how much you'll be able to do."

"That's okay. I wasn't going to do anything with her stuff. I have a disk of this new computer program that I wanted to mess around with."

"Okay. Suit yourself."

"I always say, *Mi deska es Su deska*."

"Huh?" Chet asked, reminding himself of Lacy.

"You know, *Mi casa es Su casa*? So, *Mi deska es Su deska*."

Chet watched as the woman, still giggling from her strange sense of humor, booted up the computer. He bet Lacy rued the day that she wanted to stay on this case since it meant working with this odd woman. Lacy's telephone began ringing, and Agent Olsen just stared at it.

"Agent? You can answer that if you don't mind," Chet said.

Picking the receiver off the cradle, Agent Olsen smiled into the telephone and said, "Hello. You've reached the desk of Detective Lacy Fuller. She isn't in now, but if you'll leave your name and number, the Detective will call you back."

Chet sighed. Heck, Lacy's voice mail could have done that. What was the deal with this woman?

"Okay. Do you have a last name, Homer? Excuse me? Why, of course this is a real person. Why would you think otherwise? I'm not sure when she's going to be in. Avery? Yes, he's right here. Would you like me to transfer you?"

Oh, for God's sakes, Chet thought. This woman was really something. Thinking that she would probably cut him off if she tried to transfer Homer, Chet stood and walked two feet over to Lacy's desk.

"I'll just take it here, Agent Olsen," he said patiently.

"Okey dokey!" she said, handing Chet the telephone.

"Homer? Hi, this is Chet. What can I do for you?"

"Well, Detective Avery, I'm worried about Miss Lacy, and I can't get her to answer on any of her phones."

"Oh, she's fine, Homer. I just talked to her about an hour ago. She's probably on her way into the station as we speak."

"Does she usually have her cell phone on when she drives in?" Homer asked.

"Always. Why?"

"She's not answering that either," Homer said.

"Well, Homer, I'm sure she's just fine. If you had a number where she could reach you, I'd have her call you when she got in. I'll just have her come over to your spot when she gets here."

"I do have a phone now, Mr. Chet. Miss Lacy bought it for me. It's the smartest little thing I think I've ever seen."

"That's great. I'll have her call you as soon as she comes through the door."

"Well, see, that's not all. I've got this feeling that something's wrong. I get these feelings sometimes, and a lot of times things happen."

"Okay, Homer. If it'll make you feel better, I'll try to reach her, too," Chet agreed, sounding unconcerned.

Realizing that Chet wasn't going to be very receptive to the fears brought on by his special 'gift', Homer thanked him and hung up.

As Chet hung the phone up, he noticed that Agent Olsen had the program on the screen and was happily humming while she typed in commands. What in the heck she was humming was anyone's guess, thought Chet. It sounded horrible. He laughed inwardly once more about Lacy getting paired with this ditz. He couldn't wait to see her face when she came through the door and saw the woman sitting at her desk.

True to his word, Chet called Lacy as soon as he sat down at his desk. After leaving a message, he tried her on her cell phone. This was a bit unusual, he thought. Typically, he was able to get Lacy anytime that he wanted to. Suddenly, he had a thought that made even his ears blush; what if Lacy had spent the night with Dr. West?

They had gone to that funeral together the previous day. Heaven help Homer if he actually was able to track down Lacy and she *was* with Sharon. He noticed that Agent Olsen's rendition of whatever the heck song it was had gotten louder. Sighing, he opened the kudzu case file and began scanning the results of the autopsy.

Sharon was brewing a pot of coffee and playing with the kitties with a laser pen. They were so adorable when they chased the little electronic red mouse all over the place. She particularly liked to hear the chattering noise that Ella made when she got tired and discouraged about never catching the little light. The boys never seemed to get disgruntled. In fact, they would play until they were all panting if she would let them. The sudden ringing of the telephone brought Sharon out of her playful mood. Few people ever called her at this time of morning unless something was wrong.

Thinking that it was too soon for Jessie's biopsy to have been done, Sharon wondered if there had been an emergency at the hospital that might require she come in.

"Hello?"

"Hello, is this Dr. West?"

"Yes, it is."

"Dr. West? This is Homer Files, Lacy's friend."

"Of course. How are you doing, Homer?"

"Well, I'm worried about Lacy."

"Why? What's happened?" she asked, sounding alarmed.

"I'm not sure, but I get these feelings. I see these images of folks, and sometimes something bad will happen to them," he said, hoping she would listen better than Chet had.

"My great aunt used to have visions. What did you see with Lacy?" Sharon asked.

"All I ever see is the face, Ma'am. Remember that day that Lacy was shot? I'd had one that day. I was going to tell her about it, but by the time I saw her, she'd already been hit by the bullet. Thank the Lord that she was wearing that vest."

"Okay, well, I'll give her a call and see if she's okay."

"I don't think she'll answer, Dr. West. I've tried on that new little phone she got me, and she's not answering at home or on her cell phone. Mr. Chet said she hasn't gotten to work yet," Homer said.

"Well, I do still have a key to her apartment. Would you like for me to come and get you and we could go over there and see if she's okay?"

"Yes, Ma'am. I'd like that very much if you don't mind."

"Well, I've got to have a cup or two of coffee and I'll be right over. Are you in your usual spot?"

"Yes, Ma'am. I'll wait on the curb for you."

"Okay, Homer. It'll take me about a half hour to get ready, but I'll hurry as best I can."

"Thank you, Dr. West. You're a true friend."

"Thank you, Homer. So are you."

Hanging up the phone, Sharon wondered about Lacy. What could she be doing? After fixing herself a cup of coffee, she sat at the kitchen table and looked at the crossword puzzle that her father always left folded and ready for her to work. Each morning, he would walk up the driveway and get the morning paper. He'd find the puzzle and set it aside with a pencil for Sharon because he knew how much she enjoyed working puzzles.

More often than not, by the time Sharon got up, the kitties had swatted the pencil off the table and played with it on the linoleum. Last year when they had bought a new refrigerator, there were twenty-seven pencils beneath the old one. Sighing, Sharon decided not to take the time to work the crossword. She did, however, work the word jumbles because they took far less time. Within twenty minutes, she'd worked the jumbles, downed three cups of coffee, and dressed. After leaving a quick note for her father, who had probably driven Penny to the post office, she left.

CHAPTER 33

As Lacy drove toward the storage building, she was feeling an adrenaline rush that was even better than a runner's high. This was going to be so great! She thought she should call Chet and let him know that she'd be late. Only then did she realize that she hadn't brought along her cell phone. Well, shit. She always took her phone with her. She guessed that in the excitement of the moment she'd forgotten to grab it. Oh well, maybe when she got to the building she'd call him. There was no sense in him worrying about her.

As she pulled up to the storage building, she noticed only one other car in the lot. It either belonged to the attendant or to Agent Olsen, she surmised. Lacy got out of her car and headed into the office. There was a small bell on the counter that Lacy rang. Nobody surfaced. After trying again, she decided that perhaps the attendant was inside the unit with Agent Olsen. Noticing a floor plan on the wall, Lacy quickly located unit 135 and walked out the front door at a brisk pace.

The door was down to unit 135. Agent Herndon had said to knock twice when she arrived. Lacy did as instructed and waited. This might be the most exciting moment of her law enforcement career, she thought. Hearing a small noise behind her, Lacy began to turn toward the source of the sound. In a split second, her world was black.

Chet thought that he had finally figured out what song that Agent Olsen was humming and was just about to ask her when he noticed a sickened look cross over her face.

"Oh, my God! That can't be right," she said, shakily.

"What is it?" asked Chet, assuming that he'd be told that it was none of his business.

"Oh, God," she repeated.

Maybe, he thought wryly, it was a picture of God. At that moment, the agent spoke.

"I was using this program that I was telling you about? Well, the thing is, with this program you can take a photograph of a person and edit the image to reflect aging, weight loss or gain, changes in hair color, stuff like that. I was playing around with the picture of the AIDS Assassin and look what I got." She pointed to the screen.

Standing, Chet walked over to Lacy's desk and saw the image of an attractive man who looked nothing like the photograph of Chris Frazier that had been released to the press.

"Hmm. That's nifty alright. Still, you're just guessing that he changed his appearance like that. I don't think I'd be giving that photo to your boss."

"No. You don't understand. It's him," she said urgently.

Chet patiently said, "I know. What I'm saying is, what if he didn't lose weight? What if he didn't dye his hair blond? This is an image based on 'what if' chances. The probability that Chris Frazier looks like this now is-"

Cutting him off before he could finish, Agent Olsen said, "One hundred percent."

"Excuse me?" he asked.

"It's him. I've seen him. He came here yesterday to speak to Lacy. He sat right there in that chair and wanted me to leave them alone together. I thought he was cute!"

"What are you talking about?" Chet asked, alarm creeping into his voice.

"Yesterday, this man came in named Irving Kriell who said he knew Chris Frazier. He wanted to talk to Lacy in private, so I left. I'm not sure what they discussed because she had to go to a funeral. It was this man! I've got to call Agent Shuttles."

Realizing that Homer's fears might have been founded, Chet couldn't help but feel a panic. What if something had happened to Lacy? As Agent Olsen used Lacy's phone to contact Agent Shuttles, Chet tried Lacy's home number once more.

Sharon and Homer pulled up to Lacy's apartment building. There was usually parking available along the streets in Atlanta during the daytime hours through the week, so they were able to get a good spot. Exiting the elevator on Lacy's floor, they began walking slowly in unison to her apartment. Sharon rang the doorbell and they waited. After a few moments, she looked at Homer.

"I don't think it would be breaking and entering since she gave me her key," Sharon offered.

"No, Ma'am. If it is, I'll say I did it."

Taking the key and fitting it inside the lock, Sharon was surprised to notice that none of the three deadbolts were locked. She entered the apartment first, followed by a hesitant Homer.

"Dr. West? I just had another image of Lacy. This time, it faded to black. I've never had one do that on me before," Homer whispered.

Torn between asking him what it meant and her desire to canvas the apartment in case Lacy was there, Sharon decided to do the latter. Snow approached and seemed to sense the apprehension that Sharon felt. The hairs on the white cat's back stood on end, and he began sidling away. Animals were such good indicators of one's mood that Sharon couldn't help but hope that Snow's reaction was because of her anxiety and nothing more. As she walked toward the bedroom, she wondered if Snow could possibly have had an image of Lacy in danger like Homer had. She would never know.

Returning to the living room, she saw Homer sitting in the recliner and petting Snow. Sharon sat on the couch and looked at Homer.

"She's not here. What do you think the image fading is a sign of, Homer?"

"I'm just not sure, Ma'am. Why, my Mama and my Grandma never mentioned that they had one to fade like that."

Feeling the need to rid herself of nervous energy for a few minutes until she could devise a logical plan, Sharon asked Homer to tell her about his powers.

"Well, it all started when Grandma was twenty-nine. She and Grandpa had five daughters. They wanted a son badly, and they had just had one. He was two months old. She had put him down for the night and was sitting outside on the front porch, rocking. She said that she looked up and saw a little white casket floating down the road in front of her. Then she said the image of her little baby came to mind. She ran inside, and he was afire with a fever. She took him to the doctor, and they put him in a tub of ice. Still, he died. It was probably meningitis. The next day when she went to pick out the casket, there was only one infant selection. It was the spit and image of the casket that had floated by her house the night before in her vision."

Sharon noticed the hairs on her arms were standing on end. That must have been how Snow had felt a short while before. What an eerie story. How could someone live their lives that way, having such images?

"That was the first time for Grandma. After that, she would wake up some mornings and say that something terrible was going to happen that day. Mama did the same thing when she got grown. I do it, too," he explained.

Before Sharon could say anything, the telephone rang. While they waited for the answering machine to pick up, Sharon looked at Lacy's coffee table. She must have been here recently because her laptop was still powered up. Sharon noticed a business card from an Interior Designer. Lacy hadn't mentioned that she was going to redo her apartment. Looking at the name on the card, she was vaguely aware of hearing Chet's voice on the answering machine.

I.B. Kriell. Sharon's mind, still in problem-solving mode from the morning jumbles, worked on the name. I.B. Kriell. If you unscrambled the last name, it was I.B. Killer. At that moment, she tuned into what Chet was saying.

"...so that guy that came to see you yesterday? That's him. That's Chris Frazier. He's altered his appearance. There is no I.B. Kriell, Lacy. Whatever you do, call me when you get this message and don't-"

Sharon picked the phone up and spoke.

"Chet? It's Sharon. Oh God! This I.B. Kriell guy? Did you say he's not a real person?"

"Dr. West? Is Lacy there?"

"No. Homer called me because he was worried about her, so we came over to check out her apartment since I still have a key. So, did you say that this guy isn't a real person?"

"Oh, he's a real *person* alright; he's just using a false name. I checked the database and there is no I.B. Kriell. Agent Olsen said that the guy who came to see Lacy yesterday posing as Irving Kriell is really Chris Frazier, the AIDS Assassin."

Sharon said, "I do jumbles, you know those scrambled words? Well, if you unscramble his last name, you get Killer. It's like he was giving her a clue: like he was saying I'm a killer."

"Oh, shit! I can't believe that Lacy would try to hot shot this thing knowing how important this case is. I've got to think that something is wrong."

"Me, too, Chet," Sharon answered.

"Agent Olsen and I are going to come over to Lacy's apartment. We'll be there in ten minutes. We'll figure out a game plan."

"Okay. Homer and I will be here."

Hanging up the telephone, Sharon felt as if she had a bowling ball inside her stomach. What if something had happened to Lacy? With a sigh, she sat on the couch again. Looking at the laptop, Sharon had an idea. What if Lacy had left a note on there? If she had been abducted from her home, that might explain why the computer was still on.

Picking the computer up and moving it into her lap, Sharon ran her index finger in small figure eights across the touch pad until the screen was illuminated. The image of an online service was prominently displayed with the message that the user was logged off due to inactivity. Lacy must have been online right before she left and hadn't even taken the time to log off the computer.

Sharon clicked the button to log on again and was relieved to discover that Lacy had pre-programmed her password. As soon as she was greeted by the online service, Sharon put the cursor on the arrow at the top of the page to see which sight had last been visited. It was a website that offered driving directions that Sharon herself also used frequently. Remembering that Lacy had printed a copy of the directions to the funeral the previous evening, Sharon wondered if that was the last time she'd gone to that site. Selecting web address, Sharon was directed to the homepage. The past few searches performed by the user appeared in descending chronological order. With relief, Sharon noticed that there was an entry above the south Georgia search. Selecting that location, Sharon heard the doorbell ring.

Homer slowly rose and carried Snow with him to the door. Chet and Agent Olsen both bounded into the apartment. Chet looked wild.

"Sharon? We've got to figure something out soon. Agent Olsen can't reach any of her fellow agents this morning because they are in their briefing meeting and apparently ignoring her calls. Until one of them calls back, it's just us."

"I think I've found something. Her computer was on when I got here, and she's done this search for driving directions. I don't know when she did the search but I think it was after she got directions to the funeral yesterday."

Looking at the address, Chet was encouraged that it was close by.

"What if that isn't where she's gone and we drive there?" asked Chet to no one in particular.

Agent Olsen spoke. "I can tell you when she visited that url."

Chet looked at the woman in amazement. "You can?"

"Sure. It won't take but a minute."

Sharon handed the agent the laptop and noticed her fingers nimbly pressing the keys. Homer, still petting Snow, was looking on in amazement, as was Chet.

"About one hour ago. I'd say this is where she is."

Chet turned to Sharon and said, "You two stay put. Agent Olsen and I are going to check this out. I'll leave you my cell phone number in case Lacy calls."

After quickly scribbling his number down, Chet and Agent Olsen ran from the apartment.

Please don't let them be too late, thought Sharon.

CHAPTER 34

Lacy awakened with the worst headache of her life and fought the urge to vomit. What in the hell had she been doing? Had she gotten drunk the night before? Trying to move her hand, she realized that she couldn't. As she lifted her head, she realized that she was sitting in a chair in a small, dark room. Slowly, she remembered the events of earlier in the day.

She'd been coming to a storage building to meet the FBI. This must be the inside of one of the rooms. What had happened when she arrived? She remembered that she couldn't get anyone to answer in the office and had gone to the storage unit. She couldn't remember anything after that. Suddenly, a bright light came on in the corner of the room. When Lacy looked in that direction, she was relieved to see Irving Kriell standing there.

"Mr. Kriell? What happened here?" Lacy asked.

"Oh, I'm afraid Mr. Kriell is no longer with us. I'd like to properly introduce myself. My name is Chris Frazier," the man replied coolly.

Suddenly, Lacy realized why the man who had called himself I.B. Kriell had looked familiar. She'd spent hours studying his face on the Metropolis ID badge. Although he no longer resembled the photo of Chris Frazier, he'd been unable to alter his crazed eyes. Lacy wondered how she had failed to notice those eyes yesterday.

"I don't know what plans you have, but the FBI will be here soon," Lacy said confidently.

"You think so? Did a certain Agent Herndon call you on your cell phone this morning and set up this little meeting? Did he tell you that Agent Olsen would meet you here?" Chris Frazier taunted.

"How do you know?"

"Oh, and you're supposed to be so smart! That was me, Detective. I used the cell phone number on the card you gave me yesterday. It was easy enough to say I was Agent Herndon because I had just seen him on the news last night. I must say, it was quite a convincing piece of information that I had you meeting up with Agent Olsen here. I'm so glad I had the chance to meet her when I came by to see you yesterday. It made things much simpler."

A feeling of anger overtook Lacy as she realized that nobody knew where she was. How in the hell had she let this happen? She was at the mercy of a madman with no hope in sight. She thought about Snow and Sharon and felt sad. She thought about her mother and how she would never get the chance to talk to her and find out if she really was proud of her. She thought about Homer and how he'd be left to fend for himself in his golden years. She thought about Chet and how he would be so disappointed in Lacy for getting herself into this bind. A feeling of determination rose within her.

Lacy looked at the evil smirk that crossed Chris Frazier's face and asked, "What do you want from me?"

"Oh, that's easy. You told me that you had talked with Justine. I want you to tell me where she is," he said.

"No," Lacy said.

"Oh, I'm sure I can persuade you to be more helpful, Detective."

"No. You're probably going to kill me anyhow. If you think I'm going to tell your crazy ass where your wife is, you'd better think again," she said angrily.

Lacy noticed the man's jaw muscles begin to move. She had pissed him off. That wasn't a wise thing to do. Maybe she could give him a false address for his wife and he would leave her there, alive, while he checked it out. That would at least buy her some time. He couldn't kill her until he verified the information, could he? Wouldn't he want to keep her alive in case she had lied to him? That's what a sane person would do. Of course, he was anything but sane. Thinking that she needed to reverse his anger until she could come up with an idea, she spoke.

"I've got to hand it to you. That was quite an elaborate scheme you came up with. I had no idea who you were when you came in yesterday. How did you have the nerve to do that?"

"It was easy. I even gave you a hint. If you unscramble the letters of the last name Kriell, it forms killer. So, you see, I. B. a Killer. You're right; I am going to kill you. It's up to you how I'll do it, though. If you're nice and tell me truthfully where my wife is, I'll inject a big dose of HIV into your veins. You'll then have a number of years before you die. If you say that I'm crazy again or if you don't tell me where my wife is, well, I'm afraid that I'll have to torture you slowly."

Lacy had always felt that a person's eyes were the window to their souls. Judging from the pure evil looking back at her, she realized that Chris Frazier was the most insane person she'd ever met. She would have to face the fact that she was going to die. More likely than not, it would be today. He had said that even if she told him where his wife was, she was still going to be infected with HIV. That probably meant that he would check out the validity of the address she gave him *after* he had injected her with the virus. If he discovered that the address was phony, he would come back and kill her. Slowly and painfully, he had suggested. If she gave him the true location, he would probably kill his family.

Finding herself in a no-win situation, Lacy said, "Okay, I'll tell you. But first, you've got to tell me what you did to me and how you managed to pull this whole thing off."

"I hit you in the head with a metal flashlight. I was scared that I'd put you into a coma when you were out for so long. That wouldn't have been good for either of us. As far as how I did this, why don't you tell me, Detective Fuller? You seem to have the whole thing figured out."

Lacy wondered how long she'd been unconscious. She noticed that it was taking several seconds for her brain to comprehend the conversation. It was time to get on with this sick game. Once she found out how he had introduced the virus into the blood for certain and he gave her the shot, he would leave to try to find his wife. Maybe without him there, she could find a way to get free. Worst possible case scenario: she would still be bound to that damned chair, and he'd come back pissed off that she had lied to him and kill her. Best possible case scenario: she could free herself from the restraints and somehow from the confines of the storage unit in time to go to a hospital and start treatment for the HIV virus. She doubted that she'd be able to realize the best possible case scenario under ideal circumstances, much less with this horrible headache.

Deflated, she said, "There's a device, a sterile docking device, which enables people to remove a portion of a unit of blood into a syringe without leaving evidence. You used this device to inject the virus into the unit rather than for removing blood from the unit. The donors continued to test HIV negative since they really were HIV negative. Am I right?"

"Bravo, Detective. That's quite impressive. Unfortunately, you're like all of the others; you have no idea what it's like to have people treating you like shit because you're gay and sick with this *gay man's* disease. You will, though, soon enough. Remember, if you lie, you die an even more horrendous death," Chris Frazier said matter-of-factly.

With resignation, Lacy said, "Do you have something to write this down on? I don't know the exact address, but I can tell you the name she's going by and the town she's living in."

Looking pleased, Chris Frazier got a pen and note pad from his briefcase and said, "I'm ready when you are, Detective."

"She's living in Tennessee, a little town called Piney Ridge. It's close to Gatlinburg. She works at a little shop that sells t-shirts on the main strip under the name of Lisa Stone."

"And?" he said, expectantly.

"I told you, I'm not sure exactly where she lives. She wouldn't tell me."

"I think you're lying. Why would she go to Gatlinburg?" he asked suspiciously.

"She said she wanted to go someplace where she didn't have any family because it would be harder for you to track her down," Lacy lied convincingly.

"If she just works in a store, how can she afford to pay for child care on that salary?"

Lacy's head was pounding, and the nausea seemed to be getting worse. She was sweating profusely. She wanted nothing more at that moment than to take a short nap. Still, if she had any chance at all to live, she would have to continue.

"She works in that shop because the owner lets her bring the children with her, and she doesn't have to worry about child care."

Putting his note pad and pen inside his briefcase, Chris Frazier was quiet for a moment. Lacy hoped that she'd been convincing enough. When she saw him removing a large syringe from the briefcase, she assumed that she had been.

CHAPTER 35

Chet and Agent Olsen pulled into the storage building parking lot. Immediately, Chet spotted Lacy's car.

"She's here. That's her car!" he said excitedly.

"I don't see anything out of the ordinary in her car. Let's go into the office," he said hurriedly.

Finding no one inside, Agent Olsen reached for the bell.

"No! Don't do that! We don't want to alert this guy that we're here," Chet said urgently.

"What if there's an attendant who'll be able to tell us which unit he has?"

"We'll just go through that door and see if they're in the back. If not, I guess we'll have to figure it out on our own," he said.

Both Chet and Agent Olsen removed their weapons from their holsters as Chet opened the door. The small room housed a little coffee pot, a chair, a small refrigerator, and a miniature television, but no person.

"Okay. We'll just have to walk around the complex and listen to see if we hear anything."

"Detective Avery? Did you notice that there was a little map of the buildings on the wall in the front room?"

Agent Olsen asked.

"No."

"There is. It had little stickers on a bunch of the units. Maybe that indicates the units that are occupied?"

"Maybe, but it doesn't matter. This sick guy could easily have gained access to any unit he wanted to if he's done something with the attendant," Chet said worriedly.

"That's true. What I was getting at, though, is that the units lock from the outside. We could look for units that aren't locked as a starting place since he couldn't lock himself inside if he would have to be outside to lock it."

Chet thought for a moment. Agent Olsen did have a point in her convoluted way. He said, "Okay. Let's get moving then."

"Do you think we should split up so that we can cover more ground faster?" she asked.

"No. I think we should stay together. Follow me."

Agent Olsen removed the map from the wall, glass frame and all, and lugged it along with them. Chet wanted to scream, but decided that it wasn't such a bad idea considering it would have taken time to remove it from within the frame.

After a few minutes, they learned that the little dots did indicate the units that had been rented. They also observed that there were standard issue locks on all of the units that hadn't been rented, presumably to keep vagrants from using the little rooms as living quarters. The locks on several of the occupied units were different. Both of them slowed up at the same time as they approached unit 135. There was no lock on the outside of the door. Looking at each other, they slowly crept toward the door and strained to listen. After a second, they heard a muted voice.

Motioning for her to follow him, Chet walked a few feet away from the unit and spoke softly. "I think we've found them. If not, then we'll have some explaining to do to whoever *is* in there. Here's the plan. I'll pull the door up, and you be in position with your gun pointed inside the unit. Are you a pretty good shot?"

"Top of my class," she replied.

"Good. Okay, let's do this."

As they approached the building, Chet noticed the shooter's stance that Agent Olsen had taken. The woman was far more of a competent asset than he would have ever guessed possible. Slowly sliding his fingers beneath the bottom of the aluminum door, Chet looked at Agent Olsen. With one quick nod, he pulled the door up as fast as he could and jumped back to unholster his weapon.

Agent Olsen yelled, "Freeze!"

Inside the unit sat Lacy, hands bound behind her and secured to a straight-backed chair and Chris Frazier holding something in his hands. Chet didn't know what it was, but he did know it wasn't a gun, which was good news.

Agent Olsen yelled again, "Drop the weapon and put your hands on your head!"

With an indignant look, Chris Frazier dropped the syringe and raised his hands.

"I said on your head!" Olsen screamed.

Placing his hands atop his head, the madman glared at Lacy. Chet ran forward and cuffed Chris Frazier while Agent Olsen kept her gun aimed at him. After ensuring that the man was immobilized, Chet looked over at Lacy. She looked spaced out. What had that idiot given her?

Rushing over to her, Chet began undoing her restraints.

"What did he give you, Lace? Can you talk?" he asked, concerned.

"Yeah. Um, he didn't give me anything that I know of. Well, maybe a concussion."

Quickly, Chet raised his hands and gently felt the sides

and top of Lacy's head. He discovered an enormous bump on the right side near the top of her head.

"I've got to call for an ambulance, Lace. You've got a heck of an egg on your head."

With that, Chet glared at Chris Frazier and made the 'officer down' call to his dispatcher while Agent Olsen walked over to Lacy and placed her hand on her shoulder. In her other hand, she held her gun still pointed at the suspect as her cell phone began to ring.

"Agent Olsen? Aren't you going to answer that? What if it's AIC Shuttles?" Chet asked.

"Well, that asswipe can wait. It took him this long to call me back, so I'm going to take my own sweet time getting in touch with him," she said defiantly.

Chet noticed a smile form on Lacy's face and knew that everything was going to be alright.

CHAPTER 36

Chet called Sharon and Homer to let them know that Lacy was okay. Sharon asked Chet to have the paramedics take Lacy to Brookshire so that she could oversee her treatment. Within minutes, several emergency services vehicles arrived on the scene. Lacy was placed inside the ambulance wearing a neck stabilizing brace, and Chris Frazier was put into the back of a police car. As Chet watched the ambulance pull away, he noticed that Agent Olsen, freed from her serial killer babysitting duties, had once more begun humming. This woman was truly unique, and he decided that he somehow liked her. Always a believer in sharing positive feedback, Chet moved closer to Margie Olsen.

"Agent Olsen? I just wanted you to know that you were outstanding this morning. The way you did that composite on Lacy's computer and made the Chris Frazier/Irving Kriell connection was amazing. It would be a pleasure to work with you anytime."

Margie smiled, then blushed.

"Thank you, Chet. That really means a lot to me." Looking slightly flustered, Agent Olsen added, "I should probably call AIC Shuttles back. Excuse me."

Watching the young woman walk away, Chet thought that if everybody spoke their minds when they had something good to say rather than only to complain, people would be better accustomed to receiving compliments. Poor Agent Olsen had looked dazed. Well, actually, she always looked kind of dazed, so maybe his compliment wasn't the source of that look. With a sigh, Chet walked toward the office. As much as he wanted to be with Lacy at the hospital, there was still a missing storage facility attendant whom he needed to find since Chris Frazier had refused to answer any questions.

Sharon parked her car illegally near the ambulance bay. As she jumped out, she noticed one of the security guards approaching her.

"Hey, Jack! I've got a bit of an emergency here. I'll buy you a pizza if you'll park my car for me. Deal?" she said.

"Hmmm. Let's see. Park a Jag, get a pizza. Well, it's a toughie, but you're on."

Tossing her keys to the smiling guard, Sharon said, "I'll be in with the injured police detective. You can bring the keys in to me or I'll hunt you up before I leave. I appreciate it."

Smiling, Jack said, "No problem, Dr. West."

Sharon went to the desk and asked if Lacy had been brought in yet. Upon learning that she hadn't been, she jogged down to the staff lounge and put on a fresh lab coat. She decided not to take the time to don a pair of scrubs because she wanted to be there as soon as they brought Lacy in. Closing her locker door, she quickly left the lounge and went back to the desk just as an ambulance was pulling up. God, she hoped it was Lacy.

Pacing to and fro, Sharon was glad to see that the patient on the gurney was Lacy. As soon as the doors opened,

Sharon approached Lacy and felt a tear fall slowly down her face.

"Hey, Sweetie," she said.

Looking into Sharon's eyes, Lacy held out her hand.

"I thought I was going to die."

Through a new onslaught of tears, Sharon said, "Me, too."

"You're crying, Sharon," Lacy finally observed.

"I know. They're happy tears. I was so afraid something had happened to you because of what Homer said."

"What happened to Homer?" Lacy asked with concern.

"Oh, nothing, Sweetie. He's actually over at your apartment waiting for us to come home."

Before Lacy could ask what Homer was doing there, a doctor entered the room and began examining her. Next, she was whisked down the hallway to have x-rays and a cat scan. When she was finally returned to her room, she was glad to see Sharon still standing there.

Taking Lacy's hand in hers, Sharon asked, "What were you thinking about when that idiot had you? Chet filled me in on the basics."

"Good old Chet. I was so happy to see him. Um, I think I was worried about Snow. I was sad that I wouldn't get to see him again." Softly, she added, "Or you."

The doctor entered the room at that moment and said, "Well, Detective Fuller, it seems you have quite a concussion. The good news is that there doesn't seem to be any signs of intracranial bleeding. The bad news is that you'll probably have what's called post concussion syndrome which can be a royal pain."

Looking quickly to Sharon, Lacy hesitantly asked, "What does that mean?"

A moment lapsed during which the two women just looked at one another. Finally, Sharon replied, "Post concussion syndrome can cause a variety of different symptoms, including memory loss, moodiness, headaches, dizziness, and depression to name a few. It can last for weeks or even several months."

Dr. Toomey added, "I'll want to keep you overnight for observation, maybe repeat the CT scan of your head tomorrow morning just to make sure you aren't bleeding."

Lacy and Sharon watched as the doctor left the room. Within the hour, Lacy was admitted, and Sharon followed her to her room. Moments later, Chet knocked on the door and entered.

"Hey, Lace! Hi, Dr. West. How are you feeling, partner?" he asked with a smile.

"I've been better," Lacy said.

"No, Lace, you've felt better, but you've never *been* better. Do you realize that you captured this lunatic?" Chet said, beaming.

"No, Chet, you did. I would have been just another victim if you hadn't arrived when you did. So, I'm dying to know, how did you figure it out?"

Smiling, Chet looked to Sharon and asked, "Is she on any kind of sedative because she'll need to be when I give her the answer."

Lacy repeated, "Well, shit, Chet! How did you do it?"

"Well, actually *I* didn't. Agent Olsen did," he said with a laugh.

Lacy looked stunned and blurted out, "You mean that dumbass from the FBI figured the case out?"

"Yep. Actually, she's much smarter than you'd think."

"Apparently, but that's not really saying much," Lacy said.

After a few moments of silence, Lacy tentatively asked how the agent had solved the case, and Chet told her the whole story.

"Yeah, so there I was thinking how funny it would be when you came in and this goofball whom I *knew* had to be getting on your nerves was using your PC. All of a sudden she just froze up and started saying, 'Oh my God' and she had used some FBI program to morph Kriell's face with Chris Frazier's. From there, we just retraced your steps. Homer and Sharon had called earlier, and we all met up at your place. It was kind of like a movie. But, yeah, you can thank Agent Olsen for your salvation," he said, chuckling.

Hmm, Lacy thought. Only after a few moments did she remember that Homer was at her apartment, and she still didn't know why.

"So, why was Homer at my place?" she asked.

Chet said, "I think that Dr. West should take that question because she's the one who actually listened to him and planted the seed of urgency into this whole matter."

Lacy looked at Sharon and waited for a response.

"It seems that Homer is sort of psychic. It's a long story, and I'd rather he tell you than I. At any rate, he called me because he had a vision that something happened to you. We went over to your place, and I let myself in with the key you'd given me. Chet called, and I overheard on the answering machine that you shouldn't be with this Kriell guy."

Chet uncharacteristically interrupted Sharon. "Sharon had it all figured out, too. She had unscrambled Irving B. Kriell's name and *knew* it was I. B. Killer. So, I went over, and Agent Olsen, who by the way is a computer goddess, too, was able to see when you last visited the map direction website. We got the last address you'd looked up and found out it had just been that morning, so we went on over. Well, I guess it was just *this* morning. This sure has been a long day."

Sharon echoed, "Amen."

After a moment, Lacy said with a sigh, "So I have to be thankful to Agent Olsen?"

Chet responded, "Yes. And Homer and Sharon. It was neat. It was almost like it had been orchestrated by a higher power that we all had our little pieces of the puzzle and, within a few minutes, all of the pieces were in place.

You don't know how lucky you were, Lace. That crazy jerk babbled like a baby once we got him to headquarters, and he absolutely *hates* you. He thinks that if you hadn't been involved with this case, he would have been able to continue along on his one-man crusade indefinitely. He'd even hooked up with an HIV positive guy in Florida whom he had convinced to sell him his blood so that this mess could be perpetuated. Before that, he had used his brother's blood until he died. Unreal. At least he didn't kill the storage facility attendant. We found him bound and gagged in Frasier's car. He was pissed, but alive."

Lacy lay there quietly and could feel Sharon and Chet looking at her. She hated it when people just looked at her. Before she could think of a smartassed remark about how staring was rude, Chet spoke again.

"Oh, and as I was leaving the department a little while ago, Agent Olsen said that she was going to come by to see you after she grabbed a bite to eat. It's an unofficial visit. Captain Sumlin was able to talk the Feds into obtaining your official statement at a later time given your injuries. So, when she comes by, just remember to be nice to her."

Looking every bit as annoyed as she felt, Lacy said, "Jesus Christ! Everyone I know always says for me to 'be nice'. Am I really that big of an asshole?"

With a smile, Chet said, "On that note, I'm going home. I'm so glad you're okay, Lace. You did excellent work, and I'm proud to be your partner. If you need anything at all, just give me a call. Oh, and you might want to watch the 11:00 news. It'll probably give you an even bigger head than you have now with that giant lump, but it should lift your spirits. Besides, you deserve to have a big head tonight."

Bending down to hug Lacy again, Chet bid Sharon a good night and walked out of the room, easing the door closed behind him.

After a moment, Sharon reached over and took Lacy's hand. Lacy responded with a small squeeze. Hearing Chet's and unmistakably Agent Olsen's voices in the hallway, both women looked toward the door to see Margie Olsen walk in.

"Hi, Detective Fuller! I'm so glad you're okay. Whoa! Look at those puffy bags underneath your eyes! Do you know what's good for that? Fresh cucumber slices. Oh, and also tea bags. It has to be the caffeinated kind, you know?" the agent said.

Lacy reminded herself to be nice, so she settled for only a slightly smart remark.

"Oh? Well, all I've got in the room is the decaf, but if you'll just look in the fridge over there I have all sorts of fresh, sliced veggies! I'm sure you'll be able to put your hands on some cukes."

Agent Olsen quickly scanned the room, then began to giggle.

"You're silly! You don't have a refrigerator in your room!"

Lacy replied, "No shit, Sherlock."

And with that, all three women broke into laughter.

After a somewhat lengthy and surprisingly minimally annoying visit from Agent Olsen, Sharon volunteered to walk Margie out. Sharon stopped as the two women reached the nurses station and said, "Agent Olsen? I know that Lacy and Chet have thanked you for all you did, but I'd also like to say that you did a fantastic job today."

With a blush, Margie stood in silence for a moment before responding.

"Well, I know that I come across sort of ditzy at times; well, most of the time I guess. But, you know, I'm not stupid; I'm just slow to assimilate. I think it's a medical condition and that there's probably a name for it. Maybe you could refer me to somebody? I mean, it gets old having people always underestimating me, you know?"

"I'm sure it does, but I don't think you give yourself enough credit. If you were truly *slow*, you wouldn't have morphed the images together in time to save Lacy. Actually, I think you utilize the creative part of your brain far more than most. Seriously, why would you have thought to do that photo imposition thing in the first place?" Sharon asked.

"I get bored easily. I was waiting for Lacy and was just messing around, and it just happened."

Sharon put her hand on Agent Olsen's shoulder and said, "Margie? I don't think I would want to change a single thing about myself if I were you. And as for Lacy thinking you were a dumbass, well, she thinks that of most people, and you've proven her wrong. I don't think that happens too often."

With a smile, Margie said, "I've got to admit, I was surprised that she thanked me in there, especially after the cucumber thing. What was I thinking? I appreciate your kindness, Dr. West. I've got to go back to Bureau headquarters now. I'll check in on Lacy tomorrow."

As Sharon watched Margie leave, she couldn't help but smile. What a unique individual. After a moment, Sharon requested a cot be brought into Lacy's room so she could stay the night. Sharon called her father to ask that he feed the animals for her since she wouldn't be home. She softly kissed Lacy's forehead and lay down.

CHAPTER 37

The next morning, Lacy was awakened at the crack of dawn and taken down for another CT scan. Afterwards, a neurologist came to her room, examined her, and pronounced her fit to be discharged. Sharon was lounging on the cot working a crossword puzzle and drinking the coffee from Lacy's breakfast tray while Lacy was watching cartoons on the television. A nurse entered the room carrying a large bouquet of flowers.

"Detective? These are for you," she said, placing the arrangement on the windowsill and handing Lacy the card. She then directed her attention to Sharon. "Dr. West? There are some people here to see Detective Fuller, but one of them is a little girl. She said that she didn't care what the policies were; she wanted to see her friend and give her a present. She asked if I'd talk to you about it."

Rising from the cot, Sharon put the coffee down and looked at Lacy, who was still staring at the card.

Finally, Lacy asked, "You sent me flowers?"

"Yes, I did, and there'll be more where those came from."

Sharon winked at Lacy and followed the nurse outside where she was met with a smiling Homer holding the hand of Cicely. A few feet away stood Tyrone with his head downcast. Sharon told the nurse that it would be okay for Lacy to have the visitors, and they all followed her into Lacy's room.

The moment Cicely entered, she ran over and shoved her little stuffed cat into Lacy's surprisingly willing hands.

Lacy spoke, "Hey, Kiddo! I'm glad you brought Sylvester with you. I was missing Snow. Sylvester will keep me company until I get to go home. Hi, Homer. Hi, Tyrone."

Bitsy grinned from ear to ear.

Homer walked over, bent down, and hugged Lacy gently. She hugged him back very tightly and seemed to delay letting go. When she finally did, there were tears rolling down her face.

"Now, Miss Lacy, don't you cry. Homer's here, and he'll take care of you."

Bitsy yelled, "Me, too! Remember, you drive and I take care of folks!"

Lacy looked at the little girl standing defiantly with her arms crossed and smiled. She said, "Of course you will. All of you will have to take turns because I'm going to need a lot of help for a while. Bitsy, what happened to Sylvester's eye?"

With a frown, Bitsy said, "Mama made me wash him. She said you didn't need to be around any germs. I think his eye fell out when I was drying him."

Sharon quickly spoke up, "Well, you know, I *am* a doctor. I can probably find a donor, and we can do an eye transplant on Sylvester. Then, he'll be good as new."

With a furrowed brow, Bitsy asked, "That's what they want to do with Mama; give her a new kitney. Maybe you can fix her before you fix Sylvester?"

Sharon remembered that the little girl had asked once before if she could help her mother. She bent down, looked Cicely in the eyes, and said, "I'll come over to your place and check your mother out. I promise I'll do everything that I can to help her get well. Deal?"

Bitsy took Sharon's proffered hand and shook it, agreeing, "Deal."

As soon as Sharon stood, her knees popping loudly in protest, Bitsy was off to visit Lacy closer. The joint noises weren't lost on Homer.

"Lordy, Dr. West, you sound like me," he said with a smile.

"Yeah, Homer, I think it's a by-product of getting older."

Bitsy took that moment to chime in, too loudly for Lacy's comfort, "Mama says *you're only as old as you feel,* but I feel old enough to visit Miss Lacy, and that lady out there almost wouldn't let me. Where's your egg?"

Lacy looked at her questioningly and said, "My what?"

"Homer said you have an egg on your head. I don't see it. Are you hiding it? Grams lives on a farm, and she has eggs. They're usually hiding under a chicken. Is it under your head?"

Laughing, Homer said, "I was explaining that you'd been hit in the head and that you had an egg. I guess she took it literally."

"What did I take?" asked Bitsy in her customary shrill, loud little voice. Lacy closed her eyes. Sharon knew the visit was probably causing poor Lacy's headache to worsen by the second. She walked over to Bitsy and said, "The egg on Lacy's head only shows up when it's quiet in here. I think it gets scared being around other people."

Bitsy said, "Oh. I want to see it, so I'm gonna be real quiet."

Lacy looked at Sharon and mouthed, *Thank you.*

Tyrone approached the bed slightly and said, "Lacy?

I had my interview for that position you told me about. I just went for my drug screen on the way over here. Thank you for believing in me. I'm glad you're okay."

Before Lacy could speak, Bitsy said, "Shhh, Shroom, you'll make the egg hide!"

Tyrone smiled and whispered that he was sorry. For several minutes, nobody spoke. A tapping at the door caused all heads to turn in unison. It was the same nurse from earlier carrying a stack of papers.

"Detective Fuller, these are your discharge papers. I'll need to go over everything with you before you leave. Do you have somebody to drive you home?"

Sharon quickly responded that she would play chauffeur.

Homer announced that they should be going, and everyone, including Tyrone, hugged Lacy goodbye. On their way out the door, Bitsy looked at the nurse and said, "I feel old enough, so I'm old enough to see her. Mama says so. And you scared the egg away!"

As the trio exited the room, the nurse asked, "What was *that* all about?"

A smiling Lacy just said, "Never mind. Let's sign some papers and get me out of here."

Sharon helped Lacy into her apartment to be greeted by a vocal Snow who began weaving in and out of both women's legs as they made their way to the recliner. As soon as Lacy sat down, Snow hopped in her lap and began purring and dancing.

"God, it's good to be home," she said, smiling down at the cat.

"I bet it is. Can I get you anything?"

"No, I'm fine. I think I just want to sit here and enjoy being alive for a while."

Lacy decided to call Captain Sumlin before settling in for the day.

The Captain answered on the third ring.

"Sumlin speaking."

"Good morning, Captain."

"Lacy? Are you at home? I called the hospital, and they said you'd been discharged."

Lacy wanted to tell him that no, actually she was inside a UFO, but decided to be nice, as so many people had suggested.

"Yeah, Captain. I just got here."

"Well, let me just say that I'm proud of you. You exceeded my expectations on this case, Fuller. So, how are you?"

"I'm fine. I've got a hell of a headache and am still dizzy as shit, but at least I'm not nauseated anymore."

"That's good. That's good. Um, listen, I don't know how you're going to feel about this, but I think it's best that you hear it from me first. Shelly Stevens is going to walk."

"What do you mean?" asked Lacy.

"Well, I mean that her lawyer, Martin Strausser, met with the DA, and they decided that, since her actions directly led to the capture of a serial felon, they would drop the murder charge and go for involuntary manslaughter. She'll plead guilty by reason of insanity and will pay a hefty fine, do some community service, undergo counseling, and basically, not do any hard time. She will be under house arrest and be required to wear an ankle monitor," Sumlin said.

Lacy looked pissed. "You've got to be kidding me. She *killed* someone! She admitted it! What about the victim?"

"It seems that Todd Stevens' parents don't want to press any charges. They said that their son's purpose in life must have been for the capture of this evil man. They said it was for the 'greater good' that he died. I think they want to see if they can get him martyrdom or something like that. They're pretty religious."

Lacy was too stunned to speak.

"She really will have to pay a price. Plus, don't forget that she's sick. I thought you liked the Stevens lady?" Sumlin asked.

"I do, Captain, but she just beat a murder charge."

"Well, Lacy, I'll give you the good news now. You remember those punks who attacked that homeless man? They've been sentenced to three years. It seems that Mr. Files wasn't the first vagrant they'd attacked."

Lacy knew that had it not been for Shelly's intervention, those punks would still have been roaming the streets mistreating others. Plus, she *did* like Shelly Stevens, and she could understand, at least somewhat, the woman's actions. After hanging up with the Chief, Lacy filled Sharon in on the details of their conversation.

Sharon shook her head and said cynically, "That's the justice system for you. Kick somebody and get three years in jail; be wealthy and kill someone and get off scot-free. I bet she's going to want Snow back, too."

Lacy was again too stunned to speak. She hadn't thought of that. She'd grown quite attached to the entertaining white cat with his permanent pissed-off face and was actually considering adopting him. She would miss coming home to his antics and waking up with him snuggled around her head. After a few minutes, Lacy said, "I think I'm ready to lie down for a while. Can you help me to bed?"

Sharon answered, "Sure. I'm going to run home while you're dozing and pack an overnight bag."

Lacy raised her eyebrows in silent question.

"I'm going to stay tonight. I think you need someone with you, and I'm definitely quieter than little Cicely. Besides, it'll kind of be like a grade-school sleepover," Sharon joked.

Lacy had never had a grade-school sleepover, but the thoughts of seeing more of Sharon elated her. Rising with Snow tucked gently in her arms, she retreated to the bedroom, changed clothes, and crawled under the covers. Snow curled up in a fluffy ball on her chest.

Sharon asked if there was anything more that Lacy needed before she left.

"No. But Mexican food wouldn't suck if you could pick some up on the way home. Not from that Tex-ico place, though. Yuck!"

Bending down to kiss Lacy's cheek, Sharon petted Snow as well and said, "You got it. I'll see you in a bit. Sleep well."

Lacy started stroking Snow, who was contentedly bathing a foot and purring. When she heard the front door close, she said in an utterly ridiculous voice, "*Guess who's gonna spend the night? Won't that be fun?*"

As soon as the ridiculously spoken words came from her mouth, Lacy thought, Shit! I just talked cat talk.

ACKNOWLEDGMENTS

I would like to extend my heartfelt gratitude to those who were instrumental in helping me throughout the various stages of seeing this novel come to fruition. My incredibly wonderful family: Ida, Jay, Jim, Carol, and Auntie Poe – thanks for your unfaltering love, support and also for teaching me to follow my dreams. Diane – for the awesome opening sentence, the plethora of editing assistance (yes, I still remember the nap), support, and so much more. My second family: Willie, Anna, Kellie, Tommy, and Troy – for your unconditional love, eternal support, guidance, and friendship. My posse: KiKi, Kelly, Shanda, Charletta, Colleen, Jessica, Lisa, and Cheri – for your enthusiasm, friendship and support. My sweet pets: for allowing me to share their lives and incorporate their antics into my novels. Michael Garrett: for your wisdom and guidance.

A very special thank you to Karen – for believing in me, pushing me to be the best I can be, reminding me to follow my dreams, and rekindling my desire to write. Had our paths not crossed, this novel would have remained in a drawer and my dreams would likely not have been realized. You have been a Godsend.

Image by John Ridings, Ridings Photography

ABOUT THE AUTHOR

*Lee Kelly has worked in the medical and pharmaceuti-*cal industry for more than twenty years. Originally from Alabama, she currently lives with her four cats and dog in Atlanta, Georgia. This is her first novel.